STOLEN LOVE!

Before Jane could stop him John Hardin's clumsy hands circled her waist and his mouth began its hungry search of her lips. She tried to think clearly through the fumes of martinis, to remember that this was her husband's friend—that Eric was thousands of miles away, at sea on a dangerous mission. But John's insistent love-making was upsetting her emotions, beating down her will-power.

Why not? cried a voice inside her. *Eric will go with some woman.* The familiar room—hers and Eric's—began to whirl recklessly. *Why not?* she asked herself again . . .

FROM THE REVIEWS

A NOVEL

TORMENT

(A CONVOY THROUGH THE DREAM)

SCOTT GRAHAM WILLIAMSON

WILDSIDE PRESS

For Grace Williamson

Originally published under the title
A CONVOY THROUGH THE DREAM

PART ONE | DEPARTURE

1: *Please Let Me into Your Terrible and Lovely Machine!*

It was during the half-forgotten time near the middle of the most recent of the World Wars. Many men fought and planned and talked and killed and died, wondering why. Men were at war and cities were at war. From an altitude of five thousand feet the white dome of the Capitol appeared to be the center of an X of boulevards, and the broad strip of the Mall hung below it like a bright kite-tail. Washington was a mosaic of brick red and ash gray, spotted with ovals of green grass and the cuprous green geometry of government building roofs, the whole crosshatched carelessly and fading mistily at the edges; a great stain of weak mixed dyes on the vernal velvet terrain that surrounded it.

From a lower level there were the structures of the city, and within them the symmetry of stresses, the static warfare of tensions, compressions and shearing which compose a solid building. And there was the big dome itself, colonnaded, pilastered and curve-ribbed, surmounted by an awkward statue of Armed Liberty, its back turned forgetfully toward the center of the city. Passing through the two iron hemispheres and the peeling paint of the Brumidi fresco, one could enter the South Wing where the House of Representatives was in session.

Only seven members were at their desks, and they were being addressed from the floor by a man who read words into a microphone, patiently and semiarticulately.

"Tomorrow, as all Americans know, is the one hundred and fifty-third anniversary of Polish freedom. It was on May third, 1791, two years after the creation of our own constitution . . ."

Some of the representatives were reading newspapers, others were talking to one another; yet each was imbedded in the melange of his own narrative, almost isolated within the turbid cowl of his separate consciousness.

"It is especially fitting that we here pay tribute to that day which, in the bright history of valiant little Poland, is the equivalent of our own Fourth of July. The common bonds of love of freedom and pride in national honor have long existed between us. It is hardly necessary to remind *any* American of the contributions of Thaddeus Kosciusko and Casimir Pulaski to our own Revolution!"

"Like hell it isn't!" a gentleman from California muttered to the man at the next desk. "I'm an American—I think."

"He's just reading for the *Record* so he can mail it to his Polish constituents. Why doesn't he turn it in? Doesn't he know there's a war on?"

"Does he? Wait until he gets to our brave Polish-American boys in the armed services!"

The mumbling voice rolled on through the public address system. "Today, brave little Poland, the first to resist Hitler, awaits the liberation that is surely coming. The mighty armies of the United Nations are massed for the invasion . . ."

Such a scene in the chamber of the House of Representatives was, as always, very exciting. One could feel the lines of power running out from this vaulted room to every part of the world where there are human beings, perhaps ultimately reaching even to places where there are no people at all, deep in the rich seas and high on the desolate peaks. Perhaps the earth itself rolled dangerously in a haphazard cradle woven of such words as were spoken here in this room. There is a dreadful fascination about the principles of amplification, both electronic and human, controlled by the difference between plate and grid variations of potential or by the more surprising factors of mankind's peculiar political circuits.

Outside this center of world force there was the sweet air above the clean green oblong of the Mall and the clear water of the great pool. The water reflected the priapic concrete of the Washington Monument, its internal duct busy with ascending and descending tourists, its external surfaces simply and beautifully vertical.

At the intersection of Fourteenth Street and Pennsylvania Avenue, a clerk from the Department of Commerce stood waiting for the traffic signal to change. He heard a strange and persistent sound coming down from the sky. This was the sound of an airplane.

Hardly anyone looked up. He could remember when in the time of his childhood all the people in his neighborhood ran and knocked on each other's doors when there was an airplane approaching. And everyone, wives and mothers, husbands and children, ran for an open space whence they could watch the little black cross moving magically and dangerously through the sky. It had seemed impossible and wonderful then. A man was up there in that thing. They wished him well, repressing firmly their natural desire to see him crash into the earth and disprove forever the frightening dream of flight.

Now hardly anyone looked up. The streets were crowded with government workers and they were all accustomed to hearing the sound of airplanes over Washington, especially now that the United States was in the war. This was, the papers said, the nerve center of the fight against the Nazis. It was an everyday sound like that of the electric fans above the heads of the multitude of clerks.

Yet at this instant, unique as is every instant, the young man from the Department of Commerce heard the sound of the plane as though those cylinders spoke into their exhausts for him alone. The fact of the matter was that he listened and looked and felt an orgasmic thrill go through him at the sound and sight of the B-17 flying above him.

It was a great bomber. American. Manned by brave men. Men gambling, forced to gamble—heroism or cowardice or death or all or nothing—locked in that trap of duralumin genius. This, our machine, bold, bright, hard, clear. And the power of those motors!

If men have invented all these puissant monsters, then the least that seems due them is a bit of vicarious joy in their power, the ultimate relief of subsiding into the inhuman strength of a machine of not less than 4800 horsepower.

7

He had stopped in the middle of the sidewalk, indifferent to the fact that he was blocking pedestrian traffic. He looked down at his well-polished brown shoes and then up again at the bomber. He listened to the challenging sound of the four wonderful motors.

His body became all tense as he stood there. And then, very slowly, all relaxed. A sound like a reluctant and muffled sob came out of him, and he said to himself, "Oh, God, God, God! I wish they'd take me!"

The plane made its way out of the visible area between the buildings, and the young man resumed his thinking about which cafeteria he should go to for lunch. There may have been something indecisive in his character. He always found it difficult to decide between Scholl's and the one in the new Post Office Building.

2: There on the Other Side of the Hill

The earth turned on its axis and moved the Capitol slowly into the fringe of the hemisphere of night; the lights went on in the multicellular evening of the city. The congressmen went home; the clerks went home. And in a basement apartment on Thirteenth Street Northwest, Eric Clark returned to his wife Jane. She was concerned with him at the moment, and he was concerned with the war. Both loved, but with confusion and diverting memories, half-lies and passionate needs, with all the incongruent realities of the rational flesh and the wayward dream. By no means an extraordinary couple, and yet the little pattern of their lives was quietly interlocking with that of the breadth of human history.

The dependable and conservative double boiler was the center of Jane Clark's cooking because she never knew at what hour her husband would want to eat. She chopped some ice, washed it, and put it in two highball glasses. No frigidaire here. But it had been fun turning this cluttered, depressing basement into a gay and individualized apartment that was really their own. They had tried to make advantages of all the disadvantages. They had sawed and chiseled the gingerbread of scrollwork and appliqué off the Edwardian furniture and painted some of it Chinese red. They had eliminated a false fireplace and replaced it with real bookshelves. Woodwork had changed from blood-clot brown to bright ivory. Walls and ceilings once muddy cream were now in clean pastels of green and blue. There were three rooms in a row: front room, kitchen, and bedroom. The oil-burning furnace in the kitchen was no longer hidden by an Oriental screen, but fitted in functional adequacy into the total design. The various pipes just below the ceiling gave the place something of the interior aspect of a ship.

Jane mixed a gin and ginger ale highball for herself and put the other glass into the ice compartment. The first swallow of the drink added to the anticipatory excitement in her body. She was a tall girl with straight black hair and eyes the color of wet moss in shadow. Her movements were deliberate and not too offensively efficient. The first impression she made was usually one of self-controlled sadness without self-pity. Her twenty-eight-year-old face already showed conformations of sorrow reinforced by lines of humor. Yet the sum of her personality seemed somehow incorrectly added. One felt that she had given up something somewhere and had made the best of it; something so obscure, perhaps, that she herself could not define it. She was not unhappy, nor did she appear to be so. On the contrary, one could see that she was living a life she fiercely cherished. And that life was for the most part her husband, Eric.

When she first met Eric he was only twenty-four and had just started his first teaching assignment—sociology at UCLA. She was in her senior year. The first thing she thought when she saw him was that he reminded her of the young Abraham Lincoln. His face was by no means so gaunt and stark and ugly and noble as Lincoln's. Perhaps it was merely that she did not see him singly; she somehow identified him with the total world. At any rate, Eric was the first person she had ever known who could be serious without being dull, and funny without being ridiculous or mean. There was an air of conviction about him, even though he never pretended to know anything that he did not know, never stated any axiom as unquestionable, and really had only tried to teach his pupils how to be their own teachers and find their own directions. Some of the students disliked him because he did not give them simple memory methods of getting through his course; others liked him because he was quite free with his passing grades. It was almost impossible to fail in his class. Jane wanted him, loved him, and married him.

They had had a good time together. They had moved on from UCLA—Stanford, University of Chicago, vacations in the woods, explorations of new cities. One would have thought that Jane had never had other desires. She met him at every point, she felt—mentally, sexually, and morally. And now there was the war, and since he had been turned down by the Army Eric had gone to work for the Office of War Information. For a year now they had lived in Washington. They found it the dullest city they had known.

Eric had loved the sound and color and smell and meaning of many cities. Jane knew that and in a remote way she resented it. He was a lover. She had learned that. And she felt sometimes that he loved her only as he might have loved one of those cities. Because of his capacity for love. She wanted him to love her alone, but at the same time she feared above all things that she might place limits on his mind and earn the resentment that she knew would follow. Sometimes the whole thing made her weary. Their love was good, but it was never easy.

Now she felt her body ache with wanting him; it was so physical a pain that she could not at certain moments stand erect, but had to bend forward slightly as though she had a cramp. She prayed silently to some nameless saturnalian deity of her own that Eric would come in feeling the same way she did; that he would take her straight to bed, even before dinner. She felt this way very often. And what was most exasperating was the knowledge that Eric was no less passionate than she. Nor was he less monogamously so. It was only that there were so many external things that could divert him. He had a thousand curiosities, purposes, and relatively impersonal needs, and each one was at certain moments capable of taking him away from her. Not that Jane did not share those other things, but she felt they belonged in a lower category. They should not be more imperative than love. And if they were—then what was love?

10

When she heard him at the front door she took the other glass out of the ice compartment and began to make two fresh drinks. Her heart beat faster and she tensed, knowing that he was here and it had happened again. She was always a little surprised that he had come home again. For even though they had never been apart since their marriage, she thought of him as a wanderer. Possibly she could not have loved a man who did not seem likely to disappear at any moment.

She heard him drop his trench coat on the studio couch in the front room, and then he was here with her in the kitchen and she gave him the drink. They kissed, and with his free hand he touched her hair and face. "Are you drunk?" he asked.

"Dead drunk," she said, relaxing in his arms. But she could tell that he hardly heard her words.

"I don't want to eat for a while," he said. "Let me have a few drinks and you eat whenever you want to."

"Ascetically? Sans love?"

"Sans me for a little while. I have to finish that broadcast. It's scheduled for short wave if I can only get it right enough to turn in. Leave the stuff on the stove. I'll eat before I go to bed."

"You don't love *me* any more, do you, honey?"

"Yes."

"But not as much as broadcasts."

For a moment she felt the pressure of his arms slacken with annoyance.

"Get to work," she said. "Eat whenever you want. It'll stay hot. And so will I."

"Good," he said.

"What kind of day did you have?"

"Nothing new. Routine editing. But this—this broadcast —I really want to get right."

"Can you tell me what it's all about? Or will that spoil the inspiration?"

"I've already told you. The enemy. It's a thing to be read on the short wave. What is the enemy?"

"What *is* the enemy, Eric?"

"That's what I'm trying to figure out."

"But you seemed so sure about the war."

"Sure, I'm sure about the war. But I'm only sure which side I'm on."

She kissed him and put her tongue in his mouth; he pushed her away.

"I'm *your* enemy," she whispered.

"Please let me work," he said.

"The food is in the double boiler," she told him. "Salad in the icebox. Whatever you do, don't go to bed without eating."

He kissed her forehead.

"I hate you," she said.

"Now I really have to get to work."

"I'd rather be married to a truck driver."

"I really have to get to work," he repeated. "The stuff I've written so far is idiotic. I'm going to quit my job if I can't get this straight, because I'll know in that case that I've got no right to be working on propaganda and telling other people what it's all about when I don't know myself."

"Please don't quit, darling. At least you're better at this sort of thing than most of them are."

He kissed her throat and felt her familiar breasts with his fingers. Then he pushed her away again and said, "But damn it! I don't really know what I'm doing. Help me by leaving me alone tonight."

2

Eric sat down at his worktable and turned on the radio. He drank his highball. On the table were papers, tablets, notebooks, a box of 3-x-5 file cards, a noiseless Remington portable, ash tray, cigarettes, a stapling machine, and a glass containing pencils. He contemplated these things as he drank his gin and ginger ale. All the tools with which to make or destroy a world, he thought; nothing is lacking. He finished the drink. Except, perhaps, the man.

The radio had hummed and growled into receptivity, and now the sounds of the second movement of Beethoven's Seventh Symphony came out of it. Eric was still very tense, but he knew that in a few minutes the liquor and the music would begin to make him sane. He returned to the kitchen and quickly mixed another drink. The hoarse whisper of the furnace sounded reassuring.

Jane was eating and reading the latest issue of *Time*. He kissed her hurriedly on the back of the neck and the damp hair clung to his lips.

She squirmed in her chair and said, *"Please,* Mr. Clark! I'm concentrating!"

"Cinema, I see."

"It's America's art form, isn't it? It says here that Bing Crosby makes a *wonderful* young priest. So nice to the *old* priest!"

"Good," he said, hurrying back into the front room in order not to miss the last of the second movement.

He sat down again before the implements that mocked him. The music marched with all its unmatched dignity through the vibrant air of the warm room, a fateful and wonderful statement of sound.

This is very serious music, Eric thought, yet there is no denial of laughter in it. Any humor may be here. Any comic or grave thing.

All the frustration of his clerk-ridden day in the Office of War Information struck back at him: the priestlings of useless detail, the thousand little quibblers and quoters of directives who fought against the others—fought fiercely, as desperate little rodents will fight; patiently, as termites eating away the essential foundations of a good house, clawing or gnawing at everything with no more in their minds than the hope of better semiannual efficiency ratings. So very many good things of his had been lost in the clerical maze, had been wrapped around with red tape as a fly is wrapped in the quiet web of a spider.

At this moment, he thought, in Italy and in the South Pacific . . .

Men are dying. But of course that is not the point. Men are dying here in Washington, scores of them every day. But in German Europe people are being burned like cordwood. There is no human dignity at all over there now except such as has been driven underground. No man can call his soul his own, no man is more than a thing. And our own men. Facing the indescribable fight. Most of them not knowing

13

why. But knowing a million times better than I do the greatest fact of this moment—almost the only human fact. Facing ... an ... enemy ... that ... really ... wants ... to ... kill ... *you*. Kill ... you ... now. Dead.

Who is the enemy? he thought. If I can write it, then I will know. How can you fight an enemy you can't identify? First he's on the other side, then on your side. Today he's a *führer* and tomorrow your brother.

The music ended and there were some brief news items. Four-thousand-plane raid on German industrial centers. The isolated Anzio beachhead still seventy-five miles north of the main front in Italy. Then the radio said in a deeply religious voice: "Shakespeare once asked something about 'What's in a name? A rose by any other name . . .' and so forth. But, folks, that just goes to show that Shakespeare never heard of Klapengrubber's real pumpernickel bread! For the name of Klapengrubber has stood for the very best in pumpernickel for over two decades. Remember! The name for real old-fashioned pumpernickel is Klapengrubber's!"

Eric turned it off.

He saw that what he wanted to say could not be written as a speech; it would have to be a story. He had written and sold a few stories touching on social problems that had concerned him, but he had never thought of himself as a writer. He was a sociologist, a student, a teacher. But tonight he believed quite suddenly that what is called "fiction" is less fictitious than nonfiction, because the latter can give only real or unreal facts and irrational or rational conclusions, whereas stories and plays can to some degree give the actual experience of living on which attitudes must be based.

He could no longer think of it as a speech. Imagine a radio announcer saying in a religious tone: "Folks, some wise guy once said that 'Man is his own worst enemy. The dog is man's best friend. Every man must kill the dog he loves. A man's best friend is his mother. And an enemy by any other name would smell as bad.' But had this wise guy ever heard of anything worth while? Had he ever walked a mile for Camel cigarettes? Had he ever smoked the ones that are toasted? I mean the firm, round ones? And did he know the real importance of good old-fashioned Klapengrubber's genuine pumpernickel bread?"

How to identify this war? A score of past wars fought through his brain: brutish wars and gallant wars, purposeful and purposeless, wars in which there was no choice but whim, and wars of fateful decision. There were fine medieval wars in which one side would not think of attacking until the other was ready. In the early morning before a battle each side would parade. The first to get up in the dawn would blow loudly on their trumpets to awaken the enemy camp; messengers would make inquiry as to whether the enemy were fully prepared for combat. These were good wars of contest by willing contestants. And there were brute wars waged by the strong upon the helpless—armed idiots who could not distinguish between the inanimate and the animate. There had been witless crusades of righteous shopkeepers and their lost children in search of a magic cup, and there had been planned mass murders executed by erudite engineers of slaughter. Many wars of men against men, a few gay contests, and many bewildering nightmares of dumbly irrelevant violence.

He chose a long yellow legal-size tablet and wrote with a soft layout pencil: *The enemy is there on the other side of the hill . . .*

Then he went back into the kitchen to refill his glass. Jane had washed her dishes and gone to bed. Mixing himself a double gin highball, he felt a mouth-watering pang at the smell of sausage and corn that came from the double boiler. But he resisted the temptation. I can't stultify my brain with food, he told himself. I'd only want to go to bed. I'd put off thinking until tomorrow. Go to bed and digest and enjoy the warmth of a friendly female body. That's all I'd want—with my belly full of calories.

He returned to the front room and sat down at his worktable. He felt a sensation of escape. The good pure tablet and the willing pencil. He again began to write.

The enemy is there on the other side of the hill and he is waiting and he will try to kill you. You must kill him first. Is his name Fritz or Hans? Don't ask his name when you find him. Just kill him. He might say that his name is Katzenjammer. Then where would you be?

That morning the dawn came rolling up like a tide of

molten copper out of the low Italian hills, and where the gray-green shapes of olive trees still clung to the bomb-torn terraces the new light plated their ashen limbs with gold. Each man in the company at this hour was lonely and quiet. It was not awe that stilled him, but time and timelessness, a spectacle of space and a vision of death that diminished the moment and cut him off from his friends. No wonder it was hard to remember who the enemy was! Yet the enemy was there—on the other side of the first hill.

The sky grew greater with light and color and the forms of clouds. And George MacDougal, with the others, felt alone. He was not afraid during this brief time, but it was a very vulnerable time for him because he did not know who it was over there. He was vulnerable to himself.

He had to go through it like a catechism, trying to re-member. They are there on the other side of the hill. He had seen them in action before. Distant gray figures that crouched and ran against another hillside amid puffs of smoke from mortar shells and the echoing iron rip of ma-chine-gun fire.

Several hours had passed and Jane sat propped up in bed, the bathrobe open over her naked torso, the covers pushed down to her waist. She had been smoking and reading *The Importance of Living.* Now she closed the book violently and dropped it on the floor.

Eric is right, she thought, this is just a lot of tripe. The Rotarian's Confucius.

She picked up the glass of white wine from the bed table and drank some of it. He's right about everything, she thought. Too damned right. That's why I hate him. She was restless. Her entire body felt maddeningly alive and irritable.

She began rather anxiously, as though she were painting hurriedly with the dimming pigments of memory, to remem-ber Jimmy. It was in her sophomore year at UCLA that she had met him, and it was in the same year that he had had to go away. He was small and quick, with a look that marvel-ously combined apology and arrogance, fear and contempt. His eyes were always red-lidded, his hands shaky. But he had a voice that was cunningly assured even when he was at his lowest ebb of vitality. She knew as soon as she saw him that he was an utterly worthless character. But she also knew that he needed her.

If only Eric could be a little weak-eyed, shaky, and vicious once in a while! Even when he pretended—as tonight—to be terribly distraught, he really wasn't. Some technical point perhaps. But Eric always knew what he was doing. Eric was only fooling when he pretended to need her. He knew what was happening in the world; that was one reason she loved him. But he didn't really need a thing in the world; and that was one reason she hated him. Eric was strong, very strong. And Jane's breasts often ached for the sucking utter worthlessness of Jimmy.

Just at this moment of Jane's remembering, the bedroom door crashed open and Eric came in. He was solidly drunk. He had almost fallen through the door, but now he closed it meticulously, with that solicitude which only a drunk can bestow upon an inanimate object. With self-conscious skill he walked over to the bed and sat down on the edge of it, resting one hand on the far side of her body, leaning toward her and peering down into her face.

She felt a hot urge of abysmal womanhood in her blood. This was almost like an answer to her thoughts! He *was* capable of being dissolute, drunk, helpless, wrong, lost, and weak. She saw him swaying over her and she was ready to take care of him, forgive him, love him.

She extended her hand to steady him. "Get your clothes off, sweetheart," she said.

He continued to stare down at her, formulating something.

"Need help?" she asked.

He took hold of her hand and carefully placed it back on the blanket.

"Yes," he said.

But his voice was not drunken. And it forced her to look for the first time into his eyes. What she saw there dispelled all her satisfaction.

"I need help," he said, "but it isn't here."

"You mean—not me?" she asked, in a hurt voice.

"I mean it isn't here," he repeated. "Washington, the United States, the OWI, Thirteenth Street Northwest, what I have been doing and what I have not been doing."

"Oh, Eric—you're just upset. You've had too much to drink."

"That's right."

"Come to bed. You need sleep."

He swayed a little more over her and looked at her face with eyes that were quiet and completely sober in his torturedly drunken body.

"Sleep," he said, "is what's wrong with me. I don't know what's going on. I'm just a pimp for all the goddamned academic dishonesties of the world."

"Now, Eric," she said, an undertone of triumph coming back into her voice, *"you've* always known what was going on. You're just tired now. You come to bed!"

He shook his head as a fighter does after a hard punch to the ear. "No, Jane," he said, "I've been in bed long enough. We all love it there in the warm, snug covers. But death is too close, and it's too much like death in there."

"You're crazy," she said, angry that he could not see the *life* between these particular covers.

"Yes!" he said, "thank God! I just hope it lasts!"

"You'd better get undressed."

He took hold of both her shoulders and leaned heavily on her.

"Listen," he said, "I just came in here to tell you something, not to discuss generalities. See? What I came to tell you is that I'm going away. As soon as I can. I can't get into the Army or Navy, but I *can* get into the Merchant Marine, and that's where I'm going."

This must be drunken talk, she thought. She was sure that he would get over it when he sobered up, and yet she was frightened. It wasn't like him. And it wasn't like her memory of her first lover, either. "Let's talk about it tomorrow," she said.

"We'll do all the talking right now," he said. "Tomorrow I'm resigning. I won't want to talk about it any more."

Her eyes filled with tears. "You mean you're going out on a boat somewhere?" she whimpered.

"I mean," he said, "that I'm going to get as close as I can to wherever the war is happening."

"And leave me alone—alone?"

She saw now that even when his body was an unsteady and dissolute thing, the same Eric spoke from inside, like ventriloquy. She hated him and hoped that he would be killed in the war. It would serve him right. Her mind stopped there. She dared not think of afterward.

"Alone?" he said. "Of course you'll be alone! Don't you recognize what world we're living in? Alone! Alone! Jesus Christ! This is a world where a man can knock on your door and your wife is taken out to be used in an army brothel, your brother is taken as a slave, your sister for the satisfaction of a passing regiment, your father is taken for a ride in the death-wagon for something he is rumored to have thought. They knock on your door, Jane, you *hear* me? And they do whatever they want!" His voice was fierce and crazier than she had ever thought it could be. "It isn't a little domestic scene that's going on, Jane! It isn't, for Christ's sake, a little lover's quarrel!"

"What is it?"

"If I knew, I might not have to go away."

"But you might get *killed!*" She knew she should not have said that, but it just occurred to her all of a sudden that it might really happen and it seemed very strange. Who would want to kill Eric? Nobody, of course; it was the war. And that was the strangeness.

He made a great effort toward bodily sobriety, shaking his head again and trying to sit up straighter. Something changed in him during this moment and his voice now affected her as being distressingly tender.

"We're all going to get killed," he said softly. "You know that as well as I do. The only question is, with what possible dignity—and purpose."

Jane put her hand over her own eyes, all at once feeling that she could not live without Eric, that all her dreams of Jimmy had been silly, worthless, sophomoric imaginings.

"I couldn't live without you," she whispered, and she meant it out of some fresh source of meaning. "I couldn't live without you."

Even his body was recovering now: he was erect and steady. "You'll have to live without me," he said. "We're all in this nightmare together. Don't try to fool yourself; there's

19

evil all around us, death of the spirit, indignity and defeat."

Jane sat straight upright and with both violent hands pushed Eric back upon the bed. She wanted to see his body fall . . . helplessly . . .

"Goddamn you!" she said, "with all your goddamned words about indignity and defeat and evil! What about *me?*" She was nearly hysterical. "You want to think of a *lot* of people, but you haven't the decency to think of *one!* You're just a goddamned professor who gets drunk! Take your drunken body out of here! I don't want to sleep with you! Get out! Get out! Get out! I hate you!"

He stood up and now he could control his muscles. "Listen, Jane," he said, "I know why you're angry." He steadied himself against the bed. "I know what you mean. It's tough for you. It's tough even just being a woman at all. I love you, but there's more than that."

He walked stiffly out of the room then and left her alone. She could hear him mixing another drink in the kitchen. She felt very lonely, unwanted, meaningless, lost, unloved. He had left the bedroom door open this time, and she became aware of an acrid smell. Something was burning.

She got out of bed and found her mules and fastened the belt of the robe. In the kitchen she found Eric sitting at the table staring blindly into his drink. He was really drunk now that he had said all he could say to her, just plain drunk. The smoke in the room stung her eyes. The double boiler had gone dry and now the mixture of corn and sausage was burning. She turned off the gas. The boiler was red hot.

Then she went over to Eric and took the drink from in front of him. She started to pour it into the sink, then changed her mind and put it in the icebox. There was no protest left in him; his head was heavy and he knew that he was drunk. Jane began to undress him. "You're good to me," he said thickly.

The very words Jimmy had once used! Strange and rather sickening to hear this long-delayed echo. "Good to me . . ."

"Come on, honey," she said, "help me get them off."

His body was leaden and hard to handle, like a marionette with all the strings connected wrong.

"Smells like hell in here!" he said. "Smells like somebody's burning something!"

20

3: The Captain Is a Lonely Man

Deciding to go into the Merchant Marine was a simple matter for Eric, but the process of getting in was a tiring labyrinth of offices, cross-examinations, countless forms to be filled out in duplicate, triplicate, and octuplicate, pictures to be taken, documents to have signed and countersigned and counter-countersigned. Confronting over and over again the turgid enormity of clerkdom. Many salaried robots of indifference, a few patiently good-natured persons, and a great number of miniature dictators, each—with idiot preoccupation—squeezing the little pimple of his clerkly power.

First there was the business of getting an official release from Civil Service and having himself put on Military Furlough status. Then came the acquisition of a radio officer's license. Because of the fact that Eric had had an amateur operator's license when he was a boy, he could now be granted a temporary wartime license, called a TLT, by merely passing the code test.

There followed a period in Baltimore. First he had to get his "Z papers." This necessitated lengthy interviews with the Navy, Coast Guard, War Shipping Administration, and Port Commander. Photographs had to be made, exactly two by one and a half inches, and fingerprints were taken over and over again, just as they had been before he went to work for the OWI. Then there was a session with the State Department concerning his application for a seaman's passport. And following the acquisition of these quintessential papers there was an interview with the Coast Guard Intelligence Division in order to obtain a little card without which he could not be admitted to a dock.

He joined the Baltimore Local of the American Communications Association and was assigned to a ship. Then almost everything had to be repeated: seeing WSA, the Port Commander, and so on and so forth. In all these offices he saw striking posters about how desperately the Merchant Marine needed men, and he heard statements to the same effect frequently broadcast over the radio. But the official hurdles seemed without end. At last came a physical examination by the shipping company's doctor that almost brought all his efforts to naught. For this particular doctor did not approve of Eric's physiology in any way. He listened to his heart with dismay, gazed into his pupils with revulsion, tapped his reflexes with disgust, and contemplated his urine with horror. His blood pressure was too high, his kidneys were inefficient, his pulse too fast. But in the end the doctor signed the medical slip and Eric Clark was in the Merchant Marine.

The days of preparation had, of course, been filled with other and more interesting phenomena than the irritating tangles of red tape and the inert malice of government clerks. There had been the good feeling of adventure.

He was a man who was about to go voluntarily away to war—leave his wife, his home, his work. This simple circumstance clothed his ego in an ancient and gaudy raiment. For even the very dullest and most disgruntled fellow who has ever gone out to the very dullest and stupidest war has at some moment felt upon his spirit some semblance of this shoddy but luminous legend. Eric knew this objectively and hated it, but felt its power nonetheless. He knew that such romantic nonsense does not survive long in the filth, fatigue, and butchery of war's reality.

2

Every sound, every smell, every tactile perception in the darkness of the stateroom was different from anything he had known. There are these worlds! he thought. Endless numbers of them, each complete. To be under the enlarged stars on the arid desert at night. To be in a smokily frenetic Harlem night club. To be under the wet pines in a northern forest. Flying over the Hudson River Valley in a stratoliner. Sitting on the porch of a small-town hotel. To be locked in a prison cell. In a room of the Waldorf-Astoria. North, summer, south, evening, winter, woods, concrete, places and times, endlessly, endlessly. To be in any one of these environmental molds is to have one's nature cast, for the time being, in a new shape, painfully, pleasantly, indifferently, but recast nevertheless. The existence of these multimillion entities of time and place and circumstance amazed Eric as much as did

the knowledge of those inwardly generated worlds of consciousness which he knew to be created and destroyed by
every human being day in and day out. No wonder that man
is a lonely stranger in this infinitude of concentric and overlapping worlds.

At this moment Eric felt himself caught in a foreign web,
a complex of perception that differed in almost every respect
from that in which he had been living for a long time. He
was in the lower bunk in the cadets' room of the Liberty Ship
SS William Benson. He had long since turned out the bed
lamp over his head, and the room was almost completely
dark. Yet he could feel the painted steel closeness of the
overhead above him, the warm steel of bulkheads and deck,
the precarious narrowness of the bunk, the porthole glowing
like a vaudeville moon. There were ship smells: paint, rope,
metal, oil, and cargo. The cargo was coal and it was being
loaded now from overhead cars that dumped it into the holds
with a frightful rattling rumble at intervals of about thirty
seconds. He knew that he must close the porthole or else be
covered with the black dust—he could feel its grittiness now
on his lips—but he felt too stifled to lock himself entirely
into this box of iron darkness. He felt the troubled wonder
of modern man who knows at last that he is a man within a
machine. He felt the great bulk of the ship around him—a
metal thing, but alive with the thinking and dreaming and
laboring of men. He heard it creak and sigh against the night.

He felt a smothering sense of loss. The comfortable feeling
of recognition his former work had given him. The warm
and bright basement apartment that was a collaboration of
his and hers. All that was gone. The paint on the walls, the
pictures, the rugs, the kitchen utensils, the shelves of books
—all had been influenced by his needs and related to his
identity. Here on the ship there was nothing that was of him
or for him. Probably he felt less secure in his own spirit at
this moment than did Oscar, the moron, who had managed
to sign on as a wiper. His professorial basis of function was
all swept away. For there were no classrooms or editorial
desks here. The ship did not need to be explained.

And more important than all else was the harsh with-
drawal of the woman. The warm, close body that had been
there, breathing, living, aching onward toward death. The

legs on legs, arms under and over, hands hungry, insatiably curious and knowing, soft hillocks of otherness, bottomless darkness ready to be illumined. The eternally strange alloyed with the tenderly familiar. His lover, his wife. Separated now, an erotectomy without anesthesia. The hand reaches out and cannot believe that there is no breast to touch. The thigh seeks its special and irreplaceable answering warmth. The hand searches again, angrily and then hopelessly. All gone: the innumerable shadowed subtleties that had made her recognizable and lovable, the humor and habit and specific tensions that were Jane in Eric.

All gone now, torn away, as flesh can be torn from flesh, by force or by decision. And Eric now suddenly in a forceful and foreign world, feeling the wonderful ship around him, hearing it groan and rub its iron skin against the pier.

3

In the dark of late evening on the tenth of May, Eric had gone up on the flying-bridge deck, but he stayed back against its stern rail, out of the way of the captain's possible wrath. The ship was getting under way. The great steel hulk of it was still creaking against the coal dock, but its umbilical cords had been cast off and it was now attached to the anxious strength of the two tugs. The seeing, smelling, feeling of this act of departure were wonderfully exciting to Eric; so much so that he was freed from all his nightmares of strangeness and even from his acute loneliness for the woman-presence of Jane.

When he had first come aboard the ship it had seemed to him to be only a new and different kind of building. Now it was beginning to shudder and tremble with frankensteinian life. It was *not* a building. It was a vast thing that moved— over twenty million pounds of solid afloat in the fluid strength of the river; and as it gave evidence of mobility it gave evidence of *being*. Out of a thing there emerged the first indications of an identity.

The tall silhouette of the captain strode back and forth, from one wing of the flying bridge to the other. He carried a megaphone in one hand but never used it. Once in a while he yelled to the first mate on the bow or to the pilots of the little boats that were now puffing with the exertion of dragging the Liberty ship broadside into the stream. At length they were away from the gross stability of the dock. Motion; the shore lights shifting; the grateful trembling of the steel decks; luminous plumes of steam from the tugboats; the traffic-cop shrilling of the bos'n's whistle, shrieking of the steam whistles of the tugs, imperative deep-throated answer of the ship's own whistle overhead against the stack, vibrating the brain in Eric's skull and spitting water over him like warm rain; shouts of men from the dock, the ship, the boats; the gravity and boldness and nobility of departure into unknown visions and dangers; smell of hemp and smoke, wet paint, and stale salt water . . . Good-by! Good-by! Good-by!

Eric knew that captains do not like anyone on the sacrosanct flying bridge who is not needed there. Yet that was the only good observation post, and so he hoped to hold it for an hour or so. He tried to be as nearly invisible as possible, placing himself behind one of the ammunition boxes near the gun tub on the starboard side. As the captain walked back and forth—his thin, high-cheekboned face showing occasional high lights in the faint and shifting light—Eric felt once in a while an angry look thrown in his direction. But he was not ordered off the flying-bridge deck. He tried further to camouflage himself against the gray anonymity of the ship's structure.

The telegraph rang metallically—SLOW SPEED AHEAD —and the half-born entity took over partial control of its own body. Like a slow rhythm on two enormous kettledrums, the engine could be heard and felt—*tah*-tuh, *tah*-tuh, *tah*-tuh, *tah*-tuh . . .

The freshening smell of the bay breeze made Eric breathe deeply. A shiver of pleasure ran through him as he bade farewell to the poisonous life of the cities, the monoxided streets and nicotined rooms, offices where the air is machine-made, a whole counterfeit world carried on in ugly tunnels under the surface of life. He recognized how long he had been out of touch with the ancient quadral reality of earth, water, fire, and air.

He remained behind the ammunition box near the starboard gun tub, feeling the cleaner air in his lungs and watching the changing configurations of lights on both banks. He was unfamiliar with the region and had but little idea of what these groupings of lights meant or what these prolonged darknesses separated. At length they passed close to a point where he could see a floodlighted statue of heroic size. He knew this to be the Muse of Music at Fort McHenry near where *The Star-Spangled Banner* was written. He had visited the fort with Jane on a week end in Baltimore. And a little later there was a great blinking of electric-blue lights with comet tails of orange sparks, and he knew that this was a shipyard, working all night, all day, to make more ships and more and more.

Further down the Potapsec River, approaching the expanse of Chesapeake Bay, the lights grew fewer, the air keener and colder, the ship more alone. Eric shivered and turned up the collar of his jacket.

He had a dim companion now—Peters, the second radio officer. They had murmured only a few words of recognition, but the fellow seemed to want to stay close to him. It was the first trip for both of them. As they passed the last bright group of shore lights, Peters turned to Eric and grasped his hand. "Well," he said in a tense, serious, embarrassed voice, "this is *it*. We're on our way. I feel that we're gonna be pals through this, you and me. I hope we make it. Good luck, old man."

Eric was repelled by this sentimentality. He felt his own emotions stifled in a trite overflow.

They shook hands. "Good luck," Eric said as cordially as possible.

The quality of adventure was lost, and he decided to go below. He murmured good night to Peters and found the companionway down to the bridge deck and his own cabin. It was a room about eight by ten feet, with a double closet, washbasin, medicine chest, leather-upholstered bench, desk, two chairs, two bunks, and a single porthole. The electric fan was going at half speed, and Chuck, the junior engineer, was snoring in the upper bunk. Chuck had almost missed the ship because of a personal tragedy about which Eric had heard only the bare fact that he had lost his fourteen-year-old son a few days past. Now the poor fellow was worn out and slept as though he himself were dead—but in some unnatural manner, tossing and muttering and twisting, trying to free himself from the cadaver. He had stuck a snapshot of his boy up under the electric conduit that led to the desk lamp.

In the drawer under his bunk Eric found the one bottle of liquor he had brought with him. He poured a hefty slug of the black Jamaican rum into the glass he found in the metal holder beside the washbasin. He was feeling depressed and lonely. The exultation that he had gained from the vital drama of departure was entirely gone, and as he analyzed himself he felt fortunate to have experienced it at all. For he was learning how completely the adult identity is built out of all the myriad memories of its social past and all the conditioned responses of its familiar present. He had been a well-recognized professor of sociology before the war—in fact, an up-and-coming young leader, almost an *enfant terrible*. But there was not a soul on this ship except himself who knew about all this, and it was very doubtful that there was a person on the ship who cared anything about it. There were probably damned few who even knew or cared what sociology was. He was here as third radio officer, with a job to do that was entirely alien to him. Yet it was a job on which the survival of this ship, with all its lives and cargo, might sometime depend. He would be judged only as to his magnitude in this unknown constellation. And, perhaps, by more personal weighings based upon a system of social values of which he was also ignorant.

He was feeling very lonely for Jane; a very simple kind of loneliness now, something he had never foreseen. He did not really miss the academic world where he had been a recognized figure, nor the OWI world where he had been an accepted minor power, but he did miss—with physical pain—the apartment that Jane and he had made together and all the good, warm connotations of their life. So many flesh-soft things between them that nobody else could ever possibly understand.

He drank the rum, wishing he had had enough sense to bring more of it, and listening to Chuck snoring with terrible, death-hungry inhalations in the upper bunk.

Goddamn it, Jane! he thought. I want you, I want you!

He began to have visions—vague at first—of her being unfaithful to him. Why shouldn't she be? he thought. I made

27

my leaving of her a lifeless thing. All I really said to her was that it was something I had to do. She has just as much right to do things *she* has to do. Why shouldn't they involve sex?

A vivid vision of Jane's possible infidelity struck him like a sudden wave of desolation that unexpectedly engulfs a swimmer in a quiet and familiar lagoon. He wished again that he had thought to bring more liquor on board.

He was amazed now at the memory of how he had always taken Jane for granted. Their marriage had been more her design than his, and for that reason, perhaps, he had accepted her as a safe haven. He had taken her love as a substitute for the dream of enchantment that he had slowly come to think of as unfulfillable. And now, quietly, she had become that dream. They had built a love out of the ordinary processes of living that was more magical than the most rarefied of his adolescent visions. He knew this now but he had never told her. So what did she have to adhere to?

Jealousy gnawed at him with its dirty rodent teeth, and ugly pictures enacted themselves on the unwilling screen of his reverie. He took his own sexuality in its simplest form —an emotion that had always seemed normal and clean to him—and implanted it into Jane. And there it suddenly grew into something incredibly vile. He saw her violating all their delicate structures of delight by one simple act of giving herself to another man. The movement of the ship became the metronome of his helplessness; the voyage now was no more than an impotent journey into the acid sea of doubt.

There was no way now to return and tell her why she should not let another man touch her body. It was impossible to explain in a letter, because it was in fact no more and no less than a pain that had taken possession of him. And a pain is not like an idea: there are a thousand ways to justify an idea, but a pain merely exists and to explain it is embarrassing. *Just don't do it,* he thought. *Please don't do it.*

The junior engineer stirred, woke up, and lit a cigarette.

"Hi," Eric said. "How's sleeping?"

"Hi," said Chuck. "We under way?"

"Yes. How about a drink?"

"No thanks. You save it. We got a long ways to go."

"Oh, I'll probably finish this before we get outside Chesapeake Bay. Let me give you a shot. Help you sleep."

"No thanks. I just sort of woke up for a fag."

"Okay."

"I sleep solid," Chuck said, "so don't mind about turning on the light or working at the desk. I hear you been a professor in a school or something, so you probably want to use the desk. I won't be using it, so you can use all of the drawers in it for your papers. And don't worry about the light. I sleep sound."

"You sure you wouldn't like a little drink?" Eric asked. "Really helps you sleep, you know."

"No thanks," Chuck said, putting out his cigarette and turning his face to the bulkhead. And it was apparent from his tone that he knew he could not rely upon any chemical subsidy to help him through his pain.

Eric sat down at the desk and began to write a letter to Jane:

This is written with but a vague chance of having it mailed on this side of the ocean. We have left Baltimore. Where we are going, I could not say even if I knew. A special fear touches the edges of my loneliness with cold —because you said that if I went away we would lose something, something would change. I am not afraid of the enemy nor the sea, but only of losing you. So I ask you to free me from this fear. Keep everything that we have had—as I will keep it. Love me, be faithful to me with all your flesh and dreams and memories—as I shall be to you.

The maudlin quality of this paragraph sounded quite unlike him. Rereading it gave him a queer, empty feeling, as though he had misplaced his personality. He folded the page disgustedly and put it in the drawer. He sat there for a while, staring blankly at the black porthole, finishing his drink, listening to the *tah*-tuh, *tah*-tuh of the engine and the soft whir of wind from the overhead ventilator. Then he decided to go down to the officers' saloon for a cup of coffee.

This was a fairly large room with three tables lengthwise and one crosswise. A long green leather-upholstered bench took care of seating on one side of the tables, and on the other side were swivel chairs bolted to the deck. A large frigidaire occupied one end of the room, and a corner was taken up by a small serving pantry where there were drawers and shelves of dishes, a restaurant-size coffee urn, an electric toaster, and a waffle iron.

Eric poured a cup of strong black coffee, put sugar in it, and took it to one of the tables. The captain was sitting alone at the crosswise table, and near Eric were the third mate and third assistant engineer.

Captain Brogan was a tall, slightly stooped man who looked like a Midwestern farmer. He was thin and his lean, angular face was deceptively young. It was a face of almost Hollywood handsomeness, yet there were plainly stamped upon it marks of real loneliness and brooding and a kind of outdoor neuroticism that could never have found their way into the feeble world of celluloid. A strong face that seemed in some obscure way very close to the breaking point. And yet, as Eric studied the captain, he felt certain that here was a man who—no matter how close he came to it—would *not* break.

The captain is a lonely man, Eric said to himself. And partly he was thinking of Brogan and partly of all captains.

"That Three Aces Bar," the mate was saying to the engineer, "is about the scurviest gin mill and sin mill of all the so-called fleshpots of Baltimore, Maryland, U.S.A.!"

"I didn't spend much time there," the engineer said. "Just a few beers with Johnny. The rest of my time I shacked up with a girl I knew a long time. Portuguese."

"Well, you were lucky! That Three Aces! God-a-mighty! I picked up a glamour girl there and took her to my hotel."

"Yeah?"

"Yeah."

"How was she?"

"Well—for one thing—her tits hung down so far you could strop your razor on 'em!"

The third mate, Hartley, had a face like an Americanized gargoyle. He loved words and would build up a whole conversation of lies just in order to have the satisfaction of delivering himself of a single striking phrase. The third engineer, however, was a quiet man, a big-nosed, bald-headed Norwegian named Benson. He had a wife and three sons

30

of whom he had heard nothing since the German occupation of Norway.

At the phrase ". . . so long you could strop your razor on 'em!" Benson laughed perfunctorily, and the captain's lips barely twitched in amusement and contempt. Probably Eric was the most appreciative member of Hartley's small audience. The man has a real gift for imagery, he thought.

Eric sipped his scalding coffee and, when he put it down, watched the slight, slow shifting of the fluid in the cup, first higher on one side, then on the other. He felt the effort of the ship's engine in pulses that entered his spine forty-eight times a minute. A room in motion is not a room at all, he thought. Having freed itself from complete subjection to the motion of the earth, such a room is more like a satellite or a comet—bound, yet having a measure of independence.

From the depths of the ship came the clang of an iron triangle being struck. It was ten minutes before the change of watch. Benson stood up and stretched. Then he went below.

Hartley poured himself another cup of coffee and put some cold water in it because he had to be on the bridge at eight.

"Well, Captain," he said boldly, "where we going?"

The captain was a man who thought quickly but felt no compulsion to reply quickly. There was half a minute of silence. Eric felt the pause painfully, but he was quite alone in his suffering.

Then Captain Brogan said, "You know as much about it as I do, Third."

"Well," the third mate answered, "my guess is England. We'll be over with all that limey tail again, learning to drop our aitches every time we drop our pants!"

The captain's mouth twitched again in that peculiar union of slight amusement and abstract contempt.

The pilot came down from the wheelhouse for a quick cup of coffee. He was a red-cheeked man with an air of land-locked security about him that one does not find in men who sail in deep water. He rubbed his hands together above his cup and said amiably, "Getting a little chilly topside, Captain."

The captain had been drawing invisible designs on the table with a toothpick, and he continued to do so. He had long since given up the practice of making politely meaningless replies. The pilot waited uncomfortably, but what possible reply was there to his remark? "Is that so?" or "Is it?" or "Well, well!"—any number of such senseless responses, any one of which would have made the captain feel stupid had he been compelled to use it.

The pilot was accustomed to social idiosyncrasies among seafaring men, however, and so his embarrassment was only momentary. He turned to Eric as though it were to him he had been speaking in the first place. "It *is* sort of cold in the breeze," he said.

"I imagine so," Eric replied.

And that settled the matter.

Eight bells signaled the end of the star watch, and the first mate came down from the bridge. He was a tall, lean, powerful old Dutchman named Vangaussen. There was a deep groove of scar tissue across the top of his bald head. He seemed to be an agreeable man—diplomatic, just, and highly capable, with a secret sense of humor which kept him in an almost continual state of quiet amusement, though he seldom revealed its source. He had the dignity of a man who is good at what he does, and knows it, but without vanity. He had almost no accent most of the time, just a somewhat unusual emphasis on the parts of a sentence.

"Well, here we go," he remarked, "with another load of coal. Probably we're going to Newcastle, eh, Sparks?"

"Probably," Eric said. "Or maybe Pittsburgh!"

. The first assistant engineer came up from below, wearing only an undershirt on the upper part of his beefy pink body. After he had prepared his cup of coffee he sat down at a table and remarked to all, "Well, I hear from the wiper that we're headed for the Med!"

"You can't trust wipers in these things," said Van, the first mate. "If you really want to get exact advance information about a ship's destination you got to go to the steward's department. You got to ask either the dishwasher or the third assistant cook!"

The first assistant, Duprey, was a curly-haired American of remote French derivation. He was a good engineer, touchy and self-centered—though not narrowly so—with a good lust for life; a man who loved exploration and exploit.

He was not easily approachable. No shipmate had ever dared to call him "Frenchy," "Curly," or any similar nickname. It was always either "First," or just Duprey. The "black gang" already respected him much more than they did their chief.

The deep-throated immediacy of the ship's whistle shook the saloon with two five-second blasts, and the pilot put down his cup and hurried toward the wheelhouse.

"What does that mean?" Eric asked.

"Nothing much," said the First. "Just that they've sighted a submarine or a floating mine."

"Or the Japanese fleet?" Eric suggested.

Seafaring men dearly love to find a gullible man, and it is a great pity that so few gullible men ever go to sea.

"Don't let him kid you, Sparks!" said Van. "It just means we're about to pass a garbage scow on the port side."

A small Italian wearing a soiled white shirt and a wrinkled pair of gray uniform pants came in and began to make a cup of cocoa. This was George Fiorini, the steward. He had the manner of a small boy playing gangster—and enjoying it. He carried his cup across the room and sat opposite Eric.

"That was a good meal you gave us tonight, Steward," Eric said conversationally. "First good steak I've had for a long time."

Immediately he sensed a social chill in the air of the room. He glanced at the faces of Duprey, Van, and the captain. The engineer gave him a scathing look, and the comradely temperature of the other two men had dropped close to absolute zero. He thus learned that he had violated a terrible taboo by praising the ship's food.

George, the steward, broke the icy silence by saying, "Yeah? Well, before the trip's over you'll be callin' me a goddamn belly robber, just like the rest of 'em!"

"Maybe," Eric said. "Maybe I will." He was grateful to the Italian for trying to rescue him from his own social error. He decided to return to his cabin and turn in for the night. He would not have to serve a watch until they were at sea. He said good night in a general way, but only the steward responded.

He had almost mastered the maze of narrow companionways and iron ladders which at first had seemed so labyrinthine, and now he made his way up to his cabin without difficulty. He fastened the door on the hook that held it five inches ajar, and felt his way toward the desk lamp, trying not to awaken Chuck.

He sat down at the desk and found the letter he had started to write to Jane:

. . . be faithful to me with all your flesh and dreams . . .

He listened to the uneven, dream-of-death, tortured muttering and snoring of the man in the upper bunk. He listened to the pulse of the engine.

Rereading his letter, it sounded even more feeble and foreign than before. He could hardly believe that there were such areas of insecurity within his own soul. Yet he knew that, if he had a chance, he would mail those words to Jane unchanged. In spite of all the wisdom and pride that warned him against it, he knew that he would write to Jane in this abject manner, stupidly pleading for her sexual fidelity as though it were something that could be given as alms to a whining beggar.

He removed all his clothes except his undershirt, placed them on the bench, turned out the lamp, and crawled between the cool sheets of his bunk. The junior engineer in the upper berth was talking to himself now, filling the darkness with words of protest and pleading.

Eric tried to think about some of the men he had met on the ship: the captain, First Engineer Duprey, Third Mate Hartley, the steward; the lonely and angry, the capable and explorative, the sardonic and eloquent, the bitter, sex-hungry clown. He tried to imagine how his impressions of them would change after months of close association; he tried to foresee what their interaction on each other would be, and how differently or similarly they would each respond to the unknown world at the other end of their voyage. But it was an effort for him to think of these things. His mind kept returning, like a sick dog rooting in offal, to ugly images of his wife's possible infidelity. And outside of these flagellations he felt increasingly the strangeness of metal enormity all around him, bearing him—on his back, as if in an act of levitation—toward its element, the sea. Scanning the darkness

34

restlessly, his eyes fell upon a luminous area, ghostlike, above
and to the right of his head. Or was it a little pattern of filtered moonlight? No—as his eyes grew accustomed to the
absence of other light he could read the letters:

ESCAPE PANEL
KICK OUT

And much as his mind had brooded over the complex
meaning of war, this was the closest his body had yet felt to
the simplicity of war's violence. As the night grew older the
words repeated themselves over and over in his dreams—
escape, escape, kick out, escape—twining themselves like an
alien vine through the rooms of a haunted house.

4: Life and Loves of a Queen Bee

For three days now the SS *William Benson* had been
anchored at Lynnhaven, near the mouth of the Chesapeake
Bay. The men on the ship could see a strip of gray sand that
faded back into the low, brush-covered shore line. No sign
of human habitation. There were several other ships anchored here, and every day a few more. This was the convoy
rendezvous. There was always a mist over the sea and shore,
and sometimes only the immediate circle of restless water
was visible. This world of water, shore, and mist—in which
the anchored ships seemed grimly intrusive—was dominated
by the insistent sea gulls. They circled, swooped, and hovered,
endlessly uttering their protests in raucous shrieks like the
ululation of a thousand rusty hinges. In counterpoint there
was the mournful tolling of a bell marker buoy to seaward.
This was a world of gray desolation in which even the angry
gulls were not at home.

Eric was miserable. The sense of loneliness, of severance
from everything that was relevant, of being an impostor in a
world that did not need him, had ceased to come in desperate
pangs and had now become a part of the atmosphere he
breathed.

The fact that the ship was anchored made everything much worse. As they had crept down the bay toward the rendezvous, he had thought: *A ship is a prison that moves.*

Now it was not moving.

They had left Baltimore in a great hurry, but it turned out that they were only the second ship to arrive at the rendezvous and that they might remain here for weeks until the others assembled. The prospect was frightening. Eric hated the ship now for its immobility. He began to long for motion with an aching, sexual hunger.

He had given the pilot a lengthy letter to Jane, but no sooner did he see the fellow climbing down the rope ladder to the waiting boat than he thought of a score of things he had failed to say to her. Still ashamed of this maudlin need for his wife's warmth and reassurance, he began at once to write another letter that seemed to him even more urgent and even more shameful than the first. He exhorted her not to be unfaithful to him, swore eternal fidelity, and expounded upon the fatal marital and cosmic consequences of one erotic slip. He was disgusted with himself but could not master the biologic compulsion that drove his pen. He hoped to get this last letter mailed on the day of departure when the captain and chief radio officer would go ashore to the convoy conference.

For hours every day he stood on the boat deck, bridge deck, or flying bridge, at the stern or the bow, staring at the water or shore line and listening to the irascible gulls. Once in a while the monotony was relieved by the arrival of another merchant ship at the rendezvous or by the sight of naval vessels coming in or moving out to sea: cruisers, baby flattops, DE's, destroyers. At other times a coast guard launch would come out to look them over. And everyone would be hopeful that it was bringing mail or sailing orders. But it always went away again without coming over to them. The ships were gray, the water and sky were gray, all shrouded in gray mists and haunted by gray gulls.

The coffee urn is now the center of warmth on the fog-chilled ship. It is here that the men meet and talk and size each other up. No man asks personal questions of another, yet this measuring process is their constant preoccupation.

And Eric begins to understand why this is so. He sees that on a ship, more than almost anywhere else, the character of every man is directly relevant to the survival of every other man. Therefore this searching into one another's souls is not an academic matter. In addition to the question of bodily survival there is the factor of confinement. There are thirteen officers on this ship and they are foredoomed to eating and working and relaxing together for unpredictable lengths of time, without any possible escape except death. They must find one another bearably interesting, or at least inoffensive. Their eyes search already for those who must be crudely or subtly quarantined. They are ruminating their own extensions of tolerance. As they talk with each intimate stranger they are gauging his weaknesses, probing for his breaking point, the exact stress past which he cannot be relied upon. They are analyzing his resources and estimating his coefficient of boredom, slyly comparing prejudices, seeking some comfortable congruence. The thing that grows out of all this searching and testing is the spirit within the steel body of the ship.

In spite of his depression, Eric felt unusually healthy. For a while after he had finished the rum he had brought on board he had really missed liquor. It was not a chemical thing like the cravings of an imprisoned dope addict. It was the loss of a habitual and ready-made relaxation, the loss of that daily hour in which he could, by the wonderful simplicity of drinking a few ounces of liquor, insulate himself from irrelevancies and feel thus easily concentrated upon what really concerned him. He had missed this wonderful trick of soul-freeing, as might a religious man who had suddenly lost his faith in prayer.

2

Let me have men about me that are fat, sleek-headed men, and such as sleep o' nights. . . . But not one of the fat men had a sleek head or slept very well at night. Not one of them was what Julius Caesar would have wanted to set himself at ease. The purser was, in fact, only what is generally called stout—a porcine young lawyer who had decided to join the Merchant Marine when his draft board classified him 1-A. He figured that as a purser he could at least maintain a part of the well-fed aplomb that he had so painstakingly achieved as an up-and-coming legal expert on trust funds and endowments. He had no delusions that it would be safer, but by joining the Merchant Marine he had at least escaped the indignities of basic training and had achieved officership after only a short course at the Maritime Academy.

Chief Engineer Curtis was definitely fat, with a real belly on him. An old-timer, a faker, a chief engineer who abhorred engines and ignored them as much as possible. A great teller of stories about the good old days when he was strictly a tanker man. False, grandiloquent, and mean; a man who was never liked on board his own ship but who could make more new friends in less time than anyone else once he got ashore.

And the second assistant engineer, whose name was Finley, but who had already been christened by Duprey as *"Der Auspuff Kessel"*—a term the First had learned while bringing back a captured German merchant ship—"waste-gas kettle." This man was really enormous. Guesses as to his actual weight varied between three hundred and fifty and six hundred pounds. Nobody could figure out how he could get down the narrow ladders into the engine room. He was very nearly as wide as he was tall. He continually groaned and grunted and sweated, belched, hiccupped, and farted. At mealtimes he usually ordered each of the main courses twice with a couple of extra side orders and desserts. Most of this intake seemed to come out of him in a gaseous form. Harry Shruck, the chief radio officer, a fastidious man, had to sit next to him at meals and did not like it at all. On the other side, the bench would be occupied by Benson, the Norwegian Third, but he was seldom there at the same time as *Der Kessel*.

Eric tried to place each of these men somewhere in the unique yet old pattern of the voyage. But he could see only that they were men like himself, caught first of all in the net of their own personal narratives and now suddenly cast into the white-hot, inexorable mold of history.

The sunset was unusually beautiful on the tenth evening after their arrival at the rendezvous. This was the twentieth of May. There were great banners of gold flowing up from the crimson horizon, and separate little clouds sailed into all this color like brave galleons going into battle.

Eric leaned against the boat-deck rail, looking west, watching the chromatic drama of sky and sea. Trite, he thought. Hollywood could do better. Whatever else God may be, he is definitely inferior to Walt Disney when it comes to handling sunsets.

He resented the sky and the sea and the ship. He felt like a prisoner convicted for a crime of which he is entirely ignorant.

Only a few minutes ago he had come up from the saloon where he had been drinking coffee and talking with *Der Auspuff Kessel* and the steward, and now he felt a total loss of human companionship. When he talked with these men, he knew that he was not *really* talking to them, nor they to him. It was only an exchange of formulas. These men on the ship never spoke in general terms. They never said: "Life is this way." "A man does such and such under these circumstances because . . ." "Love is . . ." "Death is . . ."

Life, love, death, man, time, beginning, end, change. Such generalities—the bases of all human reality—were never mentioned. What I did, what you did, we, she, he . . . did, said. That was all. And this made Eric very lonely. He felt himself truly a foreigner among a strange people.

In his current letter to Jane he had written:

> *God! How I would welcome some good affected phonies from Greenwich Village! Do you realize that the lousiest pretender who ever sat around the Village Vanguard trying to look like Van Gogh is closer to reality than any good solid he-man? These men with whom I now live— they react to stimuli but are not concerned with anything essential to the total structure of life, for the good reason that they are unaware of the existence of ideas. They are aware only of attractions and repulsions.*

That was what he had said in the letter, and he was ashamed of it. He felt that in writing such words he was betraying the great democratic tradition. It's just that I don't understand them yet, he told himself. These are, after all, the very men I've pretended to be talking about as a sociology teacher.

But no matter what he told himself, he felt very lonely as

39

he leaned against the rail on this tenth day of their anchorage, looking now at the yellow water and then at the fantastic sky. Trite, he repeated to himself. Very dull.

The naval officer in charge of the gun crew strolled over and stood near Eric. He was a small man who wore his tropical grays as though they did not belong to him. He had watery round brown eyes like those of a dowager's Pekingese.

"Pretty, isn't it?" he said, indicating the sunset.

"Not bad," Eric replied. And he was thinking: Can this timid-looking little man be the one in charge of shooting down airplanes and sinking submarines that may attack us? It seemed impossible, and yet it was so.

Eric walked away and stood behind the number four lifeboat on the starboard side. He really did not like to resent seas or sunsets or men. He knew that such resentments were idiotic. They were against everything in his own nature and made him feel like a snob and a fool.

The second mate, whose name was Burley, was smoking his pipe near by and now he came closer. He looked somewhat like Popeye the Sailor, mainly on account of a very bad set of false teeth which gave him a synthetic prognathism. Eric had discovered from previous conversations that this man lived within a series of hatreds which were seemingly endless. But perhaps hating is better than indifference, he had thought.

Burley wanted to talk. "Well," he said, "it's a relief not to carry ammunition for a change."

"Yes, I imagine. Is coal a safe cargo?"

"Safe? There's no fuggin' cargo in the world that's safe in wartime. Coal's heavier than water. It sinks."

"Lumber is best, I hear."

"You hear? Well, whoever told you that was a damned liar. Lumber shifts easy, and it catches fire."

"Well, anyway, coal isn't TNT."

"It might as well be when it's loaded into one of these tubs! *Liberty* Ships! Liberty shits—that's what they are. Fastened together with solder. Just touch one and it falls apart and sinks in a minute. Just look here."

He led Eric over to a bulkhead and pointed out a seam. "Welded by machinery—like by a goddamn sewing machine.

Break apart any time. Might as well be sewed together with thread."

"They do turn 'em out fast, all right."

"Know who makes 'em? A bunch of goddamn draft-dodgin' bastards in the shipyards. Fifteen, twenty dollars a day! Stickin' together these deathtraps and callin' 'em *Liberty* Ships. Just fine! They make 'em and we go down in 'em. You don't catch any of *them* out here sailin' 'em—unless it's to avoid the draft."

Eric repressed his resentment of this viciousness. He was not out to preach, he told himself, he was out to learn. And anyway, what was the use?

"Yes, I guess these prefabricated jobs aren't so good, but they've got to have them in a hurry," he said vaguely. "By the way, who is this ship named after?"

Burley took the pipe out of his mouth and spit into the water of the bay. "William Benson?" he said. "Probably some goddamn Bowery bum. That's what most of these ships are named after. Pimps and bums!"

"Well," Eric said thoughtfully, "that seems like a nice democratic way of naming ships."

Burley changed the subject. "I hear you're a school-teacher," he said slyly. "You're probably dying to see a few books."

"That is a fact!" Eric said emphatically.

"Well," the second mate told him, "I happen to have discovered where the ship's library is. It's hidden down behind the fresh-water tanks. Hundreds and hundreds of books. Want to see 'em?"

"Of course. Let's go."

Like two conspirators they went down ladders and through passageways into the depths of the ship. And there in a small, steamy room they found stacks and stacks of books. Probably more than a thousand of them. Good novels, obscure works, stupid tomes, fanatical tracts.

The second mate gave Eric a look of triumphant secret-sharing. And Eric was happier than he had been since coming on the ship.

Much as he felt that Burley was a fool—with all his witless prejudices—Eric could not now deny a feeling of brotherhood with him. For here, at least, was a man who, however crudely, lusted after books, a man to whom these stacks of damp and molding volumes represented mysterious treasures of vision.

The two men began to handle the books, glancing at the titles and stacking them in neater piles.

"You ain't a Jew, are you?" the mate asked.

"No," Eric said, "I'm not. Why?"

"Oh, nothing. Just some of these books. Written by smart Jews to put things over on people. You got a big nose— if you'll excuse me for saying so—but I never thought for a minute you was a kike."

Eric hated Burley again, hated him for his dull prejudice and dangerous ignorance. Yet he did not quite feel that the man's remarks were as vicious as they sounded. And this was because he knew that Burley was prejudiced against damned near everything in the world.

Then the second mate suddenly surprised Eric by approving of something, namely: Benjamin Franklin. He was holding Van Doren's biography of Poor Richard.

"By God!" he said gleefully, "this is a great book! Interesting from cover to cover. I never realized till I read this book that this Franklin guy was a *horny* bastard! Horny as hell! Did you know that?"

"No, I didn't."

"Well, just read it and see."

Eric added it to the stack of books he was taking with him.

"I wish there was something here on bees," said Burley wistfully.

"What?"

"Bees. Bumblebees, honeybees. I've read nearly everything written about the lives of bees. Know anything about them yourself?"

"Practically nothing," Eric replied, and he was rewarded by a grimace of satisfaction above Burley's outthrust mandible.

"Well—for example. There's only one queen bee, see? And when she begins to get hot she starts flying up toward the sun. She flies higher and higher—way higher than birds can go—with all the males trying to follow her. She's stronger than they are, see? So she keeps ahead of 'em, trying to exhaust all but one. So they all get pooped and drop out till there's only one strong little bastard left. Then she slows down and lets him catch her. They have their party up there high above the clouds—then the male dies. He's only good for one party."

"Very interesting and sad," said Eric.

"But the important thing to remember is this," Burley continued, speaking very slowly and impressively and hissing slightly through his false teeth, "that the bee is the only creature in the universe that's willing to die for his first piece of tail!"

Eric laughed, with the comradery of scholarship. "Oh, I don't know about that, Burley!" he said. "Ever hear of a character named Romeo?"

The second mate slapped him on the back, laughing uproariously and trying not to lose his teeth.

"I guess you got something there, Professor. You really have!"

3

When Eric went down to breakfast on the eleventh day of the anchorage off Lynnhaven, he immediately sensed a new vitality in the air. For a week now a feeling of depression and irritability had been a part of every breath of the gray mist they all inhaled. But this morning he found that mist dispelled by a whiff of anticipatory ozone. It was the day of the convoy conference. The captain and chief radio officer would go ashore at ten A.M. When they returned, the captain would hold another conference with his own officers here in the saloon.

After breakfast Eric sat in a canvas chair on the boat deck enjoying the rarity of sunlight. Chief Mate Vangaussen came and sat beside him.

"Well, Professor, how you like the seafaring life?" he asked in his joking but unmalicious way.

"I haven't seen the sea yet," Eric said.

"Oh, the sea!" said Van. "The sea, Professor, is just a lot of water. Same as this. The seafaring life is life on a ship— even if it's in the middle of the Sahara or on a mountain like Noah's Ark."

"It's okay," Eric said, "but it would be much better if we were moving. This being anchored is not so good."

He was somewhat relieved to note that the mate had ceased to call him "Sparks." Not that he relished the title of "Professor," but there were two other radio officers aboard, both of whom were called "Sparks" or "Sparky."

"Well, moving on one of these wonderful Liberty Ships is not much different from standing still," said the chief mate. "You won't notice any change."

They talked idly for a while, without embarrassment, without fear of silences. The conversation swung around to Van himself, and he told Eric whatever he wanted him to know; and that was not much.

Though he appeared to be about forty years old, he was sixty-two. He had gone to sea from his birthplace of Amsterdam at the age of fourteen. He chose to skip a good many details: how he had become an American, how he had risen to the rating of chief officer, and the origin of that livid scar that creased his bald skull.

At the age of fifty he had retired. He was married to a good woman whom he referred to as "The Commodore," and they owned a small orange grove near Anaheim, California. They had been consistently prosperous and happy. Their hobby was raising thoroughbred Doberman pinschers. But early in 1943 Van had returned to the sea.

At the age of threescore and two he was, in plain terms of muscle, the strongest man on his ship. He was the only man on board who could chin himself with one arm.

"Why did you come back to sea?" Eric asked him.

This was a crucial question to Eric because he wanted to know if this man could tell him what *enemy* had been evil enough and close enough to make him, at his age, relinquish his happy prosperity for a life of danger and severance from everything he now loved.

"Well," the mate replied, thoughtfully and slowly, "you see, I always got along fine with my neighbors. I help them, they help me—that's the way it is with orchard men. It's different from the way it is in cities. You help each other and lend each other things and think nothing of it. Except that— well, neighbors are more like relatives, you might say. So when the war came— They all knew I was a retired seaman.

They began to look at me in a funny way. Maybe they didn't, but I thought they did. I knew how many ships they'd have to have to win, and how few ship's officers they'd find already trained."

He sighed and began to pack his pipe with fresh tobacco. Then he continued: "I tell you, Professor, no man is rich enough to afford to lose the respect of his neighbors."

"I guess you're right," Eric agreed.

The mate laughed softly and added, *"Or* his wife!"

"Very true," Eric said. "Very, very true!"

At this moment the two of them heard a launch approaching and they got up to stand against the rail. It was the coast guard boat that took the men to the convoy conference where they would receive their secret instructions. They watched as Captain Brogan, in a civilian suit, and Chief Radio Officer Shruck, appareled in a natty blue uniform with lieutenant's bars and campaign ribbons, descended the rope ladder onto the pitching deck of the launch which then pulled away and cavorted like a spirited pony over the choppy water to the next merchant ship.

Van and Eric returned to their chairs in the gently warm sunlight.

"You sailed with Captain Brogan before?" Eric asked.

"Ever since I came back to sea," the mate said.

"Seems like a good man."

"Damn right he is. But he's had bad luck."

"How?"

"Well, he lost one of the first American merchant ships sunk after Pearl Harbor, for one thing. That was on December eighth."

"Yeah?"

"Yeah. The Jap sub knew there was no danger, so it wouldn't waste a torpedo. It just came up about three hundred yards off the beam and started throwing shells into the ship. Slow. Taking its time. It spent all afternoon tossing forty-seven four-inch shells. The Americans shot at the sub with pistols and rifles. Of course, they might as well have used cap pistols. When it started getting dark they abandoned ship. Japs tried to machine-gun the lifeboats but lost them. The captain's boat was at sea eighteen days. He was one of five survivors from his ship."

"God!"

"And then he lost his next three ships one after the other. I was on them, those next three. But it was never so bad as the first one must have been. We didn't spend much time in lifeboats—that is, those of us that got off. But after the fourth one Brogan went to the Company office and told them he wouldn't sail another ship in the Pacific. He told them his luck was bad there. So they transferred him over here to try his luck in the Atlantic. This is his first try."

All these words from Vangaussen had been said in a quiet, undramatic voice with overtones of obscure humor. There seemed to be nothing his secret amusement could not include.

At this moment the mess boy, whose first name was Harold, came around a corner of the housing. He was not supposed to be up here on the officers' decks unless on business—but he was a quick inventor of business.

"Fresh coffee, gentlemen!" he said. "Better come down and get it while it's good!"

He was a lanky nineteen-year-old with one of the most mobile faces Eric had ever seen. So great was the mobility of this lean and nervous physiognomy that one could hardly remember the boy from one meeting to the next. He had been a junior at NYU before joining the Merchant Marine.

"The coffee's especially for you, Professor!" he said to Eric. "So you'll give me good grades when I go back to school!"

It was difficult to determine whether he was being arrogant or merely ebullient. He was a strange kid and there was a fever in him.

They began getting up steam about noon and it was good to feel the increasing trembling of the ship. Strange and dreadful truth—but the men on a ship live according to its throbbings. They are the thralls, not of a machine, but of a plexus of human relationships that trembles and moves, yet may sometimes grow frighteningly quiet.

At four P.M. the captain held his conference of officers in the saloon. They all sat at the clean tables and the captain sat in the center. He was not a public speaker. It was obvious how much he disliked this duty. Sunlight came through the portholes at a low angle in dusty beams that gave the scene a religious tone and make Eric think of a *Last Supper* as it might be painted by some modern artist.

The facial expressions of the men ranged variously from stiff challenge to simple gravity. Eric was surprised to observe no embarrassment at this moment among these men who were so easily embarrassed by emotion.

The captain, now wearing civilian pants and white shirt, cleared his throat and said: "I guess most of you have heard that I'm supposed to be a tough captain. I don't know, myself, and the fact is, I don't care. I do know that any of you can come and see me any time you want, about anything that's on your mind. All you have to do is come up and knock on my door.

"But there are a few things I'm strict about. First of all, I want this saloon kept clean. There'll be a bucket for dirty dishes, and I want them in there. There'll be no linen on the tables after dinner.

"This isn't the Navy and it isn't the Army and it isn't the Marines. Every man is free here as long as he does his work. But this also is not a fishing boat! So I expect you to be decently dressed when you come in to eat. I don't want the engineers coming in here in their undershirts.

"And I want also to say to the engineers—and they should tell this to their men—that the Abandon Ship signal does not mean that the men can leave the engine room. You must keep headway. You down there will be told through the speaking tubes from the bridge when you can leave the engine room! Anyone who fails to understand this will be shot if I can arrange to see him."

Eric had never observed such an attentive audience. In fact, it was the first time he himself had ever listened to a speaker whose every word seemed to be so vitally significant. The captain continued, and now he spoke more slowly, his voice matter-of-fact yet final: "I don't make any rules on my ships that aren't necessary. The important thing is this: We've got a job to do—and it's not a pleasant job."

Eric noted how this man, who had within him an imagery of personally experienced horror, carefully avoided even such words as "dangerous." Instead he said, "not pleasant." But the men knew what he meant. His reticence drew them all closer together.

"I guess you understand me," the captain said. "You can do whatever you want if it's got nothing to do with the operation of this ship. But there are a few matters where I insist upon your discipline, and on those matters I insist upon *perfect* discipline—down to a gnat's ass!

"Where we're going is still supposed to be a navy secret, so I won't tell you. But that doesn't matter. If you get there, then you'll find out. And whatever you find out, you probably won't like it. But we've got a job to do, and we've got to do it."

The men in the room were silent and waiting. Each man in his own way seemed turned inward, wondering why, after all, he was here on this iron venture toward disaster.

The captain stood up.

"That's all," he said.

5: Darkened Cities of the Brain

It seemed monstrous and futile, this steel hulk, rolling slightly and tugging at its anchor in the outgoing tide. Moving through the starboard side of the hull and inner bulkhead, one could enter a room of the crew's quarters. It was an iron room with four bunks of pipe and canvas, and each bunk had a spotlight reading lamp at its head, so that a man could see without disturbing those who were sleeping.

Now only one of these lamps was burning. Two bunks were occupied by men who slept. A third was empty. On the fourth, a lower, sat a boy named Oscar. His hair had been clipped and his skull was enormous—like that of the Man of the Future as portrayed in science fiction stories. His nose a white lump, his Oriental-lidded eyes very small, his mouth a loose rosebud of pale pink, his skin covered with pimples, soft down on his cheeks, and scattered tufts of stiff yellow hair growing here and there. He sat with his receding chin in his yeasty hands and he was whispering aloud.

"Clean up that mess—clean up that mess. Clean up that dirty mess or we'll shoot you with a submarine. I know what that means. I worked on one of those Jap submarines before the war began. I was married to a beautiful girl too, a moving-picture girl, and we had four children. I know what they mean. Listen! Four into forty goes ten times. Ten, ten, ten. I know it, I *always* knew it. You laugh at me, but none of you know ten. Not the way I know it. Ten, ten—I really know what ten means. Ten more times. Ten forward and ten back—that makes three strokes divided into thirty dollars—and that means ten." He laughed, repressing his laughter into his belly, afraid of getting into trouble again.

Looking into his memory, one could see a treasury that had been looted by impersonal vandals, a careful file system reshuffled by a delirious cardsharp, a good frame of type that had been pied by the wanton hand of chemical destiny. "I know about ten," he was repeating to himself with crafty smiles. "Ten is ten—and ten times once over is ten again!"

The door opened and the fourth crew member who shared this room entered and began to undress. His name was "Kentucky," and it seemed that he was, in spite of his newness at sea, the nimblest man on board ship. But he was not happy.

"Foah Christ's sake! Oscah!" he said. "Why don' you take a showah? We cain't stand it in heah with you if you ain'l *nevah* goin' to wash!"

Oscar laughed with forgetful loudness. "Sometimes I wash my hands *ten* times a day!" he shouted gleefully. "Ten times! In a week that's seventy. In four weeks two hundred and eighty!"

Kentucky stripped to his underwear and swung up into his bunk. "Well, you bettah try washin' somethin' moah than you hands once in a while," he muttered. "Stinks like a daid mule in heah."

Oscar took off his shoes after considerable difficulty with the laces, and then got into bed with all his dirty clothes on. He fumbled for a long time with the toggle switch and finally pushed it in the direction which extinguished the lamp. Then he lay there, breathing deeply and saying the multiplication table in a barely audible whisper. In his enormous brain case the dream fragments whirled about like multitudinous snowflakes in the unpredictable gusts that blow up and down the crisscross alleys of a winter city.

There were little flakes of pure pain that melted into pud-

49

dles of tremulous laughter. Geometric crystals of memory that met and fused into patterns ever more elusively complex. Heavy flakes of desire that were swept around cruel corners and stunned against alien stone.

There was anarchy within this large brain. Every thought, impulse, and memory chose to live its own individual life, and was thus briefly inflamed and soon singly extinguished. The body of this haunted idiot was a clumsy thing, almost useless as far as work on the ship was concerned, jerked this way and that by all these separate explosions of consciousness that were the diffuse reality of his soul and yet were not far distant from that of any man. Only the multiplication tables remained as an unbroken theme. Ever since he had learned them in the Baltimore Special School for Subnormal Children he had clung to them as a unifying force. The chief engineer and captain had not dared to refuse to sign him on, for there is nothing so certain to bring bad luck to a ship as the mistreatment of an idiot.

Kentucky, in the upper bunk, was wide awake. He was a farm boy, strong, good-natured, and only cruel through ignorance. His mind was as troubled as Oscar's. Only he had an over-all pattern, a framework of prejudices and convictions, whereas Oscar had only the multiplication tables.

Kentucky was a great show-off during the daytime, but now in bed all he kept thinking was: What am I doing out here?

His father needed him back on the farm and why, really, should he be out here on this damned thing that would float through the water all night, all day, toward destinies he did not know nor want! Why?

He knew they thought he was okay as a sailor here because he could climb anywhere any time and do what was needed. But he longed for the quiet fields of tobacco and the mastery of good plow horses. He was arrogant during the day, but now he knew that he was locked in an iron box that floated, far from the good soil, and he was uncomfortable.

The idiot beneath him did not improve his composure. "Seven times nine is sixty-three, eight times nine is seventy-two, nine times nine is—"

"Shut up!" Kentucky yelled. "Stop your goddamn countin'! I cain't stand it! You stinks and you counts all the time! I gotta get some sleep. Now shut your mouth befoah I stick mah foot in it!"

Oscar faded out on nine times nine is eighty-one and became quiet, his theme of survival swinging inward and becoming more secret. To himself he said silently, with pain-racked triumph, "And ten times ten *is* one hundred!"

The captain's quarters were two decks higher up. They were quite spacious. He had an office, a private shower and toilet, and a sleeping room considerably larger than any other on the ship. His electric fan was running full speed, and he lay naked on his bunk. He was only half asleep, and a twenty-five-cent mystery story was in his lax hands. A body had been found. And the question was, who had killed this quiet old southern colonel? It seemed curious that such stylized approaches to the subject of death could so interest a man who had quite recently seen so many real men really die. What unforeseeable naïveté retained his interest in these dull formulas, these innumerable testaments of a popular religion in which homicide is the Holy Ghost and the sacred idols are all cadavers?

Searching the tortured discipline of his nerves, one might find the hint of an answer. In mystery stories the captain sought a minimization of death. He was haunted by a knowledge of the straining death of great ships and their men of flesh and blood. And in reading these books that said death was a cute little parlor game he found momentary relief from such gigantic memories.

Now as he drew closer to sleep the visions of the four ships that had sunk under him drew closer to his bitter memory of love. Closer to the image of the wife who had been for a while the only person in the world he had ever worshiped or trusted. He had found her after a youth of passionate disbelief, and he had *believed*. For about six months he had lived in a state of goodness and completion and decency that he had never before thought possible. Then it ended. She had scuttled the graceful ship of love as offhandedly as one tosses overboard the butt of a cigarette. Thereafter this lovely blond animal, this sweet phantom of emptiness, had libeled and robbed him. All this was intertwined now with his wartime loss of four ships.

A great ship, uptilted, slowly sinking beneath the surface of the sea, is to its captain and its men the end of a faith. And there is a limit to the number of faiths any man can lose. Captain Brogan did not feel that he could lose again and live. He had said to himself that if he lost this ship and remained alive he would never sail again. What he would do he did not know. He might become a shipyard construction worker or a whoremaster. But he would never command another ship just as surely as he knew he would never fall in love with another woman.

The mystery novel fell from his limp hand and he emitted a loud snore. He was asleep. Yet this was no indication that he had eluded his own structure of pain. On the contrary, he was now launched into the dream world where he was not even the *captain* of anything but only the helpless witness of an endless pageantry of disaster.

Ascending vertically, one might see the ships of the great convoy disappear beneath a stratum of clouds, level as the prairies, phosphorescent with moonlight. And above would be the clean black sky and its uncertain stars and steady planets and the unabashed floodlight of our dead satellite.

One might pass back across the earth and, re-entering evening, visit again the basement on Thirteenth Street Northwest, where Eric Clark had lived with Jane and where Jane now lived alone. There was an atmosphere of sterility.

Jane Clark was eating an unsatisfying meal of hamburger and canned peas, accompanied by a bottle of the most expensive American wine she had been able to find, a red wine from the Napa Valley region. She was reading the *Washington Post*. She had been out all day looking for a job. She was tired. She was many new things. And quite perversely it appeared, now that she was alone and celibate, that she was more female than she had ever been before.

Yet when there was no Eric to come home in the evening the meaning of the basement apartment had disappeared for her. All her actions in this place—her very breathing and being—seemed like shadowy silhouettes of what had once been three-dimensional living. Cleaning the rooms was nonsensical, cooking was burlesque, eating was a task, going to bed was merely crawling between two sterile sheets, bathing was no more than a habit, and getting up in the morning was only something that was slightly better than staying in bed.

After she had finished eating the unsavory food, she poured herself another glass of the *pinot noir* and began to reread Eric's last letter:

> *I am now not afraid of the enemy nor the sea, but only of losing you. So I ask you to free me from this fear. Keep everything that we have had—as I will keep it. Love me, be faithful to me with all your flesh and dreams and memories—as I shall be to you.*

She looked at the words written in ink on the white, smudged paper, and the words and the ink and the paper were strange to her. But most of all, the words. Who *was* this man who had written this letter to her and signed her husband's name to it?

It was, she felt, someone she had always known. But it was certainly not Eric. She had known only two men intimately. Could this be Jimmy? That was manifestly impossible.

Then slowly she recognized who it was. In drifting brain fumes of wine and weariness and memory, partly in inconclusive words and partly in dismembered imagery, she identified her clamorous suitor.

He *was* Jimmy. Not the Jimmy who had been, but the Jimmy she had wanted. The Jimmy she had yearned for and tried vainly to mold out of a brittle and feeble reality.

Ah, the long-remembered Jimmy! He had gotten himself into every possible scrape at college. Caught in a gambling-joint raid. That hadn't really mattered. Then he was accused of selling goods stolen from the school supply store. But nothing had been proved.

Something of the femaleness of Jane had responded to this febrile and weak young man as it had never responded—and might never respond again—to any other man. As far as rationalizing about it went, she was ashamed. But deeper, way deeper, she was proud. He *had* needed her.

At that time she had planned a career. Sometimes she thought of herself as a painter, sometimes a writer, sometimes an actress. She would take care of him, be misunderstood with him, by the whole world. Because she knew that he was not really bad, but just unwilling to adjust himself to a prosaic world.

He borrowed small sums of money from her—which he never repaid.

She went frequently to his furnished room. She gave her virginity to him, and it seemed almost irrelevant. She never told him and she doubted that he was aware that he was the first man ever to have her. She had wanted to tell him and make it important, but she felt sure that he would only laugh and pat her on the buttocks. Yet he did need her.

Sometimes he cried. These were moments of dissolution, rare moments in which all his brashness melted into a scared babyishness. And then she would treat him like a baby. Feed him with her milkless breasts and soothe him with anxious hands.

"You're good to me," he would say. And those were the only occasions where he seemed to know any kind of gratitude.

Then he was accused in a campus rape case. The girl was bruised and frightened. She identified Jimmy as her assailant, but later changed her mind. It was dark, she said, and she could not be absolutely sure. Jane was sure. Yet she had not called Jimmy a liar and she had not told him she was through with him.

He had made the break himself, meanly, badly, as he did everything. "I'm going away," he told her.

"Where?" she wanted to know.

"What's it matter?" he asked.

She offered to go with him and he laughed out of the corner of his mouth in a way he must have learned from the movies, but he was genuinely amused.

"What for?" he asked.

Yet in spite of this contemptuous question she knew that he needed her. And she could not bear to think of him crying—without her.

After he went away she lived for a while in a sort of somnambulism. Her dreams of being George Sand or Mary Cassatt or Jeanne Eagels faded away into a pale mist of relinquished melodrama. But she could not forget Jimmy nor anything she had ever done with him.

She seemed to have lost a multiple thing. She no longer wanted to be a famous painter or writer or actress, and she no longer hoped to possess a needful thing she could warmly nurture.

But she had wider reserves of awareness than she herself had suspected. And when she met Eric she visualized a world in which words and ideas were more important than actions and desires and fears and loathings and sacrifice. So she had married her sociology teacher.

Objectively she realized that her husband, Eric, had now —by some alchemy she could not fathom—become the archetype of what she had wanted from her first lover. For a moment this struck her as being a highly amusing situation. Her wonderfully strong Eric suddenly becoming weaker than her wonderfully weak Jimmy!

What Circe of danger or desolation had so beautifully demeaned him?

The world around her became animate again. She poured another glass of wine and drank it as though it were the fermented essence of personal happiness. Eric, her own Eric, really needed and loved her that way!

She toyed with her glass and her dreams, knowing that— whether or not she was truly happy—she was at least alive for the first time since he had gone away. The beating of her own heart no longer seemed monotonous, inhaling and exhaling no longer bored her.

Dear Eric, she thought, poor Eric. I hold you closely, I touch you, I hold you like a baby. Have no fear at all. My arms are around you. With all my flesh and dreams and memories. Yes—yes—always!

She put her fingers to her eyes, feeling that they must be wet. But her eyes were not wet. She looked around the apartment, trying to identify each object with Eric. The electric fan he had repaired when its commutator began to spark alarmingly. With just a bit of sandpaper he had made it work again. The alcove where the stove was, hung with red and white checkered oilcloth—like the stage of an Italian puppet show, he had said. The double boiler in which he had managed to burn his dinner that night when he got drunk and decided to quit his job here in Washington and join the Merchant Marine. The enamel was all cracked now in the bottom section.

Yet there was something false in all this painfully born happiness of Jane's; something such as an artist feels when his brain tells him that what he is doing is absolutely right and yet he *feels* something wrong. He fights against such a vagary, though he knows secretly that it is true. And finally he admits it.

With Jane this process did not take so long as though she were painting a picture or writing a story. It took only two more glasses of the good, clear, garnet-colored wine.

This is, in a way, Jimmy, she thought. Not the Jimmy who was, but the Jimmy I wanted. And this is really Eric. But it is *not* the Eric I wanted; it is the Eric I did not want!

I loved Jimmy because he was weak, but he was not weak enough. I loved Eric because he was strong, and now it turns out that he is not strong enough. Does that mean that there is no man in the world strong enough to love and no man weak enough? Must all women then be satisfied with disgusting admixtures of strength and weakness, unpalatable dilutions of masculinity? She felt simultaneously victimized and disloyal, cruelly amused and bewildered.

She poured the last of the wine into her glass, holding the bottle upside down and watching the drops fall more and more slowly from the green neck until the last one would not fall but hung there tremulously, catching the light like a liquid gem. Wishing to destroy this lovely jewel, she rubbed the rim of the neck with her finger and then hastily wiped her finger on a paper napkin, suddenly remembering the secret amalgam of shame and satisfaction she had once felt as a child when she had pulled the wings off a beautiful black and yellow butterfly.

PART TWO | VOYAGE

6: The Silence Where the Killers Wait

"Good mawning, prease, Honoraber Professaw!" said the high-pitched, ryhthmic Japanese voice. "Hahving this mawning first-crahss eggs recentry produced by Honoraber Purser! You are wishing some, fried on each side, prease?"

Eric was not startled.

"Well, if they were laid by the purser," he said, "I'll try them. And bacon and toast and orange juice and coffee."

Harold, the mess boy, was an impersonator. He had been on Major Bowes's Amateur Hour and had entertained at numerous college events. He was never the same nationality two times running. One minute he was an Oriental, next minute a Mexican. Eric had met him as a Greek, Englishman, Chinese, Southerner, Swede, and in an obscure impersonation he could not identify until Harold had confessed that he was making his first effort at being an Eskimo, and that he knew next to nothing about Eskimos.

"Honoraber orange juice are from cahns," Harold said. "So, begging your most humber pardon, sir, is more advisaber you should partake of grapefruit which are fresh."

"Okay, then give me the honorable grapefruit," Eric said. And Harold bowed stiffly, hissed, grinned crazily, and scurried into the galley.

Eric was both pleased and slightly worried by this precocious youngster. He had been watching him closely and had talked to him as often as possible.

Harold was not just trying to show off when he changed from one kind of person into another. He reminded Eric of certain highly strung children who begin a game playfully but soon become absorbed into it in some feverish, wild, and fateful fashion, as though they are possessed by desperate demons of need.

Eric was the last man down for breakfast this morning, and Harold had already removed the linen from all the tables but his. They were six days at sea now and everyone was pretty well acquainted with everyone else's habits.

After Harold had served Eric's food he brought his own plate of ham and eggs and sat down at the other side of the table. This was against regulations, since this was the officers' saloon, but inasmuch as Harold spent all his working time serving food in this room he could see no reason why he should not eat here. So far nobody had objected. Certainly Eric would not object. Diffidence and impertinence were curiously blended in the mess boy's attitude toward the officers.

Toward Eric, however, Harold had a special attitude, a special excitement. There was a nervous need in him that reached toward the older man; there were insistent questions in him that never left him alone, and he felt perhaps that Eric might answer a few of them and leave him a little less troubled.

Eric had recognized all this and also the shyness that went with it. He led the boy on, gently as a good mother, asking about his studies, laughing at his nervous jokes, waiting for the time when his false brashness would give way to trust. He learned all about what subjects Harold was studying at NYU and what professors he had liked and what had bored him. Usually when Harold found himself approaching what really concerned him he would shy away and turn on an almost hysterical humor. But that skittishness was diminishing.

This morning after he had finished being a Jap he was almost unafraid with the "professor." Because he wanted to have time to talk, he slowly cut his fried eggs into small pieces before beginning to eat.

"What got me," he said, "was when I realized that *seeing* is something that happens in my brain. It's a chemical reaction in my brain cells. And hearing is the same. And touching, and knowing—and everything. As far as I can ever know, they're just chemical reactions that happen inside my own brain."

He began to cut his ham into bite-size pieces. "If I had in my brain the chemical reaction of seeing you there and hearing your voice," he said, "it wouldn't make a goddamn bit of difference whether you were there or not! It would be exactly the same! Not a bit of difference!"

"Well," said Eric, "it might make a little difference to me, you know. I'm definitely certain that I'm not just a chemical reaction within your brain."

Harold put down his knife and fork and forgot all about his breakfast. "Yes—but you *could* be!" he shouted. "Even the sound of your saying you weren't a chemical reaction within my brain could be a chemical reaction within my brain! That's what scares me. Nobody can really tell what's real and what isn't!"

At first Eric was about to give him a snug, smug statement of reassurance. But then he thought: Do *I* know what's real and what isn't? If I knew even *that* much, would I be out here on this ship at this moment?

"You're right," he said, "the true nature of reality *is* a mystery. Apparently, anyway, we can only work toward a human reality. Absolute reality is beyond us, for a variety of very sufficient reasons. And even the conception of an extensive *human* reality is difficult. Because each of us lives within the separate world of his own consciousness. It's as though we were each the center of a great sphere, but that all these spheres are interpenetrating, all overlapping or concentric, mingled together in the totality of consciousness."

Harold sat staring at this new image, not seeing the saloon any longer, as his fried eggs grew cold and the grease congealed on his ham.

Eric went out on the main deck and walked slowly forward, making his way between the crates of deck cargo. It was a perfectly clear morning. They had long since left the Gulf Stream and the air was crisply cool. The warm steel deck, daubed with red lead where the gray paint had peeled off, rose and fell very gently beneath him, giving him the sensation of becoming now a little heavier than usual, and now a little lighter.

On the bow he stood on the iron block that guided the starboard anchor chain, and peered down at where the cutting edge of the great ship split the water of the Atlantic Ocean. That narrow area of conflict between man's ship and

God's ocean, or man-fabricated steel and nature's vast salt water, presented a fascinating spectacle. First the water would build up ahead of the prow in an increasing hill, then it would give way to each side in a suddenly hissing and whishing spread of foam. This momentous drama of gravitation and movement and viscosity recurred with an irregular rhythm, as the factors of swell and current and wind were never quite the same. Scene after scene rushed toward extinction, losing its identity in the unique configuration of its successor.

Eric peered down at this narrow and wonderful area of struggle, and thought: One could watch this forever and never see the same picture twice. Though this is what is usually called monotonous, the truth is that it is only possible to feel monotony when you are unable to see the difference between one moment and the next. To the very dullest person everything is monotonous, and to the most aware person nothing is monotonous.

The endless opposition and surrender of the cobalt-blue water, with its million white bubbles of resistance and defeat, exerted an almost hypnotic attraction. Occasionally there were intrusions of gold-brown seaweed or pale sea animals. The play of foam was like a wonderul unrehearsed ballet which, at every moment, has never been before and will never be again. But the end of this, thought Eric, is idiocy. Follow through on this and all our most intelligent citizens might take to contemplating each other's navels or engraving the Bill of Rights on the head of a pin.

He tilted back his head and looked at the sky and smelled the clean air. The air that blew in his face, the air of the Atlantic Ocean, did not have that smell that is so good when one on land approaches the coast and finds, at long last, the good smell of the sea. This had worried Eric until he figured out that what he, as a landlubber, thought of as the smell of the sea was really the smell of the beach. This ocean air was wonderfully clean, though it lacked the tonic suggestiveness of beach air. Eric looked around now at the other ships.

There was no desolation of sea out here. There were ships everywhere. One hundred and eighty merchant ships in this single convoy. Scores of fast American DE's and Canadian corvettes running around them like collies protecting a herd of sheep. Masts and superstructures of ships as far as the eye could see. It was like a city. A forward-moving city. Ships of many nations, British and American and Norwegian and Greek and Dutch, bravely flying their different flags. Each of these steel structures was complex beyond all individual imagination. Yet here they were. Many men had created and brought together what no one man could even dream. To Eric this was a scene of incomparable grandeur and dignity; this coalition of man and material, of human strength and world vastness, this forest of ships moving forward, forward, forward, silently and proudly, with a giant pride that even the sea could not mock.

2

By midafternooon the good weather was not with them. In the morning one could have said of the sea, "This is only water, a desert of water."

But by noon the ocean was no longer merely an expanse. Heavy gray swells swept toward them from the south. The sea was beginning to show its strength, barely but significantly flexing itself. The sky grew gray and lowering, so that each succeeding hour saw the ships passing through a thinner stratum of visibility. And now Eric knew that a ship is not a free thing in an element of friendly buoyancy; a ship is a reckless challenge to mighty and indifferent powers. Looking at this new aspect of the sea, it seemed as though there might be inaudible thunder rumbling somewhere within its depths.

The evening was only a narrow strip of burnt orange on the western horizon, and then the black night was upon the convoy and there was no longer any sea or sky. And this was their greatest danger. One hundred and eighty big ships without lights, moving on zigzag courses through darkness so impenetrable that a man could not see his own ship, let alone any other.

It seemed impossible, and of course collisions were not uncommon, but no deck officer or seaman could understand why they were not a thousand times more frequent.

Now Eric was on watch in the radio room—or "shack," as it is called—and he could feel the urgent swells of deep sea water beneath the ship and the throb of the great triple-expansion engine pushing it forward through the dark. All around him, from the deck and bulkheads, and connecting with him through the swivel chair, up through his spine, he could feel the thrust of the ship.

The radio room was about twelve feet square. Three sides were filled with apparatus. The available space was only about four by six feet. Metal and Bakelite panels rose from the deck to within two feet of the overhead. On these panels there were fourteen meters, five pilot lights, twenty-three switches, fifty-four knobs and dials. This was the incredibly alien place in which Eric was sole master for four hours out of every twelve. This was the sensory center of the ship.

Eric was alone with his job. He was the only inhabitant of this nerve center of oscillatory circuits and hertzian awareness, and he was in charge of it. He felt himself to be the nucleus of a cell, the center of some strange unit of electronic warfare; murder and defense deriving from capacity and inductance.

I am really alone here, he thought. I am the sensory as well as the extrasensory perception of this ship. If it is headed for the fire, the hot warning of that impending pain will come first through my nerves. He saw himself as the accidental arbiter of this calculated plexus of prescience.

He felt aloof and alone and insulated here in the radio room. He felt silence, and that was peculiar because the place was full of sound. Both the high and low frequency receivers were on at all times. The h.f. came through a speaker located under the typewriter table, and the l.f. came through the phones which Eric usually wore around his neck —for it is only in the movies that radio operators sit with headphones clamped tightly on their ears.

From these two supersensitive mechanisms there came the noise of static, varying from the amplified sound of frying bacon to shattering crescendos like concentrated gunfire; there were also groans, wails, snappings, rasps, whistles, sudden shrieks, and occasional prolonged notes of pure pitch.

How is it, Eric wondered, that a ship is the noisiest place in the world, and yet it *feels* silent? He sat there listening, trying now to hear all the sounds that came from outside this room. The sounds of the sea and the air, the ship and its men.

He thought that he could hear the whisper of foam spreading back from the bow—but this must have been imaginary. Certainly, though, he could hear the wind moaning very faintly around the housing and making a louder fluttering sound in the wind scoop that blacked out the single porthole.

He could hear the dynamo-like hum of the gyroscopic compass in the chart room. And always, of course, the reassuring *tah*-tuh, *tah*-tuh, *tah*-tuh of the engine. These were explicable, but there were also many sounds that Eric could not identify. There was slow creaking, rapid rattling, sporadic clanking, and untraceable swishing and gurgling. All part of the physiology of the ship.

Then there were the sounds of men on the ship. Once in a while there were voices from above, and they had a strange ventriloquial quality. There was the hollowness of footsteps on the deck over his head, and the thin slap of shoes on the smooth steel rungs of ladders.

A whole world of sound. And the sounds within the radio room spoke to Eric now in intimate though cryptic language. He understood the meaning of every howl and rasp and dot and dash. But it had not been this way in the beginning. There had been some bad moments.

His duties were to see that all the apparatus was functioning properly, to make an entry in the log every fifteen minutes, to keep constant watch on the distress frequency of five hundred kilocycles, and to cover the BAMS schedules —Broadcasts to Allied Merchant Ships—which occurred on various frequencies at prearranged intervals.

On the first day at sea when he had been confronted with his first general area message from NAM, the navy shore station, something entirely horrible had happened to him.

He had received the area call signal, BAMS2A, and had made ready with a clean sheet of tablet. The message was sent precisely. He got the heading all right. Then came the text, in five-digit cipher.

He wrote down the first eight groups, and then all at once his heart began to beat very fast and the muscles of his hand began to stiffen. He began to sweat. He could see from here forward that he would never be able to read his own handwriting. The figures were either cramped hieroglyphics or enormous scrawls. His hand was a tight, shaking knot of pain; the stiffness extended up his forearm to his elbow. He began to miss entire groups. His mind would suddenly be closed by some awful sphincter of inability. He was deadly afraid that one of the other operators would come in and witness his breakdown. When it was all over Eric was wet and trembling and weak. For a few minutes he did not know what to do. And then he did something more cowardly than he had ever done before in his life. He retyped his log and omitted the fact that there had been an area message on the NAM schedule.

Of course he knew that it could not have been vitally important to his ship or it would have been addressed to the secret call of the convoy instead of just to the general area. But he also knew that to be a very lame defense, for every message was important to every man on every ship in every convoy. Maybe routine—and maybe life-or-death. Yet he had faked it, pretended in the log that no such message had ever occurred. It was the first shameful act he could remember since childhood.

When he was thirteen he had sold his pet opossum to some laborers for fifty cents. They put a rope around its left hind leg and dragged it off, and it was hissing and spitting with terror. The laborers laughed and talked about the stew they were going to make. The opossum floundered in pain, and they kicked it. Eric would have given all the fifty-cent pieces in the world to retract his criminal betrayal of that sleepy animal. But it was too late.

When he falsified the log to cover up his own inability to copy the message, he had felt the same self-disgust. Yet he knew that if he admitted the shameful truth it would work as it does when a man admits sexual impotence after a single failure. He would be judged, and that judgment would permeate his consciousness and his flesh. Then he would *never* be able to do his job.

He began to think about cowardice. Was it fear that had caused his failure? He thought not. He now saw the great importance of training. He had failed because he had been confronted with a totally unfamiliar emergency. That unfamiliarity was his undoing. It is the purpose of army training for example, to make even the murder of one man by another a familiar and accustomed process.

And now, though his shame did not diminish, he knew that his decision had been functionally correct. For his hand had become steady, his ear alert, and he was probably quite as efficient as the other two radio officers on the SS *William Benson*.

Now every squeak and dot and squawk and dash spoke to him very clearly and simply. He was at last really the master of this weird center of electrical awareness. These supersensory devices had become extensions of his own consciousness.

He noted the position report of the United States Army hospital ship *Algonquin,* and recorded it in the log. He knew the satisfaction of assurance that he could do his job at this particular moment of conflict. And yet, he thought, certainly I am not any *braver* now than I was when I broke down trying to copy that first message. Maybe I was afraid, and maybe I still am.

Fear is something that should always be admitted, he thought; cowardice, never.

He felt again the motions of the ship. It rolls and pitches slightly. But what is more important is that it throbs and trembles. The deck is always breathing beneath one—always this breathing and trembling, shuddering and sighing—and one might well miss this sensuous coloring of life when one is again on rigid earth.

Here in mid-ocean Eric at last began to feel at home. And if he knew fear now it was at least not the fear of his own incompetence. He could function here, and hence he could transfer all his fear outside himself. He could be afraid of something entirely foreign that was hidden under the surface of the sea and flying in the gray sky. Something alien that really wanted to kill him.

And now, at this moment, he could hear only two sounds in the radio room. His consciousness had become irrelevantly selective, narrowed, perhaps, by the sickness of remembered shame. Every other sound on the ship was erased by the prophetic persistence of two cruel sounds.

One was the ticking of the chronometer on the wall. This was one of the most accurate clocks in the world, and it had a balance wheel in it that ticked off the real seconds of Eric's real life. This clock ticked and Eric listened to it and knew that it was ticking off the numbered moments of his own time on earth and that of everyone else who was then alive.

Then the other sound. Rattle . . . clack. Rattle . . . clack. It was a pencil rolling in a desk drawer as the ship rolled from side to side. The great feminine breathing and twisting of the ship was causing this little sound in the drawer—the pencil rolling back and forth. Eric found that such a small and futile sound in such a large ship gave him a sense of loneliness that was completely inexplicable, different from anything he had ever felt before. A thin sickness was at the core of this loneliness, and yet it seemed to rise slowly away from him on wide black wings of impersonal grandeur.

3

Shortly before midnight Peters came into the radio room to relieve Eric, who was preparing to conclude his section of the night's log.

Peters was a small, pimply fellow, twenty-two years of age, with a large head and earnest red-lidded, beige-colored eyes. He had a lofty forehead and a weak chin. Yet there was in this unprepossessing face some element of strength—or at least, confidence—which would have been hard to identify if one had not known that Peters was what is called a "radio ham." In other words, he had grown up from childhood in a world of quartz crystals, transformers, oscillators, filters, grid leaks, variable condensers, IF stages, heterodyne principles, beat frequencies, decrement, modulation, decibels, ohms, mhos, henrys, farads, shacks, rigs, and the like. That is to say, the world of amateur radio. He spoke the language of that world, and he was perfectly self-assured in it. He felt that everyone outside this familiar realm was somewhat strange and not quite real. He could not understand why Eric, who after all was functioning here as a radio man, did not seem to be able to enjoy lapsing into the only true language. He respected the older man, but felt that the guy must be holding something back. Peters tried again and again to break down Eric's seeming unfriendliness. Now he sat on the lifeboat transmitter and waited to take over the watch.

Eric typed his last log entry, then took the sheet out of the typewriter, signed it, and stood up. Peters stood up too. "You know," he said, "I been planning my new rig, my post-war rig, just working on the general layout. Tell me—what d'you think of the Sky Chief compared to the SX-28? I mean in terms of all-round performance."

Eric could hear the anxiety within the young man, and felt quite clearly his need to speak the only language that could ever give him a true sense of reality. But, alas, Eric had not the faintest notion of the comparative merits of the two communication receivers. In fact, it was more or less by accident that he happened to know them by name.

"I don't know," he answered lamely. "I suppose they both have their good points."

Peters gave him a look of weary resignation and said, "Yes, I suppose so."

"Well, good night," said Eric. "It's all yours!"

"Thanks, pal," replied Peters. And this seemingly cynical remark was not cynical at all; in fact, it was quite heartfelt and wistful.

Eric went to his cabin. At sea the doors were almost always kept ajar on the five-inch hook to avoid having them jammed closed in case of an explosion. Inside the room the air was fetid. The so-called wind scoops that fitted into the portholes and were designed by the Navy to admit air and to black out light, were quite efficient in the latter function and utterly useless in the former. There was a heavy smell of human breath and warm painted metal in the room. Eric turned on the lamp above the basin and washed his hands and face. The small room, rolling as it was from side to side, pitching slightly lengthwise, and lighted only by this weak globe, seemed weird and eerie. And there was Chuck in the upper bunk immersed in another of his endless nightmares. He made some awful sounds and half-articulate phrases. He would suddenly exhale almost all his breath and then gasp, "But why? Whyzunuff . . . whyzunuff . . . whyzunuff . . . God!" Then he would groan and make a ghastly gurgling sound. "Shouldabin," he would gasp, "shouldabin . . . shouldabin . . . shouldabin . . . God!" Then he would wheeze as though something within his own pulmonary system were closing down on his access to the air.

Eric turned off the lamp and felt his way across the stateroom to the other end, where he turned on the desk lamp. He wanted to write to Jane, but it seemed too futile to write a letter when it could not possibly be mailed until they arrived where they were going, and that would be weeks from now. He sat down at the desk and rested his head in his hands. He would have given almost anything in the world for the nerve solace of a pint of liquor at this moment.

Eric had learned many things about the other officers and some of the crew by now. He was familiar with many tensions, internal and external. He even knew what had really happened to Chuck. It was a simple and brutal and yet unexpected story.

Chuck had divorced his first wife, the mother of his fourteen-year-old son, many years past. The boy had grown up in a nervous atmosphere of marital ruin. Yet he had seemed normal, even above the average intelligence. But only a week before the ship had sailed, Chuck had married a girl of twenty—fifteen years his junior. The boy had been at the wedding and had not appeared to be upset. On the contrary, he had seemed to take a great liking to his father's young bride. Then, two days later, the boy had hanged himself in the home of his real mother. He had used the cord of an old-fashioned portiere. That was what had happened.

Chuck came suddenly and startlingly awake. "What?" he shouted. "What you say?"

Eric stood half erect so that Chuck could see his face and thus feel reassured in coming out of his nightmare. They stared into each other's eyes.

Chuck had a compact, workman's face, the sort of face that seems to have been born all tired out and yet capable of endless dogged work. His hair was a neutral light brown. His blue eyes were large, pleading, and empty. The two men stared at each other over the rim of the bunk.

"Oh," said Chuck, "it's you!"

"Yes," Eric answered apologetically. "It's me. I just got off watch."

They were still face to face, the one man lying tense and

naked in his bunk, and the other, fully clothed, half standing to look upward.

"I thought somebody was screaming," Chuck said. "Any trouble?"

"No," Eric said. "I don't think so. Have a cigarette?"

"Thanks."

Chuck took a cigarette from Eric's package and lit it and lay back, puffing deeply and staring at the overhead. Eric sat down.

"Goddamn it!" Chuck said. "You dream things that are so goddamn queer!" He was remembering his dream for a while and calming down. Then he said, "This is a crazy question, but tell me something—did you ever hear of anything called *fustishu?*"

"How d'you spell it?"

"I don't know. F-u-s-t-i-s-h-u, I guess. Or maybe f-u-s-t-i-s-s-u-e."

Eric was puzzled. "What does it mean? How's it used?" he asked.

"Oh, it's probably nothing," Chuck answered, his throat tight with embarrassment and loneliness. "It was just a part of that goddamn dream."

"How did it go?"

Chuck puffed smoke at the overhead, summoning his visions to the unaccustomed task of narration. Then he said, "It was in this undertaking parlor, like the one where we sent him. And I was there in the waiting room and he came in. My boy, I mean. Everything was just the way it was— except for that. And I said, 'How can you be up walking around when you're dead? Aren't you supposed to be lying down?' And he looked at me as natural as life and said, 'Don't worry about it, Dad,' he said. 'They embalmed me with *fustishu* and when they use that you can stay up and walk around for a while.'

" 'How d'you feel?' I asked him. And he said, 'Fine. I feel fine. I don't want you worrying about me. I feel fine and everything's perfectly all right. But the *fustishu* will wear off about four o'clock today and then I'll have to go back to being dead. But don't worry about it,' he said. And that was all there was to the dream. Or anyway, all I remember. Crazy, wasn't it?"

Eric was at a loss as to what he should say. He felt deeply sorry for the unhappy man in the upper berth and he would have liked to give him some sort of reassurance; perhaps some suggestion that the dream image of his son might really have been the boy's disembodied spirit manifesting itself and trying to tell his father that everything was all right. But Eric's disgust with the occult was too deep-seated to allow him this generosity.

"No, it isn't crazy," he said. "It was an interesting dream. It may be that there is such a word as *fustishu*. I'll remember it and see if I can identify it when we get back to the States. Might mean something interesting. It may be a foreign word you heard somewhere."

"Yes," Chuck said, "but why—why embalming fluid and —and stuff like that?"

Again Eric felt a surge of pity for the man and tried to achieve the compassionate hypocrisy that would permit him to say something mystical, but his gorge rose at the thought and he could not do it.

"I'll be damned if I know," he said. "As you remarked a while ago, we *do* dream the goddamnedest things."

Chuck sighed. He had hoped that this man, a professor, could tell him something he did not already know. He was disappointed.

Eric said good night to Chuck and went down the two ladders to the main deck for coffee. There were four men in the officers' saloon when he entered. He drew a cup of pitch-black fluid from the steaming urn and took it to a table; he stirred in canned milk and sugar. The first mate said hello to him.

Third Mate Hartley was holding forth in his accustomed and highly graphic style of monologue. "So this Captain Scudder of the Isthmian Line, he is really a grade-A government-certified sonofabitch. They actually say that he died about twenty years ago, but the lousy old bastard didn't have six friends to act as pallbearers, so they couldn't bury him. That's why he's still sailin' for Isthmian."

Hartley, with his early American gargoyle face unsmiling, hesitated only briefly after making a point such as the foregoing, and even this brief pause was not a wait for laughs.

He knew his audience too well for that. The best he could hope for was a grin or a snort. No, the hesitation was merely a point of craftsmanship, a pause to allow his imagery to take full effect. Duprey was listening, smiling to himself and drumming lightly with his fingers on the table. Vangaussen was leaning back in his chair and smoking a cigarette, entertained by that inward amusement, the source of which was one of his best-kept secrets, and it was difficult to guess whether any of this amusement now derived from Hartley's monologue. Sealman, the purser, was amused in a condescending way. He leaned into a corner with his legs sprawled on the leather-covered bench, continually working at his Dunhill pipe and smiling the superior smile of a trust-fund and endowments lawyer who finds himself, through the fortunes of war, a compulsory citizen of the proletarian world—a world utterly lacking in trust funds and endowments. He continually inspected, packed, tamped, emptied, filled, and relit his expensive pipe.

"I'll tell you the truth about this old bastard," the third mate resumed. "And this is a fact. He let out a fart once in the South Atlantic that was so terrific that it's still marked on the charts!" He paused again, then he went on: "Well, anyway, as I started to say, we were going up this river—the Amazon—and I was on watch, but this old bastard insisted on staying up on the bridge. And I tell you, the mosquitoes were so thick you couldn't see through 'em. Solid. Yessir, the air was solid protein. And it was all buzzing. My face was so swollen it felt like a baby's spanked ass, and my eyes were just about shut. Slits, you know? I felt like a fuggin' Oriental. So I says, 'Captain, if you're gonna stay up here and steer this ship through these mosquitoes, I think I'll go below.' And he says, 'The hell you will! You're on watch and you'll stay on watch!' And I says, 'But the regulations say that if the captain comes on the bridge he automatically relieves the mate of his authority!' And he says, 'You can take your fuggin' regulations, Mr. Mate, and wipe your fuggin' blowhole with 'em! You'll stay topside!' 'But, Captain,' I says, 'I can't *see* any more. What's the use my being up here if I can't see anything?' 'See, hell!' he says. 'Don't have to see to run a ship! That's the lookout's job!' 'But, Captain,' I says, 'I am so bit by these mosquitoes that I'm just about

71

finished. And he says, 'Mosquitoes, hell! I ain't had a single bite!' And then I says, 'Well, for Jesus Christ sake! Why should you? You been dead for twenty years. Why in Jesus' name would any decent mosquito want to bite you?' So he says, 'Go below, Mr. Mate! I can see you ain't fit for active duty in the United States Merchant Marine!' So I went below. And do you realize that that old cob is still sailin' ships for Isthmian? A zombie. Bet he'll outlast all of us!"

"Yeah, I know him," said Duprey. "A crazy old stinker, all right, but no worse than old Captain Carlson."

"You mean the Deacon?"

"That's the man."

Then they were off on another story, for—as Eric was learning—the legendary captains constitute one of the larger sections of seafaring narrative. "That reminds me of old Captain So-and-so," was the opening line of sagas without end.

During all his earlier life, Eric's friends had been persons who talked most of the time in other than personal terms, or who spoke in personal terms mainly to illustrate some principle or arrive at some conclusion. He still missed that manner of talk, finding it now only with the mess boy. Yet he did appreciate at last the fact that mariners in general really do have a better sense of narrative, a greater interest in the oddities of human character, and a more exuberant awareness of the possibilities of language, than any other group of men—including sociologists and writers. He was beginning to classify their stories, to place and enumerate them, as men of academic background are wont to do. He had discovered that the great legends of seafaring men were primarily concerned with feats of arrogance, physical strength, stubbornness, eloquence, and drunkenness; with famous and kindly whores; with good luck and bad luck. Then there was the minor talk which dealt with cities and ships, less a folklore than a fraternity of mutual recognition. "New Orleans? Sure!" . . . "Remember old Paddy's Bar down on Bourbon Street?" . . . "The *Black Arrow?* Sure, I remember her—an Elco tanker. Old Turkey Joe was first assistant on her for years!" And so on. But this was just the small talk.

What struck Eric as peculiar was that none of the great
72

legends dealt with courage. With danger, yes. And with stubbornness and damn-foolishness in the face of danger. But
not with courage. It had somehow come about among these
men that courage, as such, was the only thing in all their
experience that was too embarrassing to talk about.

Eric had had another cup of coffee, and his mind had
wandered away from the talk in the saloon—back to Washington and Jane and male-female tenderness and the distant
life of togetherness. But now his mind came back to where
his body was—in the middle of the Atlantic Ocean—and he
heard the last of some remarks that Duprey, the first assistant, was making to Chief Mate Vangaussen. They were bitter remarks, with a weight of black hatred behind them,
but to Eric they were entirely esoteric. Something about fixing or not fixing a connecting rod on the L.P. cylinder.

Duprey, Vangaussen, and Hartley decided to turn in, and
Eric was left alone with Sealman, the purser.

Sealman was a man whose soul was supported by a skele-
ton of success-worship, clothed in an ectoplasm of country
club culture, and enlivened by quantities of quiet and well-
mannered malice. Eric began to ask him what it was that
Duprey had seemed to be so bitter about.

He had found the right source in Sealman, for the purser
loved to discuss differences and quarrels between other people. He refilled his Dunhill pipe and tamped it with exquisite
care. Then he said, "Didn't you know? The black gang—so
called—is split wide open."

"No, I didn't know. How come?"

Sealman took special pleasure in revealing something to
Eric because he felt that the latter, being a professor, was of
his own class. He experienced a camaraderie of intellectual-
ism and professionalism for which he was avidly hungry.

"Yes, indeedy," he said, "the engine department is as divided as Guelph and Ghibelline!"

Then he worked at his pipe again while he waited for this
evidence of erudition to sink into Eric's consciousness.
"Guelph and Ghibelline!" he repeated. "On one side is Chief
Engineer Curtis and Second Assistant Finley—or *Der Kessel*,
as they call him. And on the other is First Assistant Duprey
and Third Assistant Benson. They tell me that most of the
ordinary men down there are on Duprey's side."

"Yes, but what's the quarrel?"

"Oh, nothing much, I guess. For us in the deck department it probably wouldn't make much sense."

"Well—for example?"

"It seems that Duprey and his faction want to make certain repairs at sea, whereas the chief thinks that all these things can wait until we get into port. At the moment it appears that a connecting rod is loose and Duprey thinks we ought to drop out of the convoy to fix it, whereas the chief says that that would be just like committing suicide over a sliver in your little finger. At times the old boy's rather witty, isn't he? The submarines trail us, you know, waiting for stragglers. If you drop back you're just a clay pigeon."

"Won't the escort give you protection?"

"One little merchant ship? I should say not! Anyway not with just a load of coal. Of course, they might if we were just dropping back during daylight hours for a quick repair job. Duprey thinks they would. That's his argument."

Knowing something of these men, Eric felt that the fissure in the engine department was not essentially concerned with security; the difference really originated from the fact that Duprey and Benson loved engines, whereas the chief and *Der Kessel* did not. The black gang naturally sided with the more functional of these attitudes; they themselves were slaves and devotees of the engine, whether they loved it or not, and they were compelled thus by the nature of their existences to reject the sterile iconoclasm of those who denied the supreme importance of their deity and their helpless ward, the Engine.

"I think I'll turn in," Eric said. "See you tomorrow."

The purser was examining the dead gray ash in the bowl of his pipe. "Pleasant dreams," he said. "And *auf wiedersehn!*"

"Right!" Eric said. *"Buenas noches* and *bonne nuit* and *kali nikta!"*

The foreign phrases made them both happier, but especially Sealman.

4

The following day there were depth charges at frequent intervals. They could be felt rather than heard—each one like a minor earthquake. The ship would be moving through its liquid element, and all at once it would be gripped and shaken by something very solid. A little later a short, low growl would come up out of the sea. It was a dark day, but the water had subsided to long, low, oily-looking swells that moved regularly in on the port quarter. Here and there, astern and on the port beam, the little destroyer escorts and corvettes could be seen dashing about in circles and figure eights, and behind them, as they dropped their charges, the tall, slow-motion plumes of sea water would blossom like miraculous white plants, then subside and vanish.

About three o'clock in the afternoon something black and long was seen to rise from the depths, and everyone who saw it raised a cheer, believing that the escort had surfaced a German submarine. But it turned out to be only a wounded whale. It thrashed about for a while, then lay still and drifted out of sight to the westward.

After dinner that evening, Eric stood on the boat deck, leaning against the starboard rail. The sky was leaden gray and the sea was violet gray, and on the horizon straight ahead was a flat layer of purple clouds that looked deceptively like land.

The hundred and eighty merchant ships were holding tightly to their checkerboard positions; there were no stragglers now that the rumble of danger was in the sea. The *SS William Benson's* position was 105. That is to say that she was the fifth ship in the tenth column. There had been no explosions now for over an hour, but the DE's were still circling instead of making their usual straight runs up and down the length of the convoy and back and forth across it.

Taking his gaze away from these distant things, Eric shifted his attention to the throbbing iron fact of his own ship. As it was approaching sundown, the entire armed guard crew were at their battle stations. Looking astern, Eric could see the boys in their blue dungarees and steel helmets lounging and talking in the two twenty-millimeter gun tubs and in the more elaborate emplacement of the four-inch stern cannon. A sailor was hauling down the flag, and when this was accomplished the ship somehow seemed more vulnerable and less brave.

Eric reached inward and outward with his mind to know the meaning of a ship, one among many, carrying men from peace toward war: the complexity of it, so solid, so tenuous; an iron fact, an iron faith, moving forward into the silence of the waters where the killers wait. The men cling to the ship, feeling its power, listening to it, trusting it, ready to defend it—as sons, as fathers, and as lovers.

The engine is going *tah*-tuh, *tah*-tuh, *tah*-tuh, seventy-three times per minute, the enormous heart of the ship—and then suddenly it falters, it stutters, and the heart of every waking man on the ship falters. And then the engine stops. There is a dreadful quiet.

The other machinery on the ship—the pumps, dynamos, and so forth—is still operating, but no one can hear it because all the listening sense of everyone on the ship is directed toward only one sound—and that has ceased. The ship loses headway and the column behind her swings to the starboard to avoid collision. Whistle signals are exchanged.

To Eric it seems now that they are moving rapidly astern as the convoy passes them. He can feel the great dead hulk under him, as helpless as the dead whale they had left behind earlier in the day.

He turns as Captain Brogan comes down the ladder from the bridge and runs into the boat-deck quarters. The captain's face is wooden; only his body is full of violence. Eric follows at a distance.

The captain storms into the stateroom of the chief engineer, and Eric stands back in the passageway listening to the sounds. Evidently Chief Curtis has been asleep. He hears the captain's voice, tense, ruthless, and dangerous.

"Listen, you slob, get up off your fat ass! Notice anything wrong? You don't? Well, your goddamned engine isn't running! What are you going to do about it?"

There is some startled mumbling from the chief. Then again from the captain: "Don't sit there fumbling with your shoes, you half-witted sonofabitch! Get down in that engine room!" Eric follows at a safe distance.

The tropical heat below smells of fuel oil and hot insulation. There are the methodical sounds of pumps and generators and the hurried sounds of men at work with wrenches and hammers.

Duprey, his face and naked torso glistening with sweat and oil, a stillson in one hand, meets the chief and the captain at the bottom of the ladder. Eric cannot hear the beginning of the argument, but he stops on the center landing and listens. He hears the chief bumbling, "All right, First, all right, I'll take over now! That damned rod! I'll take over!"

Then Duprey's voice, very firm and clear, almost as though he were reading from a prepared script: "Listen, Captain! You want this ship to run again—quick—don't you? All right then—keep Curtis out of here until we get it fixed."

Amid the weakened breath of the hot machinery, Eric listens to the fateful pause of the moment of decision. The captain will be breaking every tenet of discipline and the hierarchy of rank if he does what Duprey asks. But the captain has had four good ships sink under him and has heard the dying screams of many good men, and he knows that Curtis is a fool. Therefore the moment of decision is not long suspended. Brogan steps down onto the engine-room deck so that he will be on the other side of Curtis. "Go to your quarters, Chief!"

Red-faced and cursing to himself, the chief engineer comes puffing up the ladders. The captain stays behind, perhaps for fifteen seconds; then, starting up the ladder, he says over his shoulder to Duprey, "Fix it, and fix it quick."

Eric went back to his former place on the boat deck. Now the convoy was a distant city on the horizon: the many superstructures of the rear ships and the scattered banners of smoke from those ships too old to burn cleanly, and the watchful corvettes, all fading away in the east. A single DE had stayed behind and was slowly circling the SS *William Benson* as she lay wallowing in the swell.

It was still light enough to see the boys in the gun tubs. They were no longer talking. A supernatural sense of loneliness had come over the helpless ship. She was now no more than a *thing* upon which some seventy men were adrift and in danger; and the peace and resignation that always goes with sunset was with them and deepened their loneliness. When the ship's engine had been running they were all together, a team. Now each man was separate, adrift in the vastness of his own memory.

Gazing now upon this wallowing corpse of steel that was his ship, Eric felt how truly tenuous is the minute-by-minute survival of an entity, whether it be a man or a ship. How the vast structure of every man's life depends at each beat of his heart upon the strength of the tiniest of capillaries in certain sections of his brain, a glandular duct, a filament of nerve tissue no thicker than a hair. And the vast structure of a ship with all its men depends for its survival upon a single electrical connection, a circuit breaker or a valve, a small tube, a simple shaft of steel. Feeling the helplessness of the stricken ship, each man felt ashamed and lonely within the fragile structure of his body.

It was growing dark. They could no longer see the convoy. The DE was circling them in larger and larger circles. Now it began to signal with its blinker. Eric could read it.

The signalman sent slowly, and Eric spelled it out under his breath: G-O-O-D-B-Y A-N-D G-O-O-D L-U-C-K

Then the little escort ship turned eastward at full speed and gradually disappeared into the night. They were alone. A new silence that had somehow been held at bay by the presence of the DE now descended upon them. Good-by and good luck. The vast but narrowing circle of the sea welcomed them, for the sea is hospitable; it has a depth of greeting. The lonely men dared not look at one another. They grew more ashamed. There was nothing to do but wait. The gunners stayed at their battle stations. All around them now were only dark waters and heavy silence.

7: *What You Think I'm Gonna Do with This?*

From the height of five thousand feet the *SS William Benson* appeared to be no more than an elongated speck, somewhat like a single isolated bacillus in some dark media.

Lower, lower—and it was a ship again. But not really a

ship any longer—only a buoyant structure of steel that rose and fell, slipped sidewise over the swells, drifted with the currents and winds of mid-ocean. Yet entering it, one would know that this dead thing was still full of the same living men.

The quality of the human atmosphere was far different from what it had been before. These new and richly car-bureted vapors seemed mostly compounded of quiet fear and renewed memory and inarticulate loneliness. But the most suprising change was the increase of spiritual separateness. The lostness and danger of the ship brought the men closer together in decency and affection and tolerance, but at the same time drew them further apart into the intrinsic isolation of their separate souls.

On deck it was the second mate's watch, and the lookout on the bow was the boy called Kentucky. He should have been standing on the deck of the forepeak, but instead he sat on the gunwale with his long legs hanging overboard. He kept asking himself what was the use of having a lookout on the bow of a ship without an engine. It was the maritime law, that was all. There were plenty of lookouts for sub-marines; each of the ten gun tubs (one right over his head) was fully manned, and the navy signalmen were at their stations and the Armed Guard Commander was on the flying bridge with his battle phone that connected with each of these gun positions. There was no sense in having a mer-chant marine lookout on the bow, Kentucky thought, but that was the law.

In his boat-deck quarters, Chief Engineer Curtis was miserably unhappy, and this was something he thought he had learned to insulate himself against. He lay on his bunk drinking yet trying to conserve his last bottle of bourbon, and thinking sadly about himself.

It seemed that from the very beginning everyone had been against him. When he did something his mother thought was wrong, she'd say, "Wait till your father comes home!" And when he made his father mad, the old man would say, "Wait till your mother hears of this!" He was afraid of the girls but not of the boys. The boys knew he wasn't afraid of them, so he never had to fight. The girls knew he was afraid of them, so he never got one. But he loved them all while he was afraid of them.

When he hurt Evelyn, that little girl who liked him for a while, it was only because he had to. She had brown eyes and long ringlets, but he was afraid that inside of herself she was not paying enough attention to him—that, like the others, she didn't really love him. He picked up the clod when they were playing and he said, "What you think I'm gonna do with this?" And she said, "You're going to hit me." He thought it was terrible that she should know so well what he was going to do. "That's right," he said. Then he hit her.

The tears ran down her muddy face and she turned away and ran. He hoped she would tell her mother, but he knew she wouldn't. He knew that he would have told his mother if he'd been she.

That was the way it was from then on. Even Evelyn knew—after he hit her—that he was afraid of her. So he never really had a girl. Not even Evelyn. And he began to hate them all. And after he knew for sure that he hated them, then he wasn't afraid of them any more.

The first job he could get was in a garage. But he hated that too. The boss would say, "Take up the bearings on this Model T." And he would say, "Okay, Mr. Lowell."

But he hated it. He knew that he should keep the lower halves of the bearings matched with the same connecting rods he took them from. But he didn't give a damn. He'd file them all down and make them tighter. The boss just said *take up the bearings,* didn't he? So Curtis took them up. He hated the damned greasy machinery. He had a feeling all the time like: What's the use? One damned Ford or another. People thinking *their* damned bearings and valves and timers were important! It made him sick and tired.

But what was important?

Nothing, he thought. Nothing. For a while he wanted something to be important, but he gave up long before he found out about the Merchant Marine and, just to get away from home, went to sea as a wiper on a Standard Oil tanker. Then it was just sticking, putting in the time, and memorizing the stuff to pass the exams. He wanted to be a chief because he saw it was a soft job. And now he was one, a chief. He wanted to be the boss of the black gang, and he was.

And *they* had the nerve to order him out of his own engine room! While an upstart foreigner like Duprey took over. But he was not in the least surprised, because he knew from the minute he signed the articles that Captain Brogan was against him. Just the way he looked. And now, of course, he's playing ball with the others. Ruining the discipline on his own ship.

But why can't *I* feel more interested in the engine? Curtis thought. We're bound to be torpedoed now. Are other people—like Duprey, for instance—*really interested* in engines? Is anyone really interested in anything? When I think of the engine I get a tired feeling. When I think of anything you have to pay attention to, I get that feeling.

On the ship he liked to take it easy because—well, he'd earned the right to it. And on shore he liked to drink with people who really understood him—intelligent strangers.

But there'll be no more shore drinking for old man Curtis, he thought; nor any of the other lard-heads on this barge. Because we'll never make it. We're sure to be torpedoed now that the escort has left us behind. They didn't give a damn about us. Just a goddamn cargo of coal, that's all we are to them. A cargo of coal and a bunch of suckers. And now it's about all over. It was strange, but this unhealthy man was less afraid of the torpedo and the sinking and the death-strangulation in dark sea water than were most of the other men on the ship.

There was activity in the engine room. Men worked with quiet desperation here at this point from which the derelict ship now hung suspended above the wet abyss. Yet if one browsed among the hot and intricate works of metal—the great triple-expansion reciprocating steam engine, the condensers, the pumps and generators—one could not but feel that the immediate drama of these men and their survival was somewhat minimized within the grander drama of physical laws and the wonderful ways in which they have been applied by the ordered and passionate minds of other men long since dead. The wonderful law of the expansion of gases, the facts of gravity and atmospheric pressure, of buoyancy and the magnetic field and specific heats—the Watts boy and his teakettle—thousands of other laws and experiments and the men who discovered and made them. All those wonderful dramatic climaxes of human consciousness were involved in the construction of this engine room.

One could hear the men grunting and muttering soft curses now as they worked with wrench and hammer and cold chisel at the traumatic center of the ship's paralysis.

The steward, George Fiorini, was sitting alone in his room and eating out of a can of tuna: Chicken of the Sea. He was lost in that confusion of memory and projection which seems to be the natural state of almost every man; that weird juxtaposition of sultry daydream, effortful thought, and ancient inertia.

He was thinking mostly about sex. Crude visions of what was to him a crude act, though behind it lay an infinitely subtle world of pain and a poignant longing he could never define. He was thinking what it is like when you first get on top of a new woman. And he doubted if he would ever do that again. He would soon be dead in this deep ocean, he thought. No more women.

Well, it had not been too good anyway. To hell with it. But still it had been the best part of the life he had lived so far. At least it always seemed as though it *would* be wonderful—up to a certain point. And then it seemed lousy. But there was always next time, when it *might* be the way you felt it should be. Well, anyway—to hell with it. He tried hard to think about religion for a change.

For twelve years now he had been going to sea, most of the time before the war on west coast passenger ships. The tourist excursions to Alaska and Hawaii had been the most fun. All the ardent little schoolteachers and stenographers out to get the most out of three or four years' savings. Every one of them with ants in her pants, George remembered with a sigh. On land they'd yell rape if a man winked at them, but on shipboard they'd go to bed with any man they could get to push them over. It was always "Georgie" up until the day before making the home port. Then it was "Steward" again. That was a laugh.

On freight ships it was a question of waiting to see what

you could find in the next port and then getting all you could while you were there. Most of the men would rush first for a bar. No matter how horny they were, they wanted some liquor first. But not George. He'd tell the other fellows that he'd meet them later somewhere. Then he'd head straight for the nearest crib. He liked to drink, all right. But that could wait. As far as liquor was concerned, he could take it or leave it alone. But the great urge of the other thing was as irresistible as breathing, and its empty echo as inevitable as death. He put down the tuna can, crossed himself, wrinkled his brow, and again tried hard to think about religion. It's now or never, he thought.

Two decks above was the stateroom of Chief Radio Officer Malcolm Shruck. Here was a man who was but little changed by the new danger of the ship. He lay on his bunk, the light on, staring at the overhead with wide-open eyes.

He was a thin man of thirty; pale, beginning to become bald, extremely nervous, perhaps the most polite and least sociable man on the ship And the sudden new danger in which he found himself had had only two minor effects.

Above all else Shruck was efficient. He believed that every man owed it to himself and his job to perform in the most efficient possible manner. He was no bootlicker or apple-polisher. In fact, he usually regarded bosses with an impatience that was near to polite contempt. Rather it was the *Job* he deified. Whether unimportant or important, there was a sacred relationship between him and the Job.

So now he had made certain that every piece of radio equipment was functioning correctly. He had checked everything himself. He made certain that both the other radio men were aware of the need for unusual alertness and that they were familiar with the special call for convoy stragglers. He himself was determined to stay fully dressed and ready to take over in case of an alarm. That was the external, almost automatic, part of his reaction.

The other part was merely a deepening of the swamp of evil memory and monotonous imagination in which he had now lived for several years. The terrible repetitive thinking about his wife, Fevroula.

Though only one-quarter Greek, she had this Greek

83

name, which means *flower*. And she was like a flower to Shruck, every flower in the world. He loved her devotedly. And she loved him. But not exactly devotedly. She was too much like a flower for that. She had her phases of bud and blossom and fallen petals. She loved to be Fevroula, the flower, and the adoration and desire of men were soil and sunlight to her. She could not live without them. She lied unconscionably. And when he caught her, she simply looked as though she had made a bad move at checkers. And all in such a feminine and appealing manner that he felt ashamed of himself for taking advantage of her error.

Somewhere within himself he knew full well that his wife budded and bloomed and fell only in the eternal and somewhat lonely springtime of promiscuity. But he had never admitted it to himself. The submerged knowledge of this truth was the bitter food upon which his unconscious feeling continually fed. Yet what he said in terms of words to himself was that nobody in the world had such a pure and loyal love as he and Fevroula.

He hated to hear the other officers talk crudely about love. When they talked about whores and leered about "shacking up" with this or that woman, he listened with revulsion. But when they sneered at marriage or the possibility of true and faithful love, he grew tense and pale with hatred for their crudity. He tried not to show this. He didn't want to be thought a crackpot or to be unpopular. But he simply could not stand that kind of talk. He certainly approved of sex, and he and Fevroula had had the best of times in that direction. But he could not stand the crude, laughing words of the men; it was like standing by helplessly while some half-animal idiot paws over the moon-white body of your only true and eternal love.

He had been chief of a communication center for the FCC, and there had not been so much grossness among the people who worked with him there. So he blamed it on the environment. This is the Merchant Marine, he thought bitterly. What could I expect? What could they possibly know about love? They've never experienced it. Their idea of love is just getting drunk and then climbing into bed with some diseased whore. I couldn't ever do that. I'd be impotent from humiliation. I'm not animal enough for that.

Such was his controlled and continual anger toward his shipmates. Yet he was polite to them—even tried to be friendly—for that fell within the scope of his reverence for his Job.

The small area of agonized memory began to sting again like the focal point of a burning glass. Fevroula frequently accused him of being neurotic because he objected to *her* male friends but would trust her with any of his own. And he knew that he did have that reaction. When she introduced him to a Mr. So-and-so or Lieutenant Such-and-such, he was taken with irresistible seizures of jealousy. But when she took to one of his own male friends he was filled with irrational relief. She knew this very well; it made her smile and shrug her shapely shoulders. "Ah, Malcolm," she would whisper. "Poor Malcolm."

But in recent months this reaction of his had been changing. More and more the questioning, repetitive visions that he fought against were concerned with the very friends he had introduced to her. Men he had slapped on the back and told to be sure and take good care of Fevroula while he was away!

What is she doing at this minute? Who is she out with? What is she doing to enjoy the warmth of their approval? He began for the hundredth time to revisualize the last time he was out with Fevroula and Chris Arenberg, his old friend and lodge brother. Certainly Chris could be trusted if anyone in the world could. An older man, serious, dependable, and loyal. Malcolm had asked him many times to see that Fevroula was not bored or lonely while he was away at sea; to take her out, entertain her, cheer her up.

Now he remembered the last time the three of them had gone out to a night club. Each time he had come back from the men's room Chris and Fevroula had seemed to be involved in some warm and intimate talk until they caught sight of him, and then they had leaned quickly back in their chairs and faded again into the formal surface banter of mere acquaintanceship. Why? He had gone over this and a score of other details innumerable times, arriving nowhere, not really wanting to arrive anywhere.

He felt the unnatural helpless rolling of the abandoned ship and the absence of its heartbeat, and he knew that they must be very near to the quiet killers who follow the convoys. He knew that at any moment there might come the shuddering impact of a torpedo.

Did he care?

He cared about getting out the SSSS message. Getting it out efficiently. He was tensely prepared to see that this was done. Beyond that, the helplessness of the ship only augmented a helplessness of his own. He felt he had been wallowing in a cruel yet impersonal element long before the ship's engine stopped. For more than three years now he had not been able to control the direction of his thoughts.

8: The Red-Haired Enemy

It was half an hour before midnight when the heart of the ship began to beat again. Eric was on watch and First Mate Vangaussen was sitting on a stool beside him in the radio room. The mate was idly thumbing through the secret radio instruction books, pretending now and then to be engrossed in a page of schedules or a chapter on convoy ciphers and codes.

When the first throbs of the engine came to them they dropped all pretense of preoccupation and looked at each other, each man holding his breath for fear the wonderful sound would stop. They dared not acknowledge their relief until nearly half a minute had passed. Then the mate passed his hand slowly over the livid crease on top of his bald head. "Jesus Christ!" he said.

Both men sighed deeply and felt new life enter them, as though they had received a transfusion from the iron veins of the ship.

"Duprey knew what he was doing," Eric said.

Every man on the ship, from Oscar, the half-witted wiper, to Captain Brogan, felt the same wonderful release and rebirth as the ship again grew meaningful with motion. They had been embalmed in separateness, and now the loneliness drained from between them and they were together again. There came the trilling of the bos'n's whistle, the sound of purposeful feet on the ladders, shouted orders, all the coming back together, the great renewal of unity through the restoration of the ship's power.

"Yes," the mate said, "Duprey is a good man. He always has a respect for his engine."

Ordinarily Eric's scholastic background would have given him a twinge of annoyance at the implied animism of Vangaussen's remark. But at this moment it sounded like the most intelligent of all possible observations.

"Thank God for that!" he said. "Curtis is obviously a fool, and if the captain hadn't overruled him it probably would have been the end of us."

Several minutes passed while Eric copied some incoming traffic. He had intercepted an SSSS. A ship was under attack by a submarine and had reported that it could not remain on the surface for more than another hour. That was way back in the South Atlantic, north of Puerto Rico, but still it had to go into the log. The sinking ship was not in convoy. Eric was fascinated by the sound of the signal sent out by this other operator. His personal equation of courage and fear and hope and desolation could be heard in every dot and dash and pause. This could not be entered in the log, but only the barren outline of the signals. For the record.

"But it may still be the end of us," the mate added. "Don't forget that we're still alone. We may never catch up with the convoy."

"But at least we're moving."

"Yes, we're moving. And that's good."

Eric slept that night, a deep and satisfying sleep. Next morning he awoke and removed the wind scoop from the porthole and looked out with the happy assurance of a healthy child. And sure enough—there was the convoy. They were back in the city of ships. It was a mystery to him how they had done it, but here they were. And the truth was that he had expected it all the time.

He dressed and went down to breakfast feeling very fine. He thought to himself that never, in time of peace or war, had he felt such self-assurance. On his way down to the saloon he met several other men, and in the course of their greetings he learned that a peculiar and exhilarating bravado had come over everyone. They had eluded the killers and were back in the herd. By chance or by cunning, what was the difference? They were still afloat and alive and they were proud of it.

The steward usually ate in his own room, but this morning he seemed to feel more gregarious than on ordinary days at sea, and Eric found him seated at his table. The little Brooklyn Italian was mopping up soft eggs with a piece of bread. He was in high spirits. He leaned back and patted himself on the belly.

"Well, Professor," he said, "let's talk about screwing!"

Eric laughed. "Okay," he said. "What aspect of that vast subject shall we take as our morning topic?"

"Any ass-pect, Professor, any ass-pect at all. You ought to know a lot about it, being a professor, that a guy like me can never find out laying around in cat houses."

"Well, I could give you some cases from Krafft-Ebing."

"Krafft who? I thought he made cheese!"

"Well, in his spare time he wrote a book about a lot of rather queer people. That was a hobby of his."

"So let's hear about it."

"Well, did you ever hear of a man who could only enjoy himself sexually by seeing a horse fall down on the ice?"

"Did you say a horse or a whore?"

"A horse. This man used to spend all his time in the winter hanging around where they used dray horses and the streets were slippery, waiting for one of the horses to fall down so that he could enjoy himself."

George was filled with wonder and pity. "Jesus Christ!" he said. "What a life! Now if that guy had been a rich guy he could have bought himself a private ice-skating rink and a herd of work horses and had himself one hell of a good time all year around!"

"Right! That's the capitalistic system for you! Unequal distribution of wealth, unequal distribution of sex."

"Go on—tell me some more."

"Well, there was another case about a man who could only make the grade by having a naked woman wash doll clothes in front of him. She'd scrub them and rinse them and wring them out while he watched, and that would do the trick."

"Didn't she have to wring him out a little bit too?"

"If she did, it didn't get into the book."

"Say, is this the kind of stuff they teach in college nowadays?"

"Sure."

"What d'you call it?"

"Abnormal psychology."

"Well, I'll be goddamned! And all these years I been thinking I was lucky only to have to go through grade school. You give me a real yearning for education, Professor. I wonder if I could take a correspondence course?"

They were interrupted by Harold. "Good-uh morning, Signor Professori!" he said. "Such-uh bella dia! What I can bring-uh for to feed-uh you face this-uh fine-uh dia?"

"If you think you're talking like a wop," said George Fiorini, "you're crazy. And *I* ought to know."

After his eight-to-noon watch Eric decided to take a sun bath. He stripped to his shorts and set up a deck chair on the "captain's deck," as they called the narrow space that extended back from the superstructure at bridge-deck level. Eric had once horrified Duprey by calling this place the "back porch." Now he lay there with his eyes closed, feeling the warm touch of the sunlight and the little waves of coolness where vagrant breezes touched areas of perspiring skin.

He was wondering how long the present atmosphere of bravado and comradeship would last. Not long. Probably by tomorrow all the original irritabilities and animosities would have returned.

During these twenty-two days aboard the SS *William Benson* his awareness of the men with whom he lived had changed considerably. But what seemed to him more important than his changing view of each man as an individual was his changed perception of the organism of the group.

What had at first appeared to him to be a closely knit body of men, inevitably unified by the factors of confinement, interdependence, and extreme danger, now appeared to be a thing wormholed by petty hatreds and spiritually unified only in-so-far as two or more individuals could share prejudices. He could not at this moment think of a single instance of friendship between any of the officers that was based upon mutual approval of something. Yet there were innumerable friendships of mutual dislike.

Even Duprey and Benson were drawn together not nearly so much by their competence and liking for machinery as by their contempt for Chief Engineer Curtis.

In this little society of fourteen men there were cliques and countercliques, fissures and cross-fissures. All the merchant marine officers were against the Armed Guard Commander because he was a navy man. "The Navy's bad enough itself," they said, "but these gun crews are the *wastebasket* of the Navy. This is where they throw all their misfits." Also they said that he prowled the decks most of the night and that even when he went to bed he would never turn his light out. They implied that all this was because he was a coward. Whenever he came suddenly into the saloon, the men stopped talking, gulped down their coffee, and left him alone. This drove the lieutenant into closer association with his own gun crew boys. He even played cards with them in their mess room. That just went to prove further, the merchant marine officers said, the slipshod, undisciplined inefficiency of the navy gun crews.

Nearly everyone was against the steward. They said that he was saving perishable foods such as fresh fruit, and that later he would just have to throw the stuff overboard; that the meals were monotonous; that he used fancy French and Italian names for ordinary chow; that he ate in his own cabin because he wanted to eat steak every day and only put it on the menu twice a week; that he was dirty; and that he was nothing but a goddamn guinea.

There was constant bitterness over the use of water in the showers. This was the one subject on which the other engineering officers agreed with their chief. They claimed that the water would not last unless certain hammerheads learned how to take a shipboard shower. You're supposed to turn the water on just long enough to wet your body, Eric learned, then soap and scrub yourself, then turn the water on again to rinse. The chief was always threatening to turn it off down below except at certain hours, but inasmuch as the engineers took four or five times as many showers as anyone else they could not agree that turning off the water was the answer.

There was a bitter personal hatred between Sealman, the purser, and Second Mate Burley. It was apparently one of those instantaneous biological animosities. The mate was always making remarks about Sealman's fatness. "You know," he said once, "the reason you're so sluggish is because your glands ain't working right. I read a book about it. You ought to go see a gland doctor." And at another time he observed, "If the cook would just put you on a platter and put an apple in your mouth he could serve you for dinner." The purser did not at all like being termed sluggish or being compared to a pig. He retaliated by correcting Burley's grammar at every possible opportunity. It boiled down to a struggle between self-appointed representatives of the fat, intelligentsian, pompous professional class, and the equally —though less academically—intelligentsian, thin, dogmatic proletarian class.

Resentments of all sorts grew out of card games. Shruck would not play a game if Duprey played, because of some petty disagreement in an early game. Several men refused to play with Hartley because he liked to make side bets on a pot after he had tossed in his hand.

Extending outside the officer group there were many other connecting fissures. Shruck complained bitterly to the captain because the navy signalmen came down at night and used the toilet that was supposed to belong to the radio officers and the deck officers on watch.

The navy gun crew had cruel words to say about their own lieutenant. He played favorites, they said. Dished out the easy stretches to his favorite boys. They suspected that he was a homosexual, though this favoritism was their only evidence.

The three seamen who shared a cabin with Oscar, the moron, were always complaining that he refused to take a bath, that he wet his bed, that he was a grave danger to their health and they were going to take it up with the union.

As for the captain, his animosities were unpredictable. On one day when he met Eric in a companionway he would greet him as though he were a close friend. On the next day, meeting at the same spot, he might look at his third radio officer as though he were some gruesome thing that had come up from the deep sea and crawled secretly and loathsomely aboard the ship. He flew into a terrible fury at the Armed Guard Commander because the navy gunners made so much noise jumping in and out of the gun tub above the captain's bunk. Yet at other times he seemed imperturbable.

Eric knew that what he had become aware of was only a small fraction of all the social conflicts on the *SS William Benson*. So much enmity among so few men!

He began to recall the story, the basis for the radio script he had started to write about the "enemy." In a way it was that story that had brought him here. He wouldn't be stretched out here in this deck chair, sailing in convoy across the Atlantic, if he had been able to write the end of that story to his own satisfaction. But good holy God! How to determine the real enemy in a vast world war when there was so much enmity in a small group of men working for the same cause and on the same job?

He went into his cabin and found the manuscript of the story and took it back to where he had been taking his sun bath. He moved the deck chair into the shade.

He read the manuscript slowly and it seemed surprisingly artificial; there was something subtly and painfully lacking. Perhaps it was only his own sense of guilt in writing so glibly about dangers he had never experienced. He reread the last paragraph of what he had written.

> *Then, days later, George MacDougal saw through his eyes again and knew the other world, diluted and thin. It was a kind world of bedpans and shots in the arm and people leaning over him, kind people who seemed to be concerned about him . . .*

Eric put down the manuscript and began to think about biological enmities such as that between Burley and Sealman. Every man seems to have a few *natural* friends—and enemies. He went to his room again after tablet and pencil, returned to the deck chair, and began to write some more.

2

> *And one of those who leaned over him was the nurse named Ethyl and she was very good. A man who is coming out of one world and into another does not ask himself*

92

questions about the girls he has loved and the girls he has not loved. He does not even ask right away the identity of this generous girl who is leaning over him. A girl radiates something, and it is something sweet and good to a man who is passing from one world into another. Part of it is smell, but only a small part. It seems to be less a smell than some kind of radiation. Not mystical, but just like an electric heater—it comes out of her somehow. There is something warm and also a cool milk-white effulgence. Some girls understand this and some do not. But a man feels gratitude when he is wounded and meets a girl like this and he might even be maudlin about it. She is so good that in a way it is almost too much for him to stand.

But when he wakes up enough and feels that it is also personal, then it is really tremendous. And Ethyl made George feel that way; she seemed to want to do little favors just for him. And when she brought him the bedpan or things like that she had a special way of making it natural so that it didn't make him feel ashamed.

She was a funny girl in a way and George felt she was like no one else. She had brown hair and blue eyes and a sort of petulant mouth and small sharp breasts. She understood men although she did not give the impression that she had been around a lot.

One day when George was at a very low point and was almost losing himself in the other world again, Ethyl volunteered to manicure his fingernails. This was the last thing that the medical officer in charge of the hospital would have thought of. She took great pains with his nails and kept talking to him. And while she worked over his fingers she supported his hand against her breast. He could feel her heart beating through the warm cushion. And this was so good for him that in all likelihood it may have saved his life. For the other world was calling and its end was darkness, but now he refused it.

Then there was sanity again for a while, but more fear because of a certain new fact. The fact was that he now knew that his enemy was in the hospital. Now he had discovered what he had lost just before storming the hill of San Vittorio. It was all wrong of course but it was a fact; he had found the enemy right here.

They had had to reopen his wound again and again because the drain would not work. A number of doctors had done it, most of them only vague shapes in the mist of pain. But there was one, the redhead, whom George recognized. When he thought of this doctor his own hair stood on end and he wanted either to die or to fight the unspeakable creature—to kill him.

At last he knew. This man was his *enemy. He felt a chemical hatred and fear of this man. He knew that he had recovered an essential loss: for himself, he had discovered the enemy. And now he was out to defeat it. They had told him that this redheaded doctor was to reopen his wound at eight a.m.—this butcher, this enemy.*

He felt fear such as he had never known before. He began to plan how he would leap up and protest: "I will not be butchered by my enemy!" But he was afraid to tell Ethyl. She seemed to condone the miserable plot. They took him into the operating room and put him on a table and Ethyl left him alone and he waited. He planned that when he saw that red-haired beast he would leap from the operating table and denounce him as a butcher and a Nazi. He would not subject himself to the enemy's knife. He suffered the prolonged agony of waiting—minutes, seeming hours—hours of fear—fear of the ugliness and strength of the enemy—waiting for the door to open, and finally it did open.

But it was not the enemy. Instead it was a tall thin fellow with black hair and dark eyes. It was Dr. Benjamin. George liked this man. He had seen him only a few times but he had known at once that he trusted and liked this doctor.

The great wave of relief that burst upon him left a bitter salt. This, he had not expected. Maybe he was crazy. Perhaps he was suffering from battle neurosis, a psycho —for suddenly, lying there on the operating table in this strange room where the broken plaster had been hastily whitewashed, he felt guilty. He felt that he had offended the redheaded doctor because he knew now that it wasn't true. He wanted to demand that the redhead should do the work, but on the other hand that would not be polite to Dr. Benjamin. He fought with this question.

Then the redheaded doctor walked in. His skin was pink and hairy and the sleeves of his white jacket were rolled up above his elbows. To George this pink skin was very repulsive. The doctor came over to the table and put his hand on George's shoulder. On earlier occasions George had felt the touch of this man as the sneering condescension of an enemy who knows that he has the power of life and death over you. Now the touch of this solid hand soothed him and filled him with maudlin apologies.

"I thought maybe you could do it," he managed to mutter. "They told me . . ."

And the redheaded surgeon explained that he had intended to do it but that there was an emergency he had to take care of.

When George came out from under the anesthetic he felt wonderful. He had never in his life felt so talkative. It must have been the preoperative morphine that was still working in him. He wanted to talk to Ethyl and tell her about the enemy and how in fact he had been wrong about the whole thing. What a relief it was. She came and stood by his bed very quietly and he told her. She said that she understood perfectly about the enemy.

But she was not on duty the rest of the day and when she left his talkativeness was gone and he began to wonder if he had been talking crazily. He began to wonder if she had really understood him all this time or if she had just been humoring him.

9: Under the Gauze Cone

"I sigh, old chop, pawdin me faw interruptin', but cawn it rilly be true, as they tell me down in the bloody scullery, that we'll pawss through the bloody Straits of bloody old Gibraltar within the week?"

This was, of course, Harold being an Englishman.

Eric put down the tablet on which he had been writing. "That seems bloody well likely," he said. "But what is a bloody sight more likely is that if the captain catches you up here he is going to say and do some bloody things that will make you bloody well miserable!"

"But, sir!" said Harold, now affecting the manner and speech of an old family retainer who has been unjustly accused of stealing the ancestral silverware. "But, sir, how could you imagine that I would come up to these quarters without legitimate reason? Surely you must know that I regard the officers' quarters with as great a reverence as I have for their own sacred persons! I came only to awsk if you would honor my humble efforts at coffee-making by consuming a cup of the fresh brew. We simple folk of the scullery should be very happy if you would descend and honor the main deck with your patrician tread—"

Eric had to interrupt this flow of talk, since there was no indication that it would ever stop of itself. "Okay," he said, "but you get the hell out of here now. I'll come down when I get some clothes on."

Down in the saloon he prepared his cup of coffee, and Harold came and sat opposite him. "What's on your mind?" Eric asked.

"I'm worried," Harold said.

"What about?"

"Semantics," Harold said. "I read *The Meaning of Meaning* when I was in school, and I could take it all right, but now I'm getting worried about the meaning of the meaning of meaning."

"What in particular?"

"Well, I've got a book with me called *Semantics and Human Conflict,* and its main point is that if we all understood the same meanings from the same words, if we all understood what each other was up to, then there wouldn't be any war or any poverty or anything like that."

"And what do *you* think?"

"Well, it seems to me that we know pretty damn well what the Germans mean and what they want. But we don't want them to have it. Suppose we said, 'Okay, you heinies have made yourselves perfectly clear. You want to take over the world. You're all supermen and you want us to be your slaves. Okay, we ain't dumb. We get you. So come on and take over. Why should we fight now that we understand each other?' "

Eric laughed, though he saw that Harold was quite serious and genuinely worried. It delighted him to know that this young man could really be worried about questions which are commonly regarded as abstruse and unreal but which are actually crucial and as real as the blood in a man's body.

"Perhaps you're taking the book in too literal or too simple a way," he suggested. "Maybe you're skipping some qualifying statements that may be essential to understanding what the writer really means."

"I wish *you'd* read it," Harold said.

"I'd like to. Who's it by?"

"Gustave Frederick Hammermann, Ph.D."

Harold went to his cabin to get the book, and Eric took his cup into the pantry to refill it. For some years past, coffee had made him very nervous. During the past months in Washington even a single cup would wind him up so tightly that he could think only of violent physical action; it made him want to hit something. But here on shipboard, away from city pressures and office hurry and fatigue too easily solved by alcohol, he could drink as much coffee as he wanted and have only a pleasant lift from it.

2

Eight days later they were all making bets as to whether they would pass the Rock while it was still light enough to see it. There was much talk as to whether the big sign of the Prudential Life Insurance Company would be lighted or not, and probably there was not a single American ship in the convoy on which this antiquated maritime joke was not being worked over and over again for the benefit of the novitiate.

They did pass through the Strait while it was still light. The convoy changed its arrangement and became long and narrow, only three ships wide. On their left they could see the great gray somber fortress of Gibraltar with its geometrical rain-gathering system on the eastern slope of the rock. And off the starboard beam, a small white city of Spanish Morocco.

As darkness approached and the Rock was left behind, Eric stood with First Mate Vangaussen, leaning against the port rail of the boat deck. They could still see the southern coast of Spain. There were lighter splotches, like spots of chipped gray paint, which were small Spanish towns on the darkening Mediterranean shore.

"Well, Professor," said the mate, "you see them villages over there?"

"Uh-huh."

"Well, one thing you can be sure of is that if we can see them they can see us. We're probably the biggest convoy that ever came through here. So you can be mighty sure that some little falangist bastard is already sitting at his radio set telling Herr Doenitz and Herr Goering all about it."

"You think we'll get it?"

The first mate was not a man given to building up fears or rumors of fears. He spoke with regretful certainty. "Sparks," he said, reverting to Eric's earlier title, "we're in easy air range now, and this is a very big bunch of ships. Four days ago was D-day. Our people have just got a toe hold now in Normandy, and a lot of this equipment may be for opening up another front in the south of France. To ask if we'll get it is like asking if Monday will come after Sunday."

At twenty minutes to midnight Eric left the radio room and went to the cabin on the same deck shared by the first and second radio officers. Trying not to awaken Shruck in the lower bunk, he reached up and shook the shoulder of Peters. The second radio officer groaned in his sleep and pulled away. It was some time before Eric could bring him fully awake.

Back in the radio room he prepared to conclude his section of the log. He had served his first watch in the Mediterranean and nothing unusual had happened.

Then he heard the second radio officer in the toilet on the other side of the bulkhead, coughing and vomiting. A few minutes later Peters opened the door of the radio room and stood there holding onto the casement. His face was pale and his eyes bloodshot. "I'm afraid I messed up the head," he said. "I woke up sick. I don't know what it is." Eric saw that the man's body was shaking; something was really wrong with him.

"You go back to bed," he said. "I'll take your watch."

"Oh, I don't want you to do that, old man," Peters said.

"You go to bed. You wouldn't be any good here. Go down to the purser's first and see if he can diagnose you and give you some pills. He's supposed to be the medic on board, you know."

"But you must be tired."

"I feel wide awake, but if I get sleepy I'll wake up Shruck and split your watch with him."

"I better clean up the head. Shruck won't like it."

"You go back to bed. The room steward can take care of that in the morning."

"Well—thanks, old man," said Peters. He started to close the door, then reopened it. "And seventy-three!" he added.

A few weeks past Eric would have been mystified by this cryptic remark; now he knew that among radio amateurs it means "good-by and good luck," or any similar sentiment.

He was rather pleased that he would be allowed to continue through the twelve-to-four watch because of this chance illness of Peters. Whether or not anything happened, these were exciting hours and he wanted to be awake. He switched the distress frequency into the loudspeaker while he went to the toilet. The companionways were dim and ghostly at night, lighted only by faint red lamps about six inches above the deck. Phosphorescent signs with arrows pointed *out*. Heavy black canvas was buttoned around every exit.

To walk around inside a blacked-out ship in convoy in the Mediterranean was, to Eric, strange and theatrical and very real. He felt extraordinarily happy, and as he stood over the toilet watching his parabolic curve of fluid sway slightly because of the rolling of the ship, he wondered why this tense, thin, eager happiness was in him. It was because the convoy would almost certainly be attacked.

Yet most assuredly he had not felt this way when the engine had failed. On the contrary. When they were left behind by the convoy and had all expected to be attacked by submarines, he had certainly felt no exhilaration, but only a lost loneliness and hopeless melancholy. What was the difference in these two situations?

He returned to the radio room and switched the low frequency receiver from the loudspeaker into his earphones. The difference, he thought, must have something to do with gambling. They had all known that if the submarines caught them after they had been deserted by the escort they had no chance at all. They would simply be sunk. No odds, no gamble. Now they were in convoy again and if they were attacked some ships would get it and some would not. The majority probably would not. Which ships would be sunk? There were odds to establish. Nothing was certain except the danger. To be certain of death is not exciting, but to participate in a lottery with death is quite another matter.

Ever since he had talked with the first mate about the nearness of attack in the Mediterranean, Eric had felt this entirely new and exhilarating excitement. It was like a little ripple of secret laughter running through him. He actually seemed to feel some hitherto unknown puppet wires tugging at the corners of his mouth, making him smile. All of this was new to him, organic and human and subtle. He was one of many taking their chances together, gambling with a death that might come *now* instead of the inevitable *then*. It was one of the most exalting experiences he had ever known. It gave him a new quietude in some peculiar way.

Feeling that he must express something of what he was feeling and thinking, he began to write a letter to Jane. After a few preliminary remarks he described his excitement and then wrote:

IN FACT, I HAVE FOUND A PECULIAR TRAN-QUILLITY HERE IN THE PROXIMITY OF VIOLENT DEATH. I FEEL AN INEXPLICABLE SMILE TUG-GING AT MY MOUTH.

He wrote on and on, only interrupted by the BAMS schedule at 0300 GMT. The letter to Jane was written all in emphatic capitals because there are only upper-case letters on a radio room typewriter. Finally he finished the letter:

I DON'T WANT YOU TO BE WORRIED, NOR DO I WANT TO GIVE YOU A FALSE IMPRESSION. IF I TOLD YOU I WAS PERFECTLY SAFE HERE IT WOULD BE A WORTHLESS LIE AND YOU WOULD KNOW IT. SO I MUST TELL YOU HONESTLY THAT

*I AM IN GRAVE DANGER BUT THAT MY OWN
CONVICTION IS THAT I WILL SURVIVE. I HAVE
NOT FULLY ANALYZED THE STRANGE EXCITE-
MENT OF THIS HOUR. IT IS MORE SURPRISING
THAN A NEW DRUG. IT CERTAINLY IS SOME-
THING I NEVER TAUGHT TO MY CLASSES IN SO-
CIOLOGY. NOR DID I TEACH IT TO YOU, MY
LOVELY ONE—BECAUSE I DIDN'T KNOW ANY-
THING ABOUT IT. IT MUST BE AN EVIL FORM OF
EXCITEMENT, BUT SO IS SEX IN CERTAIN OF ITS
ASPECTS, AND WE MUST SOMEHOW LEARN TO
MAKE ALL THESE PERVERSE ELEMENTS PART
OF ONE GREAT AND TRIUMPHANT AND TRULY
HUMAN STRUCTURE.*

As he wrote he began to become very sleepy. He did not
want to be. His head grew heavy and he struggled to keep
his eyes open. He had been making his log entries in pencil
on a separate sheet, but now he put the log sheet back in
the typewriter and began to copy. His excitement faded as
real fatigue invaded all the areas of his brain.

With a jerk he brought his head up from the table. He
had fallen asleep. He was suffused with a feeling of guilt. He
glanced quickly at the chronometer. It was 0348 Convoy
Time—which was at present the same as GMT. Twelve minutes to four A.M. It was time to call Shruck, but he had to
fill in his log. He had the same fearful feeling of guilt as
when he had faked the log entry at the beginning of the trip.
What had happened while he had been asleep? What would
he have to falsify?

Tensely he listened to the sounds about him and felt the
movement of the ship. Everything seemed to be all right.
The regular beating of the engine was there and the strong
forward motion of the ship. It was like one of those childhood dreams of escape: he had made it again—there was
still time.

Then he looked at the log in his typewriter and to his complete astonishment found that he had made the last entry
only fifteen minutes ago. So there was nothing to fake.
Thank God! He felt such gratitude that he decided to give

the chief radio officer an extra twenty minutes of sleep. He took his time about finishing the log. Now he had only a sleep-dazed enjoyment of the moment and the gamble.

Then the headphones around his neck began to buzz with a loud, slow signal. TUD3 TUD3 TUD3—that was the secret convoy call. It was deeply imbedded in Eric's mind from his study of the mimeographed convoy instructions, but somehow he had never felt that he would really hear it. He picked up a pencil and began to copy. He was vividly wide awake and tense now. He could feel his heart beating—not faster, but with deeper surges. TUD9 TUD9 TUD9—that was the call to convoy stragglers. DE TUD1 TUD1 TUD1—it was the convoy commodore that was calling. AAAA AAAA AAAA AAAA—0400 AR.

Eric stood up and took the speaking tube off its hook and blew into it. The voice of First Mate Vangaussen answered from the upper wheelhouse. "Yes?"

"This is the radio room," Eric said. "Enemy aircraft approaching."

"Okay, Sparks," the mate said.

Eric sat down again. He had done it, and he knew at last that he was all right on his job here. Then the general alarm went off. Seven short, brutal rings of the bells that were placed all over the ship. Almost immediately there was the sound of running feet, muffled shouts, the shrilling of the bos'n's whistle.

All the complex thinking Eric had been doing about danger and gambling and so on and so forth was extinguished. Now he had only one thought, and that was: *This is it.*

TUD3 DE TUD1 AAAA APPROACHING 30 DEGREES NORTH OF COURSE MAKE SMOKE AR

Again at the speaking tube, and this time it was the helmsman who answered. "Yessir?"

"They're coming in at thirty degrees north of our course. Tell this to the Armed Guard Commander, and tell him to light the smoke pots."

"Yessir."

As Eric sat down again Shruck came rushing in, wild-eyed, his shirttail out, nervous, dazed, but prepared to be thoroughly efficient in a moment or two. "Let's see the messages," he said. "What're you doing here? Where's Peters?"

Eric handed him the scrawled messages and explained to him that Peters was sick. Shruck took over the operating position and Eric sat down on the lifeboat transmitter which stood against the wall.

The captain came to the radio room door, which was now open and fastened on the hook. He was wearing his kapok life jacket and his hair was mussed. He looked much older than Eric had ever seen him before. He did not look excited or afraid or brave, just older. "Let's see the messages," he said. "And put on your life jackets. You think this is a fire drill? Put them on and both of you stand by."

The captain went away and Peters came staggering to the door. "What is it? What's going on?" he asked, his face as white as limestone, his eyes fever-bright.

Shruck was concentrated over the receiver as though to intercept a distant signal, so Eric told the second, "Enemy aircraft somewhere in the vicinity. You go back to your bunk, but keep your clothes on and wear your life jacket."

Shruck turned with terrible anxiety toward Eric. "Are you *sure* you got it right?"

"I'm sure."

"Well, we better get it into the log right now."

And Chief Radio Officer Shruck began typing Eric's penciled messages into the log as though this clerical performance were the one thing that might save the ship.

The purser, Sealman, came bustling in. His fatness seemed somehow incongruous. It's a lean situation, Eric thought, and this man insists on being fat.

He was carrying a big box with him. It was made of steel and had holes all over it. "Give me your secret code books," the purser said.

"Why?" Eric asked.

The purser was breathing heavily. "To throw overboard," he said. "All the money goes into this box too, and all the convoy orders."

Eric began to gather together the three code books and the mimeographed convoy signal instructions, and he noted that the sieve-like box was full of paper currency. The purser wore a pistol at his belt. There was a momentary resurgence in Eric of that small current of perverse laughter, and it prompted him to ask, "Are you scared, Mr. Sealman?"

The purser's class solidarity with this other intellectual could not withstand the immediate moment, and he shouted angrily at Eric, "Put the books in there, will you!" Then he waddled wildly away into the lower wheelhouse.

There was a stillness. No bells, whistles, shouts, running feet. Eric got up and walked into the wheelhouse. The purser and Second Mate Burley were there. They all stood looking through the narrow slits of shatterproof glass. They could see nothing but blackness.

"Listen," said Burley.

Eric held his breath, trying to hear better.

"Here they come," said Sealman.

Eric could hear it too: the low hum, at first no louder than that of a single bumblebee. He returned to the radio room and sat down again on the lifeboat transmitter. In the event that the ship were abandoned it was his job to carry this transmitter into the number one lifeboat.

Shruck's face was very red; he was moving with strained but unfaltering efficiency. "What's up?" he asked.

"We can hear them."

Peters reappeared at the door. "What's going on?" he asked weakly. "All over?"

"Go back to your bunk," Shruck said, "but keep your clothes on."

"Okay, old man," Peters replied. "And seventy-three!"

Now they could hear the sound of planes even in the radio room, and Eric had nothing to do and therefore he was afraid for the first time. He just sat on the box of the lifeboat transmitter and waited and was afraid.

The exhilaration was entirely drained from him. The way he felt was remotely familiar. At first he could not identify it, but then he recalled the operation he had had as a child. And he knew that what he was feeling was the sensation of being wheeled into the operating room and then having the gauze cone put over his lower face and having the fumes of ether swirl into him. He has known for a long time that it is going to happen. Next week or tomorrow or at eleven A.M. But as they wheel him into the sterile, white, pain-scented room he really knows for the first time that it is *now*.

And *now* is entirely different from any other time: it is

not even in the same class of being. The past and the future are closely related, but *now* is of a complexity and subtlety and wonder and awfulness that cannot be compared with anything else. For *now* is that single point of nakedness at which the soul touches chaos.

The dreadful humming grew still louder, and even this recalled the operation he had had when he was ten years old, because it was the very same sound he had heard as he went under the ether. Then suddenly all sensation was extinguished in a tumult of sound; the eight twenty-millimeters, the three-inch gun on the bow, the four-inch on the stern, and the guns on all the other merchant ships and escort vessels opened fire simultaneously. One of the twenty-millimeters was attached to the deck directly above the radio room; the steel deck acted as a sounding board, and it was almost as though the muzzle of the gun were within inches of Eric's head. The ship vibrated and shook like an animal in its death throes. Then came the reverberant *karrumpf! karrumpf! karrumpf!* that must, he knew, be the bombs. Some were distant and some sounded close by; with all the other din it was hard to guess how close. Eric sat with his face cupped in his hands, his jaws clamped tightly together, waiting for the instant of extinction or pain or unconsciousness. His word-thinking brain was again caught in an idiotic repetition: *Get it over! Get it over! Get it over!* But there was also some part of his mind that was imperturbably interested in only one incidental phenomenon, namely, his own reactions. This observant part was, however, outcast and disembodied. The ether cone of the brain-deafening *now* covered everything.

The torrent of noise ebbed and flowed; there were muffled shouts, a few coherent phrases. "There he is! Get him! Get him! There they come! Goddamn! Get him!" And then just as the noise seemed to be dying away there would come another explosion and an answering burst of unholy sound, like a great blind beast lunging back at a small, cruel, and quick opponent. But finally it all died away and there was quiet.

Eric lifted his head from his hands and looked at Shruck. The chief radio officer was sitting as rigid as a model in a wax museum, the model of a very efficient man suddenly immobilized in paraffin. He melted into life slowly; then he smiled at Eric and said, "Well, Clark, that was that—wasn't it?"

"Yes," Eric said. "It was."

At this moment Sealman, the purser, came in carrying his iron box full of money and secret documents. His fat face was flushed and beaming. "Well," he said, "I always wondered how I would stand up under it, and now I know! They dropped flares over us. Bright as day. It's all over and I wasn't scared!" He put his metal box on the table and began taking out the signal books. Second Mate Burley had come in behind him, chewing on the stem of his pipe and looking unhappy. He heard what the purser said and gave him a look of glowering contempt.

"Wait till you take down your drawers," he said, "and *then* tell us how scared you were! I can smell it already!"

The purser turned toward the second mate, a copy of code book CIMS in his hand. "Speak for yourself, John!" he said, flushing even more deeply.

"My name ain't John and I already spoke for myself," said Burley as he left the room.

The purser fished out from the box the mimeographed convoy instructions and waved them at Eric. *"That* poor man," he said, "is too illiterate and stupid to know whether he's afraid or not!"

"I know damn well *I* was," Eric told him.

Sealman put the papers on the table and closed his steel box. He looked hurt and bewildered. "Well, I feel a lot better now that it's over," he said meekly.

"So do I," Eric agreed.

He was alone with Shruck again for a moment. Then the captain came to the door. "You can go to bed," he said to Eric, "but keep your clothes on."

"What happened to the convoy?" Shruck asked.

"Too dark to know," the captain said. "There were a lot of planes. We saw one tanker blow up—five ships back in our column. The closest drop to us was about two hundred yards astern. We got three of them, as far as I could tell. At the end some of our fighters came in from the direction of Oran and we got a visual Cease Fire order from the commodore. They're gone now."

All this was an unusually gracious articulation for Captain Brogan, and he regretted it almost before he had finished. His face became sullen. "Stand by!" he said gruffly. "I want a clean log of what happened in here!"

Eric said good night to Shruck, though it was approaching dawn, and then went to his room. He took off his life jacket and hung it on a hook. He sat down on his bunk and began to remove his shoes. He was suddenly again very sleepy. His fingers were numb and clumsy; he could hardly keep his eyes open. The upper bunk was unoccupied. Eric turned off the light and lay down without pulling back the bedspread. Then, through the sleep haze that seemed to be wrapped around him like warm, dry gauze, he saw a red light glowing in near space. The slow-motion processes of his turgid brain struggled to interpret this phenomenon. What difference? What did it matter? The sweet gift of darkness was more important. Then he knew that it must be the light attached to the shoulder strap of his life jacket accidentally turned on. He staggered out of his bunk and turned the little cap of transparent red plastic which switched off the light. Mustn't wear down the battery.

As he felt his way back to the berth a sudden sound cut into him like a rusty steel knife wielded by a madman. It was the general alarm again. And the seven brutal spurts of metal fear tore to fragments the warm veil of approaching sleep.

He turned on the light and began to put on his shoes. He was swearing crazily to himself. "Goddamn," he said, "goddamn—goddamn them, the bastards. Once is enough, goddamn them—" He got into his life jacket. On his way out of the room he stopped and opened the medicine chest and took out his comb. Then he went on into the radio room.

Shruck was concentrated over his receiver. Eric glanced at the log in the typewriter and saw that there had been another AAAA at 0451. He sat down on the lifeboat transmitter and began to comb his hair. He did not wonder at the time why he was doing this. It seemed natural, as though he had been wanting for a long time to comb his hair and this was the first opportunity. The time was 0458.

The words he had written to Jane came back to him. *I have found a peculiar tranquillity . . . I feel an inexplicable smile tugging at my mouth.* Now he did not feel any kind

107

of tranquillity, nor did he feel any smiles, explicable or in-explicable, tugging at his mouth. He felt that it was all awful and dull and sick. How easy it is to lie, to write glib sentences, he thought, when you don't really know what the hell you're talking about. He felt a bitter annoyance toward any man who could have written those fatuous words about *peculiar tranquillity* and *inexplicable smiles.*

The purser came in again to get the code books. This time he looked dazed and ill. Eric put his comb in his pocket and followed Sealman slowly out into the wheelhouse and then onto the port wing of the bridge. It was quite light outside. There was as yet no sign of planes, and the two men stood there breathing deeply of the fresh air.

The *SS William Benson* was now the front ship in the third column. They were all making smoke, and the white ectoplasmic clouds spread from the pots on their sterns, trailing behind them in mile-long streamers and covering all but the lead ships. The sky was almost white except where the approaching sun was welding a ribbon of orange-hot copper around the eastern horizon.

The five front ships, plowing steadily ahead and pouring the thick masses of chemical fog from their sterns; the reverent silence of the dawn; the vast gray antiquity of the sea —all this was like the background for some strange religious spectacle, a grave, poignant, and aloof moment in time.

10: An Empty Space

Jane Clark, wearing brand-new black satin panties, sat before the dressing table in her basement apartment. She had been there for an hour. Never before in her life had she applied make-up with such extreme care. She had washed off a light violet-tinted powder and replaced it with a dark shade of pancake make-up. She had tried her usual bright copper lipstick, removed it, was now applying a much darker color with considerable purple in it. Lately she had been paying attention to beauty hints in various publications. She powdered her lips and brushed them dry, then applied the lipstick to the center of her mouth, spreading and shaping it with a lipstick brush. Avoiding any dip in the center of the upper lip, she created a flattened curve that exaggerated the already adequate width of her mouth. To the lower lip she gave a much deeper curve. Carefully blotting all this by pressing her lips together on a Kleenex, she powdered her mouth again and put on the second coat. This was again powdered and then brushed smooth with a camel's-hair brush.

This process she had learned only last week in a beauty item entitled: "Here's the Way Actresses Make Their Lipstick *Really* Kissproof!" Never before had she taken a serious interest in her toilette. In fact, she had been rather careless. She took care of her skin, which was somewhat dry, but had used lipstick only casually except when she was going out with Eric in the evening. She had never used powder—other than bath talcum—or rouge or mascara or eyebrow pencil or eye shadow. But just recently she had been feeling that all these things were very, very important.

After she had applied the mascara—observing the new depth of her eyes and thinking how ridiculous mascaraed women look after they have been crying—she began to work on her eyebrows. Her original aversion to false faces struggled weakly for the conservative approach, but her new interests won easily, and she added an extra half inch to the length of her carefully plucked eyebrows. Her new coiffure was an up-do, and it required considerable thought, effort, and contemplation. Jane's taste in clothes had always been simple, and it remained so. If there was any change here it was that she was a little more concerned about quality. She wondered if, after all, having paid such low prices, her clothes could really look as well on her as she had thought they did. For this evening she chose her black crepe dress with the high jewel neckline and three-quarter sleeves. She put on the gold rope-mesh necklace that had once belonged to Eric's grandmother.

Then she went into the kitchen and began to mix a martini. Formerly she had usually made highballs when she or Eric wanted a drink, for the good reasons that they were quicker to mix and took longer to drink. These reasons no longer seemed valid.

These changes in Jane had not occurred without her knowledge. She thought about them continually. In fact, her sudden drive toward diversion was to a large extent based upon a desire to *stop* thinking about them.

She had a date tonight with John Hardin. John had been Eric's immediate superior in the OWI. About ten days ago he had come around, avowedly to see Eric and ask him when he would be leaving with the Merchant Marine. To wish him Godspeed—as he put it. He had appeared mildly surprised when Jane told him that Eric had already gone. He had waxed movingly though reservedly appreciative of Eric's courage in quitting his job and going overseas into the war zones. He had invited Jane out for a drink, and they had gone to the nearby Ambassador. There, in the High Hat Room, John had become even more appreciative of Eric's courage and all his other good qualities. Especially his earnestness.

"Eric took things very seriously," said John Hardin. "He was always the most solemn guy in the office. But really, he was right! In times like these—well, things *are* serious. So I felt all along that people who tried to make fun of—of attitudes like that—were wrong. Don't you agree with me?"

Jane did not answer, and he added, "Of course—I know you do."

Jane was not fooled in the slightest degree. She had not forgotten Eric. She knew full well that she had shared in more natural and playful humor in a day with Eric than this marionette could conceive of in a lifetime.

John Hardin was a man of about thirty-five years, of medium height, dark, mustached. He wore beautifully tailored tan gabardine suits as a rule, with prewar Irish linen shirts, hand-woven wool neckties from New Mexico, and a heavy scent, which she later learned was called "Russian Leather." His once lithe body was now accumulating bulges, but his face was still lean. He had been an account executive in one of the biggest New York advertising agencies before the war. Jane did not forget that his present job had most likely saved him from the draft.

"Yes," he had said as he toyed with his cocktail glass, "Eric is really an idealist. You might say he's a reformer. He thinks everything's wrong with everything and if you're solemn enough about the whole setup you might be able to improve it."

This angered Jane at last. "Eric isn't solemn," she said, "and you know damned well he isn't! He probably sees a great deal more humor in the world than you do. I don't think you can really know what humor is unless you begin with some sort of gravity. I guess I read that or heard it somewhere—but it's true."

John Hardin saw at once that he had gone too far and he quickly reversed his field. "Of course, of course, of course!" he said. "I know that old Eric had the best damned sense of humor in the world! He used to tell some of the best damned jokes I ever heard. Oh, Eric wasn't a sour-puss by any means! If that's what you thought I meant, please excuse me for being so inarticulate!"

With a sick feeling above her stomach she had recorded his use of the past tense. Not: Eric isn't. No, no. He must say: Eric wasn't . . .

Jane, at this first date, was not deceived in any way. She knew that John Hardin had not come to inquire about Eric, but that he had come in the hope of finding her alone. She knew that John did not admire Eric, but envied him and coveted her. She knew that John would like to sneak in and gain by circumstance all that Eric had won by the quality of what he was. The world is full of this kind of men and their feeble little plots, she thought.

She knew what John was up to. Primarily, of course, he wanted to go to bed with her. The only thing she was not quite certain of was whether he wanted most to go to bed with *her* or with Eric's wife. And that was a very important question.

That first night she had felt only a slow and contained contempt for this clever man. To him, she thought, a woman is just another scalp to hang at his belt. And if he happens to hate or envy her husband, then she represents a super scalp. He both hates and envies Eric, but in addition, she decided, he really *wants* me.

She looked deeply into the stem of her cocktail glass that night and said, "But you, Hardin—surely you're just as earnest about winning the war as Eric is?"

"But naturally," her escort said. "Who isn't? It's got to be won! Otherwise we'll all live in a concentration camp. Ha-ha!"

His laugh made concentration camps seem very improbable. The war became, what with eight martinis, all a light, fluffy game, and she wondered what Eric had been so concerned about. Was Eric really solemn?

"I have to go home now," she had said.

Because she knew that no matter what Eric was he was now out there somewhere where the enemy could kill him. And it was no matter to discuss with this covetous man over cocktails in the High Hat Room. She demanded to be taken home, and John Hardin took her home at once and made not the slightest protest. In fact, he made it almost a religious performance. This fine girl, Jane, wife of my good old friend, Eric, who is overseas, *must* be carefully taken home.

And put to bed.

But she left him at the door. "No, I'm all right," she said. "I don't need any help."

"But my dear," he mumbled, "I know you think I'm juss a shallow person. But right now all I want do is see you get bed all right. Tuck you in your li'l trundle bed. Kiss you goo'-night. Like a brother. Thassall. Thass really all. I got too much respeck for Eric think anything else no madder how lovely you are. An' you *are* lovely! I could juss hug you . . ."

He was staggering now on the pavement under the street light in front of the basement entrance. She reached for his hand to say good night, but he lurched away. She thought victoriously that she could drink more than this experienced roué could. But then she wondered how many drinks he might have had before he came to see her.

The truth was that she had been sick with worry about Eric. Only the night before she had gone to the movies alone, and in the newsreel she had seen it happen and had known for sure that she could never again love anyone as she had loved Eric. But what was this past tense? Even she was using it. She had seen pictures of a convoy, and an ammunition ship was hit and—it was destroyed, and then there was a picture of the empty ocean with only an area of turbulent foam and a few pieces of driftwood. It was a good shot taken through a telescopic lens, and the newsreel company was properly proud of it.

As Jane sat alone in her kitchen, feeling the make-up on her face like a dry mask and sipping her very dry martini, she asked herself a question. She asked it in words, grammatically, with all the punctuation in place. "Since I know better than ever before that I love Eric, and since I know what a phony John is and exactly what he's after, *why* am I going out with him night after night?"

She asked this question of herself, but no grammatical and definite answer came to meet it. The question hung in the air before her, slowly diminishing, leaving an empty space. She poured the rest of the gin and vermouth from the cocktail shaker into her glass.

Well, there was the boredom of living alone with nothing to do. But tomorrow she was to start work for the Department of Commerce. That would take care of some of this *useless* feeling. Secretarial Assistant, the job was called.

And—there was going places. Eric had never cared much for night clubs. He liked to drink and he liked the theater, but he found most night clubs expensively dull. Jane had felt the same way about it until now. It was only recently that she had had this urge, like the need for a drink, to lose herself in brash music and colored lights and crowded dancing. Like alcohol, it was both stimulation and anesthesia. It was a surcease from worry about Eric, from loneliness, and from the aching pressure of womanhood. Only John Hardin offered her this drug, and she accepted it.

And what about John himself—did he attract her in a man-woman way? It seemed to her that he had every quality she disliked. And yet, wasn't there something pitiful about him? He *was* a phony. His intelligence was the most meager fraction of Eric's. He certainly was not physically attractive in the accepted sense. He in no way resembled Apollo nor even a romantic movie star of the more decadent type. He offered no promise of male prowess. And yet he did attract her in some vague and shameful manner. He had the deft and lewd assurance of a man who has had many women who did not really want him. Jane's surface feeling toward him was one of mild revulsion. She knew that his greatest technique was that of waiting—waiting for the vulnerable moment. And this amused her in a dark way. He'll have a long wait for me, she thought.

She decided to mix another shaker of drinks so that she could offer one to John when he came to get her. They were going to see *Tobacco Road* at the National Theater and then to a night club. The thought of desiring John sexually made a wave of silent laughter run through her body. That pudgy, insidious snail of a man! She tasted the new mixture.

Sexual desire since Eric's departure had been a constant pressure, but every time she faced the thing it wore a different mask. There was the direct aspect. It was the strongest, for some reason, in midafternoon. About three o'clock it always came, heavy and slow and wet; she would visualize over and over again the way it had been—the ache, the grateful thrust, the tender and awful objective—the pain and chaos and solace of completion. All this was a humid dream that was always near her, arrogantly waiting to take charge of her life. She had tried masturbation, but this only left her more nervous and hungry than she had been before she went through with the dead mechanical process.

She heard John's knock at the door and went to answer it. "I've mixed a couple of martinis," she said. "Shall we have one before we go?"

"By all means," he said. "I'd love to have a cocktail mixed by your lovely hands!"

She felt two thought-emotions simultaneously. One was: I'd like to poke him in the jaw with one of my lovely hands. The other was: I wonder what *he* looks like? Probably very repulsive.

In the theater she let him hold her hand although it seemed silly. It was a matter of social economics; he was spending money on her and so she must give him something, such as the warmth of her left hand. She felt the pressure of his fingers vary with the progress of the play, never crudely, but in muted and subtle counterpoint to the cruel and obscene tragedy of Jeeter and Ada and Ellie May and Love and Flora and Duke and Bessie.

When Duke said, "Ellie May's horsing. That's horsing from way back yonder, hey, Pa?" When Love and the sex-starved girl with the split lip were squirming toward each other on the ground with movements of terrible body-ache

114

and self-extinction, John was very careful not to squeeze her hand at all; his fingers were relaxed then and noninsistent.

In the Kavkaz there were soft gypsy music and dim light and the rarefied sweet pungency of vodka. Jane was beginning to feel let down when they arrived at the Russian night club, and she needed a drink. The vodka was good for her.

"We must have *shashlik,*" John said. "But first let's have a few more vodkas to pick up our spirits after that depressing play."

"I'm surprised you found it depressing," Jane said. "I thought you'd see it only as a comedy—or just a dirty play."

"You *do* think I'm shallow, don't you, Jane?"

"About an inch deep," Jane said, with a sudden frank cruelty which surprised her.

John laughed, and his laugh, as always, was as mechanical as the sound made by a doll that will say *mama* when you put it on its back. "Maybe it can be measured in inches," he said. "But let's not limit it to *one* inch!"

"All right—*two* then."

"Spasibo!"

"What does that mean?"

"Thank you—in Russian."

"You speak Russian?"

"I was born in Petrograd."

"You certainly don't look like a Russian to me. Where are your whiskers and thick accent?"

"I left them in Petrograd. I was brought over here when I was five years old."

"Isn't Petrograd called Leningrad now?"

"It's still *Petro*grad to me."

"I see—you don't recognize the revolution."

"Please, my dear, no politics. We're not out together to discuss politics."

"What are we out together for?"

He looked at her steadily as he turned his empty glass slowly between stubby fingers. "To have a good time," he said. "To forget the world's troubles and our own. To be natural and human for a few brief hours."

Jane thought to herself that *Tobacco Road* was hardly a play calculated to make one forget the world's troubles, but

115

she said nothing about this. It occurred to her that John might have had in mind some quality of the play other than its social significance when he decided to make it part of their evening.

"What was your name in Russia?" she asked.

"The, same," he told her. "That is, the same last name, but in Russian John is Ivan."

"It's hard to imagine you being called Ivan."

"Ivan the Unterrible!"

The orchestra played a fanfare, and a huge man dressed in boots with red pants tucked into them and a bright yellow tunic buttoned tightly around his throat, entered the spot-lighted circle on the small dance floor and bowed to loud applause.

"I wanted you to hear this man," John said to Jane. "I think his voice is as good as Chaliapin's was. Name is Sofanov."

"My forrst nomber," the singer said, "vill be 'Provodniki,' de vorrds by Aleksyey Tolstoi."

"What does that title mean?" she asked.

"The Convoy," John said, and Jane started with surprise. It seemed impossibly coincidental that the first song this man sang tonight should have that name, when the whole background of her own present consciousness was taken up with that distant convoy in which her lover moved across some unknown sea toward some hidden destination.

The basso sang in tones that were really moving, organ-like, and final-sounding. After the Russian version he sang in English:

"Dey move ahnd deir shahdow move wit dem, vile drown by a parr awv old hahck, two light creeping vahgon keep vit dem, de escor' close aht deir bahck. Dey seeng awv a freedom ahs bow-ndless ahs de steppes reeple-mark by each gawst. De darkness hahs fallen, steel faintly, I hear deir chains cleenk in de dawst . . ."

Jane asked what this had to do with convoys, and John told her that the title referred to the guards escorting a group of criminals to Siberia. "Very touching, isn't it?" he asked.

"But we don't seem to be able to keep away from things serious."

"Aren't all Russian songs sort of lugubrious?"

"Not really; they may sound that way, but lots are really gay. Of course, this place, since the war, has gone sort of pro-Red, and so they don't go in much for the gayer songs of pre-Bolshevik days. Too bad. *Mais, c'est la guerre.*"

"My God, they certainly don't!" Jane said. "I don't know whether this is pre- or post-Bolshevik, but it certainly is not happy."

The singer had reached the English version of his second number:

"Ahnd nah aht lengt our lowng silence ees brawken, our pahdvays diverge ahnd ve part, you ahnd I. My heart cries, my heart cries, daht awn vorrd reman to be spawken. De vorrd daht ees sahd beyon bearink; ah, sahd beyon bearink: Good-by, good-by, good-by . . ."

John was annoyed. "Looks like we came to the wrong place," he said. "I wish the gypsy singer would come back. At least we can't understand her."

The gypsy did come back, and there was again music that brooded over sultry and narrowly focused personal destiny rather than the wide melancholy of the steppes of the human soul. They drank many drinks before they ordered food. Jane knew that she was getting drunk but felt curiously separate from her drunkenness and able to control it. She felt now that she was playing a daring game at which she was wonderfully skilled. She knew that this man was not taking her out in order to let her study Russian and gypsy music, and she knew what the words "natural" and "human" meant to him. But she felt very capable. She saw herself as a skilled tightrope walker. Little ripples of secret laughter ran through her veins, and she wanted to see how close she could come to giving way and falling into this man's crude and obvious snares. A woman of the world playing with an inferior Casanova, toying with his puny plans of conquest. It was fun.

The waiters brought the *shashlik* in on flaming skewers,

117

and after that they had *baclava* and thick black coffee and more vodka. John was showing his liquor now.

He would forget all his seducer's cunning every now and then to lapse into reminiscence. His childhood, his adolescence, his first marriage. It seemed that he had always loved *beauty* above all things and that the beauty he conceived had always been rudely shattered by insensitive persons who entered his life or were already connected with it and who did not love beauty at all, but on the other hand wanted only to *smash* it. All this was genuinely sad, and at times Jane forgot that she was a clever woman of the world walking on a tightrope above the pit of the giant gynophagous lizard, and she felt that it was indeed very melancholy that all our beautiful, fragile dreams are so often trampled upon by the crude tread of those practical and selfish persons who do not love beauty at all. Her consciousness was sinking with that of John Hardin into a bayou of miasmic self-righteousness.

"I guess I'm juss a fool," he said, "an' I know how shallow you thought I was, but I have *always* strive find the beau'ful somewhere in life. Maybe tha's why I drink so much. Always wanted to fine the beau'ful an' it always turn' out lousy. Only a few times beau'ful, and then brief, very brief. But you, Jane—you're the kind of girl could make it always beau'ful for a man. You're intelligen' an' lovely an' you know what the score is. You could be a frien' an' a pal an' a real lover besides. Tha's what a man needs."

The huge singer with the basso-profundo voice came out again and began to sing in Russian.

"Oh—at last, at last," said Hardin, "he is now singing a *gay* Russian song. I toll you they had gay Russian songs! Lis'n. It's all about some man who loss his horse, cause 'nother man took it away—comic song."

Jane nodded and smiled. She felt that John Hardin was not a bad fellow now . . . really. We are all human and all caught in the same hopeless quandary; it must be high time that we all understood one another and signed some kind of truce of decency. But she did not lose her wariness, not at all. She continued to balance with cunning frivolity upon the taut steel wire of self-possession. The wonderful organ

118

voice of Feodor Sofanov now sang in English, and she could understand part of it.

"De knight-errant vahs slain by a meescreant's hahnd; de knave spied de true knight afar o'er de lahnd ahnd vaited teel nightfall to strike hees fell blaw, ahnd flahng de dead mahn in de torrent belaw. Den clahd in de armor he'd vawn by fahl force, de murderer mahnted knight-errant's good horse. Ven o'er de breedge he vould erge heem een flight de steed rear opp vildly ahnd neigh een affright. Ahnd vainly de rohbber strock sperrs to eets flahnk . . ."

"Jane, you really don't know how it is," John said melancholically into his glass of Pennsylvania vodka. "It's so won'-erful out with you. All the other girls got no brains. You un'erstand things. You got a mine—goddamn good mine in your head in addition to a beau'ful body—and you simply can't realize what a relief is to a man like me. Grow awfully, awfully tired of brainless li'l girls who don't un'erstand anything—juss don't un'erstand. Awfully tired—and now less have juss one more li'l shot good ole Russian liquor."

When they got out of the taxi on Thirteenth Street Northwest she invited him in to have one more martini, but then when they were inside she thought what was the use of mixing it, so she poured them a couple of straight shots of gin in highball glasses. He was in the kitchen watching her. Jane bumped into the side of the doorway on the way back into the front room. She laughed. It was fun to be drunk, because she didn't care. What was the difference? Drunk or sober, what was the difference?

The room swayed around her. She was on a merry-go-round. Sometimes she saw two John Hardins swinging past. She giggled aloud as she thought, My God! Isn't one enough?

"What you laughing at?" John asked.

"I juss saw two of you," Jane said. "Was funny seeing two —two li'l Ivans."

"I'd like see a million of *you!*" John said.

"What could you do with million?"

"Juss look at 'em—worship 'em—tha's all."

Jane's eyes filled with tears and she had the sensation of being someone else—some sentimental fool, in fact. "You worship me, Ivan?" she asked in a pathetic voice that was not her own.

"Certainly, I worship you! Worship you like an angel. Lemme juss show you, juss show you once!" He drained his glass and then got down on his knees on the cement floor. "Worship you like a saint," he said.

He put his arms up around her waist and began to rub his cheek against her knee. "Like a saint, juss like a saint," he kept repeating.

She tried to feel for a moment his hands on her hips, his face on her knee, but it was as though her blood were diluted with liquid rubber. She only partly felt things and then they bounced away. He was trying to push her knees apart.

"No, no," she said. "That isn't the way you worship a saint."

"Oh, Jane!" he said, breathing very heavily. "Less not be saint! Tha's way I want worship you!" He began to cry and rub his face against her thigh. She could see spots where his tears darkened her dress. "Isn't bad—really isn't bad. Want to worship beau'ful girl like you this way. 'Smose beau'ful thing in the worl'! Please un'erstan', Jane, *please* un'erstan' me!"

And all the time he was trying to move her knees apart.

In spite of her physical drunkenness a clear, undrunken voice spoke in Jane's consciousness. *Why not?* it asked.

Eric will go with some whore, the voice said. He'll have to go. Not because of lust so much as because of curiosity. He won't think that just because he happens to be married to me he can't find out what's going on in whatever country he happens to land in. And that's one of the ways of finding out. I don't want this thing in front of me. God knows I don't want it from this crying weakling. But after all, I'm curious too! I want to know what he'll do. I want to see how he worships me. And I'm tired, tired, tired, and—I just want to be taken care of—worshiped—taken care of . . .

The room that she and Eric had created in this basement whirled around her with a lewd and funny recklessness as she relaxed her thigh muscles. What's the difference? she thought. And the world revolved from carnival delirium to amoral curiosity and then to humid fatigue. Why not? she thought. Why not, why not, why not . . . why not, why not . . .

And she gave way as a dam breaks, letting him do whatever he wanted. It was dull and evil, hot and sick and futile.

Afterward she despised or liked him no more and no less than she had before. "You'd better go home now," she said. "We're all out of worship. You can phone me at my new office tomorrow if you want to."

During all this she had not allowed him to kiss her on the mouth, and now when he tried to, she pushed him away. He smiled wisely.

"Good night," he said. "Good night, my love!"

Jane did not miss the note of triumph in his voice, nor was she unaware of the nature of his victory. This man was not thinking that he had done this to her; he was thinking that he had done it to Eric's wife. And later, as she lay awake in bed with the liquor slowly wearing off, she did not mind at all that he had won over her, but she was nauseatingly resentful that he should feel himself triumphant over Eric. She cried quietly for a while, and then got up and vomited.

11: You May Be Torn Apart by Their Reality

Palermo as seen from the ship in the heightening light of morning was like the backdrop of an Italian opera, with some peculiar subtractions and additions. There was the old Roman arch, the palm trees and other greenery, the many tile-roofed, stuccoed buildings with balconied façades, the church with its domed campanile and cross. But subtracted were the fronts and sides of many buildings. This subtraction, however, added much to the color and charm of the scene. For the inside walls of the apartments thus revealed formed cubistic designs in a great assortment of lovely pastel tints: pink and green and blue and yellow and violet. Beautiful to behold in the bright morning of a Mediterranean summer. And there was much fallen masonry in white and brick red and tan, all forming grotesque patterns of the most delightful variety. And on the big hill where the aqueduct came down there were many deep ochre bomb pockets this side and that side of the pipe. And the entire backdrop now appeared to be suspended by cables from the whalelike silver shapes of innumerable barrage balloons. It was a wonderful and tempting prospect to men who have been locked in the floating prison of a ship for thirty-eight days. They could see the miniatures of people, horse-drawn carriages, jeeps, and some black-gowned figures entering and leaving a partly destroyed church.

Eric stood at the starboard rail of the boat deck with Vangaussen, looking at this operatic spectacle. Van had arrived at many ports in many lands at peace and in war, before he settled down to be an orange grower. But this was Eric's first war port.

Of course they had stopped for orders off Oran, but they were far offshore and could see no more than they had when they passed the other cities and towns of North Africa. Algiers was an expanse of tiny cubes thrown against some hills, Bizerte was distant dry rubble, and between the towns were the brown cliffs and green capes of the coast with now and then the solitary white ruin of some Moorish fortress. But Palermo was different; they could see its life.

At Oran the British had taken over the escort duties and one of their corvettes led the *SS William Benson* to Palermo. The corvette left them outside the harbor, and they sent in a visual signal telling their name and cargo. Six hours later an American navy launch came near by and its officer asked through an electronic megaphone, "What's your name and what's your cargo and where are you bound?"

Captain Brogan shouted back through his nonelectronic megaphone that their name was *William Benson,* their cargo coal, and their destination Palermo. This seemed to cause some dismay. The man on the launch asked, "Did you say your cargo was *coal?*"

"That's what I said," the captain replied.

122

"What kind of coal?" the naval man asked.

The captain was nonplused. Almost everyone on the ship was listening to this important conversation. After all, they had been risking their lives bringing this stuff here, and now they naturally wanted to go ashore and get drunk and forget it. After a half-minute of thought the captain shouted through his megaphone, "Just coal—ordinary coal!"

"Hard or soft?"

"Anthracite!"

"How big?"

This stumped Captain Brogan for a minute. "Different sizes!" he shouted.

"Is it barley?" the naval officer asked impatiently.

"No—it's coal!"

"I mean barley-size!"

"It's from barley on up!"

"We have no use for large coal in Palermo! Who sent you here?"

"The Navy! Goddammit! The United States Navy!"

The launch went away in disgust and there were no further orders. That night they were left outside the submarine net and there were depth charges near by for many hours before dawn. It was an unhappy night; the ship was desolate as an unwanted lover.

But now they had been signaled to enter the harbor. And it was very pleasurable. It meant that their cargo could be used after all, and they would get ashore and get drunk and find some women.

The backdrop of the city would have looked unreal enough without the subtractions and additions. But now, to Eric, it was hard to say whether it was lyrical vision or Daliesque nightmare.

He spoke to Vangaussen. "Looks sort of unreal, doesn't it?"

The first mate relit his pipe slowly and thoughtfully. He was not a man in a hurry to answer any more than the captain was; only his delays were based upon an actual requirement to consider all aspects of the situation at his leisure, whereas with Brogan the pause was an indication of disgust with the trivia of human intercourse.

"Yeah, Professor, I guess it does to us all right," he said, "But to them people that were born there I guess it looks pretty real—everything being smashed up like that."

Eric recalled the mess boy's worries about what is real and what is not. If you dream bombs are falling and they aren't, then the reality of the bombing is limited to yourself, he thought. If bombs are falling and you dream they're not, then the reality of the bombing is limited to others. Except that you may be torn apart by their reality, whereas they will never be destroyed by yours. At least not directly. He laughed a little at this kind of thinking, which reminded him of Harold's heavy burden of conflicting semantics.

"What's the joke?" Vangaussen asked.

"I was just wondering about what's real and what isn't," Eric said.

Van reverted now as he sometimes did, for no apparent reason, to a broad Dutch accent. "Vell, Spaarks," he said, "you got someding, I tink. Personally I don' know whedder I'm here or derr."

They had received another order from the navy signal tower now that they were close inside the bay. Eric could read the slow flashes of light from the tall concrete tower. And then came the shouted order from the flying bridge: *"Let go the starb'rd anch-or!"* And the iron rattle of link chain as the men on the bow let it go. Everyone on board ship felt a visceral tug of sick depression. They were not being taken into a dock; they would not land their goddamn coal; they would not get ashore today to find the special exaltation of alcoholic semiconsciousness and the methodical solace of professional love. The whole setup, they thought, was lousy and snafu.

2

It was their second night at anchor in the bay of Palermo now and everyone was disgusted with the way the war was being run. Here they were with a load of coal that nobody wanted, locked up on the ship within sight of bars and women. The days were maddening, and the men were grateful for the night.

Eric sat in a canvas chair on the captain's deck. The air

moved against his face like cool, wayward fingers. The broken buildings, the Roman arch, and the hill behind the town were still visible in the blue-gray dusk. The boats were coming alongside now to sell wine and exchange talk. He could hear the hollow, isolated sound of voices reflected from the water. Questions and answers and low laughter. There must be at least two rowboats alongside the stern.

These boats were manned by Italian oarsmen hired by navy boys stationed in Palermo. The sailors came out partly to make a little extra money selling the wine or exchanging it for cigarettes, but mainly to talk with some of their own kind who had just come from the States. The men on the ships were equally eager to talk to these strangers because they knew all the ins and outs of Palermo. The Americans from the shore and the Americans on the ship each held a new kind of magic for each other.

The boys in the rowboats mainly liked to ask, "Where *you* from, fellow?" . . . "Texas! Well, I'll be damned! A real man on board!" Then in an anxious voice, "Don't suppose you ever been up around Amarillo?"

And from the ship the earnest questions were almost entirely about women and how much they cost and whether there was any trouble with the MP's and the price of liquor and what were the best places. No one on the ship had been to Italy since the war began, so it was in many ways a new world even to the oldest seaman.

As the afterglow diminished it was supplanted by the light of a full moon that hung almost vertically above the ship, and the sentimental mezzotint of refracted sunlight became the romantic stereoscope of moonlit night. The whole visible world seemed to become more and more clear in the liquid, ennobling light of the full moon. The stern structure of the ship, the water, the inaccessible shore, all were enriched in the lucernal hour.

Eric was no less anxious than any other man to get ashore, yet now he felt completely absorbed in the delicate and macabre beauty of the moment. There was plenty of Marsala on board now and its glow in the veins of the men spread over the ship as surely as the glow of the moonlight. Every once in a while there was a white shimmering in the sky where a shifting aluminum-painted barrage balloon caught the light of the moon at just the right angle to reflect it to Eric's eyes.

Someone drew up a chair and sat down beside him. It was Peters. Eric was glad that Peters had recovered from his food poisoning, but he did not particularly welcome his company. They exchanged greetings of recognition.

"Picturesque, isn't it?" Peters asked.

"Yes," Eric said. "It is. With variations."

"Heh-heh-heh," Peters giggled. "I guess so. You mean all the wreckage and stuff?"

"Uh-huh."

"Boy, this burg really got it. First from us and then from the Germans. I guess these wops will think twice before they jump into another war!"

"I guess so."

There was a long silence then, during which Eric tried to forget that Peters was sitting close beside him, but he could feel the unrelenting pull of a sincere and feeble mind tugging at his attention.

Finally, in an embarrassed voice, Peters said, "I guess you think my interests are kind of limited to radio and stuff like that. Being a professor of college you naturally are interested in wider interests."

"No," said Eric, "it's just that I really don't know much about radio."

But Peters would not be diverted. He had something to talk about and he was determined to talk about it to Eric.

"I been studying lately," he said solemnly. "It's a book you would probably be interested in. It's called *Personal Magnetism,* and it's by a doctor—Dr. Somebody. Ever heard of it?"

"No, I don't think I have. What do you learn from it?"

"Well—I guess it sounds kind of crazy—but it tells how to bring all your hidden forces to bear on any problem. See what I mean?"

"Sort of. But what are these hidden forces?"

"Well—I guess it sounds kind of crazy—but everybody has hidden forces that they don't know about until they— until they find out about them."

"What are they?"

"Well—like animal magnetism!"

"Uh-huh."

"Animal magnetism can turn into just plain sex stuff, or you can use it for mental purposes like—like sublimate it."

"How?"

"Well, you sort of bring it up, you know, into your brain, and then you think with it."

"Sounds good."

Peters' voice was enthusiastic. "I knew you'd be interested in this stuff!" he said. "And there's another chapter on how to judge character by the shape of the facial features. It tells you what you're up against when you meet someone new, you see? How to make a good impression on them. How to impress different types, see? That's important, don't you think so?"

"It certainly is," Eric answered. And at the same time he felt suddenly sick. "Excuse me," he said, "I have to make a brief trip to the head."

He was sick in the toilet and painfully threw up his dinner. He had gone through all the sea-tossed rolling of the ship and the dull fear at being left behind and the acrid fear of the air attacks, and he had not been sick. But now all at once a terrible feeling of the hopelessness of the human situation had welled up around him: the primitive mind still so earnestly and religiously active in a world of implacable technology, the fatal gulf between the extremes of consciousness in this improbable and aspiring and tragic species.

He went back at last to the captain's deck but he saw in the untroubled light of the moon that Peters was still there, and so he turned about and went into the radio room. He sat down behind the locked door in prideless loneliness and looked at the wonderful apparatus. Everything had been turned off except the oven of the autoalarm, and its pilot light stared at him like a baleful little red eye. He decided to try the emergency crystal receiver, which required no current. He pecked away at the cube of galena with the cat whisker of the old-fashioned crystal detector and eventually he found a sensitive spot and heard some music in the headphones. He had not used a receiver of this kind since he had built one at the age of ten. But it was music all right, and the voice of a girl.

She was singing in Italian but the music was American: "Night and day . . . you are the one . . ."

Her voice was limpid and bold, asking and only partly answering. Eric heard this retreating and advancing voice against the moonlit beauty of Palermo as he had seen it before he had been driven indoors. He was quieted. He felt a great sob of worship go through him, and it was the worship of woman. This singing told him of the miracle that man and woman require of each other. But particularly of the soft, wise, and elusive enchantment of woman. He grew weak with desire for Jane. Letters were so impotent. If he could say one word, touch her only once—anything to fill in the void of the lucernally impassive night in this unreceptive bay.

Early next morning they received their orders. They were to dock at noon. When Eric came down to breakfast, Chief Engineer Curtis and the third mate were dawdling over their coffee and talking about Italy and Italians. They had both been over here before the war.

"You better check them gold-capped teeth of yours," said Hartley. "These guineas are the most light-fingered lot in the world, next to the Ay-rabs."

The chief was in a jovial mood. Hartley was one of the few men on the ship who would sit and talk with him, and soon he would be ashore in the more distinguished company of the anonymous.

"Yessir," he said, "they're a whoremongering bunch of thieves, all right. At least the Ay-rabs are out-and-out about it. You *know* an Ay-rab is gonna try to rob you. But a goddamn wop will pretend to be your best friend while he's reachin' in your pocket."

They had not noticed as they talked that George Fiorini had come into the room carrying a plate of food. George sat down opposite Eric, and now the other two noticed him. Hartley was embarrassed, but Curtis derived a sadistic satisfaction from the idea that George had heard what they had said and that George was a wop. "Well, Steward," he shouted brazenly, "ain't it a fact? Ain't it true that these goddamn guineas over here are a thieving lot?"

"Well, they got my watch last time I was over here before the war," George said, his face flushing darkly.

The engineer and the mate went out and left Eric alone with the steward. George was eating ham and eggs and did not shift his attention from his plate.

"Tell me, George," said Eric, "doesn't this foolishness about wops and so on and so forth sort of make you mad sometimes?"

George looked up aggressively. "I'm as much of an American as anybody," he said. "I was born in Brooklyn. Some of these guys that hand me the wop business weren't even *born* in America!"

"I know you're an American," Eric said. "I just asked you whether it didn't make you mad. Whether you wouldn't like to kick their teeth in when they say things about all Italians being thieves and so on? Wouldn't you?"

George smiled at Eric now that he knew there was no secret malice behind his questioning. "I used to get mad," he said. "I used to get into plenty of fights. But no more. I *did* have my watch stolen over here. And that's a fact. They're different over here from people like my family. Anyway, my people came from *northern* Italy."

The steward gulped his food and hurried away without finishing his coffee. Eric saw that he wanted to get away from this kind of talk even though he knew it was friendly.

A navy tug came alongside at noon and tied up to the *SS William Benson*. The process of docking was lengthy because of the many sunken ships that blocked the harbor. There was an Australian troop transport broken into three pieces directly between them and their dock.

A Port Security officer came on board with shore passes and a mimeographed copy of the port regulations. Most of the officers not on duty joined him in the saloon. He was a red-faced American, a first lieutenant, proud of his superior knowledge of the situation, avid for some extra cigarettes and rare canned goods. They all gave him packages of cigarettes and candy bars. Cigarettes cost fifty-five cents a carton on the ship and sold ashore for nine dollars. The steward gave him a half-dozen cans of fruit. They all wanted to know about the women.

"Oh, you won't have any trouble finding women," said the Port Security officer. "Every woman in Palermo is a whore.

It's terrific." He laughed and slapped his thigh, and the men leaned closer attentively. "All the kids are pimps," the lieutenant continued. "It's the damnedest thing. Little kids that can hardly talk. Some maybe about five years old."

Chief Engineer Curtis roared with laughter. "Just what I was saying," he said. "A goddamn race of pimps, even the kids."

George Fiorini's big-nosed face was deeply flushed. "Jesus Christ," he said wonderingly, "even the kids!"

"And what are they like, the dames?"

"Well, it's the funniest damn thing you ever saw in your life," the army man said as he munched a chocolate bar. "The guineas call these kids pilots—they pronounce it *peelohts*—and sometimes one will lead you up one damned alley and down another, and finally you'll come to some bombed-out dump and there will be this kid's old grandmother or some damned ancestor or other and that's what you're supposed to lay! Isn't that a laugh?"

"So what d'you do?"

"Oh, I usually give them a few lire and beat it."

"Is that all they got—old women?"

"Hell, no! Sometimes it's the kid sister. Just a kid herself, nice and pretty."

The chief was again overcome with guffaws of laughter. "I bet you don't walk out in a case like that, eh, Lieutenant?"

"What d' *you* think?" the army man asked.

The purser came in then with the shore passes signed and told everybody that they would issue shore-leave money in Italian lire about an hour after docking. He had a large sheet of paper on which he noted how much each of the officers wanted.

Eric was on deck in time to witness the final activity of warping the ship in against the dock. From his position on the boat deck he could see the captain, megaphone in hand, strolling calmly from wing to wing of the flying bridge. Following him was the Italian harbor pilot, neatly dressed in a tight-fitting civilian suit. On the bow was the first mate and his group of seamen; on the stern, the second mate and his group. On the dock were several Italians who were supposed to handle the ropes that were thrown to them.

The scene was to Eric, the sociologist, a concentrated drama, not of race, but of contrasting national cultures. The Italians were running about like wild men. The pilot on the bridge would scream long imprecations first at one man on the dock and then at another. Then he would pull his hair, look heavenward, and call upon a long list of saints. The men on the dock in turn were dropping the ropes into the bay, fastening them on the wrong capstans, tangling and untangling them, calling on the Virgin Mary and the spirits of their departed mothers and fathers. While the pilot screamed at one of the dock workers the latter stood with his hands pressed together prayer-fashion, crying over and over again: *"Mamma mia! Mamma mia! Mamma mia! Santissimo Giuseppe!"*

From all this it appeared impossible that the ship could ever be docked, or, in fact, that any ship had ever been docked. Captain Brogan, however, paid no attention whatever to the pilot. He gave his own orders to the tug and his men at the stern and bow winches; waited patiently for the Italians on the dock to pick up the right rope and fasten it to the right stanchion. When this occurred, his men applied the proper tension with their winches. And eventually it was done and the ship was correctly secured.

"Santissimo diavolo!" said the pilot, wiping the sweat from his brow and shaking hands with the captain.

3

After lunch the army finance officer still had not arrived with the Italian lire for shore leave, so Eric returned to the deck. The ship was to be unloaded by American soldiers. They had been opening the hatches and getting the winches and cargo slings ready. But now they had all gone back onto the dock for lunch. Their food had arrived in a truck and they were lined up with their mess kits. The food and coffee were served to them steaming hot out of enormous thermos containers. Soon they were all seated on boxes with their aluminum dishes on their knees, or were standing with their dishes on some high tables that had been built for this purpose. They were all intent upon eating.

Then Eric noticed the Italians standing in the background. They were old men and young men and children, and most of them held some sort of container, usually a large tin can with the top cut off. They stood back with a peculiar and shadowy respectfulness, watching the Americans. And whenever a soldier had finished eating, one or more of the Italians would step quickly forward, holding out his container. Some were more enterprising than others, yet all seemed agonizingly polite and humble. Some got a whole canful of the slop to take home to their families. Others, less enterprising or weaker, got none. There were some with no cans who simply stood and looked out of their gaunt heads at the food on the steaming plates of the soldiers.

Chief Engineer Curtis had been standing for a moment at the rail near Eric, but now he turned away in disgust. "Those filthy bastards will eat *any*thing!" he said.

In the midafternoon, Eric, with the others, was issued his shore-leave pay: forty dollars in the form of four thousand lire of crisp "invasion money." This was paper printed by the Allied Expeditionary Forces, currency secured not by gold or the integrity of institutions, but by guns and force.

Soon after that he went ashore with all the other officers except the deck officer and engineer, who had to remain aboard. On the suggestion of the Port Security officer who had visited them in the morning, they were headed for the Allied Officers Club.

It was strange to be on shore at last in this other world of fallen masonry and ragged people. Eric lagged somewhat behind the others, wanting to be enough out of the group to see what was around him. He could not believe in the immediate reality of it. It was not so much like something he had dreamed as it was like something he had read in some half-forgotten book many years past. It was *foreign* in a sense that he had never experienced when he had traveled before the war.

A mob of children surrounded them—gaunt, avid, ragged, dirty, amoral little animals. It was hard to feel that they were human. Whenever one of the Americans became separated a few yards from the others, one of the little boys would rush up to him and say in a hoarse, loud, crowlike whisper, "Hey, Joe! You wan' piece ass? My seester! Verra nize girl! Seexteen!"

They tried to take hold of the arms of the Americans, and the men pushed them off, laughing and swearing. "Goddamn little wop brats!" "Piece ass! Can you beat that?" "Only kids! Listen to that!" "They sure pick up English fast!" "Probably sayin' the same thing in German a few months ago!" "Gwan! Beat it!"

There was one girl among the children. She was about nine, and very thin. She was dirty and dressed in a ragged dress and her bare legs were covered with scabs. She clung fiercely to Eric's arm. "Geev me, Joe, geev me!" she said. "You fahk me! Geev me now, Joe! Please, Joe!" Eric gave her a fifty lira note and shook her off his arm with a shudder of grief, grief that was redoubled by the fact that it was not without a faint echo of concupiscence. And he recognized guiltily that even in the awful presence of this deformation of childhood, there were within each of the conquerors certain secret and shameful death-whispers of obscene glee at the utter helplessness of the conquered.

He walked faster and rejoined the group of his friends. Soon they came to the Allied Officers Club. It was in an undamaged building guarded by two MP's. Most of the Americans were not in uniform, but they showed their shore passes which had been marked with their rank, and then they were admitted. It was cool inside. An Italian waiter came to their table and they ordered several bottles of *vino spumanti.*

The Italian champagne was raw but cold, and it was served in chilled metal goblets. It tasted good to them all; it tasted like reprieve and release and redemption. They sat around a large round table and everyone saw to it that the goblets near him were kept full. They poured it like beer, fast and bubbling, easy and good.

The first man to leave was George Fiorini. He had been nervous all the time, only sitting there and drinking the first round to be polite. "I'll be back in a little while," he said to Eric. "I speak this goddamn phony language, you know, and I want to go out and test it!"

Eric was feeling a great wealth of life in himself, excesses of awareness expanding outward. Now, he thought, I will learn about this war, about defeat and victory. I will learn about the enemy, and I will at the same time get very drunk.

PART THREE | DESTINATION

12: In the Cage of the Tiger

"Up one!" yelled Eric.

"Down three!" shouted Burley, waving his goblet and spilling *spumanti* over the table.

They were imitating the signals that the mates shouted down the speaking tube to the engine room when they wanted to change the number of the propeller's revolutions per minute in order to keep the ship in convoy position.

"Up yerass!" yelled Hartley.

Captain Brogan was swaying even though he was sitting down. He smashed his fist down hard on the table. "Hartley," he said to the third mate, "I hereby promote you to chief engineer!"

"Thank you, Cap'n, thank you."

"Don' mention it."

The chief, dressed in his full commander's uniform, was slouched forward with his face pressed into his folded arms. He was snoring loudly. Two MP's came from the entrance and spoke to the captain. "Shall we take him back to the ship, sir? We have a jeep outside."

The captain straightened up momentarily. "You can take'm and throw'm in the bay," he said.

"Yessir," the MP's said, without smiling.

Then they picked up the huge body of Chief Engineer Curtis and carried it out of the Palermo Allied Officers Club.

"Down one!" Eric said. "And set 'em up in the next alley." A queer and overflowing gaiety possessed him. He felt a new and wonderful comradery with all these men here at the round table.

Now that they were all completely drunk the central and

unifying drama had taken hold of them. They were the officers of the *SS William Benson* which had arrived at its destination through hell and high water, and now that fact alone was enough to give them all a deep affection for one another. There was no malice even in the business of the captain appointing the third mate as chief engineer. It was all in a spirit of honest fellowship. Even telling the MP's to drop Curtis in the bay derived not from anything he had done or failed to do during the voyage, but from the fact that he had impolitely passed out at the table.

Eric saw the champagne world of the Officers Club revolving slowly around him, and it was the center of the total world and more especially of the total war. They had done it. Here they were. They had brought the coal.

He had quite forgotten that nobody seemed to *want* the coal.

Everything was wonderfully simplified. The enemy was whatever it was that had tried to kill them, whatever it was that they had outwitted in getting here. It was delightfully clear. The enemy was what tried to kill you while you were trying to bring across the material with which to help kill *it*. Eric enjoyed the classic beauty of this simple situation. To risk death with good comrades is the one gesture that has always ennobled temporarily even the meanest of men. It seems to be a purpose in itself. Who can deny the propriety of challenging death in good company?

Yet even in his drunkenness a voice of reason quibbled and told him that this was all nonsense: that theirs was not the dullness and drudgery and gore and filth of war; theirs was an antiseptized and only slightly relevant aspect.

The architectural and human shambles of the island revolved like a slow carrousel outside the insulation of the Officers Club, and the alcoholic anesthesia of Eric's brain admitted only that which was least painful.

He started for the toilet, which was on the second floor of the building, and on the stairway he met George Fiorini. The steward appeared to be ludicrously depressed. They walked up the rough concrete stairs together.

"What's the matter, George?"

"Oh, nothing—except this is a hell of a place, that's all."

"What happened?"

They were on the second floor now and standing in front of the doorless toilet booth. "Well," George said, "I went with one of these kids. And he took me to some dump—like an apartment sort of, but with part of one wall knocked out—and there was his mother and father. The old lady talks to me in Italian and says everything is okay and she will do it for anything I want to give them, such as a pack of cigarettes or a bar of chocolate. And the old man gets up and nods his head at me and smiles a silly grin and goes out into the kitchen to leave me alone in this room where the bed is. The kid has gone away."

"So what did you do?"

"Well, the dame was no chicken, but she was still good-looking. So I asked her what her name was. And what you think she said?"

"Smith?"

"No. Don't be funny. She said their name was Fiorini! Can you beat that? Same as mine!"

"It's a common name here, I guess."

"But Jesus! For all I know they might be relatives of mine! Can you beat that?"

"So what did you do?"

"I gave the old lady a hundred lire and scrammed the hell out of there. I felt sick."

Eric politely gestured George forward for the first use of the toilet. "Thanks," the steward said. "You're a good guy, Eric. I don't like many of the other jerks on the ships, but I like you. Jesus Christ! what I would give to find a real decent cat house!"

When Eric turned away from the toilet a few minutes later he found George Fiorini violently busy at a near-by window. The steward had found an open lug-box of oranges. And one by one he was throwing them out the window into the busy piazza below. He was fiercely concentrated. He would crouch low, his head just high enough to see over the sill, and when he picked his target he would rise, quick as a mongoose, and throw the orange that he had gripped in his right hand, emitting a low, glad grunt. Then grabbing at the box he would throw another and another, and then duck again beneath the ledge of the window. "Goddamn!" he kept muttering. "Goddamn! I almost got him!"

"Who?" Eric asked.

George looked around, surprised but not disturbed, his face transfixed with the bright and purposeful singleness of a man under the influence of a fever's delirium or an ideological fanaticism. "The guy I was trying to hit!" he said. "Who d'you suppose? You think I'm throwing oranges at Jesus Christ or Christopher Columbus?"

"But who're you trying to hit?"

George was crouching again now, intent as a supple carnivore upon its prey. Suddenly he rose again and, almost quicker than the eye could follow, threw three hard, greenish oranges. Then he ducked again.

"My God!" said Eric. "That last one hit an officer in a jeep. They stopped the jeep. He and his driver are looking around. The driver has his pistol out of the holster. They're looking all around."

George began to giggle and sob and pat himself on the cheek with his open hand. "By Jesus," he said, "I hope it's a general! Tell me! For God's sake, tell me if it's a general!"

"I am not sticking my head up again in that window," Eric said, "but I think he had silver leaves."

"A goddamn lieutenant colonel. Well, that's okay. By Jesus, this is fun! I'm gonna do this all evening."

"The hell you are! You're going to come downstairs with me right away fast before you get yourself shot by a firing squad or something."

He had difficulty pulling George away from the window. "You throw a few," the Italian pleaded, and Eric perfunctorily tossed a few green oranges down into the square.

For all they knew the lieutenant colonel and his aide might now be in the building. Finally Eric persuaded George that it was not really wise to remain up here near this open window and box of green oranges. They walked down the newly rebuilt stairway arm in arm and returned to the round table where the others were drinking.

"Where's the captain?" Eric asked Vangaussen.

"Went the way of Curtis," the first mate said. "The MP's carried him out to their jeep. Who's next? *You*, Professor?"

"I would not be surprised," Eric said, for he was sane enough to know that he was poised on the edge of real drunkenness.

He and George sat down and their metal goblets were quickly filled with *vino spumanti*.

Eric drained his and he noticed that George was also drinking with great enthusiasm. He knew that George was not really a drinking man; there was something about his drinking that reminded Eric of the way a fourteen-year-old boy smokes his first cigarette. George likes the idea of everybody getting together this way, Eric thought, but he doesn't exactly know why they do it. He feels all right without drinking and, besides, he thinks that we men should be going after girls first and not drinking this stuff that is only likely to impair one's erotic efficiency. Yet now, for perhaps the first time in his life, he really wants to get drunk—because George is sick and scared.

George was sick all right, and the most thirsty man at the table. He ordered three more bottles and threw down the money to pay for them as though it were something he wanted to get rid of.

It's time to really drink some *vino spumanti*, Eric thought. Time to drink a million gallons of this stuff because *in vino veritas* and I am just now beginning to understand everything about what war is and what is happening and how this wounded and snafu world of sick conflicts must give way to something else, to cleaner and more exciting and more human conflicts. My God! Our little time. Our single luminous hour between dark, frightened birth and dark, homeless death—and how we waste it. It's sure as hell we can do something better in that time than the things we do. He stood up to give a speech beginning: *"In vino veritas . . ."* He added that what they did here would not be long remembered, but that what they said here would be— might be—long remembered . . .

He was standing in front of the tiger cage in the dream-lit zoo and telling the people to look at the tiger and to learn a lesson from it. *Watch it move,* he told them, *watch the silence of its strength, the economy and reserve of its motion, the beauty of its contained pride. Now, my friends, if we were as good at being human as this tiger is at being tiger . . .*

Our strength is consciousness, my friends, and irrational
138

magnanimity . . . and more consciousness . . . ever ex-
panding . . . for no matter at what point it stops it is no
longer a human virtue if it is not expanding . . .

A fat man in the crowd laughed derisively. *Look out or
the tiger will eat you,* he said. *You may be more human than
us, but he is more tiger than you. His belly is ever expanding.*

The crowd laughed and Eric knew that he must climb into
the cage and show them that he was not afraid of the tiger.
He unlatched the door of the cage and entered the animal-
and-sawdust-smelling confinement and walked forward toward the beast. It grew darker and he could not see anything
but his own extended hands. He sat down on the rough
wooden floor.

It was in his lap then, crawling and mewing, and it was
not a tiger but a little gray kitten. He could feel the thorns of
its tiny claws plucking at the threads of his clothing. It was
blind and sick. Eric felt revolted and helpless as it began
clawing its way, feebly but irresistibly, into his shirt. He
wanted to push it away but he could not think how to do this
without hurting its feelings. He knew that he could never
push it away no matter how its diseased claws dug into the
skin of his chest. The crowd outside the cage was laughing
now, and the fat man's derisive guffaw was dominant, like
the piano in a piano concerto. He had failed to show them
what he meant, but now there was no way he could defend
himself against the sick kitten. He was ashamed and helpless
in front of all the people who stood outside and looked at
him until the dream cage began to dim and he felt real light
against his closed lids and heard sounds that originated outside his own brain. Then he did not want to see the light nor
hear the sounds. He tried and tried to creep back into the
cage of dreamlit humiliation. It was simpler than this other,
the reddening upon his eyelids and the foreign sounds which
were not of his own consciousness at all. Footsteps on metal,
doors opening and closing, and a rhythm of *tah*-tuh, *tah*-
tuh, *tah*-tuh . . .

He felt the sheets around him, and his head aching, and a
fluid like the distilled essence of guilt flowing sluggishly
through his aching blood vessels. When he reluctantly

opened his eyes he saw Chuck, his cabin mate, sitting at the desk writing something on a square of white paper.

Chuck looked up and grinned when he saw that Eric was awake. "How you feel?" he asked.

"Like hell," Eric said. "I think I'm dying. What happened?"

"Just a little drinking. You'll live, all right. Want me to get you something to eat?"

Eat? The idea caused Eric's stomach to contract and started a reverse peristalsis in his throat. "Eat!" he said. "My God! I never want to eat again!"

"You better. I'll get you some soup."

"Thanks, Chuck. But *please* don't get me anything."

He dropped his head back upon the pillow and tried to relax the tortured complexities of his body; every part seemed to be acting independently to tear him asunder. His arms ached with their own specialized arm-torture, his legs with their leg-torture, every part in its own way. And all the king's men could not have put Eric together again. "Listen, Chuck," he said, "I don't remember getting back here at all."

"They carried you on board. Some MP's brought you in a jeep."

Eric had closed his eyes again and all at once he felt that he was pressing first on one side of his bunk and then on the other. And he heard the *tah*-tuh, *tah*-tuh that should not have been there.

He sat up and his dry brain seemed to rattle within its heated skull. "My God!" he said. "We're under way! What time is it? I'm supposed to be on watch!"

He started to climb out of his bunk and only then discovered that he was completely naked. Chuck reached out and gently pushed him back. "Peters is taking your watch," he said. "They decided they didn't want our coal after all, and now we're on our way to Naples. And by the way, we got an Italian corvette escorting us. Ain't that a laugh? A few weeks ago they were our enemy. Now they're supposed to guard us. What you suppose they'll do if some German planes come over? It sure is funny. Everybody on the ship is laughing."

A renewed agony of headache and nausea and anarchic body parts came over Eric, and he said that it was funny all right but he could not really at this moment believe what he was saying. "Oh, Lord!" he muttered to himself. "I wish I could remember what happened."

13: Caves of Defeat

For three days they lay at anchor inside the great crescent of the Bay of Naples. The days were hot, and the nearly naked men lay about on the hatch-cover tarpaulins and on army cots on the deck and burned their skins to shades of red and brown. The nights were cool and moonlit and brought with them a desire for women that was a different thing in every man, but intense and maddening in them all.

The plume of smoke from Vesuvius seemed carved of yellow marble, so little did it move, and the silhouette of Capri looked iceberg blue even in the heat of noon. And when night erased all this there were only a few scattered lights along the shore untill the moon came up and gave them a quicksilver sea and a ghostly volcano and vague outlines of the city and the little towns to the south. Then Eric would sit on the captain's deck and listen to the music that one of the navy boys made on his mouth organ. And some of the others would be singing in gruff, embarrassed, atonal voices. "If I Had You." "Night and Day." "I Can't Give You Anything But Love, Baby." "Good Night, Sweetheart." Sad songs of longing and adoration; trite, perhaps, but also true. Heightened by the moonlight, the danger, the isolation from women, the feeling of being forgotten, such songs seemed closer than anything else to the secret center of the heart.

Eric felt the pure worship of the dream of woman and lewd craving for the body of woman no less than the most adolescent member of the crew. Only in him the dream and the need did not seem so opposed and conflicting, even in the daytime. In most of the boys it took the moonlight to make the two seem the same, or even in any way related. Eric thought about the traditional connection between the moon and lunacy and wondered if the reverse were not true; he could not but see how everyone was saner, less

141

broken up by the idiocies of history and the inertias of culture during the evenings than they were in the commonplace light of day.

The moonlight was so bright that they could see the other ships at anchor and the superstructures of many that had been sunk near the shore. *Vedi Napoli e poi muori,* Eric thought, has taken on a new meaning for many Americans who were not intentionally tourists.

On the fourth day they had received orders to proceed to Castellammare di Stabia on the south side of the bay. From the ship the little town seemed picturesque and artificial as a motion-picture set. Before four o'clock in the afternoon the sun went behind the mountains that rose steeply out of the bay, and the green cliff where the castle stood was deep in shadow; and beneath this the outlines of the town itself, with its buildings of tan and white and yellow plaster, were softened in the unreal chiaroscuro.

They had docked before noon, and then the cigarette trouble began. No shore passes were necessary here. There was no sign of British or American MP's anywhere. The docks were guarded by Italian *carabinieri.* And even before they were secured to the pier there were numbers of Italians yelling and gesturing to the men on the ship that they would pay eleven dollars a carton for cigarettes.

Almost everyone was enthusiastic about making a profit of ten dollars and forty-five cents on each carton of cigarettes. But the Armed Guard Commander suddenly discovered in himself a streak of single-minded aggressiveness. He posted a notice to the effect that he would countenance no black market dealings and that he would station a navy guard with orders to shoot if necessary. Captain Brogan had the lieutenant summoned to his stateroom and Eric overheard their talk.

"You may post guards anywhere you like," he heard the captain say, "so long as they don't *do* anything. I am in command of this ship and when anything is *done* about anything—*I* order it."

"Well," the lieutenant said in his fussy maiden-aunt's voice, "I have every intention of reporting anybody who tries to sell cigarettes!"

"Now *that,*" the captain said, "is strictly your business.

You can report anything you damned please. Reporting, in fact, is anybody's business; but when things are *done* on this ship, *I* order them. Do I make myself clear?"

"You do; and the Navy will receive a full report of our conversation."

"Good."

Eric himself came to no ethical conclusion on the subject. Certainly he would not have had anything to do with selling food or clothing to starving and ragged people at exorbitant prices. But nobody was starving for cigarettes. They were simply trying to exchange their worthless Allied "invasion money" for a commodity with an exchange value in an economy that had been suddenly reduced to barter. Was it wrong to give them something that could be exchanged for food in return for printed pieces of paper that were almost worthless? The invasion money could be reconverted into dollars by the Americans, but not by the Italians; they were not allowed to possess foreign currency. As far as Eric could see, in the strict realism of the immediate situation, it was neither a good nor a bad thing for the Americans to exchange their cigarettes for the war-counterfeited lire.

Then Duprey had a bright idea. He got the other officers together and suggested that each of them carry with them several cartons of cigarettes. And thereafter there were cartons thrust into pants pockets and protruding from jackets all over the ship. Eric was amused, but the joke was a little too close to childish sadism for his taste, and so he could not quite bring himself to join in it. At lunch almost all the officers went through elaborate performances of slowly removing all the cartons from their clothing and stacking them on the table so that they could comfortably sit down. The lieutenant sat in pallid silence and finished his meal in record time. Really it was a funny enough joke, except that the lieutenant was too much alone.

2

Eric had not looked forward to being well liked on the ship. He came from such an alien world that he did not expect to be freely accepted. But in this he was wrong. The men competed for his friendship. They seemed to sense some lack of general animosity in him as an attractive mystery.

On the afternoon when they docked at Castellammare it was the word-loving Hartley who made it first to Eric's cabin. "Well, Professor," the third mate said, "what say we go ashore and get stewed, screwed, and tattooed?"

"Okay," Eric agreed. "Are you ready?"

"Soon as I shave, shower, and shampoo, Professor! But in the meantime come down to my bailiwick and have a snort of prewar firewater."

From here on there began for Eric the strangest and most out-of-control period of his life. All his plans to observe and think and figure things out came to nothing. Or very little. His brain was anesthetized. His spirit was, unforeseeably and all at once, clad in a crazing and foreign and immoral shroud of irresponsibility.

Scores of wineshops and kids leading them into private apartments and whorehouses and the officers' clubs in Naples and the city of Pompeii immobilized in sudden volcanic death and a panting drunken climb to look into the infernal crater of Vesuvius—all shaken together in his brain and sifted through his numbed nerves.

To Hartley the places they visited were "caves," and it was an apt word. They were all intermingled in Eric's mind like a wild montage, parts of one entering the other. But he could remember the cavelike place that was a low-ceilinged windowless cellar with a dirt floor, damp and stinking, with only the light from a wick burning in a single cup of olive oil. There was only one large, dirty bed, and some wooden boxes to sit on against the wall. There were three ugly and aged women. They had front teeth missing and they smelled of cheap pomade, excrescences of unwashed sex, and the breath heavy with garlic and indigestion. The men were mostly Canadian soldiers on leave from the front, and they sat around on the boxes drinking Marsala out of sticky tin cups and watching the one who was on the bed with one of the women. The soldier on the bed had not taken off any part of his uniform, and he was sweating and straining. The drunken spectators, however, were not amused by his plight. There was no obscene banter. The scene was not pornographic. They merely watched in a dull, glazed way that which they knew to be their own sick destiny.

Then there was the occasion when the little boy told a

144

bunch of the men about the girl who did something more specialized. "Come on, Joe! You like!" They found her in a damp, eerie cave off a courtyard. She was pleasant, quiet, tubercular. She lived in this hole with her old crone of a grandmother and her scar-faced *"fratello,"* who was really not her brother at all, but her lover. The three of them were very polite, and when an American soldier or sailor came, the man and the old woman would go out into the courtyard and leave Lydia to do her work with him and earn the money or cigarettes or candy on which they lived. All this was recorded in some semiconscious way within the mind of Eric. The hopeless, malicious senility of the old woman and the poker-faced pain and surrender of maleness in the *fratello*. He had fought with Rommel in North Africa, he said, and he often amused the Americans by telling them, "We *italiani*, see? Rommel try put us up-uh front! We just-uh like run back! We like-uh run *presto*. No run through *tedeschi*, no run through *inglesi*. We shoot *tedeschi*, *tedeschi* shoot me. We *italiani* good-uh for run, run, run!" And all the time the pain on his face as plain as the scarred, pock-marked features. "We just-uh run back, see?" And the pain beneath the foolish grin was a burning thing, like a branding iron; and he had nothing to brand with this cruel configuration which was all that life had left him of his manhood.

That cave, that particular cave, diminishing, and the sound of some drunken soldiers singing "Lydia the Tattooed Lady."

And that high-class bar on the north side of the town where the back room was reserved for Americans, Britons, and the most respectable class of Castellammare citizens, that is to say, the former Fascists. The proprietor was proud of his zombies, which were always wonderfully different. He shook them in a cocktail shaker and poured them into large stemmed glasses, and they were composed of everything he had in the place selected by a process of intuitive motivation that never produced the same result twice. They were yellow, red, green, purple, brown. Sometimes the edge of the glass was dipped in powdered sugar. Sometimes they were very cold, sometimes lukewarm. But they were always strong. After five of them one day they rented a *carrozza* and started to go to Torre Annunziata. Hartley insisted on driving, and they had to get the driver drunk to convince him that it was right and proper. So at the piazza where the carriage men gathered to wait for customers, they took the driver into a bar and fed him about fifteen *espressi al cognac*. Then they put him in the back seat of his carriage and he began to sing "Santa Lucia" in a rather good tenor voice. Halfway down the highway to the next town they hit a large rock while turning a corner, and the carriage turned over. Nobody was hurt, but the tired horse lying on his side on the rough road looked very disgusted, and the driver was bewildered. A weapons carrier with three American air-force mechanics came along and they fixed the harness with some heavy copper wire, and Eric and Hartley went on with the soldiers, leaving the *carrozza* driver still bewildered and no longer singing "Santa Lucia."

In all the more interesting streets there were large signs saying "Out of Bounds" and others that said "V.D." It was a brown world of narrow stone-paved alleys, steep and twisting and puddled. There was very little wood in this; it was all brick-colored and dirt-dyed plaster. And the blended smell of garbage and dampness and stale food and carelessly distributed human excrement and the acridity of charcoal smoke. Lightless damp and stenching courtyards and worn stone steps that led up from them to heavy doors, scarred and worn by human conflict, neglect, and confusion. And ruins—ruins and fallen masonry—great gaps in the geometry of tradition and the established patterns of old streets and buildings.

Of course, in Naples, inside the Officers Club, it was all very different from that nether world of dark caves and stinking courtyards and ragged children who have become pimps in their first years of consciousness and men who stand holding empty cans in respectful awe of those who happen to control the slop of survival.

Inside the Allied Officers Club of Naples there was good liquor and a secure feeling of belonging to the most important part of a phenomenal adventure. Someone at the table was describing an Italian traffic policeman. "He'd stand there in his baggy uniform, nervous as hell, trying to guess what the drivers were gonna do, and then at the last second he'd signal them to go ahead and do what they were gonna do anyway. He knew damn well if he guessed wrong some hard-boiled sergeant might get out and bawl the living Jesus out of him. It was funny as hell!"

"Like an orchestra conductor trying to keep time to the music instead of vice versa."

"Yeah—only a damn sight funnier."

The only Italians in the Officers Club were the members of the six-piece orchestra, the waiters, and the girl who sang. The orchestra played a diluted version of American dance music with an occasional surprising flourish of swing, like the galvanic twitch of a man who is half dead. The girl was small and pretty, but her dark face was usually expressionless. For the most part she sang things like "O Sole Mio" and "Santa Lucia" and "Take Me Back to Sorrento." But the number most often requested by the men in the club was the German song, "Lili Marlene." The cornetist would play a muted taps to start it, and then the orchestra would begin in soft, funereal march style to play the melody, and the girl's low, nostalgic voice would sing the words. Then the men in the large room would grow quiet as they did not do at any other time, and the drunkest and the soberest would have difficulty keeping the tears out of his eyes. This had been a German officers' club only a few months past. Eric studied the singer closely and was certain that he saw a lambent glow of irony pass briefly across the controlled passivity of her face. No doubt she had sung the same song in German, and with the same effect.

3

One night three of them were drinking vermouth in a bar on the Via Bernotti. It was the biggest bar in Castellammare. The wine glasses were made of beer bottles cut off about four inches high, with sharp, jagged edges. The counter was zinc and about forty feet long. Hartley had lost some of his eloquence from prolonged drinking, but Duprey was fresh as a daisy because he had had to spend most of his time on the ship working on the engine. Eric felt drugged, not a participant, held apart in an edgeless dream. They had watched the performance of the chief engineer at the far end of the bar, but now Curtis had gone and been replaced by *Der Auspuff Kessel*.

The chief had been dressed in his full commander's uniform, scrambled eggs on the bill of his cap, and all the trimmings. And he had had with him several navy seamen that he had picked up somewhere. The sailors were not quite sure which were naval officer's insignia and which were merchant marine; in fact, they were not quite sure what the separation was between the two services. Consequently they wavered between awe at this democratic commander, boredom with his polemics, and contempt for his undisciplined behavior. Commander Curtis had slapped the smallest and drunkest of his charges on the back and said, "Well, my boy, drink up! And don't feel backward. Just remember that I started out as a common sailor myself. Worked up from the very lowest rung of the ladder. And you can do the same. I just wanna give you boys one little piece of advice to remember and that is this: Always honor the uniform you wear!"

"Yeah—like you," the small sailor said, laughing.

Commander Curtis was hurt, and the other two sailors looked shocked and whispered to their friend. The one who had laughed gulped the rest of his vermouth and shook his head as though to clear it. Then he faced the commander, who was now peering sadly into his wine. "Sir," he said, "I'm sorry if I spoke out of turn. I guess I'm feeling my drinks too much."

Curtis did not hesitate to forgive him. He turned immediately and extended his hand. "My boy," he said, "we all make mistakes. I've made dozens of them. It's only human. Just forget it."

"Thank you, sir," the sailor said.

"And by the way," added the chief, "do you have a shotgun?"

"No sir," the sailor said, looking frightened.

"Well, never mind," said Curtis, fingering the brass buttons of his skintight gray gabardine uniform coat, "you can use mine. I want to invite you to come to my farm after the war is over, and go duck hunting. Finest sport in the world. Don't worry at all about not bringing your own gun."

The trio at the other end of the bar—Hartley, Duprey, and Eric—had listened to all this at first with derision, then with grudging admiration. The chief and his naval friends had staggered out with their arms about each other's shoulders. And then *Der Auspuff Kessel* had come in, his enormous body swaying above the painful movements of his stubby legs. He was dressed in full blue uniform, with the ribbons of all three combat areas. He brought with him an Italian of about fifty years and two Italian adolescents. The three Italians treated him with a cringing respect which he sucked into his enormous and gaseous bulk with a kind of organic greed. He was treating them to what was called cognac—*originale.* It seemed that the three understood his English. "What ever made you bastards believe in Mussolini?" he was saying. "What ever made you think you could lick America?" he asked them, extending his question to the rest of the bar with the wave of a heavy hand. "Goddamn, that was a funny one! Don't you know America ain't never been licked in *any* war!—let alone a war with *you* kind of people!"

"Mussolini multa merda!" one of the boys said, holding up his glass of brandy.

And then the older man and the other boy both shouted, *"Sì, sì, multa merda, merda merda . . ."*

Eric in his drugged dream said to himself that he did not give a damn any more. It was all useless, and it was only good to be drunk and insane, and he did not give a damn what the fat man made them say for or against Mussolini.

"One thing I do know, gentlemen," said Duprey, "and that is that I do intend to blow my tubes tonight—if you will pardon an old engine room expression."

"Fine, fine," said Hartley, who was straining to recover the significance of his eloquence. "And thou shalt then awaken one day soon with a carnation on thy cucumber!" He waited for his laugh before concluding, "And then thou shalt be satisfied!"

Arm in arm the three of them left the bar and started to walk. The evening breezes swept fitfully out of the passageways and cooled their liquor-heated faces. "Goddamn my soul," said Hartley, "every one of these damned alleys has a different kind of halitosis!"

Walking abreast, Duprey was on the inside, Eric in the center, and Hartley in the gutter. "You notice how there aren't any dogs or cats?" Duprey asked. "Fido and Tabby long since gone into the old spaghetti sauce."

149

"I notice there aren't any pigeons either."

"I haven't even seen a rat."

"Personally, I bet the goddamn cockroaches ain't too safe."

They came to an area of faint yellow light. Two little girls approached them. The smallest one, about six years old, clung to the other and hid her head. The older one said in a small bold voice, "Hey, Joe! You want *vino?*"

The men stopped and looked at the kids.

"Good *vino,*" she said. "Cognac, vermouth."

"What the hell," said Duprey. "Let's just see where they take us."

They followed the children down a narrow alley. It was so dark that they could only see the shapes of two ghostly little light-colored dresses ahead of them. Every once in a while the girls had to stop and whisper to each other and wait for the men to catch up. They turned a lot of corners, went up and down hills and through narrow passages choked and slippery with refuse.

"Let's go back," said Hartley. "They're takin' us to hell and gone."

"How much further?" Duprey asked the vague shape of the larger girl.

"Here, Joe," she whispered anxiously. "Close—close."

Finally they entered a courtyard and went up three flights of stone stairs and knocked on a door. It was opened by a thin Italian with a scraggly gray mustache. They entered the apartment. The two little girls looked up at them triumphantly—"See, Joe? Nice-uh place!"—and then they began to giggle and scurried off into another room. The man led the way to a large round table.

Eric and his friends took off their caps and sat down. "*Vino,* vermouth, cognac?" They all asked for cognac. There were three women in the room. The oldest was about fifty. She sat in a corner mending a ragged shirt and rocking back and forth slightly on her straight chair as though she were listening to slow music outside the range of the others' hearing.

The youngest was about twenty, small and dark and compact. She had eyes that had once been demanding. She had eyes that had once been Salome's eyes sweetly asking for the bloody head of the austere prisoner served up on a bright, cold silver platter of vanity.

The other woman was about thirty years old and she was feeding her tiny pink baby at her breast. She was larger than the younger one, fragile-boned and gaunt, with large eyes that had always been sad. She might have been a camp follower in Roman times. She could have been a camp follower at any time. But she had lost her camp. She was born to the tragedy of womanhood, and there was a dark cavern of total acceptance behind her eyes. But there was also more pride in her than had ever existed in her younger sister. For she had never been ashamed. She had always felt born to the tragic fate of woman, and if she had ever had any vanity at all it had been only in her ability to endure.

The Americans told the Italians all to drink up, so the Italians bowed and smiled and they all took drinks. They all raised their glasses to each other and drank. And the Italians were frightened and cringing in their guts because they had no real protection against anything these three healthy-looking Americans might choose to do to them. The Italian police had no authority whatever. The survival of these people was suspended from the invisible thread of general human decency, and they were among the many millions of the earth who at this time were fully aware that the tensile strength of that thread is very slight. These three men in reality could do anything they wanted to do: loot, rape, murder, set fire to the place, refuse to pay; it all hung on that untrustworthy thread.

The four Italians were straining their facial muscles continually to make very polite looks that tried to say: "Here we are all human beings and understanding each other and getting along just fine! Drinking *vino*—cognac! And by the way, I have a cousin who lives in Brooklyn!"

The Americans talked among themselves and the Italians watched them anxiously, trying to catch a familiar word or interpret the meaning of a glance. And each time an American looked at one of them, that one would turn on a quick, nodding, apologetic smile, as though a controlling rubber band had been snapped taut inside the head.

"My God! but this is a scurvy race of people!"

"Yeah, but they're a people that's just been beaten."

"But suppose this was America? This wouldn't happen in America!"

"Maybe."

"You think if the wops had occupied *us* that every American would start peddling his daughter's ass?"

"Maybe."

"Hell no, brother! We'd be out in the woods with our squirrel guns sniping at the bastards."

"Okay, drink up and stop waving the flag!"

The smaller of the two little girls had crept back into the room and was standing, holding onto the skirt of the old woman with one hand while she sucked meditatively on the fingers of the other and stared at the Americans with wide, bemused eyes, dark mirrors of shy contemplation. She and the baby were the only members of the family who did not turn on the rubber-band grin when they were looked at. Hartley was looking at her now, and she stared back at him gravely.

Suddenly he raised his right hand palm outward and shouted, "Heil Hitler!" The little girl took her fingers out of her mouth and raised her hand above her head. Her face beamed with the joy of recognition, and she said in the self-conscious treble of a child reciting a familiar nursery rhyme, *"Viva il Duce!"*

The Italian leaped across the room and grabbed the child. *"Mamma mia!"* he exclaimed as he carried her struggling out of the place. The old woman quickly gave her rubber grin to the room and continued rocking to the secret music of her memories. Hartley roared with laughter. "Come on, bring the kid back!" he yelled. "Let her *viva* the *Duce* all she wants. She's the only guinea here that ain't a fuggin', hypocrite! Bring her back!" He got up and started to follow the Italian who was carrying the squirming child into a back room.

Duprey pulled him back into his chair. "Leave the kid alone," he said. "What's the use of making her do that? They'll only beat her after we go!"

Eric felt vaguely that the important part of his own entity was drugged and paralyzed. Something had given way in him after the voyage; he had entered into a vast and immoral and shameful cave of sick surrender, and he was neither spectator nor participant—he was a half-being without identity or purpose or desire.

I should have said what Duprey said, he thought weakly, as though trying to remember a time when he had had a moral function.

Hartley sat down convulsed with laughter that made tears run down his face. *"Viva* the *Duce! Viva* the *Duce!"* he kept shouting. "Bring the kid back!"

The younger girl seemed frightened, but her elder sister, the one with the baby, looked as though she were witnessing something that was very, very old.

They finally stopped Hartley's shouting with more of the bad cognac, and he lapsed into drunken quiescence.

The father came back into the room apologizing, grinning, and gesturing. The general idea of what he was trying to say was that he could not figure out where the *bambina* had picked up this fantastic phrase and salute, inasmuch as the whole family had always been anti-Fascist, and in fact he himself had worked with the underground. *"Mussolini multa merda!"* he shouted, trying to make it as loud as Hartley. And his face was vacant of all meaning except that of a clown's despair.

Eric wanted to go away. He turned to Duprey. "Why don't you go to bed with her?" he said, indicating the girl who had once had the eyes of Salome.

But Duprey was involved in some inner colloquy. He waved his hand in an impatient gesture. "In due time, Mr. Clark," he said. "In due time."

Duprey is a true mechanic, a craftsman, Eric thought. A man who gives mature consideration to the work to be done, selects his material, and approaches each job as a conscientious workman should.

They all had another round of drinks. The Italian was accumulating more aplomb. He had been studying Duprey and he pointed at his youngest daughter, she who now had slave's eyes. "You go," he said. "She good piece. You like heem. Good, good!"

But then Eric noticed that Duprey seemed unable to keep his eyes off the naked breast of the older daughter who was nursing her baby. It was not a beautiful breast. It had once been full and proud, but now it was hanging and soft and pallid and without assertiveness. The baby's eyes were closed, and it appeared obscenely helpless, as do all living things that have not yet learned deception.

She had been aware of Duprey's eyes upon her for some time. She felt neither embarrassment nor welcome; if she had hoped for anything it was merely that he would turn his attention to her younger sister. But this could not have been an important hope, because she was ten thousand years old and it had not really mattered after the first thousand years.

Duprey could not take his eyes off the poverty of that breast at which the helpless human thing sucked needfully.

She pulled the baby's mouth away from her nipple and held it up toward the table. *"Americano!"* she said. *"Questo bambino americano! Bene, bene, americano."*

Hartley was evil and slobbering now and he wanted to be mean to these people. "No *americano*," he said. *"Tedesco!* Heine! *Tedesco!"*

Duprey turned on him fiercely. "Shut up, you goddamn fool!" he said. "Leave her alone. It's none of your goddamn business who made the kid. Go back to your stinking cognac and leave her and her kid alone!"

Hartley stood up and made an oratorical gesture. "Well I'll be buggered and bewildered!" he said.

"Shut up!" Duprey said harshly. "These people understand that kind of stuff. You sit down and drink your cognac!"

"You go to hell," said Hartley as he sat down and drank his cognac.

Duprey turned to Eric. "Listen, Professor," he said, "you speak this lousy language. Tell the old man that I don't want his younger daughter. I want the other one."

"I only know a few words," Eric said.

"Well, say them. Tell the old man."

Eric called the Italian over to the table, but it would not have mattered if he had not known any Italian, because the father understood from his vague gesture of the right hand toward the girl with the baby. He nodded his head gently. *"Sì—eef ufficiale desidera,"* he said sadly, and then he spoke a few words to his daughter.

The girl stood up slowly, as though her legs were cramped, as though something were happening to her that she had always expected and yet it had never quite happened this way before. But her eyes showed only the emptiness of life-long acceptance. She took her cloth-wrapped baby and placed it in the center of the wooden drinking table. The grandmother had put down her sewing and extended her arms, but the daughter disregarded those arms and placed the baby on the wet table between the men.

Duprey and the older daughter walked off into another room, and the ones left in the front room exchanged embarrassed and cajoling glances. "I'll take on the old man!" said Hartley, laughing his way out of his stupor.

The baby on the table began to cry and vomit. Eric looked at it out of the fog of his anesthesia. It was a helpless, pink, puckered miniature of every human being who has ever lived upon the earth. There is no one who could not have been born into this, no one anywhere who might not have been placed upon this wet wooden table in just this way at just such an hour, Eric thought.

He was standing up now, looking down at the living thing on the table. He wanted to pick it up, but he was afraid. It was wrapped in a white square of ragged cloth. All at once it stopped crying and vomiting its milk and waving its arms. It became quiet. It opened its eyes wide. They were blue, a wonderfully clean shade of cobalt blue. It stared directly into Eric's eyes. There was an instant in which this small, newly born entity and Eric Clark gazed directly into each other's eyes, an instant in which they were simply two human beings caught in the same tragic circumstance of birth.

Something within the drunken and dulled nervous system of the grown man suddenly gave way, burst like a swollen tumor of pain within him. "Good God!" he said aloud.

He turned to Hartley. "I've got to get out of here," he said. "I'm going now."

Hartley was nodding dumbly to himself. "Why'n you take the other one, the keed seester?" he asked.

The Italian man came forward, frightened and rubbing his hands together. "Whatsamatta?" he wanted to know. "Ees wrong, *signore?* You-uh mahd on oss?"

"No, no," Eric said. "Everything's fine. You're a fine man."

He dropped a thousand-lira note on the table and staggered out, blind with pain and illness.

Outside he saw nothing of the dark streets of Castellammare until he had arrived at the small park that covered a short spit of land extending out into the bay. He walked under the trees down to a place near the water and lay down on the grass near a hedge of oleander. For a long time he lay there, face down and vomiting. He disgorged what there was of liquor in his stomach and then he began retching over nothing. That went on for a long time, and he thought it would never stop, but finally it did and he remained there with his head on his arms.

He turned over on his back and he could see the pale pink blossoms on the hedge above him. There was a high mist, and a moon somewhere above it was making a soft, diffuse light on the cool plants and the old earth. He could smell the grass and the soil and the bushes. There were some birds flying back and forth over him, swooping and darting through the darkness. They looked like bats.

My God, what has gone wrong with me? he wondered. Was I so scared by what happened to us on the ship that it destroyed everything human in me? What in God's name have I been doing?

The birds swooped and darted about among the oleander bushes and against the luminously gray sky above him, closer and closer. More and more he thought that they were bats. Or birds acting like bats.

He tried to remember what a bird was like, how its motions differed from the evil and blindly intrusive flights of bats. He was sick again. He turned over on his belly and began again to vomit nothing. He could smell the green smell of the grass and the black smell of the wet earth close against his face, and his whole body strained in anguish to expel something that was too elusive for the aching peristalsis of his viscera to take hold upon.

14: The Ends of the Earth

Then there were three nightmare days and three haunted nights through which Eric fought to clear his depleted body of poisons and to save his wavering mind from that autonomous symbolism of pain which is one of the thresholds of madness. He had somehow returned to the ship and crawled into his bunk. He had refused drinks from Hartley and Duprey and others who had come to see him. Even the captain had come in with a treasured bottle of real Kentucky bourbon, and Eric had turned it down. He wanted it. He was almost dying for the immediate solace of a drink, but some strong factor of self-preservation told him that if he tried to live any longer within the tumescent insulation of a drugged brain he would go to pieces altogether in a very short time.

It became an important part of the ship's legend that "the Professor" was suffering from a super-hangover. But it was not like any hangover that Eric had ever had before, and he knew that the amount of alcohol he had consumed was not its most important cause. There were many hours when he could not think at all. He simply clenched his jaws, gripped his fingers into fists, and kept from groaning. But when he *could* think, he thought that alcohol was the least of the villains in the old melodrama of consciousness, for there are more than a thousand other ways of avoidance, and all of them are more successful than liquor. There are always the medicine men with their innumerable dogmas of religion and prejudice, national and familial totems, and all those other communal sanctuaries or prisons of the primitive mind within and around us.

Harold and Shruck attentively brought soup and coffee to Eric at frequent intervals. On the fourth day his hands had stopped shaking, and on the fifth he awoke calm and at peace with his own body. He dressed and shaved carefully. He put on his gray tropical uniform, then changed his mind and got out his civilian suit of worn brown tweed. While he was re-dressing, he was interrupted by Hartley.

"Ah-ha, Professor! I see you're ready to return to the fleshpots!"

"Not exactly."

"I'm on my way too. Let's have a little glass of *originale* together at the zombie shop."

Eric wanted above all else to go back into Castellammare alone. "No," he said, "I want to go alone today."

"I understand completely." said Hartley, leaning a bit forward in the doorway and winking his right eye. "But let's have a short one before you go there."

"Where?"

Hartley stepped into the stateroom and slapped Eric on the back. "I know, I know, pal!" he said. "You got some private stuff lined up. Okay, so keep it a secret—but let's have a friendly drink first. Might put a little extra lead in your pencil!"

Eric slapped Hartley on the shoulder. "Right," he said, leering back at him. "But you see, my friend, this special stuff is going to meet me near where I come off the dock. So no time for drinks. See?"

They winked at each other again. Men pay a high price for comradery, Eric thought; I wonder if it's worth it?

He walked up the dock rapidly in order to minimize the amount of coal dust that was bound to filter into his suit. They were unloading the coal in canvas slings and it was a slow and inefficient process. During these past days he had listened painfully to the relentless repetition of taut steel cable against the steel spindles of the winches, followed by the looser chainlike rattle as the empty slings descended into the holds. Over and over again. It would take several more days to unload the ship.

As Eric walked along the quays toward the center of Castellammare di Stabia, he felt an increasing glow of inner excitement. He was seeing the place itself for the first time. A new city is like a new sweetheart, he thought. It is unthinkable that one should explore her mysteries in the company of others.

Even in his earliest years this had been true with him. He recalled, for example, how he had first visited New Orleans with his family when he was seventeen, and how restlessly he had waited for the moment when he could escape from them to wander at will—or almost without will—through alleys and lives of the Vieux Carré. With others, even the most *en rapport,* there is always a gross compromise of response. To explore a new city one must be infinitely sensitive to the winds of chance and absolutely feather-free to drift on them as one pleases, directed only by the subtlest fibers of the will.

In regaining the right to see alone, Eric felt that he had regained his own identity. There was also another sharp and wonderful pleasure: the use of his mind as a controllable implement. Before this, in all his time here in Italy, he had dulled its edge with drunkenness and restrained its movements within the circumscribed limits of a group compromise. He had forgotten for a short time the wonderful excitement of personal consciousness—consciousness that reaches back through the past before birth and into the future far ahead of death, that can leap oceans and move through interstellar space, into the souls of others, living or dead, into the flaming center of the sun and the fateful secrets of the electron, with no barrier but ignorance. He felt the recovered use of his mind as a man long paralyzed feels the recovered ability to walk, with a convalescent cleanliness, an irrepressible joy.

The town was brown and quiet under the midday sun. Behind him as he walked along the waterfront were the steep ridges that separated Castellammare from song-fabled Sorrento, and beyond Sorrento were the bloody beaches of Salerno where the first landings had been made. Ahead and to the left was the town itself, and stretching away on the other side of it was the valley that led to the dead cities of Pompeii and Herculaneum.

There were only a few people on the streets; occasionally an army truck moving at fifty miles an hour or a two-wheeled cart loaded with wine kegs and moving at less than one mile an hour. Once there was a tremendous clatter from afar and a Sherman tank rumbled by, leaving fresh white scars on the stones of the old road.

Eric recalled that this town had died along with the other two in a rain of burning volcanic ash some eight decades after the birth of Christ; that Pliny the Elder had tried to land a rescuing sea force here during the catastrophe and paid with his life for that enterprise. But this is an old town and it has died many deaths, he thought. Some century and a half before it had perished in the earth's impersonal wrath, it had been razed much more thoroughly by the vengeful spite of a dictator named Sulla. There were centuries when Castellammare was a resort for patrician Romans—half ruins, half elegance. And then the feudal glory with Frederick II who built a castle here, and Charles II of Anjou who built a wall around the town. Then there were the Bourbons, and all the others—and now Mussolini, a puppet Caesar, trembling in the north.

As Eric came nearer to the center of town there were more people, but for the most part the citizens were eating or already in their midday sleep. There were steel shutters over the windows of the more affluent shops. He noted that many unshuttered windows were newly broken, the shattered glass not yet swept away, and he knew how it had happened. A contingent of men from the British Eighth Army had been here on a brief leave from the front—which was now almost immovable, a jagged line across the mountainous region between Grosseto in the west and just south of Ancona on the Adriatic. They were damned sick of it up there and they had had enough of pretending the goddamn Iteys were cobelligerents, they said. One of the men from the *SS William Benson* had been drinking with them and so the story had spread through the ship. They had had enough of that nonsense, the limeys had said. And then they had gone through the town after the bars closed, smashing every window they could see. There were no MP's here, and the Italian police did not dare protest against anything that was done by their conquerors. Eric saw the small shops of many poor men here, men long bewildered by the double-talk of politics and wars, men who must have wrung their hands together helplessly trying to add everything up and get a reasonable answer to why such things happened to them.

He was walking toward the waterfront park. He came opposite a cart with two huge wheels. It was barely moving. The driver had a long, drooping mustache. Eric saw this driver wave urgently to a pedestrian and he watched the pantomime of what happened between them. The driver wanted a light for his pipe. The pedestrian had to climb with great difficulty onto the hub of one of the wagon wheels in order to light the pipe of the driver. The driver thanked the pedestrian with elaborate formality, then he looked at Eric with a glance that contained an extraordinarily delicate humor. There was no malice in it. All it said was: "This is rather ridiculous, is it not?" It was a quick exchange of comedy, and then it was gone and the driver drove on and the pedestrian resumed his course, but to Eric this was an indescribable refreshment. It belonged to the world of subtle awareness which he had tried to forego. He felt a gratitude toward the wagon driver, a gratitude that would stay with him as long as memory.

The park was half taken over by a British supply unit as a petrol supply point. But the north end of it was not fenced off with barbed wire, and Eric found a bench there down near the sea wall. The rediscovery of unhampered consciousness and undulled sensation remained marvelously exciting. Some fishermen down on the narrow strip of beach were coloring their nets in vats of mud-brown dye. And two little girls straddling the wall were playing with some sort of jellyfish that exuded a royal purple opulence. He looked at the town, and the great gaps of masonry seemed like wounds that were so overcauterized that they could never heal.

"Signore, signore," said a cringing voice near him. "You please-uh go me ahnd hahve *una piccola tazza di* likker?"

It was Harold. He was slightly drunk. He sat down beside Eric. "No," said Eric. "I don't want to drink now."

"Go with me and drink *un caffè espresso, Professore.*"

Eric could see that the boy was aching internally, as though something had squeezed his viscera in the wrong way. There was a peculiar madness now in his way of imitating the Italians. He was no longer imitating a vaudeville wop; something in him was trying to imitate an Italian half-drowned in the raging flood of history. His imitations were beginning to take charge of his life.

They sat and talked for a while. "I can't go with you anywhere now," Eric said, "because I'm trying to see things. And I have to do it alone."

The mess boy understood this perfectly, as no other man on the ship could have. "I'm trying to do that in my own way," he said, "and at the same time trying not to."

Then he suddenly changed and became arrogantly insistent. "Oh, come on," he said, "have one drink with me. Don't be so goddamned professorial. One drink now, and then go your own way!"

Eric was disturbed but adamant. "I don't want to do anything *with* anyone from the ship today," he said. "Whatever I do, good or bad, it has to be alone."

Harold stood up with gestures of Latin temperament. "Okay," he said, "so you pistahfaness?"

Eric looked mystified at this last word and Harold sat down again on the bench. "Goddamn these people, god-damn them!" he said. "I don't know what to do. It hurts to see things like that. I try to imitate what it's like and instead of it seeming funny it just hurts more."

"Okay—let's have it."

Harold leaned against the hard back of the wooden bench and almost closed his eyes. Then he told a story that seemed very commonplace. And yet nobody had explained it. This story took place in Palermo and it was about a family there.

It appeared that Harold and the seaman called Kentucky had ended up that night they were ashore in Sicily with a family in a house where some kid had taken them, and the two of them slowly discovered that this was a very decent family. They did not seem to be out to get anything. There was a father of about fifty, his old wife, a son of about eighteen, and daughters of about ten, sixteen, and twenty. They seemed to be very decent people and they were delighted to have the Americans sitting around their table with them. They would not take any money. The old man reluctantly accepted one package of cigarettes, but would not take any more. He insisted on furnishing the wine and brandy and food. He did not pretend to be affluent, but he had a fairly good job as a plumber and the son was working at the army airfield. They kept plying the two American boys with liquor and food and all of them talking together in pidgin English and pidgin Italian which became more and more articulate with the flow of the liquor. Harold tried to explain about democracy—how everybody could say what they wanted to, and so on and so forth; and the Italians listened, pleased and enthralled by the pleasant pictures. Kentucky did not say much, but it was obvious that he was forgiving these people for being foreigners and beginning to think of them almost as real folks. It never occurred to either of the Americans to try to make love to the girls—that is, not in the presence of their brother and parents. But they really had a good time drinking and trying to understand one another, and of course they enjoyed the great respect with which the Italians treated them. Another thing that made a great impression

on them was the strength of the seventeen-year-old girl's
teeth. They had sent out for some soda pop to mix with
brandy. It came in old bottles with caps that were rusted
on. They had no bottle opener, so this girl put the ends of
the bottles in her mouth and pried the caps off with her
flawless white teeth. It still made Harold's nerves ache when
he thought about that. But then came something much
worse.

Both he and Kentucky were drunk in a quiet way and they
announced to their Italian friends that they must now leave
and get back to their ship. The Italians looked very hurt,
especially the father. "Whatsamatta?" he asked. "You pis-
*tah*faness?"

The Americans did not understand. The son was the one
who knew the most English and finally he made them understand what the old man was trying to say. "You know—
all time at airfield Americans say, 'So you pis*tah*fahness?' "

At last they figured out that he was referring to an army
phrase: "pissed off on us." Angry at us.

"But why?" they asked.

"You no like go bed with girls? Why you pis*tah*fahness?"

Harold became cagey then, thinking that this was where
these people made their dough and that that was why they
had been so indifferent about money before. "How much?"
he asked.

But then the brother really looked insulted. *"Niente,"* he
said. ."You *amichi. Mia sorella no puttana. Amichi—amichi,
Capisc'?"*

And all the time the old man was grinning pleadingly at
them and the old woman was nodding her head and the two
girls were looking at them with open, bland looks as though
the whole thing were merely a matter of etiquette. Yet before the war they must all have lived within the strict black-
and-white world of Catholic-Latin sexual morality.

There was no money in it for them and yet they would
feel insulted if this thing—which formerly had been regarded as worse than death for young unmarried girls of this
class—did not happen.

"What is the explanation of that?" Harold asked Eric. "It
doesn't seem to make sense to me. There's a lot more to the
story. But I know that they were very respectable people

163

before the war. Probably the old man would have killed one of his daughters if she lost her cherry without getting married. And the brother would have knifed any guy who tried to lay one of his sisters. How can you explain all that?"

Harold's face showed real suffering as he said these things. His gift for impersonation was getting the better of him. His constant preoccupation with being able to sound like other people had led him naturally into trying to *feel* like other people.

"How can you explain all that?"

"I can explain it in one word," Eric said. "But I doubt if that word will be very clarifying to either of us. The word is *defeat.*"

The sky was clear and very pale above the Bay of Naples, but somewhere in the Mediterranean there must have been a storm, for the waves, which were usually no more than ripples, were now several feet high, and they slapped against the sea wall like little animals grown furious with the impotence of being only half-grown. The fishermen had taken their nets out of the dye pots and were stretching them on the stone wall to dry. The two little girls who had been preoccupied with the purple exudations of the gelatinous sea animals they had been playing with were now forced to move, and they brought their small playthings of protoplasm to the far end of the bench on which Eric was sitting. He watched them, enjoying the fact that they were almost unaware of him. They had not identified him as an American.

"Good afternoon, *signor marconista,*" said a clear school-boy voice behind him.

He turned and saw a neatly dressed, pink-cheeked boy of about thirteen. "Good afternoon," he answered.

The boy came around the end of the bench and sat down between him and the little girls. "I guess you don't remember me," he said.

"Not too clearly," Eric told him.

He did remember the boy as part of his drunken week, but he could not be quite sure about it. He seemed to remember him as one of the more dignified *peelohts,* one who led them only to sources of drink and culture. They began to talk and it turned out that Eric's impression was correct. The boy's name was Mario and his English was excellent. His grandfather had once been a well-known professor at the University of Naples.

"As you have told me that you are also a professor when there are no wars," said Mario, "I am almost certain that you would enjoy the knowing of my grandfather, Giuseppe Valdo."

"I'm sure I would," Eric said.

"My grandfather is a little much too old to think very clearly at all times now," Mario continued. "He spent many of the past years in a jail."

"He was anti-Fascist?"

"He was editor of the newspaper here in Castellammare, and the things he printed caused disapproval in the government. They warned him numerous times. But my grandfather is—how you say it?—*stubborn*."

"And what about your father? Was he also in jail?"

"No, my father is a worker in a bank in Naples, and he tries never to be so political as my grandfather."

"I see."

He and Mario talked for about half an hour, sitting on the bench. Mario was at the top of all his classes now that schools had been resumed here. His ambition was to be a diplomat. In fact, he wanted to be Ambassador to the United States. There was something of patient and obliging assurance in the boy that made Eric feel certain that he *would* some day be Ambassador to the United States.

"When I last saw you," Mario said, "you were a little influenced by liquors, and at that time we were discussing some phrases in Latin in a bar on the Piazza. The truth is that you were not saying them correctly."

Eric laughed. "That does not surprise me in the least," he said. "As a matter of fact, I almost failed in Latin when I studied it in high school, and but for the grace of God and a very kind Latin teacher I would never have graduated. But now I begin to remember the phrase we were discussing. It began: *Nihil tam absurdum dici potest quad non decatur ab aliquo philosophorum*."

"Libro *philosophorum*," Mario corrected.

"Let's go and have some coffee," Eric said.

The old man, Giuseppe Valdo, wore a skullcap and bathrobe and carpet slippers, and he was very proud of his skill at roasting last winter's chestnuts. He and Eric had exhausted the other members of the family. The daughter—Mario's mother—was a simple woman who loved her place in bourgeois society and had never conceived of the possibility of any other way of existence. To her history was an annoyance, and no more than that. If she were stood up against a wall to be shot, Eric had thought, her emotions still would be only those of a conscientious housewife who has inadvertently hired some very unruly servants. Her husband, who was vice-president of a bank, was a man of more conscious caution; he felt that business was business and that politics was a sort of Bohemianism which had from time to time become shockingly powerful through some out-of-hand perversion of reality.

There was a peculiar sterility about the apartment. It consisted of seven enormous high-ceilinged rooms with tile floors and unrelated pieces of furniture. Each room was more like an auctioneer's showroom than a place to live. And all this unrelated space made one feel cold even in June.

But the old man was all right. He and Eric were eating chestnuts that the family had kept from last winter and drinking raw homemade wine and talking quietly together. Everyone else had gone to bed.

The old man varied from time to time between senile maundering and intelligent awareness. On the wall in a small frame he had shown Eric a piece of felt with numbers sewed on it: 1338C. That was his convict number when they had put him in jail. He felt very gay about having spent all that time in prison. He was getting shaky and feeble, but not too feeble to reach for the wine bottle. He refilled Eric's glass.

"I will tell you exactly how it was," he said in his academic English. "Especially when the man came and said that they were going to kill me. He was an old acquaintance who had become a leader of the *Fascisti* here in the town. He said to me: 'Giuseppe, you must not write what you write in your paper, because times now have changed. If you go on to write like that I must tell you that something will happen to you at night some time soon—an accident. Then you will not be alive.' "

"So what did you say?"

"I said nothing. But in my paper next day I print a front' page editorial. And in that I say I will offer a reward of one thousand lire to whoever may assassinate me. Then I explain that the *Fascisti* have said that they will soon kill me and that since I would rather be dead than live in such a society as is now going on in this country, I am offering one thousand lire to be paid to whichever Fascist may choose to kill me."

The old man laughed and straightened the skullcap on his bald head. Eric laughed too. "And so they didn't. They were afraid to go after the reward!"

"Yes. I had been here a long time, and they knew the people of this old town would lose their faith in the new way of life if the new-way-of-life people found it necessary to kill an old man like me."

"That's a good joke."

"It is one of the funniest jokes of all time. But you know what makes me think you Americans are the greatest people to have arisen so far on the entire earth?"

"No. What?"

"That ink bottle."

"What ink bottle?"

"The one where you have just enough ink in a little lip at the top of the bottle, just enough to dip your pen in without getting ink on your fingers. What an idea! Only America could have an idea like that!"

Eric felt the keen and courageous mind of this old man moving toward him and then suddenly receding back into the mists of old age. He kept trying to hold the old fellow closer to him.

"In Australia," said Giuseppe, "I ran a restaurant. I did my own cooking. And Melba came there! I sent a message that I would supply her with any food she might want at the theater. A little rare broth just before going on the stage, a platter of oysters with Chablis when she came off—anything she wanted. She was very pleased. She wrote me a very kind letter. We became good friends."

"Australia?"

"Yes—I was there then—and there were lots of opportunities in the restaurant business. Better to be a restaurant owner there at that time than a professor in this country. Italy is a tragedy. That is all there is to it. I am a patriot and would like to think otherwise. But it is so. You will be surprised if I tell you why Mussolini put an old man like myself in the jails."

"Why?"

"Well—this will disappoint you. I was not objecting to Fascism. It seemed like an old story to me. I had perhaps studied too much history. I was insisting that they should take advantage of the wonderful mineral springs in Castellammare which have now been neglected for hundreds of years. And all I said about the government was that it was stupid and inefficient. That was all I said—and they finally reluctantly took me and put me in the jails. I am a Socialist in my beliefs, as Mussolini once pretended to be, and the truth is that all these things bored me and at the same time amused me. I could not see to what they would lead. And now let me peel a few more chestnuts. I doubt if you would find any elsewhere around here at this time of the year."

Eric refilled their glasses with the sweet-smelling half-fermented wine. "And what about *now?*" he said. "Does this time also amuse you or bore you?"

The old man removed the charred shell from a chestnut with trembling fingers, fingers that were almost fleshless— tendon, vein, and skin laid upon fragile bone. "It might bore me if I were not Italian," he said. "And it might amuse me if I were not human."

"What will happen?"

"So many like myself were made very happy when you people began to drive out the Germans," said Giuseppe Valdo. "The word 'America' has been like a flag of all humanity to many of us. But slowly we have seen that the Americans did not arrive here at all. They only helped the British to arrive. And now the British are up to their old game of imperial power and are trying to force our Fascist king back upon us."

"Yes, it's ironic and stupid. Of course, they're afraid of Russia. And Russia's afraid of them."

"And both are afraid of the people."

Eric leaned back in his uncomfortable Empire-style chair and closed his eyes. He was trying to believe that it was near the end of June 1944 and that he was actually sitting here drinking wine in a room in Castellammare di Stabia with an old man named Giuseppe Valdo.

"We have come to a bad time in human history," Eric said. "It is difficult to know enemies from friends."

Signor Valdo held a shelled chestnut between his thumb and forefinger and looked at it as though he were gazing into a crystal ball. "My son," he said, "this is only the beginning. This is only the period of setting the stage. The world is getting ready for a final struggle between two gigantic forces."

"Yes?"

"And our tragedy is this—that they are both evil."

They had reached the dregs of the bottle and the old man padded off into the kitchen after a fresh one. "Fortunately," he said when he returned, "new wine is very good for the kidneys—for there is no longer any time in which to mature anything."

2

Eric opened his eyes. He was in a strange room. He fixed his gaze on a plaster rosette in the center of the high ceiling. He was lying on an enormous chaise longue, covered with a blanket and fully dressed except for his coat, necktie, and shoes. Some shuttered doors partly open behind him admitted a cold gray light. On a table near the center of the room were some bottles, glasses, and saucers full of nutshells and cigarette butts. On the floor were several more bottles.

Eric smiled to himself as he visualized the old man putting him to bed here on the couch and thoughtfully covering him with a blanket. "You're a better man than I am, Grandfather Valdo!" he said to himself. Then he got up and put on the rest of his clothes. The tile floor was cold against his feet. The house was silent except for a muffled sound of snoring from one of the bedrooms. Eric wrote a note saying that he would try to visit them again before his ship sailed, and left it, weighted down with a package of Chesterfields, in the center of the table. Then he quietly left the apartment and made his way down the stairs and into the Via D'Annunzio.

It was five-thirty, and a gray mist somewhere between the earth and the sun drained all color from the morning light;

and although it was not cold, there was a winter appearance upon things. There was not yet much activity in the town. Halfway to the coal dock Eric found a small café that was open.

The place was steamy and smelled richly of damp masonry, coffee, and anisette. He sat down at a small round table and ordered some bread and *mozarella* cheese, and *caffè espresso* with brandy. His head ached slightly from the night's excess of bad wine, but he was happy. He was free now from that nightmare feeling of having burned fiercely in a vacuum, of having squandered too much irreplaceable consciousness. There was quietness in him now, an area of new experience on which his mind could ponder without shame or pride. He could taste the warm grain goodness of the dark bread, the soft, subtle sharpness of the *mozarella*, and the dark heat of the strong coffee with its vaporous overtones of brandy. His senses were unusually acute and appreciative.

At the coal dock he nodded to the gold-braided cockhatted *carabiniere* who stood "guard" there, and the latter, delighted at such kind attention, answered with a sweeping military salute. He walked rapidly under the fine rain of coal dust that was continually flung into the air as the cargo was unloaded. The ship had risen in the water and the gangway was now at a precarious angle; it was necessary to hold onto the loose rope on one side. Kentucky was standing the gangway watch and he observed Eric's ascent with a knowing grin.

" 'Dja have a tough night, Professor?" he asked politely.

"Not so tough," Eric said.

"Was she pretty?" Kentucky asked, as he steadied the guide rope.

"Well," said Eric, thinking of old Giuseppe Valdo, "not exactly. I don't think you would have called her pretty."

"Oh, I ain't particular," the seaman said. "They all look alike in the dark. Ain't that a fact?"

"That's a fact."

"Was she hot?"

"We-ell—yes and no. The truth is she drank a lot. She drank me under the table."

Kentucky roared with appreciation of this understandable disaster. "That can happen to any man," he said generously.

In his stateroom Eric turned on the desk lamp because the light that came through the single porthole was colorless and gloomy. Chuck, the junior engineer, was snoring earnestly in the upper bunk. The air in the room was heavy with human breath and the smell of sweat-soaked underwear. And all at once Eric felt very tired and lonely.

The loneliness that entered him now was that which a man often feels after a hard day's work; all the multiple connecting rods of the job have been removed, the complex mechanism which for eight hours has related a man to the external world is suddenly stilled, the thin vapors of evening descend around him, and he is alone. He makes his way homeward, no longer a participant, and he passes through the city of a thousand answers. But as he is now released from a communal participation he cannot bear for the moment to flee toward a communal solace; he is lonely for a solace that is separately and entirely his own. That was the way Eric felt at this early hour in the morning, though he could not understand why it should be so.

Then he noticed that there was a letter from Jane on the desk. The overseas air-mail service was surprisingly efficient. *Eric Clark, Radio Officer, SS William Benson, c/o Postmaster, N.Y.C.* That was the address—and here it was. He was grateful.

He sat down at the desk and stared at the letter for a long time before he opened it. He wanted to feel the physical reality of it. He wanted to treasure the knowledge that this was paper on which the woman he loved had written words for him, words out of the truth and mystery of her own precarious identity. That alone, without reading the letter, would have sufficed to quiet the worst of this unexpected ache of loneliness in him.

He read the letter. In the last three—which had come to him in a single mail—Jane had seemed to be living entirely in the past, avidly anxious to recall every moment of loneliness or humor or passion that they had ever had together. There was almost nothing of the present. In this letter, also, there was almost no mention of her present life. But instead of reaching into the past for assurance, she seemed here to

be trying not quite successfully to make cautious generalizations. Eric found it somewhat puzzling. He read parts of it
several times.

*Life is stronger than we are, and it is futile for us not to
recognize that this is so. You, darling, probably have
always known it—but I am only beginning to see it.*

A tenderness filled Eric, swelled within him like a cre-
scendo of compassionate music, and filled his eyes with tears.
My poor child, he thought, in what cruel and shameful manner has life proved its mastery over you?

He knew the answer to his own question, but at this moment he could feel nothing but tenderness and love for his
wife. There were tears on his cheeks and he brushed them
away with his hand. They were foreign to him, as though
they had been raindrops.

Chuck stirred in his bunk, groaned, and swung his legs
over the side. "Hi," he said. "How you been?"

"Okay," Eric said. "And you?"

"Okay—except I have the goddamnedest dreams. I don't
know why it is."

"Dreams can be awfully painful," Eric said.

Chuck slipped down to the deck and began to put on his
clothes. Then he washed his hands and brushed his thinning
hair, looking at his sleep-worn face in the mirror. "I don't
know why in hell it is," he said. "I can't go to sleep without
those dreams. Sometimes I wish I never had to go to bed."

Eric had not written to Jane for almost a week, and after
Chuck had gone below, he got out his fountain pen and
paper and tried to begin a letter. He made several begin-
nings and then tore the pages up and dropped them in the
wastebasket. The first attempt sounded like a report by some
third-rate correspondent, and the second was like a tourist's guidebook. There was so much he wanted to tell her
about, all the past days of living delirium and the rediscovery of personal awareness, the deep death-sickness in
the human shambles of this catastrophe. And the look in the
eyes of the baby as it lay on the wine-wet table between the
men—the conquerors—looking at Eric, not questioning and
not asserting, but looking at him out of a soul born fresh

172

and clean from infinity. Yet he could not write any of this
into a letter because it was not related to any part of their
shared experience. It was not a part of them, not even
slightly, and therefore it was impossible now for Eric to
write to his wife about these things.

Not part of us, he thought. Is love so small? Is love no
more than a narrow furnished room where two of us are at
last permitted to warm our hands at a rented fire?

He began to try again. The least he could do was to reply
in abstract terms to her own generalizations. For he knew
that those generalizations were not born of the book-dry
archives of philosophy but of the dark blood of his beloved.

Just then he heard a great shouting outside the stateroom
and the sound of hurrying feet. Someone opened his door.
He turned toward the door resentfully. It was Kentucky.
"Have you seen a wop runnin' around here?" the seaman
asked. "There's a thief got loose on the ship!"

"No," Eric said.

"Goddamn thievin' bahstud!" said Kentucky. "We'll get
him!"

Eric walked outside where he could survey the boat deck
and the stern half of the main deck. There were frantic
shouts and the leather-against-steel sound of running feet.
Several seamen were standing on the main deck, half
crouched in the attitudes of defensive football players waiting for the opposing ball carrier to break through the forward line. There were noises from inside the ship. "There
he goes! Head him off!"

The voices were full of the concentrated excitement of
boys playing run sheep run or cops and robbers. Then a small
figure of a man came running out of the main-deck housing.
The seamen who were waiting there tried to catch hold of
him, but he eluded them and scrambled up the ladder to the
boat deck directly below where Eric was standing. The seamen were close behind him. He looked about wildly. Then
another group of pursuers came out of the boat-deck housing
and the little man was cut off. They grabbed him from behind and from the front at the same instant. A seaman
twisted one of his arms behind his back. The Italian clutched
a paper bag in his free hand, holding it close against his
body.

Eric had the sensation that time had slowed down perceptibly; he saw the thief in great detail, as though this were a motion-picture scene which he, as director, could have repeated over and over again until it was just right. The ragged clothes, the thin, wild body, the hand clutching the wet paper sack. The face with all human pride removed—animal and violent. All human pride removed, but not all human dignity. There was a dignity of need, a functional dignity, in the single-minded desperation of the Italian's face. And in the suspended moment, Eric found it beautiful. And as he looked at the athletic, game-excited faces of the pursuers against the steel background of the great ship, he thought: This is the end of the world. Our stupidity and our ingenuity have moved too far apart. This must be the breaking point.

The thief's paper bag was snatched from his hands and opened. "Jesus Christ! Potatoes! Rotten potatoes!" The captors were disgusted and embarrassed. It seemed that the man had only been stealing rotten potatoes from the garbage cans.

The face of the Italian was like that of an animal that is driven to bay, yet the hunted face of the thief was more human than the dull game-masks of the pursuers.

"Jesus Christ!"

"Stealing garbage!"

"The dirty bastard!"

"They'll eat anything!"

"Turn him over to the MP's!"

"Better throw him overboard!"

"Teach him a lesson!"

"The bastard was hungry!"

"He just took that 'cause he couldn't find anything better!"

"Oh Christ—they *like* to eat that stuff!"

Captain Brogan came out of his cabin and stood beside Eric. He looked over the situation. "Put the man ashore," he said to the seamen.

"How about the MP's?" someone asked. "Shouldn't we take him into Naples?"

"Put the man ashore!" the captain repeated angrily.

Eric turned toward Brogan with relief. "The man was only stealing garbage," he said.

The captain gave him a look of dark and weary contempt. "He's a guinea thief," he said, "and I don't give a
goddamn what he was stealing!"

As the captain returned to his quarters Eric looked down
again at the crowd that was pushing and prodding the thief
off the ship. A seaman had taken the sack of rotten potatoes away from him and thrown it overboard.

Eric walked down the ladder to the boat deck. He met
George Fiorini standing there. The steward had a faraway
look on his face, as though he were walking in his sleep.

"Funny what people will steal, isn't it?" he asked softly.

"Yes," Eric said.

They could still hear sounds of shuffling feet and low
curses, the peculiarly muted rhythms of bodily violence, as
the thief was being pushed down the gangway onto the coal
dock.

"I helped catch him," said Fiorini. "I was the one that
caught hold of his shirt. He almost got away again."

Eric went around the side of the boat-deck housing to
where he could overlook the dock. He saw Harold standing
behind a lifeboat. The mess boy was gripping the rail with
his right hand and his face was contorted in a repulsive grimace. He was staring into space, quite blind to his surround-
ings. He drew back lips bloodless with terror, narrowed his
eyes with the cunning of desperation, clutched one hand
against his chest as though he were holding there the earth's
last spark of life, straining all his muscles as though the
hounds of death were already at his throat. Eric saw here
again—the thief. He did not need to look down on the dock,
but he could not escape the muffled grunts of pain and the
padded wet sound of fists on flesh that came from below.

He hurried back to his stateroom and sat down again at
the desk where he had been trying to write a letter to
Jane. He picked up his fountain pen and carefully removed
a piece of lint caught on its point. *Jane Dear—* he wrote.

Chuck returned from below and began to wash himself at
the other end of the room. "Well," he said, "I hear they
caught a thieving guinea loose on the ship!"

"Yes," said Eric, "they did."

"We ought to keep this door locked," Chuck said. "You
can't ever tell, you know."

"That's right, you can't."

"Want to come down for some java?"

"Not now. Got to finish a letter."

"The *frau?*"

"That's right."

"Well, don't tell her *every*thing! But give her my regards."

"I'll do that."

Chuck put on his shirt and went out, and Eric was alone again. The yellowish light of the desk lamp was disturbingly unnatural, as electric light always is in the daytime, and in its glow the sheet of writing paper was gilded with unreality.

Jane Dear—

He poised the point of his pen against the paper again and again. But he could not think of a thing to say.

15: *The Magic That Was Better Than Light*

There was a half-moon in the clear night sky as they sailed westward. The blacked-out ship was without escort and, having unloaded its cargo, rode high and light in the water. They clung closely to the North African coast and moved at slow speed, for there were no coastal lights, and even though they could plainly see the white towns and the pale loneliness of isolated watchtowers, they could not be certain of their position. The captain did not want to arrive before dawn at Beni-Saf, where they were to take on a ballast of iron ore for the return trip across the Atlantic.

Eric was on the flying bridge with the captain and the second mate. The captain was in a tolerant mood and the three of them were drinking hot coffee with brandy in it. The helmsman had gone below for the coffee while the mate relieved him, and Eric had with him a bottle of what the Italians had referred to as *cognac originale.* Now the night air was sharp and dry, the hot drinks were good in their throats, and the moonlit African coast was sheer picture-book imagery. Eric strained to identify the reality of this hour. Here he was leaning against the rail of this buoy-

ant steel monster, balancing the warm cup on the pipe of
the rail, talking familiarly with strangers in a world of exotic
irrelevance. What was he doing here? But then he recognized that this was one of the oldest and commonest of questions. For there is one mystery, separate and perpetual for
every one of us, and that is the mystery of how we really
came to be in the situation in which we find ourself: our
body, our country, our city, our marriage, what we are doing
and saying at any given moment. We may accept many a
specious and formal explanation, but in truth we have not
given up wondering how it really came about.

The ship is a ghost ship on a faërie sea slipping silently
past enchanted shores, Eric thought. Only it is not that at
all. This is a Liberty Ship, and like the very situation itself,
it is constructed of iron and dream and madness, far more
incredible than any myth.

He was deep in reverie, yet he heard the Mediterranean
Sea sighing and gurgling and whispering against the hull
beneath him, and some obscure perversity caused him to
invert his cup and pour the remainder of the warm drink
into the dark water. Perhaps he wanted to leave some personal impression upon its mobile permanence. His mind
wandered through currents and eddies of old words. Life is
a tale told by Oscar the wiper . . . and out of a misty dream
our path emerges for a while . . . then closes . . . within
a dream. Life is . . . a bomb. You cannot hold a theory
between yourself and an explosion. Not if the explosion is
big enough. Yet a dream which was congruent to the truth
could free the world from the slavery of poverty and dis-
ease and ignorance, or could destroy it utterly. The fact of
the matter is that we live not only in our bodies, our houses,
our cities, but also within a totality of consciousness. The
human world is no more and no less than whatever human
beings can experience. My friend Joe Edwards killed himself
because of an inescapable sentiment; and Steve Shapiro was
on his way home from the grocery store when he was killed
by a truck that jumped the curb because its steering gear
broke. Both experiences were equally valid, equally real.
You can't dream your way out of a bomb blast. But neither
can you blast your way out of a dream.

"Well, Professor!"

It was Second Mate Burley standing near him at the rail and puffing at the cold pipe which he was forbidden to light in the blackout.

"Yes?"

"I bet you're planning a book out of all this. Am I right? 'Adventures in the Merchant Marine,' or something like that. I'm a good judge of character, and I bet you dollars to doughnuts that's what's on your mind. Am I right?"

"Well," Eric answered, "I wouldn't say you were one hundred per cent wrong."

Burley chuckled wisely.

"I'm a real judge of character," he said. "I've studied psychology from A to Z. Phrenology and all the rest of it. Just from the shape of a man's nose I can tell you more about the guy than most people would know if they lived with him all their life! One look and I got him sized up completely."

"Is your first impression ever wrong?"

"Never! I tell you it would take *some* character to outsmart me by his looks!"

"Well, I've studied a little psychology, too; in fact, I taught it for a while. But my first impressions are almost always wrong!"

Burley was polite. "The fact is," he admitted, "that you have to have a feeling for that sort of thing. Some people can read all the books there are and still they won't be good judges of character."

"I suppose so," Eric said.

It was strange talking to this lantern-jawed figure in the clear cool moonlight of the Mediterranean night; so weirdly irrelevant that it seemed to have made the complete circle and approached relevance again. Somehow Burley's reference to phrenology and kindred subjects caused Eric none of the sickening sensations that he had felt when Peters spoke of similar matters. There was a ribald and cockeyed vitality about Burley. He didn't drain the life from things.

"Tell me," the second mate asked, "how many books would you say you'd read?"

"Recently?"

"No—in your whole life."

178

"I don't really know. Quite a few."

"Ah-ha! And you, a professor, admit you don't know how many! Well, I can tell you exactly my number. I've read two thousand and eighty-four books, and when I finish the one I'm on now it'll be two thousand and eighty-five exactly!"

"That's a lot of books."

"You're damned right it is. When I was on the beach for two years during the depression I used to go to the lib'ary twice a week. I used to come home with my arms full of books on psychology. Sometimes the guys on the street corner used to try to get smart. 'What's all them books?' they'd say. So I'd put down the books on the sidewalk and go up to 'em and look 'em in the eye. 'They're books on psychology,' I'd say. 'You want to make something of it?' Then I'd just stand there takin' 'em each by turn and lookin' 'em in the eye. Usually that was enough. But sometimes I had to kick the livin' Jesus out of one of 'em. They'd think because I had all those lib'ary books I must be a queer. I changed their minds all right."

Eric laughed. "I'm glad you defended your right to read books without being considered a fairy," he said.

"Usually I didn't have to fight," said Burley. "I was powerful at looking a man in the eye in those days. That was before I lost my teeth and my constitution got worn down. Usually I just had to fix my gaze."

The second mate grasped the lapels of Eric's jacket and pulled him close and stared with metallic moonlit ferocity into his eyes. "You see," he said, "it's not as strong now. But it's still pretty strong if you're not used to it."

"By God," said Eric, struggling to free himself, "it certainly is!"

Back in his stateroom Eric sat down to finish his bottle of *originale;* he turned on only the desk lamp and went below to refill the carafe with ice water. He returned and sat down at the desk. Chuck was snoring in the upper bunk, with constant changes of rhythm and intensity. He is living through some tremendous experience, Eric thought.

Eric wanted to be alone with the secret processes of his own thinking. He wanted to ask himself if he had learned anything more that would lead to the conclusion of his "enemy" story. He knew that he had learned very little.

If I should say that the enemy is within oneself, he thought, I would be stating a dangerous and trite half-truth. We *must* conquer the Nazis. The organized ones. If we fail in that we will return to feudal slavery and to the old indignity of communal superstition. If I say that every form of self-righteousness and blind self-interest is the enemy, every "patriotism" and every formal devotion to creed, every refusal to regard one's own viewpoint as tentative, every cowering into that dead end of consciousness which is called mysticism—if I should say all that in my story it would be quite true, but it would also conspire to defeat the truth. The righteous would agree and add, "But not, of course, *our* beliefs"; and the mystics would say, "Certainly, but not *our* astral interpretations"; and the patriots would say, "So very true, but we must not sacrifice the sacred sovereignty of Monaco!"

That is the philosophic truth of who the enemy is, and yet it is thus that the philosopher sometimes inadvertently becomes the enemy of society. Because this truth distributes the immediate guilt and tends to render us incapable of killing. And in our day such may well be a fatal impotence. Can we afford the luxury of diffuse definition? Or must we, in this desperate and beautiful and criminal moment of our history, speak only of the enemy that is in power? Perhaps, though he be our archetype, and the blood of his evil cruelty is in our blood, before we fight him in our ally and extirpate him from ourselves, we must defeat him in those places where he has gained ascendancy—lest we delay until we no longer have any choice in the matter.

"Fustishu!"

The shouted word broke into Eric's thought-weaving, stopped the loom and pulled 'the threaded words asunder. He stood up and looked into the upper bunk. Chuck was lying on his back with his eyes wide open. He was no longer snoring; in fact, he hardly seemed to be breathing.

"What did you say?" Eric asked.

"Nothing," Chuck answered in a thin voice, almost a whisper. "I didn't say anything. You must be hearing things."

Eric sat down. "Have a drink of brandy and water?" he asked.

Chuck sat up on his bunk, bending forward to avoid the overhead, swinging his feet over the side and flexing his toes thoughtfully. He lit a cigarette. "Okay," he said, "if you're sure you've got enough."

Eric brought the other water glass from the medicine chest and mixed a drink for both of them. "Plenty," he said.

Chuck sipped the warm rankness of the fluid. His vision was turned inward, yet he was grateful to be with someone who was outside his nightmare. He was not really a drinking man. There was no solace for him in alcohol; it was only an esoteric link between himself and that which was outside his own wretchedness. "Tastes good," he said.

"Like hell it does," Eric laughed. "It tastes like the contents of a long-neglected cesspool. But it still manages somehow to have a few beneficent effects."

"My God, Eric," the junior engineer said, "I wish there was something I could drink that would keep me awake forever. I never want to go to sleep again. Not until I die. I won't mind being dead. But I hate like hell to go to sleep."

2

The three men were standing on the main deck waiting for the chain conveyor to be lowered close enough to the hatches for them to climb onto it. No gangway had been put out. "A godforsaken-looking hole if ever I saw one," said Duprey.

"And you've probably seen plenty," suggested Hartley. "Plenty of holes, I mean."

"I see that big hole you call your mouth often enough."

"Now, gentlemen," said Eric. "Let us not enter the town of Beni-Saf in a spirit of unbrotherly disparagement."

The scene had changed completely: there was nothing at all here reminiscent of Italy. The dock, with its little elevated railway and conveyor belts, was red with the same dust of iron ore that was now settling over the ship like sudden rust. Behind the ore dock, fastened upon the brown hills, were the white houses of the town, unwelcome and alien in the bright dry heat of this barren corner of Algeria. And the few withered trees that lined the streets only served to emphasize the tenacity with which the town clung to its bleak portion of baked earth.

There were no white soldiers in Beni-Saf, not even French. The captain had been informed of this when he was briefed by the Navy before leaving the Bay of Naples. A French Moroccan infantryman, wearing a faded blue uniform and a red fez, stood guard on the dock. He seemed extremely bored; he paid no attention to the ship or the men on it. The only things that seemed ever to arouse his interest were the flies that buzzed around him. When one lit on his face he gave it a certain length of time to get off. He seemed to be counting off the seconds and minutes; if it didn't get off by the end of the count, he brushed it off.

By the time Eric, Duprey, and Hartley had climbed onto the side structure of the conveyor and along it and then down to the dock, they were encrusted with sweat-soaked iron ore. They nodded to the guard, but he stared through them, counting off the seconds.

When they left the dock and entered upon the road that led into the center of the small town, they were quickly surrounded by a small mob of Arab boys. A very different lot from the children of Italy. Beggars, dirty and ragged, unhealthy, amoral little animals. But very different. For these children were arrogant, unified, bold, and dangerous.

"Hey, Joe! You got something sell? Sheets? Sugar? Clothes? Good price!"

One boy of twelve took out of his pocket a large roll of French currency and waved it at them. Others, in an organized fashion, bumped against the Americans and quickly felt their pockets. Pushed away, they laughed defiantly and returned. Their quick hands entered pockets. They stooped down and felt the calves of the Americans to see if they had smuggled sheets off the ship by wrapping them around their legs.

These were three strong men, but they could not keep the Arab urchins at a distance. Their approaches were as well organized as a skilled play in football. Hartley took out his over-the-side knife and opened its long blade. "Go away, you little bastards!" he said.

One of the older boys, about fourteen, quickly opened a knife of his own. "You want game with knives?" he said. And the other boys watched the scene with cynical amusement. At this moment a man of about twenty-five approached them. He was dark and handsome, with eyes that were incredibly soft and brown and totally without compassion. He carried a walking stick of thornwood and wore a dark blue tunic above well-cut trousers of gray tweed. "Would you gentlemen care to have a guide?" he asked in English, almost without accent.

"I think that would be a first-class idea," said Duprey, "absolutely first-class. You are definitely hired, here and now."

The young man said a few Arabic words to the boys and they turned away toward the dock, running in a group, laughing in a way that was like the barking of half-grown carnivores in a land of shepherdless sheep. Their guide bowed, bending about five degrees from the vertical.

"My name is John," he said. "The town is mostly asleep at this hour. There are very few shops open. But we may find a bar or two, if you care for a drink."

First there was a bar that was patronized mostly by Arabs. This place had an open front; there were a dozen marble-topped tables and a zinc counter. The three men drank vermouth. They invited John to have a drink, but he declined with a combination of politeness and aloofness the like of which Eric had never seen. They had several drinks of the warm, fortified wine. There was an Arab scribe sitting at a table. He was a real motion-picture-type Arab, with a gray beard and a proud head hooded in a white burnoose. He was writing letters for various customers. He looked at the Americans in a friendly fashion, so they went over to him and admired the elegant Arabic script he was producing. They told him their names and he wrote them down on little slips of paper, spelling them out phonetically in the Arabic alphabet. They bought him several glasses of cognac.

Then they moved on to another bar several hundred yards away. This place was run by Frenchmen and the customers were predominantly French. Eric found it rather amazing that these Frenchmen seemed just like those he had known in France in 1934. Neither the unwelcoming coast of North Africa nor the recent and tragic history of France seemed to have had any visible effect upon them. There was still that French manner that he had loved on sight: the shopkeeper's realism combined with the *bon vivant's* interest in the baroque and the sensual, the cynic's resignation with the hedonist's optimism, the wry and unostentatious acknowledgement that life is extremely complex.

This was a delightful place to Eric. Everyone seemed to be having a good time. The bartender sold Hartley a pair of slippers. They were made of goatskin with pointed toes and no strap behind the heel. "How the hell can a girl keep these on?" he asked. And the red-faced mustachioed bartender said, "She must drahg the feet. You *comprend* drahg?" And he demonstrated by dragging his feet which were in felt carpet slippers. "I get the idea," Hartley said. "She's got to be slug nutty. Okay, Monsieur La Frog, it shall be so!" The heat entered the damp cavern of the bar in oppressive waves and, combined with the vermouth, seemed to make them briefly dizzy. They sat down at a table and changed to cognac. It was none too good, but it was better than what they had been drinking in Italy.

"We ought to go out after some Ay-rab tail," Hartley suggested. "Can either of you impeccable gentlemen do it in Ay-rabic?"

"I'd rather drink in French for a while," said Duprey.

Hartley nodded his head sagely. An alcoholic malice seemed to be taking possession of his usually harmless personality—a special malice directed at Duprey.

"You might be able to find the kind of stuff you go for here," he said, "but with Ay-rab variations."

Duprey wanted to be friendly. He was enjoying the bar. He spoke a little French, had bought drinks for several Frenchmen that struck him as being men of good will, and was looking for some new prospects.

Hartley was not enjoying the bar any longer; his humor had inexplicably turned sour. He was persistent. "They breed fast here, Monsieur Duprey," he said. "I'm sure you could find it. Especially with the aid of our good friend, John."

Duprey focused his attention on the third mate. "What are you getting at, Hartley?" he asked. "What the hell do *you* know about what *I* go for?"

Hartley's face, that Eric had always seen as that of a humorous gargoyle, was now evil and unhumorous, full of pain that had rotted into malice. He lifted his glass and waved it in time with his speech. "I mean," he said slowly, "that maybe you can find some Ay-rab girl here that's nursing a kid.

You know—something *you* can really go for! You can take the kid away from her and then go to town."

Duprey slapped the glass out of Hartley's hand and stood up. "If you weren't a drunken fool," he said carefully, "I would beat your brains out with the top of this table."

Hartley leaned back in his chair. His face was indifferent and mocking and cravenly confident. "Go ahead and hit me," he said. "Eric saw what you did."

For a moment Eric was certain that Duprey would kill Hartley on the spot. He saw two kinds of pain in conflict, but the liquor had saved him from external participation. He was not drunk, but he was, in a way, insulated. They are both mine, he thought, both kinds of pain. The guilt of the defendant and the righteous, envious anger of the prosecutor. They are both mine. They are me.

After striking the glass from Hartley's grasp, Duprey had lifted his open hand again as though he were about to hit the third mate across the face. But now he slowly relaxed. "You're a stupid, drunken Eastshoreman," he said, "and I won't let you make me disturb this bar. Only just remember one thing! Don't ever speak to me again. Here or anywhere else. I don't want to break your goddamn neck. I intend to have a good time with the decent guys from the ship. So just don't ever give me any more of your dirty talk."

Hartley remained leaning back, grinning but saying nothing.

"Because if you do," Duprey added, "I swear to God that I'll kill you."

"I didn't mean to offend you," Hartley said airily.

But Duprey turned sickly away and went to the bar. Eric joined him. "Well," Eric said, "allow me to buy you a drink. Existence is not simple, Duprey."

"Shit on existence!" Duprey said. *"I'll* buy *you* a thousand drinks!"

3

Eric and Duprey had long since paid off John, and now they were in the back room of Les Trois Filles where the lamps were lit and the acrid red Algerian wine was flowing freely. The bar itself had been closed for over an hour. Now Monsieur and Madame Martin, their son Jacques, and their

185

one-legged sea gull Monsieur le Duc were all at the kitchen table with Duprey and Eric. It seemed that they all liked one another very much—except that the nature of the sea gull's affections could not readily be determined; his only visible interest was in catching flies. He hopped about on the bare wooden top of the table, snapping up the wine-drugged insects with unflagging enthusiasm; he could pick one from the rim of a glass without upsetting the wine, making only the faintest click of his bill against the edge. There was a quality of neurotic intensity about the bird that was shared by the son of the family. Jacques loved to pour liquor or wine. He would turn the bottle completely upside down, and at the last split second he would stop the flow of liquid by dipping the neck of the bottle into the glass, thus cutting off the entrance of air; then with an incredibly deft twist of the wrist he would turn the bottle right side up again. All this was done with a nervous concentration far beyond anything available to the entirely sane. Earlier, before the bar closed, Eric had seen Jacques pour a thimbleful of Cointreau from a vertically inverted bottle without spilling a single drop. Jacques was a thin young man with haunted, anxious, mocking eyes. There was a bond of specialized madness between the boy and the bird.

"We lack many things," said the elder Martin, "but thank God we have wine. It is rank stuff, and we long for the beautiful wines of the continent. Before the war we shipped all our wines to France to be sold as the lowest grade of *vin ordinaire,* while here in the colonies we drank only the good wines of France. I would give all the wine in Algeria for one bottle of the ordinary white wine of Anjou."

"Well, soon those things will be here again," Eric suggested. "Already the Americans have taken Cherbourg, and yesterday the British completed the encirclement of Caen."

"Thank God for the Americans," said Madame Martin.

Monsieur Martin was a small man with blue marble eyes and a black mustache. He was polite, he enjoyed himself. It was impossible to say whether he was a strong or a weak character, yet there was no question but what he would be equally at home in heaven or hell. His wife, however, was an obviously strong character. She was a tall and very handsome woman with silvery white hair drawn severely back from her high forehead and tied in a knot at the nape of her neck. There was dignity and beauty and inexhaustible tenacity in her old face.

Duprey was an uncommonly expert man at holding his liquor, but at this time he was showing it more than anyone else.

"You're all good people," he said. "You're all decent, and it's a crying shame, a crying shame that you have to do without *any*thing. A goddamn crying shame."

"C'est la guerre," said Monsieur Martin.

"C'est la vie," corrected Madame Martin.

Monsieur le Duc nipped a fly from the edge of Eric's glass, and Jacques Martin refilled it from a bottle inverted ten inches above the top of the glass. "Thank you," said Eric, addressing his remark both to the sea gull and the young man.

Jacques had been in the Foreign Legion for a while, but he had had an experience out on the desert. Jacques did not care to discuss that experience. In fact, he did not care to discuss anything. He knew English as well as did his father and mother, but he had confined himself to three or four brief sentences during the entire night. The longest of these sentences was: "Let us all have some more wine before this open bottle turns entirely to *vinaigre!*" He did not drink as much as the others, but he had an urgent need to pour.

Eric seemed to be going through succeeding waves of drunkenness and complete sobriety. He had never seen a sea gull at close range before and the experience somewhat unnerved him. Never before in all his life had he seen a tame one-legged sea gull hopping around on a table and eating flies from the edges of the wine glasses. Its gray feathers looked shabby and flea-bitten; its compact and monomaniacal aliveness was sinister and frightening. Yet Eric felt that if he had a few more drinks perhaps this phenomenon would no longer be frightening; it might even become reassuring.

They made their way through narrow alleys, and it was very dark. The moon was hidden by clouds. They crossed the public square and then followed the road that led along the waterfront to the ore dock. Eric and Duprey followed Jacques, Duprey keeping the beam of his flashlight focused on the ground somewhat ahead of the French boy. Every once in a while a group of ghostly shapes would materialize, now to one side and then to the other. And Duprey would quickly throw the light upon them and they would slink away. Often they would come close enough to leave the fleeting vision of an arm upraised to shield the eyes, a grinning mouth, a ragged shirt. Once in a while Jacques yelled something in French or shouted a word in Arabic. The sounds of shrill, barking laughter answered him from the darkness.

"What things did we promise them?" Duprey asked. "I forget now—we talked about so many things."

"Sugar and rice," Eric said, "and coffee and a piece of fresh meat."

"They shall have the best," said Duprey. "The very best our larder affords. Decent and noble people."

"That they are."

Then they both became aware of a strange sound: it was a deep-throated, sustained vibrancy, so deep and insistent that it could be felt against the flesh.

"A ship's whistle," Eric said.

"We're the only ship in the harbor."

"What's up?"

"Benson must be working on the whistle. It was all screwed up, but we couldn't waste steam on the way over."

When they arrived at the ore dock the whistle had stopped blowing. They left Jacques and went on to the conveyor. It was not moving, but they climbed along it until they could drop onto the deck of the ship. The purser was waiting for them. He rushed forward to greet them and they saw that he had his pistol strapped at his waist.

"My Gawd almighty!" he gasped. "You made it!"

"Made what?"

"Made it back alive!"

"Alive?"

"My Gawd! Don't you know what's been going on? We've been blowing the whistle for an hour to get you back on board ship. We've got a posse organized. We were just going off to search for you."

Then he proceeded to tell them excitedly what had been

happening here at the dock. It seemed that earlier in the evening Benson, the third engineer, and the seaman called Kentucky had strolled down to the dock entrance to see if they could buy some native coins from the children. No sooner were they outside the gate than they were attacked by a mob of boys ranging from ten to sixteen. Each had his job to do. One grabbed the engineer's left arm, another his right, one the left leg, another the right; others held him around the waist. Benson was a very strong man, but in this situation he was helpless. They paid no attention to Kentucky, and the seaman opened his knife. The biggest of the boys took out a knife that was much longer. Kentucky closed his knife and put it back in his pocket. The Moroccan soldier who guarded the dock was standing about fifteen feet away. They called to him. He turned his back and lit a cigarette. The little Arabs removed Benson's expensive wrist watch, released him and slipped away into the dark. Then a short time later several of the seamen returned to the ship with information about what had happened to three British sailors in Beni-Saf about a week past. They had all been killed. Their throats had been cut and their sexual organs severed and stuffed into their mouths. There were no French police in Beni-Saf.

They were walking toward the saloon as the purser gave them all this information, and when they entered the brightly lighted room they found the posse. Most of the officers were armed with pistols. The others had sheath knives, jackknives, or clubs. They all looked a little bit embarrassed when they saw the men they were supposed to rescue. There was a lot of talk as they began to disband. The purser had seemed frightened and happy, with something of the shrill excitement of a eunuch who has been invited to an official slaughter. Now he was disappointed. Eric followed Duprey to his quarters on the boat deck.

"To hell with all this nonsense," Duprey said. "We promised those people some rice and sugar, and they're going to get it. I don't know about you, but I'm going back."

Eric's mind was still quite rational. This is utter foolishness, he thought. Those people aren't starving. All we can do for them essentially is to let them taste some rice instead of beans for a few days, some beef instead of goat, let them use less chicory and more sugar in their coffee for a while. It's stupid showing off and childish recklessness, he thought.

"Okay," he said, "let's go."

Duprey had two thirty-eight caliber Colt revolvers. They loaded these and put them in their pockets with some extra cartridges. Duprey found two clean pillowcases in his closet, and they each stuffed one of these inside their shirts to use as a sack. Then they went below.

They met the captain coming up the ladder from the main deck, and he looked at them suspiciously. "I hope there's something left in the icebox," Eric said, feebly attempting an expression of innocence. "We are really about starved!"

"Very true," said Duprey, "very, very true."

"And by the way," said Captain Brogan, "there's a DE alongside and we've got new orders. We're not taking on our ballast here. We're going to another port. So do not make the error of not being on board when we sail at five A.M."

"Naturally we will be on board, Captain," said Duprey.

Brogan looked at their bulging clothes where the pistols and pillowcases protruded. "Naturally," he said in a tone of hopeless disgust and weariness, "naturally."

There was no trouble getting into the storeroom. Duprey had a key to it because part of his job was keeping the refrigerators in repair.

The return trip to Les Trois Filles was much like the trip down. The shouts of Jacques Martin and the beam of the flashlight seemed enough to keep the Arabs at a distance.

Monsieur and Madame Martin could not quite conceal their astonishment at the fact that the two Americans had actually returned with bags of food. They exchanged glances of surprised pleasure and brought out more wine. They had put the glasses away but now they brought out some clean ones. They all gathered around the table and examined the food. The rice and sugar delighted them, the coffee aroused only a polite response, and when they came to a ten-pound package of dried prunes their faces revealed a brief disappointment.

"You are magnificently kind," said the old lady.

"*Vive l' Amérique!*" said Monsieur Martin, looking at them curiously out of his inscrutably polite blue marble eyes.

190

"Let us not allow the wine to sour," said Jacques, as he expertly filled the clean glasses.

They drank to America and France, and to each other, and to the extermination of Germans, Petainists, and *les Japonais*. Monsieur le Duc seemed even more intent than he had been before they brought the food. He was infallible; he flapped his clipped and flea-bitten wings as he went about his business. When there were no longer any flies to catch he began to peck at imaginary ones, and these he swallowed with even greater satisfaction than the real ones.

And Jacques seemed to share this unilateral expansion of spirit. He poured with phenomenal vivacity. He seemed dissatisfied each time he failed to fill a glass so full that only the surface tension of the fluid kept it from spilling.

"And one more thing," said Duprey, "one more thing to drink to."

They all picked up their glasses.

"And that is," Duprey continued, "to the extermination of all people who are *indecent.*"

The first engineer's face was red and beaded with sweat and there was a living glow of angry pain in his eyes.

"*À bas les indecents!*"

"Down the hatch!"

"Come, come, *mes frères d'armes,* do not permit the wine to become too sour."

"As if that were possible!"

"To their extermination!"

Eric wanted to say something about *within ourselves,* but the cumulative structure of unhappiness and shame that he had seen in Duprey was too vast for casual recognition or virtuous platitudes. "Let's drink a toast to a new world," he said, "a world that will be exciting enough to make war and greed *and* indecency seem very dull, too dull to exist."

While they were all thinking this over, Duprey was struck by a thought. "My God!" he said. "We forgot the meat!"

It was true; they had forgotten to go into the ship's refrigerator and take out a piece of beef.

"Oh, it is nothing," said Madame Martin. "Perhaps tomorrow."

"No, by Jesus," said Duprey, "there *is* no tomorrow. You must have it tonight! What d'you say, Eric?"

191

Eric was still sober enough to know that what they were doing was thoroughly ridiculous. But he felt that within the present consciousness of his friend it was *not* ridiculous. And therefore he agreed that they must by all means go and get some beef.

Duprey stood up. "Come on, Jacques," he said, "let's go!"

But a grayness had come over Jacques. All the vivacity of his wine pouring had suddenly left him.

"No, Monsieur," he said, "I cannot go."

Duprey was astonished. "Can't go?" he said. "Why not?"

The young man was silent, his eyes fixed on the sea gull as though he were seeing the bird for the first time.

Monsieur Martin had now turned livid with anger. He had lost all his *savoir-faire*—that poise which Eric had imagined would survive both heaven and hell—and he shook a trembling finger at his son. "Coward! coward! coward!" he shouted. "Go and help our friends bring us a little meat from America!"

But the boy's eyes were glazed with inward visions and fixed stubbornly upon the bird. *"Monsieur le Duc, Monsieur le Duc,"* he said, *"vous est très intelligent."*

The father stood up and raised his hand as though he were about to strike his son.

At first Eric had thought that Madame Martin was siding with her husband, but now she stood up and waved her hands at him with an anger that was as the sea is to the headlong brooklet. "Be quiet," she said. "Jacques is tired. He cannot go. If our friends wish to bring us some meat it will be all right for them to do it alone."

"Mais ouis, but what will happen—?"

"Fermez vôtre boit!"

All this family argument was beginning to embarrass Duprey. "Come, come," he said. "It's okay if Jack is tired. I know the way now. You just keep the home fires burning and we'll be back in a flash—with beefsteak! And nothing but the best!"

The clouds had thinned now and the steep white-walled streets of the town were illumined by filtered moonlight. Duprey walked ahead, carrying the flashlight but not turning it on. Eric no longer felt that what they were doing was absurd. He could not now evaluate the moment in terms of the reasonable and unreasonable. The moment existed. The ghost-white Arab town was around them.

Some dim shapes moved toward them as they entered the open space of the square. Duprey shined his flashlight on them, but this time they did not vanish. The light had lost its potency. It was reflected back in the gleam of knife blades. Duprey switched off his light and fired his pistol over their heads and they ran away. The pistol made a red flash, and orange sparks flew up from its muzzle and from around the cartridge chamber. Eric fired his own revolver into the air. The two reports were sharp, like the snapping of large whips, and then there came echoes from the hills. There were no more dangerous shapes. The magic had worked. This was better than light.

Was it the movies, the stage, or pulp fiction; or Ibáñez or Dumas or the Old West? Whatever else it was, it was delightful. It took Eric back to the most exciting moments of his childhood. Playing cowboy. "All right, stranger, reach for yer shootin' iron." Cops and robbers. "I shot you first so *you're* dead!" "Did not! I shot *you* first! Bang! Bang!" "Okay, mister, you're covered. Put up your dukes and leave that lovely sweet girl alone! Bang! You see? Now you're dead!" The primal ego is really at home when its body is carrying a pistol and the others are less modernly equipped. "So you will, will you? All right then—*bang!* Now you see things differently, eh?" And things, at last, are as they should be. No more nonsense.

Eric fired again, this time aiming at the moon; Duprey laughed and fired twice in the same general direction. Then they walked on downhill through the melodrama of narrow foreign streets. They were on a mission of grave importance, a mission of irrational generosity. They must get there in time to pay off the mortgage, save her from a fate worse than living, or bring the beef. Yet the real town was around them and Eric could see it, feel its pavement under his feet, and smell its goatlike perfume of confined animals and coffee and liquor and heated plaster and night coolness. This was a real place which he now saw only as a symbol in the structure of his own internal narrative, as he was but a symbol within the structure, the special dream of this place.

Duprey had been turning this way and that, apparently taking pride in his ability to find their way back to the ship. Eric followed him without thinking about direction. His only idea of location was the knowledge that downhill must lead eventually to the harbor. Now Duprey turned abruptly to the left around the corner of a building. It was as though he had made it part of his game to astonish Eric by suddenly disappearing. Eric entered into the spirit of the thing and crouched in a doorway, expecting his friend to reappear. He was smiling to himself as he crouched there holding his pistol and peering into the shadows. Duprey is playing a game with me, he thought.

Then he heard a scuffling sound and a short, grunting cry of pain. What was Duprey doing? Eric advanced cautiously toward the corner of the building and looked around it.

He saw Duprey lying on the pavement and a half-dozen dim figures bending over him. He raised his revolver and fired. There were loud exhalations and one of the figures fell. The others ran off into the darkness. Eric went forward and knelt beside Duprey. He felt around and found the flashlight and turned it on Duprey's face. There was a hole in his throat and Eric could hear the bubbling sound of the blood that flowed from it. He shook the shoulders of his friend.

"Duprey!"

The engineer's eyes were wide open and staring, and the voice that came out of him gurgled as though he were speaking under water. It reminded Eric of the childhood sounds of ducking for apples at Halloween parties.

"You better get going," the bubbling voice said, "and don't waste your cartridges. I can't get up. I got it in the belly too!"

"Don't be foolish," Eric said. "I won't leave you. Somebody will hear the shots and come down here."

"It won't make any difference," Duprey said. "You can't —you can't put a tourniquet on a neck . . ."

He made a ghastly sound that must have started as a laugh.

"They'll come," Eric said hopelessly.

Then Duprey's body began to shake with violent convulsions and he vomited his liquor. Eric had turned off the flashlight, not wanting to be too visible to those who were near them. All he could hear now was the soft, thick bubbling of blood and the evil sound of bare feet padding softly against the pavement in the shadows. He heard this murderous padding from all sides. It was a waiting sound, a giggling sound, a killing sound.

Duprey stopped his shuddering and vomiting, but now he began to breathe heavily, choking inhale and gurgling exhale. "I ought to have a priest," he said. "I'm a Catholic."

My God, Eric thought. A priest. Here and now. What a place and what a time to ask for a priest. But this man is dying. How can I give him a priest?

"Duprey," he said, "if you will take things easy, we will get a priest. You must hold on. You mustn't give up. You're going to be all right if you hold on. I'll get you a priest. But now you must just hold onto yourself until somebody comes."

Duprey had stopped breathing. Eric thrust his hand inside his friend's shirt. It was strange to feel the hairy skin and the flat smoothness around the nipple of the male breast. The heart was not beating under the warm skin. Duprey was dead.

Soon I will be dead, Eric thought. I must save my cartridges and walk downhill. Then he noticed the other body that was sprawled about five feet away from Duprey. He turned his flashlight on it.

He saw a small figure dressed in ragged clothes. He turned the light on its face. The mouth was open, the eyes were rolled back, there was a gay and gruesome look of release about the gaunt dead head of the ten-year-old Arab boy he had killed.

He switched off the flashlight as he heard the sound of bare feet moving with an increased excitement, closer, closer, closer. Save your cartridges and walk downhill.

Every once in a while they came closer, and it was like an old childhood nightmare: the footsteps of the running figure closer and closer behind him, the evil, dark thing that would destroy him utterly, destroy him with evil laughter that would echo in the black halls of eternity. And there would be nothing left of him but this laughter, nothing, nothing ever—no one would know. Now he crept through nightmare alleys and several times he fired his revolver; he no longer shot at the moon. He heard cries of pain and fear, but the barefoot death would not give him up. He felt the darkening fumes of liquor in his brain and knew that the others were counting on that to drive him into a false move. He reloaded his revolver. When he arrived at the harbor road he turned left and eventually he arrived at the ore dock. As the sounds of the others faded back behind him he transferred his attention to the Moroccan guard. As he walked through the gate he kept his pistol hidden under his jacket and pointed at the guard.

The conveyor had been raised, and it was necessary for him to drop about ten feet to the deck. He sprained his ankle slightly but he could still walk. He made his way to the captain's quarters.

He turned his flashlight on the bulkhead by the open door until he found the switch. When the light went on Captain Brogan sat bolt upright in bed. "What the hell you mean coming in here?" he asked, rubbing his eyes.

"Duprey has been killed," Eric said. "He was killed by the Arabs. He's back in the town."

Brogan sat there sleepily feeling his tanned farmerlike face. "Killed . . ." he said, and it was neither question nor exclamation.

"That's right," Eric said. "They stabbed him in the throat and other places. We were coming back from a bar in town. He's lying there in the street now."

Brogan was in no way astonished but the look he gave Eric was beyond speech. "You've just helped get rid of the best first engineer I've ever had," he said.

"We ought to go and get his body," Eric said. "God knows what they've done to him already."

"His body!" the captain snorted disgustedly. "Who the hell wants his body?"

"Well, he's dead there," Eric said. "He's just lying there in that alley. He wanted a priest."

The captain laughed in an unhumorous way and lay back upon his pillow. "I guess you haven't seen many men die," he said. "They always want this and that. When I was in a lifeboat for eighteen days after the first ship I lost, the only thing the radio operator wanted was a cigar. And then finally when we sighted the island the guy said, 'Gentlemen, if you

196

will excuse me, I must go down to the corner after a cigar.'
And he stepped overboard into the water. Nobody cared.
Before that we'd seen the third mate go nuts and we had had
to kill him and throw him overboard because he wanted to
drink blood. I had a raw potato to suck on. I guess that's
why I stayed alive. But as for wanting a priest in Beni-Saf!
You're a damned fool!"

"I didn't want a priest," Eric said. "Duprey did."

"Duprey doesn't want anything any more," the Captain
said. "We'll get his body in the morning before we sail and
we'll bury it at sea. You better go to bed now and sober
up. We sail at five. And before that you'll have to take some
of the men back to the body."

"I don't have to sober up. I happen to be sober."

"Sure you're sober. Any drunk thinks he's sober after he's
seen blood."

"Good night."

"Are you absolutely sure he's dead?"

"I'm sure."

"Well, then for Christ's sake," the captain said, "turn
out the light and let me get some sleep!"

16: The Garment of Enchantment

It took two days to get to Bône, and the belief on board the
ship was that they were going there to take on some sort of
ballast, such as worn-out airplane engines, scrap iron from
what had been mechanized equipment, or something of that
sort. Or they might, Van suggested, be going to take on a
cargo of *effects*. Many ships returned from these ports with
that sort of ballast.

Effects, the first mate explained, were the personal pos-
sessions of soldiers who had been killed. His last ship in the
Pacific had taken on a load of effects, and the seamen had
all found it very depressing. It was worse than carrying high
explosives. All day long the winches had hauled up the slings
loaded with neat wooden boxes. They were of many sizes.
Some of the dead men had had only enough of material pos-

sessions to make a box of one cubic foot; others had had enough to fill a piano crate. They were each addressed with the name of the dead man and the army depot in Kansas City where such matters were taken care of. It was said that diaries and other records had to be removed and held until after the war; the rest was sent on to the next of kin. Vangaussen did not articulate to Eric all that he had felt about that cargo, but neither did he need to do so.

Each of these boxes was the meager terminal point of a personality. Destination. A box of clothing, books, souvenirs —inanimate things that now must speak a kind of sign language to those who had loved the dead man. In every box there must have been achievement and failure and goodness and evidence of guilt. Strange ballast for a ship, strange official gifts for the multitudinous bereaved. What was left of these men? Whatever whole or separate fragments of their bodies now moldered in the soil, this box of "effects," and whatever memories they had left in the minds of those who had known them. Precarious extension, now utterly vulnerable to the corrosive currents of decay and indifference.

But it turned out that the *SS William Benson* was not to take on a cargo of effects. The Navy was to give them a different task.

They had buried the body of Duprey at sea on the afternoon of the day they left Beni-Saf. When they had found it during the early morning of that same day, it was completely stripped of clothing and badly mutilated. They had tied some scrap iron to its feet, wrapped it in a WSA sheet and, with some words from the captain, had slipped it overboard. The captain had not read the regular burial service. He had had a Bible in his hand but he had not read from it.

"Duprey was a Catholic," he said embarrassedly, "and we don't have any priests to give him the kind of a service he would want. So all I can say myself is that he was the best first engineer I ever had and I'm sorry he's dead. He was a good man, too; as good as they come. And I hope if there is anything that happens to people after they die that Duprey will get the best of everything, because he deserves it. Amen."

2

On the morning of July 6, 1944, Eric was awakened by the junior engineer shaking his shoulder.

"Come on, come on," said Chuck, "get out of that sack! Rise and *shine* for the Matson *Line!*"

Eric sat up on his bunk; he could tell at once that they were tied to a dock. "So how does Bône look to you?" he asked. "Are we taking on ballast yet?"

Chuck's face was enlivened with a queer and perverse glee. "Wait till you *see* the ballast we're taking on!" he said. "Just wait! Here, take a look out this porthole!"

Eric padded across the warm iron of the deck on his bare feet, rubbed his eyes, and peered out the porthole from which Chuck had removed the wind scoop. He saw a dock and some buildings illuminated by blinding sunlight. The dock was covered with hundreds of oil drums. He could see Arab workmen loading some of these into a sling; and then he heard the rattle of the winch cables as the drums were swung on board the ship. "What is it?" he asked.

Chuck replied slowly, savoring his words. "That, my friend, is one-hundred-octane gasoline. In drums—*and* in beach-head cans. One—hundred—octane."

Eric got dressed and went down to breakfast. He felt a little sick in the solar plexus. He had been sure that they would be going home, and now it was obvious that such was not to be their destination. The reactions of the other men appeared to be divided. Either they partook of the malicious and perverse inward pleasure that seemed to be in the junior engineer, or else they just looked depressed and slightly sick, the way Eric felt.

After breakfast Eric wandered around on the main deck and watched the loading. He stood beside one of the oilers, a dark-skinned young man with a burn scar across one side of his face and a manner of quiet intelligence. The oiler was one of those who were not pleased. He watched the loading of the gasoline drums with tired and disappointed eyes. "And to think," he said, "that I gave up sailing on tankers!"

"You did?"

"I got off *two* that were burning and then I figured I'd

stretched my luck as far as it would stretch. So I wouldn't ship out on any more tankers."

"I see."

"And this stuff is twice as bad." He spoke matter-of-factly, like a tired surgeon talking to a colleague. "When you're hit, some of the drums are split open and the fire from them heats the others. High octane vaporizes very fast. Then phooey! The whole works goes up. It's worse than TNT because everything is covered with flame. You don't die as quick."

"Only minutes of difference, I should think."

"Yeah—but I've seen men die on tankers. In the water and on the ship. And minutes can be awfully long when a guy is on fire."

There were several crews of Arab dock workers, and each had its chief. But the chiefs did not work, nor did they supervise, nor did they, for the most part, remain awake. They carried shepherd staffs and their fingers were covered with silver rings, and they lay on top of the drums in the sun and slept. Then every once in a while one would awake and sit up. He would begin to curse his men for their inefficiency, stupidity, and laziness. Then he would demand a cup of water and one of their number would bring it to him, bowing respectfully. And the chief would drink it and then go back to sleep.

There were also a number of British and American noncoms who were really supervising the work, but apparently they could not manage the job without hiring these little chieftains.

Hartley came up to Eric and put his hand on his shoulder. "Ready to go ashore?" he asked. "This Bône is a real town, I hear. Everything you want. Even beer. They've got the shore passes up in the purser's quarters. Let's get going."

"I don't think I'll go ashore this morning," Eric said. "Got a lot of stuff I want to do."

"What the hell! There's plenty of time at sea to wash clothes and write letters! Come on!"

"No, not this morning."

"Okay, you're the doctor. See you later."

As Eric mounted the iron ladder to the boat deck and continued on toward his own quarters he felt a disquieting surprise at his own reaction to this new place. He had not brushed Hartley off because he wanted to go ashore by himself. The disturbing truth of the matter was that he did not want to go ashore at all. He wondered if he had lost his nerve.

He stopped for a moment and leaned against the rail of the captain's deck where he could survey the dock from a higher elevation. He saw Hartley go ashore with Burley, and then several other groups of men left the ship. He did not want to be with any of them. Then he saw George Fiorini go ashore alone.

The little Italian was almost running, leaning forward, blind to all else but his destination, like a small dog that has caught the subtlest whiff of some distant bitch in heat. He skillfully circumvented gasoline drums and Arabs and disappeared in the dusty air where the trucks were arriving with more cargo.

During the past weeks Eric had seen George do this again and again. George was in pursuit of what he dreamed about during almost all his sleeping and waking hours in between times ashore.

Yet Eric knew from long observation that Fiorini was not bent on satisfying a simple appetite; he was, in fact, in search of love. Though he ran like a little Airedale toward the female scent, yet he was in search, not of the simplicity of mere excretory relief, but of love—divine love, answering love. The love that says with a great sigh of gratitude, "So *this* is what it was all about!" The love that recognizes, "So at last—it is you!" "And how amazing! You—really *you!*" "But how did you know me?" "After waiting for you all my life?" The laughter, the kindness, the turbulence that now and at last and finally is able to enter the unconfined vastness of the long-awaited miracle: return, fulfillment, destination, justification, and worship.

And as many times as Eric had seen George Fiorini start pantingly on this quest he had seen him return. Over and over again he had seen the Italian's disappointed face as he came into the bar where the other men had gathered. Always that look of melancholy that was beyond description. He had again not found it. For two dollars or a package of cigarettes he had again failed to buy the vision of Tristram and Abelard and Dante! He never ceased to be amazed at this. "Well, how was it?" someone would ask. And George, his face gray and very far from any humor, would say, "Oh —the same old stuff. Just the same old stuff."

A soldier that Eric had not seen before came up onto the deck and stood beside him, leaning on the rail and looking at the dock.

"Those Arab chiefs sure do earn their pay, don't they?" he observed.

"They work hard at sleeping, all right."

"They get almost all the money for the work, you know. They just give a few pennies to the men. Seems silly, but the men won't work any other way. Arabs are funny."

"I've seen people all over that went out of their way to be exploited."

"But you must admit that the Arabs really are good at it! What can those lousy little chiefs give them? Nothing!"

"The chief gives them a place in the world. He identifies them for themselves. He tells them who they are and what they believe in. That's what most men seem to want primarily—once their basic needs of survival are taken care of."

The soldier looked at Eric searchingly, as though he were a little surprised. "I guess you're right," he said. "That's what makes Nazis."

"Yes," Eric said, "and saints."

"That's why the Irish could never go Nazi."

"How d'you mean?"

"Every Irishman wants to tell *himself* what his position is and what he believes."

Eric laughed. "Oh, I don't know about that," he said. "For one thing, every Irishman has a ready-made place in the world just by virtue of being Irish. They're nationalistic and devout and they love strong leaders. Isn't that the raw material that goes to make a good Fascist?"

"I suppose it is. But in the Irish there's another belief that's stronger than their faith in what they happen to be supporting."

"And what's that?"

"The right to rebel against it."

This is no run-of-the-mill soldier, Eric said to himself: he has ideas.

They introduced themselves.

"Joe O'Neil."

"My name's Eric Clark."

"English?"

"By remote descent—about six generations ago."

"That's long enough to be forgiven."

"My mother's name was Casey."

"Well, well! So that makes it really forgivable."

It turned out that Sergeant O'Neil was liaison officer between the Americans and British in this British-controlled port whenever there was a problem of shipping out American army cargo. It seemed rather suprising to Eric that a noncom should be entrusted with such responsibility. But it was not surprising to O'Neil.

"We get sort of informal," he said. "Colonel Hennesy likes me. He's the one that got my stripes back for me last time."

It further developed that O'Neil was staying on the ship until it was loaded. They had given him the medical room to sleep in. He had been studying engineering at Cal Tech when the draft got him. His father was a manufacturer of plumbing supplies, and he had intended to go into the same business as soon as he got out of college. He dreamed of designing the toilet of the future, he said. Something that would really reward its user with a sense of security and aesthetic satisfaction. Eric identified his own immediate past and found that O'Neil was respectfully pleased to meet an ex-professor, though he was by no means obsequious. "Aren't you going into town?" he asked.

"Not today."

"Would you care for a drink?"

"Well, it's a little early, but . . ."

"But?"

"But let's have one—if you have it. I'm out."

"I've got a fifth of Scotch in my bag."

Joe O'Neil was a short, compact, blond young man, with a manner that was arrogant but not truculent. Now he sat in Eric's warm stateroom and they drank the Johnny Walker Black Label with water. They did not seem to get drunk. It was still morning. All that the liquor seemed to do was to cause a more sharp division between the men and their environment. The room, the ship, the Algerian port of Bône,

203

the Mediterranean, Africa, the war, one-hundred-octane gasoline, the iron bulkheads, the noise of the winches, the small and warm and comfortable isolation of the stateroom —all this was sharpened by separation. They felt less *part* of it and more *participating* in it. The fumes of gasoline became oppressive, and Eric closed the porthole and turned on the light. They talked without haste.

O'Neil had been wounded during the long siege of Cassino and he still had a considerable number of shrapnel fragments in him.

"I never thought anything like that would happen to me," he said. "I just thought I would spend my life designing better and better toilets, and get married and settle down. I never thought people would be shooting at me."

"But I gathered from what you said before that you felt Irish enough to start a revolution."

"No—I just like to think that it *can* be done. My uncle died in the Easter Rebellion. But I'm a peaceful guy. I've never even fought with my own father. We've never had a bad word together. Just luck, I guess. But what he wanted me to do happened to be just what I wanted to do. Funny, isn't it?"

"Well—unusual."

"Then when I got into this business over here I got into trouble several times. I flunked out of Officer School. Then I lost my stripes twice. Once I just said I was going to quit the war if they were going to fight it this way. And the other time I socked a captain. I think he was a fairy. Anyway, if he wasn't, he should have been. That was when Colonel Hennesy went to bat for me. He hated the guy too. The sonofabitch! They sent him back to the Pentagon."

They had a few more drinks of the good Scotch and then O'Neil began to talk about the things that had happened to him up front and in the hospital. According to popular legend, soldiers who have been in battle do not want to talk about it. Eric had always doubted this and now he saw that it was not true, but he also saw the source of the legend. If a man is inarticulate, or articulate only in terms of the smug truisms of sheltered and respectable family life, he cannot bear to reduce the shocking experiences of mass murder to those terms. But if he is really articulate in the first place, he will have a very urgent need to talk about what has happened to him.

Eric got out the uncompleted manuscript of his story about the "Enemy" and gave it to O'Neil to read.

"I've probably made lots of mistakes in the battle stuff," he said. "So I'd appreciate it if you'd write in any corrections that occur to you." Then he lit a cigarette and went out on the deck, anxious that O'Neil should really read the manuscript.

The whisky in his veins had the effect of making the scene on the dock and the view of the city much more picturesque. Some veiled women had come down to the dock, bringing food for their men. Eric wondered if there could be a beautiful face beneath any of those dirty cloths. He doubted it. He had a feeling that only the ugly women were sufficiently pious to hide their faces. Yet there was one woman who walked like Jane, striding with a kind of boldness that remained utterly feminine. He began to want Jane, and the wanting was a physical pain above his stomach, just as though he had been struck an unexpected blow under his ribs, a blow that made the solar plexus radiate a heavy ache all through the body. He wondered what Jane was doing at this moment. Her last letter had said that she had found a job. With the difference in time she should just about be getting up and preparing herself for work. He visualized her sitting in her slip on the bench in front of the vanity, putting up her hair and applying her make-up. He allowed himself to come up behind her, as he might have done had his body been 3500 miles from where it was, and to slip both his hands softly over her shoulders, down into her slip and brassiere, cupping her breasts. In his mind he kissed the top of her head as the female warmth in his two hands flowed into the rest of his body and canceled the pain that had begun to invade him. It is good to have loved someone, he thought.

And then he was startled by his own thought. Why was he thinking in the past tense? He corrected himself. It is good to love, he thought. But a feeling of separation was entering him, sharp and irresistible as a scalpel; its pressure was distance and its edge was time. And the wound that it made felt uncomfortably like prophecy.

For the first time he noticed that there were *No Smoking* signs chalked up around the ship, and he put out his cigarette. Then he returned to his stateroom to see if O'Neil had finished the manuscript.

The sergeant had put the papers down on the bench beside him and was sitting there frowning over a freshly lit cigarette. He looked up at Eric and there was a puzzled expression on his face. "This story," he said slowly, "is about —me!"

"Really?"

"Hell, yes! These are the very things *I've* been trying to figure out, and even what *happens* to the guy is almost what happened to me!"

Eric was pleased. "Well, I'll be damned!" he said. "Imagine meeting your character right in mid-story. It's like that play by Pirandello—*Six Characters in Search of an Author*. Or maybe it's seven characters. Well, I'll be damned. Let's have another drink. Character Has Drink with Author."

"Did you have to get me hit by those shell fragments?" O'Neil asked. "That was a hell of a thing to do!"

They sat over their drinks, smiling and musing over this curious circumstance. "This is an opportunity that very few writers have," Eric said. "I can have my central character correct the manuscript for me. And what is much more important—finish it."

"I can't understand how you could know all those things," O'Neil said. "Even what it was like at the moment when I got hit; that was exactly right. It seems impossible, but that is exactly the way it was. Are you sure you've never been wounded in battle?"

"I've thought about it a lot. But I hadn't even been shot at until a few weeks ago. And nothing hit me then. And anyway, I wrote this before that happened."

"There were a few little things you were wrong about," O'Neil said, picking up the manuscript.

Eric went to the desk and found a small notebook and a pencil. "Proceed," he said. "Give me the works."

"Well, about that artillery barrage. The fact is that the heavy artillery would have been doing its stuff during the night, and at the time when your story begins—"

"*Our* story."

206

"Yeah, our story. When it opens they would probably be using only the lighter pieces—mortars and machine guns and maybe 88's and 75's. Then, when our men start across the valley they ought to have a smoke screen. It's white phosphorus smoke made by special mortar shells. Our press relations officers usually cut that out of news reports because they're afraid the public might confuse it with poison gas."

"Like the stuff we use on the ships, I guess."

"I suppose so. And then you've got to get the sounds of the German shells into it. The 105 howitzer—it's like the low rumbling of thunder that's far away. The 88 is a fast-firing piece—the most demoralizing of all, as far as I've seen. For some reason, no matter how far those 88's land from you they seem to be probing, probing just for you. The 205's come slow, like big freight trains rumbling toward you, and you always think you're right on the track. Our 155's are about the same, but they're going the other way and that's a different feeling altogether. Every time one goes over, you say 'Good! Go get the bastards!' "

"Go ahead," Eric said. "Go through the manuscript again."

O'Neil fingered through the sheets of paper diffidently. "Well, here," he said. "It says here: 'George heard the guy with the walkie-talkie sending back the command that would stop the barrage. And suddenly there was silence.' Well—there isn't ever any silence in a battle. A lull maybe, but not silence."

"Okay—good."

"And here it says: 'Then there was the foreign and evil sound of machine guns from above . . .' Well, machine guns just don't sound foreign to a guy by this time. They sound very familiar. A chattering and evil sound, maybe. It's evil, all right. But you feel you've lived with it all your life. And 'the wicked whisper of bullets . . .' You've got to remember that there's a hell of a lot of noise in a battle. Bullets don't whisper at you. They yell. It's very noisy."

O'Neil's face had broken out into a heavy sweat as he talked, and now he reached for the bottle and poured himself a drink of Scotch. "It's very noisy," he repeated, "very noisy."

Eric poured another drink into his own glass and put aside

the notebook. "And what about the rest of the story?" he said. "Who is the enemy?"

"Well," said O'Neil, "I felt like this George character in the beginning. I didn't know who I was supposed to be mad at. I couldn't figure out what I was doing over here trying to kill some guys before they killed me. That was the first stage. Then when I saw my buddies get killed—right beside me—I just knew it was the Germans. I hated them for having killed my buddies and I wanted to kill them. That was all there was to it. Then—like it says in the story—I saw some prisoners. I saw my enemy face to face for the first time. I looked into his tired eyes. I saw his broken spirit. And I recognized my own tiredness and my own nearness to the breaking point. I couldn't help but realize that he'd seen his own buddies die beside him and had hated the enemy that did it, the same as me. Then my mind was all screwed up—I couldn't figure out what we were doing. It seemed to me after I fought for a while that *some* people at a higher level had a quarrel to work out and that somehow all of us other people got roped into doing the dirty work and none of us could ever know what it was all about."

"There's a lot of truth in that feeling."

"But then when I got sent up front again—that was at Cassino—I got a different idea."

"How was that?"

"Well, I began to feel that we *were* different. He wasn't just another GI on the other side. You see, every night both sides send out medic squads to pick up wounded. They were in plain sight. Well, they used to shoot our guys. Finally our guys had to go out just like reconnaissance patrols, crawling on their bellies. But the krauts would come out standing up. We had orders not to shoot them and they knew it. Goddamn! We wanted to kill them! But it was court-martial if you did. Those were the orders! My best friend was a medic. Jake Stern. We went to school together. They killed him before our medics learned to crawl on their bellies."

The sweat was pouring down O'Neil's face and he was breathing heavily.

"Maybe it was just that they got different orders," Eric said. "In the Army you do what you're ordered to do, don't you?"

O'Neil's young gray eyes, which were ordinarily arrogant, gay, and good-natured, were now turned inward upon a bitter world. "We wouldn't have done that," he said. "No matter what the orders were, we would never have done that first. Even if we had had orders. We would have missed."

"But they were brought up differently," Eric said. And even as he said these words, with all their connotations of the lectures about environment that he used to deliver so brilliantly in his sociology classes, he felt that they must sound very foolish to this young man.

O'Neil looked as though he were smothering. "Sure," he said, "they were brought up differently. They were taught that if somebody tells you to kill unarmed medics that are going out to pick up wounded you're supposed to do it. And us? They left that out of our education. Well, my friend— that's your enemy! It's guys who *will* do that—and it don't make a goddamn bit of difference *why* they'll do it. Kill them! That's all! Kill them wherever you find them and kill them quick!"

O'Neil's face was now flushed dark red, and in his anger he had forgotten all politeness and all liking for Eric; his eyes were blind to the stateroom around him and the sweat was pouring down over the distended veins of his throat and wetting the collar of his shirt. "I want some air," he said. "I'll be back in a minute." And he felt his way out of the room as though he could not see. He rushed out of the room, and Eric, with tenderness and questioning despair, watched him go.

3

After lunch Eric found it difficult to pass the time; he tried to think of small physical tasks that needed doing. There was a washtub, a scrubbing table, and wringer down in the hold of the ship near the fresh-water tanks, and he took his dirty clothes down there to wash. The "library" was in the same space, and he spent some time while the clothes soaked in hot water straightening and dusting the hundreds of books. Then he laundered his things and took them up to hang in the fiddley where the hot air from the engine room would dry them quickly.

On his way back to his quarters he met O'Neil on the

boat deck. The Irishman seemed embarrassed and did not care to look him in the eye. "You'd better come up and get what's left of your Scotch," Eric said. "That must be pretty rare in these parts."

"Oh, I've got another ration coming," said O'Neil. "You can have what's left."

"Well, at least come up and help me finish it."

"I'm sorry, but I've got to go ashore. Business. Got to see Colonel Hennesy."

"Oh, I see. Well, thanks for the Scotch, and also for the sugestions about the story."

"Okay," said O'Neil, turning away.

Eric felt quite certain that the sergeant did not have to go into town on business; he had a feeling that O'Neil wanted to go ashore and get drunk—alone. Or perhaps with other combat infantrymen.

Eric still did not want to go ashore in Bône, and yet at the moment he did not like the idea of returning to his stateroom. He went down to the saloon for coffee. It was deserted. Everyone who was not on watch had left the ship. As Eric sat at the table stirring sugar into the thick black coffee, he began to feel more and more depressed. A few flies buzzed about the table and gasoline fumes drifted in through the open portholes to combine with the stale food smells from the galley; the iron rattle of the winches and the shouted orders and responses of the men came to him muffled and strange, unrelated to him, increasing his loneliness.

He put his empty cup in the bucket for dirty dishes, and then returned to his quarters, thinking again that he would try to write a letter to Jane. He glanced about the room, and the sight of the half-empty bottle, the two sticky glasses, and the pages of his manuscript strewn about on the bench somehow knocked from beneath him the last prop of his poise. After closing and locking the door he sat down at the desk, and he could feel the expression on his face stiffening like a mask of woe.

He asked himself why the mere sight of that manuscript had such a violently depressing effect upon him. And he knew the answer. It was because the problem of the "Enemy" story had been the original catalyst of his departure, the question that had sent him out of the intellectual and moral security of his own world, away from the things he understood and loved, away from Jane. And for what purpose? To what end? He had learned nothing, nothing at all. He was a thousand times more ignorant than he had been before!

Had he been able to do so, he would have wept; but not having really given way to tears since early childhood, he no longer knew how to do it. He poured a half-tumblerful of Scotch and sat staring at it. He did not want it.

What he wanted was the organic answer to his self: that answer which is beyond the word-world, the manifold answer to all those stresses of body and mind which composed his entity—and the questions to draw forth his own life-given answers. What he wanted was Jane. He had never been so depressed and lonely in his life. His brain was possessed by a fixed idea that he would never see her again. The ache of the loneliness was like a heart-rending music, a counterpoint of memory and prophecy, a poem of pain that destroyed entirely that cardboard structure which Eric, like every man, had set up for the polite charade of ordinary existence.

Out of the dream of his origins he tried to trace the sources of this music. He had begun school late because of a childhood illness, and so he was seven when they started him in the second grade at the Buchanan Street Grammar School. It was very strange to him. He felt aloof and embarrassed when they played the games. He wanted to go home. He could see no purpose in these ceremonies. But then there was a game where they all held hands and formed a large circle, and the girl who held his right hand wore a brown velvet jacket. Everything about her seemed to be like brown velvet. Her eyes were brown velvet. Her soul was brown velvet. And out of her hand there flowed a magic that suddenly transformed his entire world. It was not mother-magic nor friend-magic nor sister-magic. It was a magic that transformed, that beckoned, that promised what can never, never be put into words. She was very kind to him, aware of his embarrassment, aware of his worth. He was never in all the rest of his life to be looked at with such completely aware woman-eyes as those of the little girl in brown velvet. During the noon recess they sat together in the playground and ate their lunches. They exchanged food, each claiming, probably quite falsely, that they preferred the sandwiches of the other. There seemed to be nothing else to talk about. When they were through eating they sat there looking at each other, and Eric was bathed in a fluid of ecstasy. He was a thin little boy at this time, dark-haired and blue-eyed, rather grave and curious; and he had a look of extreme wisdom at seven that he was to give up by the time he was eight. They were sitting on the sill of a window, and he now began to drum on the windowpane with the fingers of his right hand; he did this thoughtlessly, making a complex rhythm to express something quiet but rhythmic within himself. The brown velvet girl watched him with delighted admiration. "How can you do it, how ever can you do it?" she asked. And she moved her own fingers in a hopeless way, striving to duplicate the expert applications of his fingernails to the plate glass. It had never before in all the long seven years of his life occurred to him that a way of tapping fingers against a windowpane could be regarded as something difficult and admirable. He was enchanted by this discovery. He tapped and tapped, straining his fingers to produce more and more complex patterns. Yet at the same time he felt a desire to be modest. He wanted her to know that it was nothing. It was something that anybody could do with a little practice. He was pleased that she took this to be a wonderful accomplishment, but he wanted her to know that he himself did not regard it highly. There were other things he could do. Things of greater magnitude. Yet he continued to drum with increasing madness until the bell rang and the noon recess was over. Then they were lined up in a boys' line and a girls' line and they diverged into different halls. He caught a last look from her eyes, and it was a look he could never cease striving to recapture; in that look was everything which in a woman is different from what is in a man—all of the indefinable magic that the one offers to the other, all the tragedy of inevitable farewell. And he never saw her again. For after this one day in school he became ill again and could not return to the Buchanan Street Grammar School. He retained only a brown velvet dream, and it was the most important dream that had ever come to him;

he could never look at velvet without celebrating a private Mass at the shrine of his first worship.

In the years that followed he draped the cloak of his first enchantment around other girls and grown women. He was never disenchanted; each successor wore it with a renewing grace. The dream did not fulfill its promises, but it maintained its strength by promising more and more. Even in his first sexual experience Eric did not find the ugly disillusionment that has stricken so many other very young men.

When he was fourteen the first erotic outcries of his own body entered his crystal dream of woman like tongues of flame, transmuting it to fire opal. For a while he lived in spiritual confusion, not knowing whether he was being robbed or enriched. Images of defilement filled him with fear, but other visions told him that this was a part of the language of the answer.

When he was fifteen he went to a place called the Welcome Hotel. His cousin Bruce had told him how to proceed. He was dressed in a new blue serge suit and had put lots of liquid vaseline on his pompadour. He had some cigarettes and matches. The colored maid at the top of the stairs asked him whom he wanted to see and he said that he wanted to see Jean. This was what his cousin had told him to say. He was trembling and he could feel his heart pounding with terror as he waited in the red-plush anteroom. Finally he heard the rustle of a satin skirt, and a young woman came toward him. She was dark-skinned, her black hair hung down to her shoulders, and her brown eyes were tired and intelligent. She looked at him quizzically and then led him down the hall to a bedroom. She closed the door and then they sat down, she on the bed and he on a straight chair. She kept looking at him searchingly, amused but kind. He offered her his cigarettes and she took one. He took one too, but before he could find his matches she had struck one of her own and she lit both their cigarettes. He tried to keep his hand from shaking, but it was useless.

"You look awfully young," she said. "You know, we get into trouble if we have boys that are too young come here." "I'm twenty-one," he said in a tremulous voice that tried to stay in its lower pitch and not jump into its falsetto. She did not smile. "Well," she said, "the landlady is out right now,

213

and if she should find out I took someone too young she'd fire me. We got into trouble a few months ago when a high school boy told on us. If the landlady was here I could ask her—but she isn't." The smoke from Eric's cigarette got into his eyes and tears streamed from them. Above all things he did not want Jean to think that he was crying. "The smoke got in my eyes," he said. And she did not smile. Her voice was extremely soft, almost velvet. "I'm afraid I can't do it," she said. "The landlady would be awfully mad. She'd fire me. I'm sorry. It isn't that *I* think you're too young. I'm sure you're not too young to—to make love. But I can't take the chance."

His throat was too tight to speak and she walked with him out of the room, down the hallway and into the ante-room. The colored maid was not at her table; they were alone. He had the two dollar bills folded into a small square in his pants pocket and now he took them out. He felt that this girl was ineffably lovely and good. "Here," he said, "I want to give you this anyway. I don't care about the other." She looked at the money very thoughtfully and then she looked at him again. "Your face is as beautiful as a girl's," she said. "You're a strange boy." He reached out his hand, wanting the contact of her hand for a moment before it was all lost forever. She looked at him very quietly out of experienced and tired eyes, and there was a richness of womanhood that was very close to the brown velvet of his first enchantment.

"Come on back," she said. "After all, you're twenty-one." And then, terrified all over again, he followed her back into the bedroom, and this time she locked the door. They undressed and lay down on the bed. She was as gentle with him as any dream of gentleness, as warm as the soul's welcome, as tender as the last caress of a lover condemned to death. Soon he lay quiet in the bed beside her and she caressed his forehead, looking into his face with a searching look that would haunt all the days of his life.

"Did I make you happy?" she asked. And though his being was full of the chaotic seething of a tragic love and suicidal gratitude, he said, "Yes—forever." Then she walked down the hallway with him again and this time they met a fat old woman playing with three Pekingese in the ante-

room. "Jean!" the old woman exclaimed. "What *are* you doing with this boy?" Jean did not answer at once but hurried
Eric toward the stairs.

She looked at him as though she were memorizing his
face. "Good-by," she said. "You be a good boy, now. Wait
until you fall in love." He could not say anything at all as
he turned away. He could only look at her once more, and
he saw in her eyes everything which in a woman is different
from what is in a man; all the indefinable magic which the
one would like to, but cannot, offer to the other, all the tragedy of saying farewell in the same breath with hello, and a
shadow of very tender irony. "Good-by," she said again, in
a low voice. "You're twenty-one, all right. I believe you
now." He tried to say good-by, but the word would not come
out.

A week later he went back to the Welcome Hotel and
asked for Jean, and the maid told him that there was nobody
there by that name. Then he knew that the boys' line and
the girls' line had diverged again and that he would never
again see the woman who had first extended the enchantment into something that could be touched, held in the
hands, kissed, invaded, possessed, and surrendered to. He
felt another sick pain of loss, an added treasure of being,
and a more authentic dignity.

From that time onward the renewed and extended dream
was applied successively, and sometimes simultaneously, to a
good many women; and none was a fulfillment, but each
was an exploration of it. He suffered jealousy and frustration
as well as wonder and delight; yet the worst experience did
not disillusion him and the best did not complete him, because somewhere in the back of his mind he held them all
to be no more than approximations. But sometimes, and
with increasing frequency as he grew older, an anguished
cry would break forth inside him, often at the climactic moment of love-making. And the sound of the cry was:
"Where is *my* woman? *My* woman!" This was an occur-
rence, not a fixation, and it did not interfere with his appreciation of many women; not merely a sensual appreciation,
but a reverent awareness of their separate identities. At this
same time his interest in the entire world was continually
expanding; his interest in a knowledge of things and of be-

ings, in the stupidities that men have inherited from the inertia of their methods, in the gross evils of life, and in its exultant realities. And the more he fell in love with the vastness of life the more he grew afraid of the diminishment of death—diminishment to zero. He had never been afraid of dying. He was afraid of that part of death which is not widely recognized. That is to say, not existing. Even from childhood he did not believe in the Halloween picture of death. He knew that death was not lonely, not dark, not cold, not damp, not worm-eaten—it was nothing. And this conception frightened him a thousand times more than the most fearful vision of hell-fire or tomb-imprisonment that has ever been conjured out of the burning pits of the human mind. For a long time he felt alone in this knowledge. He felt that others saw death as one of the aspects of life— dark, cold, light, warm, damp, dry, lonely, gregarious. But he knew that darkness and loneliness were aspects of life. To some persons this idea might have been a relief, but to Eric the relinquishment of his identity was the most awful of all possible prospects. A knowledge of the fact that one is *really* going to die causes one to cherish life, or to treat it lightly, or both. With Eric it was both. One knows the inestimable value of each moment and the complete futility of trying to conserve it. This was not a cerebral thing with Eric, but a nightmare of the flesh. And in the matter of love it pulled him in two opposite directions. It made him grasp at every wisp of beauty, and, in a sense, to compromise. It also created in him an insistent demand for no less than the ultimate and gave him a belief that he could *not* compromise. By the time he was twenty-four and had been appointed to teach sociology at UCLA he had grown more avid in many ways—but also a little tired. His concern with the internal dream had grown somewhat weary while his interest in the world around him was feverishly increasing. Perhaps the internal thing was not diminishing, but it had been put aside to some extent; not in disbelief, but in impatience.

At the beginning of his first teaching assignment at the University of California at Los Angeles he had not even noticed that Jane Laird was in his class. It was only when she began persistently staying to ask a question that he separated her from the homogeneity of the student group. Often the question that she stayed to ask was very close to the crux of his lecture, but at other times it was quite obviously fabricated out of next to nothing; it became a game with him to guess at what she might stay for at the end of the next class. And slowly he became aware of the girl herself. Her eyes were moss-green and rather somberly contemplative. She was tall and thin, with straight black hair. Her face was not pretty, but there was that quietness in it which is the foundation of all real beauty. There was an earnestness about her, yet she was not what is called an intellectual; hers was an inward and secret earnestness. Certainly what occurred to him was not love at first sight or even second sight. In the beginning she was a puzzle, a charming problem; and then he began gradually to see her as a quietude that was willing to receive him, a Cythera where the sick dishonesties of the social world could be forgotten, even though it might also be necessary to forget the most lyrical dreams of completion. He began to take her out and to find increasing pleasure in doing so. There was only a four-year difference in their ages, so the relationship of teacher and pupil did not remain important for more than a short time. They used to go to a Culver City roadhouse called the Red Mill every Friday night. Their approach to each other was tentative, gentle, and relaxed. One night Jane told him a story about her only former love affair. The story was about her relationship with a remarkably persuasive young man who had later turned out to be a gangster. Eric knew that objectively the story was a lie from beginning to end. She knew that he knew this, but this knowledge did not inhibit her elaboration of the myth. He also knew that she was only drawing circles around the real center of an earlier affair which must have been masochistic and futile and fundamentally dull. Since he certainly would not have wanted a girl who could entirely forego living during the first twenty years of her life, he was not disturbed by the knowledge of this former passion. Increasingly he began to think of Jane as a haven, an area of security from which to set forth again and again. He knew that she wanted to marry him long before he had decided that he wanted to marry her. He asked himself repeatedly if this was a compromise. Was he, at twenty-four, so beaten as to make a deal with life and settle for something a little less than infinity? He was still asking himself this when they went to Las Vegas and were married. That was more than seven years past now. And year by year, day by day, month by month, the structure of relationship had grown. In the beginning he had been so certain that he had made some sort of compromise with ultimacy that he felt rather grateful to the unnamed young scoundrel who had preceded him in Jane's affections. For this episode in her life somehow relieved him of a degree of responsibility: it saved him the necessity of pretending ecstasy when all he was feeling was satisfaction. But the structure grew much more rapidly than he was aware of—silently, swiftly, cell locked to cell, tissue upon tissue. The thousand little private realities of humor and association of meaning. The innumerable small tendernesses. The relief of discarding one after another of the false ornaments of the social façade. The continual expansion of the sexual experience as the body of one learned to trust the body of the other in the wordless terms of erotic loyalty and response. When Eric first became aware of this organic growth between himself and Jane, he tried to tell himself disparagingly that it was no more than a thing of habit. But a growth of habit must serve the purpose of easing the strain of new experience, and with Jane he was having experience that was continually more new. There was nothing for him to do then but acknowledge to himself that this was a truth of love beyond what he had foreseen. Visions flare and die as signal rockets flaming across the black sky; but how else does one achieve a living and working love but by the day-to-day and night-by-night addition to the sum of dream and reality? Not the average, but the *sum*. Eric could see this development now as he had never been able to see it before. And he knew that what now existed between himself and Jane was a living and clear-eyed and miraculous world beyond any he had ever created in his imagination. He knew that Jane was his woman and that he was her man beyond the faintest doubt. And now, sitting alone in his stateroom on the *SS William Benson* and listening to the sounds of the gasoline drums being lowered into the hold, he knew that he wanted Jane above anything else he had ever wanted. Yet— and this was the strangest part—he did not regret leaving her, nor his futile reason for leaving her. Because that seemed to be a part of the structure of what was right between them. They could not have been all that they were to each other had they not been all that they were separately. The exquisite and tender and secret things between them could not have occurred if she had not also been capable of having that former affair with the needful little criminal, and much less so had Eric been incapable of that irrational devotion to the human adventure that had finally torn them apart. He knew all these things now as he sat at his desk, and still he could not feel any desire to drink the Scotch in the glass in front of him.

Why had he refused to go into the city? After the killing of Duprey in Beni-Saf—was he afraid? Were his nerves shaken to some point of dissolution? O'Neil wanted to go in without him. Without . . . without. He felt certain that he would never see Jane again; yet his objective mind laughed at this. Everyone has premonitions. But it's only when coincidence makes them work that they make a big impression. I think I'll go into town, he thought. I'll walk around. I'm lonely for the sight of love. I'll walk around the town and look at things.

3

There was still daylight in the city of Bône, and its low amber rays illumined the shop fronts, the treetops of the Cours Jerome Bertagna and the nests of the great storks atop the buildings. There was a wide promenade running down the center of the Cours; it was lined on either side with trees, and there were cane-bottomed chairs and small iron tables along its entire length. Across the roadways which were on each side of the promenade at least every other place was a café or bar, and the waiters from these places took care of the customers at the promenade tables which happened to be more or less opposite their particular establishments. It was very cool under the trees, and more than half the tables were occupied. Eric walked slowly, savoring the strangeness of this foreign hub of life. Sailors— American, French and British; soldiers—British, Australian, South African, Canadian, French, American, Polish, Sikh, and Moroccan. Arab chiefs from the outlands, bearded, fierce-faced, white-robed, carrying long carved shepherd's staffs in their silver-ringed hands and followed at a respectful distance by their veiled women. French citizens of Bône gazing with persistent suavity upon the gaucherie that the latest war had spewed upon them. Americans from civilian agencies trying hopelessly to enjoy the exotic. British civilians applying their usual sporting boredom to the situation at hand. Arab and French children scurrying about, playing in petty crimes and avarices as other children play with blocks and toy trains. Women, French and Algerian, and intermixtures of all the races of the earth.

Eric strolled through this scene, and it was trance-like; he could not attach himself to it and perhaps he did not want to. Not that he felt aloof; on the contrary, he regarded everything he saw with an abnormal warmth. Still there was some quality here that was neither reality nor dream, something in himself, mesmerized and isolated.

To his right was the French part of town; he could see it through the open spaces, Parisian-like shops, Provençal homes, ultramodern apartment houses adapted to the Algerian climate. And to his left was the native quarter, a maze of dusty-tan brick and dirt alleys stretching up the hillside. He turned left into the Casbah.

There were only a few evidences of bombing in Bône. But on the street he had chosen to ascend he had to pick his way over mounds of rubble for several hundred feet. He came to a barricade guarded by two red-capped British MP's. They approached him.

"This is the safe limit, sir," one said to him.

"Is the Casbah out of bounds?" he asked.

"It's out of bounds to troops."

"What about Merchant Marine?"

"We have no right over you fellows here. But part of our duty is to tell you that you'll get no military protection above this point."

"Well, I'm just out for a walk. The sun's still up. I just want to take a look around."

The British soldier was very polite. "It's your party, sir," he said. "But men are killed up there as often in the sunlight as in the dark. And all I can tell you is that you can yell your bloody head off twenty feet above this line and there's nothing we're allowed to do about it."

"Okay," Eric said. "I'll try not to yell."

"Very good, old man, we'll appreciate it," the other MP said. "That may save us a bit of embarrassment."

They all laughed and Eric went on into the narrowing maze. He was lost now in a pale mud-tan world of narrow alleys and low windowless buildings with narrow doorways. Occasionally he passed a group of men, and as they looked at him he caught an obscure amusement in their manner, a kind of amusement that only those who understand the simplicities of belief and the simplicities of violence can feel toward others. And sometimes he would pass a beggar bent over the paralytic cup of his open hand. And sometimes he would pass a group of women and young girls who would whisper and titter and turn their faces away from him as they went by. He met a group of Arab urchins and they harassed him for a while, until they were convinced that he had nothing to sell. And this world of dusty amber grew darker and darker until it was vague with shadow.

A little form crept out of a doorway. He felt a moment of fear as it scurried toward him, but he had not brought his revolver with him and he did not reach for his knife. There was a sense of fatality upon him that left him defenseless. But the shape did not attack him. It seemed to be a child of very peculiar proportions. "Hey, Jack," said the hoarse whisper of the shape, "you sell?"

"No, nothing," Eric said. "Nothing!"

The shape made a low sound like insane laughing. "You go me," it said. "You go Black Cat, many *anglais*."

Eric followed the small figure that trotted ahead of him with its strange stiff, short-legged gait, leading him deeper and deeper into the labyrinth. He asked himself why he was following it, and the answer seemed to be that it did not make any difference. He was not looking for anything. And it might be better to find some nodal point in all this dark-alleyed mystery than to wander through endless indirection into an antechamber of nothingness. It might be better to find a place that was a place, that had a name—such as the **Black Cat**.

They zigzagged up and down, right and left, through passageways, tunnels, and stairways. Eric was enjoying the sensation of becoming increasingly lost; he was not certain whether this wandering was into the maze of the world or into the caverns of his own secret being. Whichever it was, he wanted to give way to it, to submerge himself with even the vague purpose of lostness before destiny submerged him without any purpose other than its own geometry. They came to a lighted doorway, and for the first time Eric could see the shape that he had been following.

It was an adult man whose legs had been severed just above the knees and who now walked skillfully on leather-capped stumps; a man whose face had enormous features, huge nose, wide grinning mouth, and large expressionless eyes. The door was opened cautiously by a fat old woman wearing an apron. *"Anglais, anglais!"* the little man said to her, simultaneously holding out his hand to Eric.

Eric gave him a fifty-franc note.

The low-ceilinged room was faintly lighted and the air was rank with tobacco, cheap cognac, wine, dampness, stale food, urine, and the sweat of many heated and unwashed bodies. Eric made his way to the bar and ordered wine. It was served to him in a soldered sheet-iron measuring cup. The room was crowded with men and there were many languages spoken, in gutturals, nasals, falsettos. There were several British soldiers and two American seamen. The brick floor was covered with puddles and the light came from kerosene lamps at each end of the counter. A few short-skirted girls wandered about in the shadows talking to the men. Two were naked from the waist up; the others were modestly attired.

Eric drank the acrid wine from the filthy iron cup and drew into himself the reality of this place, this little sore growing upon the surface of man's dream, this infinitesimal fermentation point in the vast vat of frustrate human desire. On the far end of the bar there was a girl. She was sitting on the bar and leaning back against the wall, quite relaxed. She wore a cheap filmy gown that covered her above the waist. Her feet were on the bar, her legs spread wide apart and naked. With her left hand she was eating from an open can of sardines. With her right hand she was stroking the inside surfaces of her thighs to the desultory and weird rhythm of an Arabic song that she sang between swallows of fish. Her eyes were almost closed. She was far away.

Eric watched her and wondered. Is the vision within which she now lives any less authentic, he asked himself, than that of a good average American clubwoman, say an average member of the Western Star? Is the symbolism by which she accepts the tragic and incredible fact of finding herself alive any further away from the truth? Undoubtedly she is drugged and drunken and depraved; but against the known facts of this nonhuman universe, who is not?

The song that came out of her now had totally absorbed her. The diminishing consonances of its seven-tone scale spoke of the pure loneliness of the body lost in a cunning world contrived by the slyness of the mind; it spoke out of an ancient and sensual recognition of the irony of resisting that which exists; it spoke of sorrows so old that they had become music.

Eric stayed in the bar for about an hour. He drank many cups of wine, and no one molested him except a few of the girls who asked him if he wanted to go upstairs with them. The wine did not seem to change him. The men moved about the crowded room, sullen and boisterous, laughing and cursing, their eyes gleaming redly in the lamplight, their lips wet with wine and unfulfillable desire. An explosive center of human flesh that might at any moment be excited into self-destruction by a single knife thrust. Eric's loneliness deepened; it passed through gloom into compassion and from there into an individual isotope of compassion that held him closely in its grasp. And this too was like an old music.

Outside, he walked through labyrinths of mist; the labyrinths were real but the mists were those of his own mind. By walking downhill he made his way out of the Casbah. He crossed the Cours Jerome Bertagna; it was alive with cosmopolitan gaiety now, and he felt it as an abrasive against his consciousness. He wandered into the first narrow streets of the French quarter. He felt the adventure of his own life —his only possession—as a thing which was now almost expended. This idea was not welcome to him, but it was like a release; he felt a hitherto unknown unity of mind and body, spirit and flesh.

He walked without any sense of direction, up one street and down another, turning now left and now right. The streets were wider here than in the Casbah, but they were unlighted except by the open doorways of shops and bars. The sidewalks were almost deserted. Sounds of singing and shouting came to him occasionally, but in between those times the city seemed muffled and the few figures that passed him appeared slowed down, as though all were involved in a conspiracy to delay the passage of time. Out of Eric's mind there flowed a warm fog, like that which came from the smoke pots when the convoy was under attack. Yet he seemed to be able to see more clearly through this fog than he had ever been able to see without it. The strangeness of this foreign city was like the familiar strangeness of suddenly finding oneself alive, alive in a universe that was by no means made for us.

As he passed a lighted space a woman stepped out of the doorway. *"Anglais?"* she asked.

"American," he said.

She was very close to him and he could hear her breathing.

"Will you go with me?" she asked in English without identifiable accent.

"I'd rather you would go with me," he said.

"You have a room?"

"No."

"Where?"

"Walk with me."

"Walk where?"

"Just walk."

She stood still, staring at him through the shadow which they had now re-entered. He found some hundred-franc notes that he had folded in his pocket and handed them to her. She stepped back into the lighter area and counted them. Then she rejoined him.

"You just want to walk?" she asked.

"Yes," he said. "I'd like to walk with you."

She was close to him again. "All right," she said. "I can walk with you if that's what you want. But only for an hour."

"How will you know when an hour is up?" he asked, laughing.

"I have a watch," she replied.

"Can it measure life?" he asked. "Can it divide death into minutes?"

"Are you all right?" she said warily, drawing away from him.

"Don't be afraid," he said. "I'm not crazy."

"You talk sort of queer."

"I was just joking."

"You Americans do have some queer humor."

"You're British?"

"I was once."

They were walking down the deepening darkness now, and he could smell her cheap perfume and her female body and feel her clothes brush against him. She told him that she had been born in England but that when she was sixteen she had married a visiting Frenchman who had brought her to Algeria where he promptly died of dysentery—and here she was.

"That was a long time ago," she said.

Eric could feel her as a woman; he felt the physical fact of womanness more intensely than ever before in his life. He felt what the war must have been to her. In her body was the means of her livelihood, a little factory between her thighs, and she the capitalist who must try to exploit it in accordance with the law of supply and demand. The incredible irony of this caricature of love, this mimicry of lust! The German soldiers who must have spent their seed in that darkness, now joined by the Americans; the creeds and races and wars intermingled and lost within that impartial cave— that tunnel toward life and toward death, that beginning and destination. He felt her shiver as her shoulder pressed against his.

"Are you cold?" he asked.

"No," she said, "but why is it you just want to walk?"

"It's just that I'm lonely," he said. "But I don't want to go to bed. I don't think it would do any good."

"I've got some good cognac in my room," she told him. "We could drink some and I wouldn't charge you any more than you've already paid."

"Not now," he said.

They walked on and on through longer and longer areas of darkness, and Eric could feel that the woman was afraid.

"Don't be afraid," he said. "I'm not going to do anything to you."

"But why not go to my room? It's warm. It's—it's cozy."

"Let's walk a while longer."

He certainly did not want to frighten this woman, but he seemed to feel the total music of the earth moving through his blood and he could not diminish it. There was laughter in this music and there was the weight of all living sorrow and the gratitude of the unforseeable moment. They were approaching another area of faint light, and when they came to it he turned and gripped her by the shoulders. "Here," he said, "stand still. I want to look at your face."

She protested and twisted in his grasp, but he held her firmly. "Stop breathing," he said. "I must see you absolutely still."

"I can't stop breathing," she said.

She can't stop breathing, he thought. She can't stop existing. She can't stop the inexplicable narrative of her life.

"Never mind," he said. "You can go on breathing."

"You're drunk!" she whispered.

He quieted her and studied her face very thoroughly under the yellow light from the doorway of the bar.

"My dear, my dear one," he said, "you are very beautiful."

Her body surged with extraordinary strength then, and twisted from his grasp. She ran away into the night and he could hear the sharp tapping of her high heels on the pavement as she ran, now fading to a ticking no louder than the sound of a clock measuring time, then finally to nothing.

17: Nocturne

Frantically she ran down the Rue Gambetta and turned to her right at the first side street. After running for two more blocks she fell exhaustedly into a dark doorway.

She sat for a while on the stairs, regaining her breath. Then she stood up and lit a cigarette. Her heart was still pounding as she waited.

She heard a man approaching and when he was twenty feet away she could see his silhouette. He was a heavy man, lurching drunkenly, now on the narrow sidewalk and then in the gutter. As he came opposite her she stepped out of the doorway and took hold of his arm. "You American?"

He was too drunk to be startled. "I'm no damned Yankee," he said. "I'm a damned fit member of His Majesty's Royal Navy, a bloody petty officer, and no damned Yankee."

"How about it?" she asked. "Let's go to my room."

"Gwan—" he said, "I don't want no more bloomin' whores. Leave me be."

But she hung onto his arm, steadying him, and he did not hit her. At length they came to another lighted spot near an intersection. They stopped, and with one hand he supported himself against the trunk of a tree while with the other he turned her around so that he could examine her. Then, nodding his head disgustedly, he looked at the pock-marked, life-weary confession of her face.

"Why, yuh dirty slut," he said, "tryin' pick up a gen'man!"

"I won't charge you much," she said.

"So yuh won't charge me much?" he mocked, assuming a manner of drunken elegance. "Now ayn't that sweet of yuh!"

"I've got some cognac—"

"Why, yuh toothless old hag, yuh ought tuh be ashaymed uh yerself! Yuh ought tuh be in the old laydies' home!"

She took hold of the lapels of his uniform jacket. "Just let me stay with you," she asked.

"So yuh got no playce tuh put yer head, eh?"

"No, no! I've got a place to sleep. I'll take you there!"

"Then what's got yuh so bloody scared?"

"I met a queer chap. Crazy I guess."

"Oh-ho! So that's it! And what did he do to yuh, if I might ahsk?"

"Listen," she said, beating her fists against his chest, "for Christ's sake, just let me stay with you tonight! I'll do anything for you."

In Italy along a ragged line that stretched from the Ligu-
rian Sea to the Adriatic, many men were trying to kill one
another. If one could have listened to the talk of the soldiers
—German, American, British, Polish, French, Italian—
looked into their brains at the memory pictures, traced the
dream fantasies through their blood, examined their syn-
apses, counted their red blood cells, measured their cephalic
indices, and compiled other information along the lines established by Alphonse Bertillon, one would not have been
able to discover by any or all of these methods why the men
on the opposite sides of this line were trying to kill one another. Not here nor in the White House nor the Reichs
Chancellory nor Downing Street. For everywhere the en-
tanglement of unfunctional institutions and outworn habits,
the dead and the living within men themselves, obscured and
diverted, made of one war a million wars, and cast the
enemy in an endless multitude of changing roles.

Straggling unevenly along the Rue Gambetta in Bône were
four men from the *SS William Benson:* the deck engineer
named Henry, Oscar the wiper, and the two seamen, Sanko
and Kentucky. As they came to a lighted space they met
Third Radio Officer Eric Clark.
"Hi, Professor!"
"Hi, boys!"
They all shook hands quite formally, as though they had
not seen one another for a long time. "Where are you fel-
lows going?"
"Oh, we're gonna teach Oscar here some of the facts of
life. Good idea, ain't it?"
"A damned good idea, as long as you're sure it's the facts
of *life* you're teaching him about."
"Want to come along?"
"No thanks. I want to walk around a while."
"So long!"
"So long!"
As the four men passed into the shadows again the three
who could have passed sanity tests felt vaguely uneasy; they
were not sure whether they had been accused or praised.
Sanko assumed the responsibility of dismissing the matter.
"The professor sure did have a crazy look in his eye tonight."

"Yeah," said Kentucky, "I reckon he had a pretty big load on. Those kind of guys can't hold it."

About a block further on, the deck engineer turned into a lighted doorway and up some stairs that led on the first landing into a large room full of benches. They sat down on one of the benches. There were about twenty other men waiting. On one wall was a large sign which read: *Soldats Français 10 f. Soldats Anglais 25 f. Soldats Américains 50 f. Autres Hommes 100 f.—Bureau de Santé.*

Most of the men stared at their feet and appeared to be embarrassed and unhappy. But Oscar was grinning, rolling his eyes and nodding his head, while the other three Americans watched him and giggled.

"Well, Oscar," said Kentucky, "in just a few more minutes you're gonna get yourself bred for the first time in your life!"

They tried to smother their laughter in the hushed funeral-parlor embarrassment of the large room, but they could not entirely repress the titters and the little gasps of glee. Oscar said nothing and did not laugh, but he grinned at them ever more widely and rocked his head more than ever.

Then the deck engineer punched Kentucky in the ribs and said to Oscar, "How does it come that you got a beautiful wife in Hollywood and three kids, but you never been bred?"

With his right hand the idiot began to play with the five fingers of his left hand as though he had just discovered their amusing and surprising existence. "Three kids," he said. "Three and two is five. Five minus two is three. That's how."

"Musta been the iceman!"

"Maybe it was the Lone Ranger!"

"Or maybe an admiral of the Japanese Navy."

A fat little woman of about forty came out of one of the several adjoining rooms. She waddled into the large room of benches and looked about. Then she headed for the Americans.

"Américains?" she asked.

"One hundred per cent," said Sanko, "that's us!"

"Je ne comprends pas!"

"Oui, oui! American!"

They began then to try to make Oscar stand up and go with the woman, but he twisted and turned. His cheeks changed from pink to white and then to red and then white again. The grin on his mongoloid face was turning on and off spasmodically, as though a flickering motion picture film had caught him now in fear, now in joy, and again in grief, with all the intervals of transition lost in darkness.

The woman was laughing with the others, her fat little face a mask of derision and petulant worry. She grasped Oscar by the shoulder and finally he stood up and followed her. The other men in the room had watched this scene without evidence of humor. Many had been waiting for hours, for they were taken in financial rather than chronological order; hence the French soldiers who were most favored economically were the most unhappy and ashamed.

The three Americans on the bench were convulsed with amusement as they watched the door close behind Oscar and the French whore. They exchanged glances and bent double with half-suppressed laughter.

18: The Miles of Sea We Travel

On a zigzag course bearing generally to the northeast, the *SS William Benson* set forth from Bône without escort. No one on the ship except the captain and the Armed Guard Commander knew their destination. And only the mates and radio officers were kept informed as to the immediate position. Yet almost everyone on the ship was making his own estimate from the speed and direction as they could be guessed at from the frequency of the engine's beat and the position of the sun during the day. A spirit of fateful uneasiness was spreading like a slow plague among them.

Eric did not know the destination, but he could follow their course because he was given the position whenever he went on watch. They made their way around Sicily without sighting its coast and then headed straight into the Ionian Sea. He kept expecting each time he entered the radio room that their position would have shifted to the west so as to arrive at some port on the southern or western coast of Italy. But no such change of direction occurred. And at length, after three days and nights, he was forced to acknowledge to himself that they were heading into the Adriatic. It did not seem reasonable that an unescorted merchant ship loaded with high-octane gasoline should be sent into the narrow sea where it would be necessary to pass within plain sight of the German-held coast of Albania, but such was inescapably the situation. And in his deeper areas of awareness Eric was not really surprised. What was happening seemed to proceed naturally and inevitably from what he had already experienced.

In Bône, Eric had come through confusion and despair into a sense of release that was almost ecstasy. It was not the release of irresponsibility that he had discovered, but exactly the contrary. In the secret conviction that his time of living was nearly done, he had found the dignity, the grandeur, the tragedy of the human spirit, burning as it does like a lost comet in the black chaos of immeasurable indifference. This seemed to free him from many false conventions of thought and attitude, conventions based upon that caution which derives from a feeling that we are to live for a long time, and perhaps—if we are just careful enough —*forever.*

In his mind he had seen the lonely rock of the earth soaring precariously through careless infinity, and all the creatures clinging to it, cunningly meting out their generosity in little beggar's cups, weighing their love on the balance of tomorrow, buying low and selling high, counting their virtues and vices on the fingers of their two hands. The new state of awareness had not left him now that they were at sea again; it had only grown somewhat more calm and more adaptable to conventional conduct. For he had also learned that the direct adoration of life frightened people. And there was no time left for that; he would approach them more gently, stick to accepted manners. One does not shout at a grazing antelope the latest news about the vastness of love; for there is not only urgency, there is also patience. Nothing in his new awareness made him feel superior or humble or serious. In fact, he felt that the creation of humor was one of the few rational human occupations. Humor and drama, and sharing together the awesome and wonderful complexity of our experience. He had no desire to issue manifestoes now, but he wanted everything to be in sharp focus, real and incomparable, as is every moment of our time on earth if we can only live it without the fear that is sometimes called common sense.

It was almost noon of their fourth day out from Algeria, and Eric was hungry. Opposite him at the table there was a new member of the ship's company. This was Corporal Benjamin Stein, who had been put aboard by the Army for an obscure reason. He was supposed to be in charge of *cargo security*, but no one could figure out what there was that he could do about a ship full of high-octane gasoline. The old-time merchant mariners on board knew considerable about all kinds of cargo; that was a part of their craft. But the Army had sent this overgrown boy from the Bronx to tell them not to blow themselves up without an O.K. through proper channels. Benny had already, in these three short days, aroused a dislike so intense that it almost outweighed the innumerable other animosities on board the ship.

"Hello, teacher," he said when Eric sat down.

"Hello, Corporal."

Stein was working over a steak as though he were a great surgeon performing a difficult operation before an audience of medical students. He made an incision here and there, then studied his work thoughtfully, considering all aspects of the situation. It almost seemed as though he were about to whip out a surgical needle and some catgut to begin work on the sutures. But then he began to eat, carefully considering each remaining piece before he took a bite, chewing conscientiously, and removing the gristle from his mouth to place it on the folded napkin beside his plate. He continued this process until he had finished what was. on his plate, and then he leaned back, sighed loudly, took a toothpick from the container, and began to work on his teeth like a jeweler meticulously removing the delicate parts from a valuable watch.

Eric knew that Stein was now thinking up something to say, and that it would begin either with a mystifying remark or with what he mistook for banter.

"Would it be all right with you if I raise my hand?" the corporal asked.

So it was to be the mystifying approach. Eric tried to figure it out. "With clenched fist or palm front?" he asked, try-ing the political angle.

"Neither. I mean with one or with two fingers."

"Sorry, but I don't get it."

"You're a teacher, aren't you? What I mean is, do I have to raise my hand if I want to go to the can?"

"Oh," Eric said, "I see. No—it's okay with me if you go any time you feel the urge."

Stein laughed and put aside his toothpick. "Tell me, teacher," he said, "as fifth assistant radio operator on this barge, what do you do that's *useful?*"

Undoubtedly Stein wanted above all else to belong to the hearty masculine world of good fellowship. But he went about this so boldly that he skipped all the preliminaries. He did not understand that banter between friends is the exercise and acceptance of a privilege by which each indi-cates his affection and asserts his position in the affections of the other, and that it serves in this way as a means of artic-ulation where direct statement might be embarrassing. Nor did he understand that banter within a group is a declara-tion of unity, of clanhood, and an implement with which to chasten undue vanity in its members. His complete unaware-ness that masculine mockery is not insulting only because it is based upon preliminary understandings caused him to arouse the ire of almost every man he spoke to on the ship.

"Oh, I keep the brass polished," Eric answered with an effort. "And in between times I soogie down the bulkheads."

Stein started an involved joke about "soogie" being baby talk, but then his attention was distracted by the entrance of the third assistant engineer. The latter's shirt was drenched with sweat and there were streaks of black grease on his tired face.

"Well, well," said the corporal, "I see you're all dressed up in your best Sunday clothes!"

The Third was usually a placid man who lived his own inward life, but now he gave the soldier a look of contempt that almost bared the fangs of violence. Eric finished his coffee and went up to the boat deck for a breath of fresh air before it was time for him to go on watch.

The sea was a dusty blue color and the low swells ad-vanced toward the starboard side of the ship with fugue-like variety and precision. The air was sultry, but there were small intermittent gusts of coolness and heat that brushed his face capriciously. Eric searched the northeast horizon, hoping to see the mountains of Albania. But nothing was visible there except the anemic blue sky. The ship was inside a hollow pastel hemisphere of sky and sea.

"Well, Mr. Clark, how do you like it?"

It was Sealman, the purser. "Like what?" Eric asked.

"Oh—the general situation," the purser said.

"Well, that's a rather complex question," Eric answered. "But generally speaking, I don't feel that our approval or disapproval will alter the aforementioned situation to any observable degree. So—like the old Confucius joke—we might as well relax and enjoy it."

"Did Confucius say that?"

"I don't think so. This joke was one I heard when the 'Confucius say' jokes were popular. I think it was 1939— when the war began."

"What was it?"

"Confucius say: 'When rape is inevitable, relax and enjoy it.' "

Sealman laughed and scratched his head. His porcine features expressed formal amusement, but Eric knew that what he wanted, almost desperately, was to share opinions with someone of his own class, someone of the professional level, or better still of its heavy intelligentsian cream; such sharing was the only thing in the world that could reassure him in the present situation.

"That's very funny," he said. "Relax and enjoy it! That's a good one! Ha-ha! But what about the Jew? Do we have to relax and enjoy him too?"

"You mean the corporal?"

"Who else?"

"He's a pretty annoying guy, all right."

"Annoying! That's what I call real understatement, Mr. Clark! He's just a Jew, that's all."

"How do you mean?"

"Doesn't know his place. Crude, gross, ignorant, offensive. He'd take over everything if you'd let him."

"You mean you think he's that way because he's a Jew?"

Sealman wished so deeply to have Eric as an ally that he

grew a little cagey and thought carefully about his answer.

"Well," he said, "you'll have to admit that the Jews in general are a pretty offensive lot."

"Some of them are," Eric agreed. "But I've also known some extremely offensive Irishmen, Swedes, Greeks, Mexicans, Canadians, and Americans. Haven't you?"

The round face of the purser smiled its country club smile and assumed its expression of well-mannered fairness. "Yes, of course," he said. "There's good and bad in every race. You're quite right. Take Einstein, for example. He's a Jew!"

Eric looked away from the fat young trust-fund lawyer and stared again at the area where the mountains of Albania should appear, but the horizon remained empty. The sea and the sky looked very, very old to him now, as though the eons of successive night and day had at last wearied them and drained them of color.

"Sealman," he said, "it is not important to acknowledge that a people has produced great men. What *is* important is to allow them the right to produce fools, weaklings, and scoundrels without having to have any special permit to do so. Don't you agree with me?"

"I suppose you're right," Sealman replied, straining toward agreement. "But they do make a damn nuisance of themselves sometimes."

Eric felt the oldness of the sea and sky in himself, but not as weariness. If a man knew that the world were to end tomorrow, he wondered, and his son came to him and asked to be informed of the facts of life, what would the man say?

A son, he thought; and a vague feeling of unquiet came into him, a shadow of organic guilt at the knowledge that he had had no children. "Whom shall I think of as my son?" he asked himself. And out of his memory he saw the faces and recalled the identities of his favorite pupils and younger friends. But none were his. And then he recalled all the children he could remember ever having known, but none seemed to belong to him; until out of the mingled mists of old and recent memory he saw two dark blue eyes peering at him from a small, puckered face. It had stopped crying and vomiting its milk and waving its arms. It stared directly into his eyes, and its question was the sum of all human questions, and Eric recognized it at last. It was his son.

"You're right," he said to Sealman, "people often *do* make a damned nuisance of themselves!"

It was time for him to go on watch then, for ever since Peters had begun to have recurrent attacks of stomach trouble they had exchanged watch periods and Eric now stood the twelve-to-four.

At ten minutes to four Shruck entered the radio room to relieve Eric. It had been an uneventful watch. The only things of interest he had been able to copy were the reports of various hospital ships in the Mediterranean and Adriatic. The hospital ships of both sides made frequent position reports to both German and Allied land stations to avoid accidental attack. And there was a peculiar electronic relationship involved here. For Eric had observed that the radio operators on both sides took a special delight in communicating with the enemy. They were, in fact, unusually polite to each other, but it was not the politeness of the dueling field. They prolonged each contact to an extent that must have been indirectly in violation of orders on both sides. It delighted the American operators to sign off with DS, for *Danke schön,* while the Germans signed off with TU for Thank you. And quite frequently the powerful German station in Venice would call GBS at Gibraltar to tell them that the weak British station at Malta had been trying to get in touch with them. To a radio operator, emotion is quite as audible in the rhythms of a "fist" as it is in the tone of voice. And it was undeniable that the operators on both sides took a special pleasure in talking together without the intervention of authority—many of them must have been amateur radio operators before the war—and that in this specialized manner some of the little men who fight wars felt that they were putting something over, no matter how slight, on the men who plan wars.

When Eric entered his room he found Chuck sitting at the desk working over a letter. After they had said hello Eric began to wash his hands and face at the basin. He could feel an embarrassed effortfulness in the junior engineer, and he wondered what profound thing he might be straining to say.

"Are you good at rhymes?" Chuck asked.

"I don't think so," Eric said. "I've never written any."

"Well, anyway—what rhymes with *travel?*" the junior asked.

"The only thing I can think of is *ravel,*" Eric told him.

"Ravel . . . ravel . . ."

"There must be a hundred other words. We ought to have a rhyming dictionary."

"Can't you think of any others right now?"

Eric tried without success. "Not now," he said, "but if I think of any later I'll let you know."

Chuck pushed the paper away from himself and put the pencil back in the drawer. "How about some java?" he asked.

"Not now," Eric said. "I want to get some air before I go below. See you later."

Chuck left the stateroom then to go below for his coffee, and Eric was alone in the place and felt not the slightest compunction about going over to the desk to see what the junior engineer had been writing. The remembrance of that convention which would once have told him that he should feel guilty about such an underhanded action was now a foreign thing to him. Why? He wished nothing but good things for his friend, and he wanted to read what the man had written. That was all there was to it.

> I'm always thinking dear of you
> When I'm out on the blue
> I'm so lonely for you.
> When I'm dreaming hours away
> My thoughts are always turning your way
> And in my memories I can see
> Your smile.
> Your love will guide me,
> Back o'er the miles of sea we travel
> I'm always dreaming dear of you
> Forever yearning to be home with you.

Back o'er the miles of sea we travel . . . forever yearning to be home with you. Eric had come into the room wanting to write a letter to his wife, and the more articulately his thoughts had resounded in his mind the more he had felt that there was nothing he could really say to her at this moment. He could not reduce to classroom definitions the few important things that he had learned since leaving Jane. If he could have spoken to her he would simply have told her that he loved her. He could not avoid an acknowledgment that Chuck had made a better attempt at this kind of communication than he could now have done.

Eric went out on deck and now he found that they were within a mile of the Italian coast; they were close enough to see the roads that wound inward over the green hills, the small carts, the houses, and even the figures of men going about their work. And there on the other side of the ship were the pale purple mountains of Albania. It gave him a strange sensation to be able to see with his own eyes a portion of the earth that was at this moment in the hands of the enemy. He went to the starboard side of the boat deck and stared at the conquered land.

Suddenly he became aware of a near-by sound that sent a chill through his viscera and made the hair stand up on the back of his neck. It was a soft sound, but all the world's idiocy seemed concentrated in it. Blind pain and tittering laughter wrestling together and smothering each other with insane caresses. "Five times six . . . heh-heh-heh-heh-heh . . . thirty, *thirty* . . . heh-heh . . . THIRTY . . ."

It must be Oscar, Eric thought, but what in God's name is he doing up here on the boat deck?

The sound was coming from behind the number three lifeboat, and Eric now made his way around the boat because he wanted to warn Oscar that he would get into trouble for being up here off the main deck. But the source of this sound was not Oscar.

It was Harold. And the mess boy's face was contorted in the crafty grimace of an idiot, his gibbering lips flecked with saliva. "Harold!" Eric said. "For Christ's sake, what's the matter with you?"

But Harold did not seem to see him; he only went on mumbling, and occasionally his arms jerked and his face twitched. Eric stepped forward, grasped him by the shoulders and shook him as hard as he could. "Come out of that, Harold!" he said. "Come out of it!"

And after a minute of this the mess boy began to resume his own personality, as though awakening from a queer somnambulism. When he was fully himself he looked embarrassed and frightened. He ran his fingers through his hair several times and visibly shuddered. "I don't know what's the matter with me, Professor," he said in an unsteady voice. "I guess I've gone nuts."

Eric was still holding onto the boy and he could feel the shivering through his shoulders. "You're not crazy," he said. "I know what's the matter with you. So don't worry about it. Let's go down to the main deck and up on the bow, so we can talk. You may get into trouble up here."

"The bow's a bad place to be if we strike a mine."

"Okay, let's go back to the stern."

"Oh—the navy crew is always infesting that place. Let's go to the bow. To hell with mines."

They made their way along the narrow path that had been left clear of deck cargo, and the fumes of gasoline were very strong until they came out into the fresh breeze at the bow.

"I don't know what's the matter with me," Harold repeated.

"I do," Eric said. "You had been thinking about impersonating Oscar. You'd been trying very hard to feel what it was like to be him, to be living in his body. And all of a sudden you *were* him!"

Harold nodded, and now the pent-up talk spilled out of him, jerkily, anxiously, needfully. "You're right. That's exactly what happened. God! It felt awful! Like being in prison, locked in a cell with a nightmare. And this isn't the first time! It's happened before. In Italy—when I started feeling what it was like to be those people. The men who turned over the bodies of their women to us because they were beaten. The hungry bastards that came with their tin cans to beg for garbage. That guy we chased all over the ship, the one that was stealing rotten potatoes. And all the kids that were pimps for their mothers and sisters. Jesus Christ! That's when it started happening to me. I'd start being one of those people and all of a sudden I couldn't stop because I *was* them! Just like you said. By God, I don't know what to do about it. They'll sure as hell have me in the booby hatch if anyone except you finds out about it."

"No, they won't. You're not crazy. Insanity is self-centered. You've just carried one aspect of sanity a little too far for your own health. We're all under a state of hypertension on account of the danger, the constant waiting for that damned alarm bell to ring. When you're back in a normal world, these things won't happen to you any more. So for now just try to forget it."

"I try—I try to forget it. But then I sort of wake up with a start and find myself doing it. If it were just these—these fits, or whatever they are—it wouldn't be so bad. But I've lost my whole sense of reality. Half of the time I can't tell the difference between dreaming and waking, or between being myself and being someone else. When I try to remember things I can't tell whether they happened to me or if they're just something that somebody told me about. I can't —I can't take hold of anything. There's nothing solid."

"Yes," Eric said, "I know. I remember when you and I first talked together. First you were worried because it was possible that the whole world was just a chemical reaction within your own brain. Then you were worried about the meaning of meaning. So I can see how this, combined with your trying to *be* other people, has broken up your sense of reality. But this is only a period in your life. The thinking in itself is a healthy thing, even though it may have thrown you temporarily off balance."

"But what *is* reality? Do *you* live in a real world, one that seems normal to you?"

"No, I don't. It seems to me that there must be a reality that includes what's going on inside of us as well as what's happening to us from the outside, a coalescence, a total human reality. But our society isn't equipped to deal with that kind of reality. That's why you and I are sailing up the Adriatic on the *SS William Benson* at this moment."

Harold looked at his wrist watch. "My God," he said, "I haven't set the tables! I'd better get going or the steward is going to have a chemical reaction within his brain that will cause him to have me logged!"

Alone on the forepeak Eric stepped onto the iron block that guided the anchor chain, and peered down into that narrow area where the cutting edge of the great ship split the waters of the Adriatic Sea. The water piled up before the prow and then spread away in unrepeatable patterns of hissing foam, over and over again but never the same, scene after scene rushing toward extinction, losing its identity in the unique configuration of its successor.

That was a damned glib answer I gave to Harold, he thought. A neat little package of truth all tied up with ribbons of smugness. *See Professor Eric Clark for well-rounded explanations of the mysteries of life and death. Have the meaning of your dreams explained and have your realities interpreted into dreams. Step right up, friends. It's free today. Everything's on the house . . .*

The dancing of the white foam upon the dark water was endlessly enthralling. My God, but it's wonderful to *see!* Eric thought. Just to have eyes that work, to see—light, color, form, texture—the wonder of it.

It was almost time for dinner now, but Eric wanted to prolong this time in the open air as long as possible. He made his way back among the gasoline drums to the ladder that led up to the boat deck, and from there he continued upward to the flying bridge. First Mate Vangaussen waved to him from the wheelhouse where he sat on a stool near the helmsman.

This was the very top of the ship, like the roof of a building; he could gaze freely in all directions except for the narrow obstruction of the upper wheelhouse. The sun was nearing the summits of the low Italian hills and there were flashes of copper flame on the water between the ship and the shore, like the fins of fiery sharks breaking the surface, disappearing, and reappearing at another point.

Eric went over and stood beside the Armed Guard Commander who was leaning against the starboard rail, gazing intently at the horizon. The lieutenant jumped slightly when Eric accidentally brushed against his arm. "Oh," he said, "it's you. Good evening."

Eric offered him a cigarette which he accepted. Then the navy man lit a match and extended it to give Eric a light, but his hand was shaking so badly that Eric could not follow with the end of his cigarette. At length he took hold of the officer's wrist and steadied it while he took his light.

"You're nervous."

"Aren't you?"

Eric repeated the question to himself: Was he nervous? "No," he said. "I'm scared, but I'm not nervous. I don't think they have any particular connection. I get nervous when I drink a lot of coffee."

The AGC looked at him out of warm, watery, earnest Pekingese eyes, and shook his head. "Maybe if you knew what I do, you'd be nervous as well as scared," he said.

"What is it?"

"Did you know that we're sailing with our running lights on tonight?"

"No! For Christ's sake, why?"

"That I can't say. I could tell you about the lights because in an hour or so you'll be able to see them anyway. But I can't tell you why."

The AGC's voice was tremulous, and it was obvious that he was a man who was not only scared but who felt himself unequal to the frightening thing that he must confront.

"Let's not be secretive at this point," Eric said. "There is really no sense to it out here—no matter *what* the regulations say."

"I'm sorry, Clark, but—"

There was a sharp, ugly laugh close behind them and they both turned. It was Captain Brogan.

"So you can't tell him, eh, Lieutenant?" the captain said. "You can just hint around like some goddamned old bitch! Well, I'll tell him! And you can put it in your damned navy report that I told him!"

"I don't care what you tell him," the AGC said. "But *I* won't!"

The captain laughed again, and it was not entirely a normal laugh. "Hell," he said, "it'll be scuttlebutt two hours from now! Why not tell the worthy professor?"

"Why not?" Eric said. "Let's have it."

"Well . . ." the captain said slowly, as though he were making a statement that gave him some deep and bitter and secret satisfaction, "here it is. It seems, Professor Clark, that the German Navy still has a few cruisers and whatnots left up here in the Adriatic. They're based at Trieste. And it seems that our high brass is desirous of sinking same. It is believed that they will commit suicide whenever it appears to them that they can do enough damage to make it worth while. And *we* are the potential worth-while damage. We are decoys, Mr. Clark. It is our purpose to lure those ships out so that they can be sunk by our Air Force. They are sending a steady stream of well-lighted merchant ships up the Adriatic coast for this purpose. We are one of a considerable number. None British, you may be sure. But even so—it's quite an honor, isn't it? I could have refused the assignment. But I was sure the rest of you gentlemen would have been disappointed if I had deprived you of the opportunity of being heroes."

Eric was surprised, but only as one is when one opens a black-bordered letter. We know that someone close to us is dead. We only wonder during the moment of opening: Who? And how did it happen?

"Then why did they have to load us with high-octane gasoline?" he asked.

"They are practical men, Mr. Clark," the captain said. "They know there's a chance of us getting through—and if we do, they want us to bring in something they need."

Eric heard from below the ringing of the iron triangle which indicated that dinner was ready to be served. "Well," he said, "I can't say that what you have told me makes me happy. I have never especially wanted to be a hero. Or at least, not since I grew up. But it's fair enough, I guess. Lots of other people are being shot at too."

The AGC giggled in a startlingly high-pitched way. "Yes," he said, "but we are sitting on the bull's-eye—and we can't get off!"

"But look at all the guns you've got, Lieutenant," the captain said. "You won't have any trouble sinking a few German cruisers with all *those* guns, will you?"

The AGC's face became even more pale than before. "This may be a joke to you now, Captain," he said, "but it may not be so funny a few hours from now." And with that he turned away and strode over to the battle phone that was attached to the forward rail of the flying bridge.

Captain Brogan shrugged his shoulders, and it seemed to Eric that the man was unusually happy. Yet he knew that it was not happiness. Brogan did not want to die. He had gone through all of the war struggling to survive, sucking on a piece of raw potato for eighteen days in a lifeboat.

"Mr. Clark," he said, "you are a very unlucky man."

"Why?"

"Because when you signed on with me you signed your death warrant. I knew my number was up. You can't change your luck just by changing oceans .For a first tripper, you sure made a bad choice."

"I didn't leave Washington looking for a safe berth," Eric said.

The captain snorted contemptuously. "For a professor you're not very smart," he said.

There was no evidence in the saloon that the truth about the ship's mission had as yet begun to spread among the other officers. The most important topic was the new notice the chief engineer had posted on the bulletin board.

For weeks past now, Chief Curtis, wearing dungarees and carpet slippers, had been padding his way down into the engine room at odd hours, always with a sly and secretive look on his face. And out of a ten-gallon milk can, some odd bits of wire, and a plumber's friend which he attached to an overhead rocking beam, he had improvised a washing machine which would work off the power of the ship's engine. Now he had posted a notice about it.

Anybody wishing to use the washing machine in the engine room can use it for the fee of two dollars ($2) per washing, providing they furnish own soap and washing does not exceed more than ten gallon capacity of container.

Signed: J. Curtis
Chief Engineer.

To some of the men this was no more than a bad joke; to others it was a disgusting display of petty avarice; but to all it was a subject for neurotic contemplation. Most of them tried to treat it as a joke, but it somehow worried them, it gnawed at them and bit into tender tissues of the soul.

"We better rush our undies and Lux up to the chief," said Hartley, "before he raises his price to two twenty-five!"

"That plunger might do him more good if he took it out of that milk can and put it in his own," said Second Mate Burley.

Just then the chief lumbered into the room and went to

his place. His face wore an expression of challenge and an effort toward indifference.

He gave his order to Harold in a low mumble, and the mess boy had to ask him twice what he had said. "Harold," the chief asked, "did you have any trouble getting into the Merchant Marine?"

"No sir. What about?"

"About your ears. You *are* hard of hearing, aren't you?"

Harold turned away without replying, and then there was a long silence in the room; all waiting to see who would make the opening remark.

As was to be expected, it was Hartley who led off. "Chief," he said, "I haven't got much dirty wash right now, but I do have one dirty old jock strap. How much would you charge me to slosh it around for a while in your bucket downstairs?"

"Two dollars minimum," Curtis said.

"How about a reduced rate," asked Burley, "for washing out used condoms?"

This sort of talk continued as Eric sat eating his steak and potatoes and canned peas. There was laughter, but there was no real humor. There was something about the chief engineer trying to add a few extra dollars to his large pay by this means, at this time, in this place—something inorganic and bewildering and disturbingly familiar—that caused a strange disquiet in the men.

Then the corporal came in, Benjamin Stein, the Jew— and his presence served to drain off some of the moment's poison into a new duct. He sat down with his usual brash manner, quite indifferent to the emotional dynamics that had preceded him. "Well, gentlemen *and ladies*," he said, "if anybody here wants to borrow a million dollars, just ask me!"

He gave his order to Harold and then concentrated on Eric who was opposite him. "You want to borrow a million?" he asked.

"Not right now," Eric said. "I don't know where I could spend it. But why all the wealth?"

"Well," said the corporal, "I was just listening to the German propaganda broadcast from Berlin, and it talks about the Jewish Communist International Bankers who are running America—so I guess I must be one of them. So in that case I guess I can lend any of you guys a million bucks."

Eric knew the dull lifelong pain that lay behind the oafish mask of this barren burlesque, and since he could think of no way of lessening the pain he tried his best to help hold up the mask. "I wouldn't take a loan like that from an international banker like you," he said, "because then the Communist part of you might get the upper hand and you'd suddenly expropriate all the wealth you'd just loaned me."

As Eric left the saloon he passed by the open doorway and serving window of the men's mess. They had already finished eating and had cleared the table. About ten of them were shooting craps on the table and there were stacks of money in front of each man: lire, francs, dollars. And the biggest stack was in front of Oscar. His shaved, enormous head was now covered with a blond stubble; his face was sweating and flushed; his eyes were alight with savage frenzy. Yet he seemed the sanest of all the gamblers. Eric watched him with amazement.

Bets were laid at constantly varying odds in three differently valued currencies, yet Oscar never hesitated for an instant in picking up his proper winnings and paying off his losses. There was a narrowed efficiency and concentration about him that reminded Eric of the sea gull and of young Jacques in that bar in Beni-Saf. Some of the men were so upset at the idea of losing money to this moron that they kept opposing him, while others, more fatalistic, gave way and made their side bets with Oscar. Eric stood in the doorway, watching. Money changed hands with astonishing speed. There were several bottles of red Algerian wine on the table, and these were passed around without glasses, but Eric noticed that Oscar was segregated to his own bottle. When he handed it around, the others passed it back and forth and tipped it up, but nobody really put their lips to it. The only sounds were the rolling of the dice and the grunted phrases, "Five hundred lire he makes it." "Take two hundred." "Here's three more. It's covered." "Lay you ten to one he don't make it on the next throw." "Here's fifty francs says he does." This is not gambling, Eric thought; this is a competition of strange forces, a struggle between formal and informal madnesses, a contest of fugitive realities. "Here's a hundred lire to cover you."

Back in his own stateroom Eric took off his shoes and lay

down on his bunk. He put his hands behind his head and closed his eyes. Chuck was again working at the desk, although since the death of Duprey had reshuffled the engine room schedules, he would have to go on watch at ten minutes to eight. "Have you thought of anything else that rhymes with travel?" the junior engineer asked anxiously.

"No," Eric said. "I'm afraid you'll have to change that word for one that rhymes easier. Change it to move, or go, or sail, or something like that."

Without opening his eyes he could feel Chuck looking at him for a moment and wondering whether or not he had read the poem, half wishing that he had, and half ashamed.

"Sail . . ." he murmured. "Sail. That sounds good. But what rhymes with sail?"

"Wail, snail, bale, hail, tail, frail, kale, fail, mail—"

"That's it! Thanks."

"What's it?"

"Mail."

Eric kept his eyes closed the better to see the vision of recent weeks swimming in and out of the unsteady focus of the conscious mind. He was trying to bring some order into a chaos of new impressions.

Chuck got up from the desk and began to put the wind scoop in the porthole.

"Almost time for me to go on," he said. "I'll fix the place up so you can take a snooze."

"You don't have to put that in," Eric said. "We aren't going to black out tonight."

Chuck was incredulous. "What kind of weed have you been smoking?" he wanted to know. It took Eric several minutes to convince him, and once he was convinced he shook his head puzzledly. "Somebody somewhere must *really* have gone nuts this time," he said.

Eric thought of observing that the powerful men who order the destinies of unpowerful men had been going nuts for a long time, and that the situation had not noticeably altered in the past few days. But that would not have been a very decent thing to say, inasmuch as they now heard the clanging of the iron triangle from deep in the vulnerable belly of the ship, the signal that meant it was time for Chuck to go down there and spend the next four hours. And that room of fire and live steam was no place to philosophize at this time on the expendability of the majority of men.

"I guess they must figure it's safe now," Eric said. "They have airfields and radar all along the Italian coast, I guess, and we're only about a mile offshore."

"Sounds damned funny to me. Lights! My God, that's awfully funny up in a place like this."

Then Chuck went below and Eric was alone in the dimness of the stateroom, alone with the gentle swaying, the vibration, the creaking of wood and metal, the smell of warm paint and gasoline, the *tah*-tuh, *tah*-tuh, *tah*-tuh of the engine, the *tah*-tuh, *tah*-tuh, *tah*-tuh of his own heart. His heart within himself, himself within the ship; himself with the others within the throbbing body of the steel ship; the ship moving toward its destiny, which was now the destiny of all within it. And what was their alliance as they sailed so close to the borders of that sea of all seas which is eternity? There were cliques and countercliques among them, fissures and cross-fissures, and there was the comradery of blind hatred. Men meanly aligned against men. Against the ones who used too much water in the showers, the ones who belonged to the other service, the one who served the food, the one who thought he was better, the one who was ignorant, the one who won and the one who lost, the one who commanded and the one who was servile, the one who was from here and the one who was from there, the one who was a Jew, the one who used the wrong toilet, the one who knew his job and the one who did not, the one who was a Catholic, and the one who spent his time and money ashore buying cameos and pottery instead of liquor and whores. Perhaps the evil did not occur so much in the fact of each man being against all who were different from himself as in his making false alliances with those who were least offensive to him, so that innocent organic irritabilities thus became mechanical and multiplied with the anarchic single-mindedness of cancer cells? Whatever it was, the evil and the good of the world were here within this ship, here within this conflux of dream and reality, this tragic alloy of life and death within the cosmic crucible of matter and energy.

Suddenly the small room was smothering him and he sat up on the edge of the bunk. A wild cry of love for all the

world broke forth silently inside him and he felt a poignant
urge to see the outdoors again before it became dark. He
caught sight of Chuck's writing on the desk and glanced at
it while he was putting on his shoes.

> And in my memories I can see
>   Your smile.
> Your love will guide me
>   Back o'er the miles
> Of sea we sail,
>   Far from the daily mail,
> I'm always dreaming dear of you
> Forever longing to be home with you.

Outside it was still quite light, although the sun had fallen
below the stunted hills. The hemisphere of the sky shaded
smoothly from fiery red in the west through coral pink at the
zenith to dark purple in the east. There was a cool, damp
breeze on the forepeak, a breeze that came from the north
and had no gasoline fumes in it but only the freshness of the
sea. All the navy men were at their battle stations in the gun
tubs, helmeted and life-jacketed figures, top-heavy and bi-
zarre against the quiet loveliness of evening.

Eric stood in the angle of the bow breathing the good air,
feeling himself alive in the mystery and beauty of the earth,
and holding the precious hour of his allotted time with reverent carelessness. He looked up at the stately fresco of the
sky and thought of Jane. He did not say to himself that he
loved her; he merely summoned her out of the cells of his
own blood to hear again the music of knowing her, and it
came to him more strongly now than at any time since he
had left her. It was a music of gaiety and dignity and desire
fulfilled and renewed, a minuet and rhapsody, of laughter
and sympathy and love; polka, elegy, and torch song—the
music of the time of Jane and himself together. He heard
it now against the hiss of foam where the bow of the ship
cut the sea, and he was lost in it completely until it was interrupted by a crude counterpoint like the crash of cymbals.

This was the general alarm: the seven brutal spurts of
metal violence for which the nerves of every man on the
ship had long been tensed during every waking and sleeping

moment. Eric was neither startled nor afraid. The sound came to him like a familiar dissonance in a modern symphony. He could feel his heart pounding as he turned and began to walk down the length of the forward main deck toward the ship's superstructure. He could not bring himself to run, though he knew that his battle station was in the radio room in charge of the portable lifeboat transmitter. Everything had gone into slow motion and he was keeping pace with it.

The figures in the gun tubs had awakened into action; the shielded barrels bobbed deftly about. He could hear the Armed Guard Commander on the flying bridge shouting into his battle phone: "They're coming in on the starboard beam. But hold your fire. They're probably our own planes. Hold your fire! Hold your fire!"

Eric could see them then, three planes coming in very low and fast over the sea from the east. He ducked behind the drums of gasoline that lined the starboard rail. Maybe they're ours, he thought. It was supposed to be ships, not planes. Maybe they're ours.

Then the roar of the plane's motors swelled suddenly close and another sound with it, and he saw the tracers arching over his head and all around him like a sudden and close web of fire. His heart was pounding hard, yet he was breathing slowly and he felt very quiet. The guns on the ship did not open up until the planes had passed to the port. Then there was a hellish clatter of gunfire that rattled the steel deck against Eric's hands and knees. He stood up and continued to move forward. He saw the tracers from the ship's guns soaring outward, seeming to move as slowly as baseballs and curving off to the left just before they disappeared. He saw the planes circle and come back at a higher level.

On the port side of the ship twenty feet from Eric some flames were rising; the flames hissed outward from the punctured drums of high-octane gasoline as though each were a separate blowtorch. He dropped to the deck again as he heard again the sudden swell of the motors. His heart now was beating so hard that each stroke was a pain in his chest, yet he was aloof from it, quiet and vividly aware. This was totally unlike the ether-cone feeling of the first attack in the Mediterranean. This is it, he thought. This is really it.

He gathered his strength to meet it and there was gratitude in him for all that he had experienced in his life now suddenly concentrated into one vivid center brighter than the fire of the burning gasoline.

The deck of the ship trembled with the recoil of its own guns firing at the approaching planes, shook convulsively, as though in a fevered effort to achieve an orgasm before it was too late. Then there was the close and terrible blast of bombs that suddenly turned the air to steel and the decks to fluid. And Eric was at last afraid in this cage of shuddering substance, wildly afraid; but strangely the sudden terror existed side by side in him with the calm gratitude for all that preceded it, and all that he had ever been was now condensed into a small knot of life and memory and flesh and dream within the converging vise of force. He held his breath, drawing himself into the tightest thing he could make of the soft flesh in which he had his being. And his mind reached out into the incredible structure of things and came back with a special gift of duration. And because of this he looked very thoughtfully into the cobalt-blue eyes of that baby he had seen on the table in Castellammare. But it was no longer of any importance who was asking the questions. They looked into each other's eyes as two human creatures born into the same terrible narrative of magic and pain; they questioned and answered each other, and there was a smile somewhere and a look of gravity. Then the gift was used up and the flame came over it all, a great destroying and purifying and awful blast of it all over everything, including the screaming, and then a loud, white-hot moment of going forth somewhere and a velvet cape that at last sheltered him from too much of everything and carried him down into the sweet relief of black.

19: Now and Never

Far to the westward, in Washington, D. C., an afternoon session of the Senate was drawing to its close. Here in this smaller chamber of the Congress one always feels a subtle dignity that is sometimes lacking in the House. A clerk was reading a bill. He spoke in the curious jargon of court attendants—articulation being irrelevant, since there was a copy of the printed bill on the desk of each member.

Most of the senators present were reading newspapers. But a fat gentleman on the left side of the aisle had put down his paper and spoke animatedly to the man at the next desk.

The fat senator said, "Say, John!"

And the less fat one said, "Yeah?"

"Did you know the whole United States—in fact, the whole world—could be destroyed by one bottle of milk?"

"What? A bottle of milk?"

"You heard me."

"Okay. What's the gag? Don't cry over spilt milk or something like that?"

The fat one was coy. He folded his newspaper in a secretive fashion. "Don't be silly," he said. "I have reference to *destroying!* Not to crying over spilling something. Get it straight, John. I'm asking you. One quart. Destroy the earth. My question to you is *how?*"

The thinner senator was studying the end of an unlighted cigar, thinking heavily.

"Let me use your clipper," he said.

The fat one searched his pockets and produced the implement, and the thin one made a great show of concentration in clipping the end off his cigar, sparring for time.

"Some kind of a pun," he said slyly. "It's either that *milk* rhymes with something else or else *destroy* does? Am I right?"

"You are not."

"Then it's a riddle. Milk represents something else and the earth represents something else. Am I right?"

"You are not only not right, but you are very far off the track. I'm not pulling tricks. I mean just what I said. A quart of milk. Destroy the earth." The fat senator was enjoying a cunning and benign moment.

But his friend was losing interest. He had lighted his cigar and picked up Bill S-1874. "All right," he said absently, "what the hell is it? A bomb?"

"Of course not!" the other laughed. "A milk bomb? It's germs!"

"This is beginning to bore me. Where d'you get such crazy stuff? Letters from crank constitutents?"

The fat man knew that he had lost his grip on this little joke that had given him a momentary sense of superiority. "It's in the paper," he revealed. "It's Ripley. Listen: 'The bacteria in a bottle of milk reproduce so rapidly that if none died in twenty-four hours they would grow into a mass the size of the earth.' And that would certainly be the end of things, wouldn't it?"

The thinner senator blew out a big puff of blue smoke and laughed. "That Ripley stuff is clever, all right," he said. "But that could no more *happen* than that you or I could blow up the earth with a pint of whisky!"

The two men laughed heartily together.

About a mile down Pennsylvania Avenue from the Capitol Jane Clark was through with her day's work in the Department of Commerce. She was tired. One of the clerks from the outer office rode down in the elevator with her and then hastened ahead, somewhat awkwardly, to open the street door for her. He was a bland-looking fellow, and she did not even know his name.

As they left the air-conditioned building, the hot air of the outside world struck them oppressively. The street was crowded with government workers homeward bound. From overhead there came the mysterious and sinister and promising sound of airplanes, but nobody looked up. Everyone was too intent on getting home.

"I'm going to eat in Scholl's Cafeteria," the young clerk said to Jane. "It's air-conditioned."

"That's nice," she said.

"Would you care to come to eat with me?"

"No thanks. I have to get home."

He laughed embarrassedly. "I didn't think you would in the first place," he said. "I saw by your ring that you're married."

"That's right," she said.

Jane entered the apartment and found it damp and empty as she had expected. She took off the jacket of her suit and dropped it on the studio couch. Then she went back into the bedroom and washed her hands and face at the basin. The moment of coming into this place was always a desolate one; it was a castoff carapace, something once living that had now been shed and was becoming desiccate. She no longer felt at home here.

She went back into the central room where the icebox was and made herself a strong gin highball. She was tired, but only on the surface. The drink was kind to her, but she could not awaken any interest in eating.

Since the evening she had gone to the Kavkaz with John Hardin she had lived in a kind of loneliness that was difficult to define. It seemed to her that that evening had taken the personal element out of all experience. Each thing that happened to her now was like a chance contact with an isolated fact. She had told John on the phone the next day that she did not wish to see him any more, and she had known that he did not care; he had gained what he wanted and was somewhat relieved to know that there was no need to continue the performance. Since that time she had tried continually to restore the personal element to the texture of her daily living. For the most part, however, it had remained little more than a structure within which she moved as an alien, a refugee from her own entity. Yet in the past few days she had begun to recapture a little, a very little, of the warmth of sensual identity.

When he comes back, she thought, we'll have quite a bit of money from his pay-off, and we'll go on a trip together. A honeymoon. California or Florida or Lake Placid. I'll love him then as I have never loved him before. I'll love him for everything that he is—I'll love him for every greatness and weakness that's in him, every joke and every compassionate sympathy. I'll caress all of that every time I touch him. And when I touch his mouth with my fingers I'll know all the generous dream and the selfish suffering that has formed it in its beautiful shape, and I'll kiss all that with my own mouth. And he'll know me too, and all those adolescent ideas that I had about Jimmy will disappear because he'll understand them and be cruel and tender with me and I'll just be myself then. And I'll love him, my *God* how I'll love him!

She grew warm and fluid with delight. And then she thought: Unless he's dead.

But she knew as deeply as she had ever known anything in her life that he could not be dead. Her body became cold with a frightening feeling, and she said to herself that such a thing could not be so. It could not. Lake Placid would be best, she thought. The clear, cold, clean air, the pure snow. We'll walk under the branches of the pine trees and it will all be real and true. It will be us, and not just impulses and forces. The trees are like Eric and they're like me too. They are themselves and they live as themselves without being tossed about in currents that have no meaning, no meaning at all. He could not be, she thought. He absolutely could not be, and I know that better than I have ever known anything in my life.

Yet her body began to tremble, and she got up from the kitchen table and went into the bedroom and opened the door of the closet. In the darkness she found the three civilian suits he had left there. She touched the one of blue serge. This was made for Eric. Its shoulders were made to fit his shoulders. There was the warmth of his form inside this cloth. She pressed her face against the coat, and though she was crying, she now began to feel like laughing with relief. "He would never leave me alone," she said aloud. "Eric would never do a thing like that."

THE END